MONTANA MOONFIRE

CAROL FINCH

D0681945

ZEBRA BOOKS
KENSINGTON PUBLISHING CORP.

This book is dedicated to my husband Ed
for his assistance and support.
Thanks, honey!

ZEBRA BOOKS

are published by

Kensington Publishing Corp.
475 Park Avenue South
New York, NY 10016

First printing: December, 1990

Printed in the United States of America

Part One

Ah Love! Could you and I
  with him conspire
To grasp this sorry Scheme
  of Things entire
Would we not shatter it to
  bits—And then
Re-mould it nearer to the
  Heart's Desire?
      —*The Rubaiyat of Omar Khayyám*
                Edward FitzGerald

Chapter 1

Virginia City, Montana
July 15, 1865

Hisses and curses spewed from Caleb Flemming's lips as he circumnavigated his office that was situated behind the lobby of his hotel. Caleb was a "pacer" who employed stiff, precise strides to wear a path from one end of the room to the other. Pausing, he read and reread the telegram that had gotten his dander up and then burst out with another round of expletives.

"Damn that woman!" His vocal outburst was followed by several muffled oaths in which he called "that woman" every degrading name in the book.

"What the blazes is bothering you? Did Tyrone Webster try to pressure you into selling your hotel and restaurant to him again?"

The deep, resonant sound of Dru Sullivan's voice brought Caleb's bitter curses to a halt. Clutching the crumpled telegram in his fist, Caleb wheeled to face the six-foot-five-inch mass of brawn and muscle.

"As if I didn't have enough trouble with Webster and his scheming attempts to buy out both you and me, I have my ex-wife to thank for putting me in a huff," Caleb sputtered. "That woman purposely waited until the last possible minute to inform me so I wouldn't show up to

7

embarrass her in front of her highfalutin friends at the wedding! God, I bet this event will be the highlight of the social season in Chicago."

"What the hell are you ranting about?" Dru queried, staring at the telegram Caleb was crushing.

Dru ambled across the richly furnished parlor, followed by his constant shadow—Whong. When the devoted little Chinaman, in his wide straw hat and queue that dangled down the middle of his back, didn't ease down into the adjacent chair, Dru gestured for him to take a seat. With a dutiful bow, Whong sank down and folded his arms into the baggy sleeves of his blousy shirt.

"I wish you'd stop scampering around me as if you were my humble servant," Dru lectured for the umpteenth time on this monotonous subject. "God-amighty, you're a man, not a slave, Whong."

Whong reflexively bowed from his chair while Caleb went back to pacing like a caged lion.

Dru bypassed another sermon about Whong treating him like an imperial majesty. Since that day ten months earlier when Dru had rescued Whong from a drunken mob of prospectors who were harassing him for their own wicked amusement, the Chinaman had been bowing and deferring to Dru. The overt displays of gratitude and affection had gone way beyond flattery. Although Dru had insisted that the Chinaman go his own way, the little man stuck to him like glue. Dru found Whong's exaggerated devotion annoying. Hell, Dru couldn't even sit down for more than a few minutes at a time without Whong kneeling to brush a speck of dust from his boots! Whong kept them polished for Dru like a waxed floor. It wasn't that Dru wasn't fond of the pigtailed man, but the guy had some peculiar quirks. His loyal devotion, for one, and his belief that he had contracted every ailment known in the northern hemisphere, for another. Whong was constantly sniffing and sneezing and he was never without at least two handkerchiefs. The Chinaman seemed to react to everything that grew or moved. His

8

nose was constantly red from blowing and he had downed so many foul-tasting herbal remedies that his mouth was permanently puckered. Whong had tried grating onions into boiled milk and had drunk four cups of the concoction a day. Then there was the horseradish-and-lemon remedy, as well as the concoction of boiled potatoes or boiled pinecones and needles. Whong was often seen stuffing his head under a towel to sniff the aromatic vapors.

Discarding his wandering thoughts, Dru focused his blue eyes on Caleb, who was still pacing.

"Damn that woman," Caleb muttered again. "Oh, how I would love to have the last laugh on that haughty . . ."

His voice trailed off and he pivoted to study the thick midnight-black hair and craggy features of the man who casually lounged in his chair. Caleb silently assessed Dru's striking physique and mentally listed all his abilities—ones that had been tested to their very limits over the years. There wasn't another man in the territory who could match Dru's resourcefulness and talents. He was a bundle of bottled vitality, a dynamic man with tremendous inner driving force. If anyone could blaze a path to Chicago before the wedding, Dru could. And what better man to accompany Tori to Montana? Caleb mused, biting back a sly smile.

"As one old friend to another, I desperately need a favor, Dru," Caleb requested.

A wary frown appeared on Dru's brow. It sounded as if Caleb was leading up to something serious. "You know I'd do most anything for you," he said cautiously. "But—"

"If this wasn't extremely important to me, you know I wouldn't ask," Caleb cut in. "I want you to fetch my daughter for me, posthaste. Today. Yesterday would have been better."

The frown settled deeper in Dru's chiseled features. "Fetch her from where?" he quizzed Caleb.

"From Chicago. That's where she lives now that her

9

stepfather has become a wealthy railroad magnate and her mother took to the life of the filthy rich like a duck to water."

"Chicago!" Dru hooted incredulously. "I have unpleasant memories about that town and you know it. In fact, I'd like to strike that frustrating incident from memory. The first and last time I was there I went several rounds with that sonofabitch whose daddy owns the meat-packing and slaughterhouse. I drove my cattle herd through hostile Indian country, forded swollen rivers, and wove around mountains to get there. And then that miserable scoundrel paid me only half what that herd was worth. I swore I would never go back, and that's one promise I intend to keep."

When Caleb pasted on a pleading smile, Dru gave his dark head a negative shake. "Godamighty, Caleb, I hadn't planned any extended vacations away from the ranch. And besides, it would take me at least three weeks to get there, even if I took a fast steamer down the Missouri and rode hell-for-leather like a pony-express rider."

"I know all that," Caleb said with a dismissive shrug. "But I said this was important to me."

"To you maybe, friend, but it ain't to me," Dru snorted derisively. "I have a ranch to run. We've had trouble with rustlers of late and Tyrone Webster's ring of thieves have—"

"For crying out loud, Dru. You have four capable brothers who can fill your shoes," Caleb interrupted. "It's about time you doled out more authority to them anyway. You've been treating them like children and you have worked yourself to a frazzle. You could definitely use a vacation."

"In Chicago?" he sniffed distastefully. "I'd rather face an Indian war party single-handed."

"Now look here, boy, if it wasn't for me, you would never have struck it rich and you wouldn't have been able to buy up enough land to support you and your little brothers. You owe me," Caleb insisted.

10

"If not for *you*?" Dru smirked caustically. "As I recall, we were wandering along a summit in the mountains when you accidentally tripped over your own feet and tumbled off the edge. I had to rescue you."

"But I was the one who found that rich vein of gold when I fell," Caleb parried. "If I hadn't knocked the nuggets loose during my fall, I wouldn't have this hotel and restaurant and you wouldn't own your sprawling ranch."

Dru chuckled in amusement. Caleb's clumsiness had exemplified the adage about stumbling onto good fortune. It was a stroke of luck that had made them wealthy after years of hand-to-mouth existence. Dru and Caleb had met in the Sierra Nevadas and became partners to search for enough gold to fulfill their dreams. And if one stretched one's imagination, Dru supposed it could be said that Caleb was the reason for the fortune they had acquired while prospecting . . .

"Who tossed in a little gold dust during those lean years when you were sending as much money home to your family in Kansas as you could spare without starving yourself to death? And who chipped in to pay the expenses for your brothers to come up here after we dug out the first day's worth of ore?"

Dru shifted uncomfortably in his chair. He knew he was losing this argument. "You did."

"And who has been buying up your livestock at one hundred dollars a head to satisfy these hungry miners' appetites? And who makes sure your man Whong has plenty of staples to prepare your meals and sees that you get supplies on time while other folks around here have to wait several weeks for orders from the freight wagons?"

"You do," Dru mumbled begrudgingly. "But I thought we did each other favors because of our long-standing friendship. Godamighty, I didn't know you were going to hold your favors over my head for the rest of my life!"

11

"For Pete's sake, Dru, I haven't seen my only daughter in ten years! The minute I came west to search for gold and try to make a better place for us, that woman up and divorced me and married the man she had flaunted in my face for eleven years. Now that sneaky bitch is planning to marry my daughter off to an uppity aristocrat—who no doubt bears her stamp of approval," he added in a bitter tone. "She wants my baby girl to live in the manner to which she herself, curse her soul, has grown accustomed. I once swore that woman had been sent up from the fires of hell to torment me, and damned if she isn't trying to do it again!"

Dru had heard similar tirades in the past when liquor and self-pity had gotten the best of Caleb. When times were hard and prosperity seemed to purposely elude them, Caleb had dragged out his liquor bottle to drown all his frustrations. On such occasions, Dru had heard Caleb curse his ex-wife for her deceitfulness. Gwen hadn't awaited his return. She had procured the divorce papers on only God knew what grounds, and there was a letter already waiting for Caleb when he arrived in Silver City. It wasn't a pretty story, and when Caleb was drinking heavily he could tear a man's heart out with his tales of betrayal and cruel rejection.

"I want to see my little girl, my only child, before she marries that uppity muckamuck," Caleb declared, staring beseechingly at Dru. "She's all I've got! And if she still wants to marry the sniveling dandy, then I'll give her my blessing, but *not* before I have a chance to see her now that she's all grown up."

"Then catch the next boat to Council Bluffs, take the train to Chicago, and see her for yourself," Dru suggested.

"I can't, damnit all, that woman has purposely given me short notice. She doesn't want me to come and stir up trouble. Besides, I'm too old for such a frantic trip. It would probably kill me, and she would like nothing better. But you have youth and resourcefulness on your

12

side. If anyone can make the journey before the wedding commences, you can. And I'll be indebted to you forevermore."

When Dru looked as if he were about to reject the request, Caleb appealed to the younger man's strong sense of obligation to his family and friends. That was Dru's most admirable trait. The fact was, Dru was loyal to a fault, just like Whong, only not quite so blatant. Because of Dru, the Sullivan brothers had been granted a prosperous life in the mountain valleys of Montana. Because of Dru's persistence, Caleb was finally enjoying his dream of making something of himself, despite Gwen's degrading insults.

"This means everything to me, Dru," Caleb pleaded, his brown eyes probing Dru's bronzed features. "I just want to see Victoria, to ensure that she's happy. Is that too much for a father to ask when he has been deprived of seeing his child for the last decade? I'll pay for all your supplies and expenses and it will cost you nothing but your time." To put the finishing touches on his plea, Caleb unfolded the unsigned telegram that he had been clutching in his fist. Then he broke into a wry smile. "Maybe this will be incentive enough to help you make up your mind. Look who that woman has hand-picked for my daughter to marry . . ."

Dru read the telegram and scowled at the intended groom's name. Wouldn't you know it was the very same man who had cheated him out of a fair price for his cattle herd—the arrogant tycoon who owned the huge stockyard and slaughterhouse beside the railroad depot! Dru had met the stuffy, haughty Hubert Carrington Frazier II and hated him on sight. The thought of anyone, especially Caleb's daughter, marrying that swindler turned Dru's mood pitch-black in one second flat.

For a long, pensive moment, Dru regarded the stocky six-foot man who towered over him. Caleb's lips were compressed into an uncompromising line and his dark eyes bore down on Dru, silently imploring him to accept

13

the proposition. He looked stern and desperate all in the same moment.

"You realize, of course, that if I do steal Victoria away, your ex-wife will probably hunt you down or send someone along with death threats," Dru grumbled.

The hint of a smile hovered on Caleb's lips. It grew wider and then became downright devilish. "That's exactly the way I have it figured," he said. "I have a few choice words to say to that woman and I'd like to spout them in her face while she is standing smack dab in my prospering hotel. I've waited forever to give her a good piece of my mind. And now we'll see how she likes having her daughter taken away from her. Turnabout is fair play, I reckon."

Dru unfolded his tall, muscular frame from the chair and ambled over to pour himself a brandy. The fact that he was even contemplating this cross-country goose-chase was ridiculous. But he was—for Caleb's sake. Dru's downfall was that he had a soft spot in his heart for stray dogs and lost causes. Though he had a strong sense of devotion to his family and close friends, that trait didn't extend to those of the female persuasion. Dru had learned long ago that most women in this part of the country would do and say almost anything to latch onto a man who had struck it rich in the gold fields. Although Dru had known his fair share of women, he didn't spare them much sentiment. That was reserved for his brothers and for Caleb. Women wanted Dru's money, and he wanted the pleasure a woman could occasionally provide. It was as simple as that. His relationships with women, thus far, were shallow and brief, and there had been no strings attached.

"That woman has kept Tori from me and has probably turned her against me. Tori won't even answer my letters," Caleb muttered. "Please, Dru. I'm down to begging you. I want the chance to tell my daughter my side of the story. No doubt, that woman has filled Tori's head with a crock of lies, just to save face. I don't want to

14

go to my grave having my daughter despise me . . ."

Caleb's sentimental tone of voice tugged on Dru's heartstrings. What they were discussing here was out-and-out kidnapping, but it didn't sound like a crime in light of Caleb's past experiences with his ex-wife. And by God, if Caleb wanted to see his daughter, then he would see her!

"All right, my friend, I'll bring her to you if it means that much . . ."

Caleb suddenly snatched Dru's whiskey glass away from him and stuffed several huge gold nuggets in his hand. "You don't have time to stand there dawdling. You've got to put wings on your feet. I hope to God Tori isn't already married when you arrive."

While Caleb hustled him toward the door, Dru rolled the nuggets in his palm and focused a somber gaze on Caleb. "And what happens if I'm too late to stop the wedding?"

"Bring Tori to me anyway," Caleb demanded. "I want to spend some time with my daughter. It's the last chance I'll have." He paused beside the opened door. "And one more thing, Dru—she's probably going to require a few lessons on surviving in the wilds. Teach her to fend for herself outside Chicago . . . just in case my little girl decides Montana isn't such a bad place to spend the rest of her life . . ."

Dru rolled his eyes in disgust. Lord, what was he getting himself into? He was going to have his work cut out for him just getting to Chicago on time. And when he got there, he would have to take a helpless bride captive. Godamighty, he hadn't considered that Tori wouldn't be as capable and resourceful as her father. But how could she be? There weren't many mountain lions, coyotes, or renegade Indians running around loose in Chicago! What the blazes could Tori know about self-preservation in the wilds when the worst difficulty she probably faced up to now was a traffic jam in the crowded streets of Chicago?

15

Caleb's mind had rapidly changed gears to mentally list the provisions Dru would require for his trip to Illinois. Herding Dru and Whong out the door, Caleb volunteered to inform the Sullivans that their eldest brother had gone off on a mission of mercy.

There was not a minute to spare. If Dru was to arrive before the wedding, he should have left the previous week. Damn that woman! She could have given a little more notice! Well, one ornery deed deserved another, Caleb decided. Just see how Gwen liked being deprived of ruling Tori's life. And even if Tori hadn't written to Caleb all these years and had put him out of her mind, he was going to see her again. A father deserved that much, didn't he?

An hour later Dru was asking himself why he had consented to this fast and furious trip and why Whong thought it was his duty to tag along. The man could barely stay atop a horse while they made a high-speed dash northward to catch the steamer down the Missouri River. Whong was an excellent cook and valet, but he was a lousy horseman. Yet, in jumbled English, the Chinaman insisted on accompanying Dru, and so here the two of them were, galloping over hill and dale on a crazed crusade.

Chicago? Godamighty, Chicago seemed a continent away from the Montana gold fields. Dru swore he had misplaced the good sense he had been born with when he agreed to this. Tori Flemming-Cassidy was probably a prissy debutante who had no desire to trek west to see her father. Gwendolyn had undoubtedly raised her daughter in her own image.

Dru could picture the fussy little snip whining and throwing one tantrum after another after she was abducted from the soft lap of luxury. Just what he needed, Dru thought, a spoiled brat of a female to tote west with the ill-adapted Whong who was out of his element in the

16

wilds and who was positively certain he had contracted every disease listed in the medical encyclopedia.

Godamighty! What a long two months this was going to be, Dru thought as he left the Montana mountains far behind. Already he was wishing he was back home where he belonged!

Chapter 2

Victoria Flemming-Cassidy stood before the full-length mirror in her boudoir while her maid and her mother oohed and ahhed over the elegant lace wedding gown. The dainty five-foot-two-inch bride remained still as a statue while her maid swept her waist-length hair into a fashionable coiffure, leaving alluring silver-blond curls dangling around Victoria's forehead and temples.

Indifference etched Tori's stunning features. *If this is supposed to be the happiest day of my life, there is a lot to be desired,* thought Tori. Her mother had earmarked the rich aristocrat for her and had arranged this marriage when Tori procrastinated in setting the wedding date. Tori's heart wasn't in this wedding, and it never had been. But as usual, she was given no choice as to what was to be done with her life. In years past, Tori had rebelled against Gwen's strict authority, but to no avail. Now it was easier not to care, not to feel anything, only to obey. Tori had buried all emotion long ago and resigned herself to going through the paces of living as Gwen ordered.

While Gwendolyn jabbered about what a glorious day this one would be as the two powerful families merged into one, Tori's delicately arched brows puckered into a frown. She supposed Hubert Carrington Frazier II was as good a catch as any. But she was hardly in any position to make comparisons since she could count the men her

19

mother had allowed to court her on one hand. Hubert was reasonably good-looking, well educated, terribly wealthy, and he was the first and only man who had ever been allowed to kiss her. But whether she and Hubert would be compatible was mere speculation since the couple had never been allowed to converse—or do anything else in private. Gwendolyn had seen to it that Tori went into wedlock as pure as the day she was born. Hubert had stolen a quick kiss here and there in the backseat of the carriage when no one was looking, but that was the extent of Tori's experience with romance.

Tori knew only what her mother had told her—which was darned little—about the affection shared between a man and his wife. She supposed she would find out soon enough, this being her wedding day and all . . .

"I cannot imagine why you insist on wearing that tarnished string of pearls Caleb gave you when you were a child," Gwendolyn sniffed distastefully. "They look hideous, and Caleb doesn't give a whit what happens to you—and he never did. You're wasting sentiment by wearing those frightful things!" Sparing herself a glance in the mirror to ensure she looked her best, Gwen focused on Tori, who possessed the beauty that was slowly slipping away from her mother. "Take them off, Victoria. They look ghastly with that expensive gown that cost your father a fortune."

Her father? Tori sorely wished Gwen would cease referring to Edgar Cassidy as her father. He wasn't, after all. Although her natural father had never written to her after he trekked off in search of gold, Tori had faithfully penned letters to him that her mother promised to post. But the only writing Caleb Flemming had ever done was writing his only daughter *out of his life*. Yet, Tori's fond memories of her father lingered. Regretfully, she removed the pearls and clasped them in her hand. They reminded her of another time and place.

"This will be the grandest, most envied affair in Chicago history," Gwendolyn gushed as she shepherded

Tori down the spacious hall.

Who cares? Tori mused sullenly. She didn't love Hubert, even if Gwen assured her that love was not a prerequisite of matrimony. In fact, Tori suspected that Hubert's two mistresses were experiencing more emotion at the moment than she was. Although Tori was expected to be pure and innocent, Hubert wasn't expected to be, and he most definitely wasn't! Two mistresses? Honestly, wouldn't one mistress have been enough for a normal man? This dual set of values for men and women was most perplexing to Tori. Occasionally she had been stung by the ridiculous urge to step down from the pedestal her mother kept her on and go carousing. Of course, the scandal would have horrified Gwen, who was so socially sensitive that the mere threat of gossip terrified her.

Tori chided herself for harboring rebellious thoughts. She owed Gwen and Edgar a great deal. Although her life had been no more than a carefully guarded prison in which she was heavily chaperoned, she had been educated at the finest women's seminary in Chicago. To compensate for her lack of association with men, she was bombarded with culture, and drilled in the niceties of proper behavior. Rules of etiquette had been pounded into her head and she had been taught every last thing a dignified lady should know about life in the upper crust.

Tori dined at the most elegant restaurants, attended every cultural event, and knew all the right people. And now this well-schooled, sheltered princess was about to marry her designated prince. In actuality, Tori felt like a lifelike doll who was prodded through the paces of living in her fairy-tale world. She was certain she was not beginning a new life when she entered the institution of matrimony but would continue the old one, with Hubert instead of Gwen telling her what to do.

Ah well, Tori mused as she slipped the string of pearls around her neck while her mother wasn't looking. She knew no other life now and probably wouldn't fit in anywhere else, even if she made a break for freedom. She

21

was stuck with Hubert Carrington Frazier II, and she could only hope he turned out to be a kind, considerate husband, even if he had no intention of giving up his two mistresses.

After Edgar lifted his stepdaughter from the brougham, he smiled down into her exquisite features. "I hope you will be happy, Victoria."

Offering Edgar a meager smile, Tori lifted the long gown and made her ascent up the steps of the church with the enthusiasm of a condemned criminal trudging to the gallows. She came to a dead stop when the clergyman, garbed in his flowing white robe, moved toward her. Fleetingly, Tori wondered what had become of John Wilson, the resident pastor, but her thoughts were drawn to the man who graced her with a smile.

The clergyman had a thick crop of raven hair and the most incredible pair of blue eyes Tori had ever seen. He was at least six feet five inches tall and as broad as a mountain. There wasn't a hint of refinement in his dark, chiseled features. The angular lines were stamped with a wild nobility that Tori found intriguing. She decided right then and there that this pastor must have served as a circuit rider at some point in his ministry. He had a rugged, outdoors appearance and a natural charm that no doubt left the females in his flock daydreaming on one or two sins for which they would need forgiveness . . .

"Miss Cassidy?" The preacher extended a bronzed hand to draw Tori up the last three steps. "I hope you and your fiancé will forgive this change of plans," he said with a low, slow drawl. "Brother Wilson suddenly became ill and he has asked me to perform the ceremony in his stead."

Gwendolyn was flustered by the news and by this ruggedly handsome pastor who did indeed look as if he belonged in some country church instead of the elegant Chicago cathedral. "But I had so hoped . . ."

22

A reassuring smile hovered on Brother Sullivan's lips. "I will see to it that this monumental occasion will be one you will always remember, Mrs. Cassidy." His rich baritone voice was full of confidence and conviction. "And since I have just met your lovely daughter on the day of her wedding, I would like to spend a few moments alone with her in the pastoral study. After we have had the chance to chat, I would also like to speak with the groom."

A frown creased Gwendolyn's brow. "Isn't that a mite irregular? I didn't know pastors were in the habit of counseling brides and grooms before their weddings."

Brother Sullivan's keen gaze shifted to Edgar Cassidy and then swung back to the bewitching bride. Tori's impassive expression touched him in a way he hadn't expected. An odd sensation swamped Dru, but he shrugged it away before focusing on the mother of the bride who looked as if she had topped forty but intended to go down fighting. Gwen was dressed fit to kill and appeared to cling fiercely to her youth by garbing herself in a gown that drew attention to what was left of her youthful figure. Tori favored her mother, but the young beauty was by far the more stunning of the two women, even with that sad expression in her amethyst eyes.

Displaying another gentle smile, Dru circled his arm around Tori's waist to usher her forward. "Speaking privately with brides and grooms is a formality of my ministry, Mrs. Cassidy," he explained. "A prayer of divine guidance for this upcoming wedding is a symbol of good fortune for the bride and groom. We will only be a moment."

While Tori and the parson strode into the church, Gwendolyn frowned at Edgar. But before she could voice her objection about the unrefined-looking pastor, Hubert Carrington Frazier I and II arrived upon the scene. Together they speculated on the preacher's unexpected request for consultations before the ceremony. The foursome glanced at the study door, expectantly waiting

23

for Tori to return.

It proved to be a long wait.

The instant the door eased shut behind him, Dru Sullivan sprang into action. In the batting of an eyelash, he ripped off Tori's trailing veil and stuffed a handkerchief into her mouth. Employing her lacy veil as a rope, he quickly bound her hands in front of her.

Round violet eyes peered up at the preacher in mute astonishment. Never had anyone done a thing to alarm her, and quite frankly, Tori was too stunned to react. When Dru yanked off his robe to reveal the buckskin shirt beneath it, Tori continued to stare. The garment stretched across his massive chest, revealing the dark matting of hair that peeked through the leather lacings. Doehide breeches that fit his lean hips and muscled thighs like a second set of skin covered the lower half of his torso, and Tori was so entranced by this mountain of a man that she simply stood there marveling at this magnificent specimen of masculinity who made Hubert look like a half-grown schoolboy in comparison.

Despite the rapt attention he was receiving, Dru scooped Tori up in his arms and, with a catlike tread, he crossed the room. Then, in fiend-ridden haste, Dru breezed out the back door toward the wagon that awaited him. Glancing in every direction at once, Dru dropped Tori in the back of the wagon as if she were a feed sack and then threw a smelly canvas tarp over her. In a single bound, he leaped onto the seat to snap the reins over the horses.

Dru supposed he should have been smiling triumphantly as he whizzed down the alley, but he was in the sourest of moods and had been so for two weeks. The journey down the Missouri with Whong had been a nightmare. Thieves had attacked their steamer, pelting the vessel with bullets that forced its occupants to swim to safety or go down with the sinking ship. Whong, who became seasick when he merely glanced at a glass of water, had been too ill to swim. Dru had dragged the Chinaman to shore and had been forced to listen to Whong carry on about how the towering giant had saved his life a second time.

Two days later, Dru, Whong, and the other stranded travelers caught a ride on another passing steamer, but the extra passengers had left the decks excessively crowded. Dru had felt like a sardine and Whong had bowed over him so many times in thanks for saving his life that Dru was sure he would go mad if he were subjected to much more praise.

As if the boat ride and delay weren't enough, Whong had contracted some exotic disease that put him flat on his back. Dru attributed the illness to one too many humble bows; the constant up-and-down motion had apparently put a strain on Whong's stomach and the man couldn't keep his meals down. But Whong insisted he had succumbed to a rare ailment that had yet to be listed in the medical chronicles.

Leaving Whong in Council Bluffs to recuperate, Dru had taken the stage because he had already missed the train bound for Chicago. The stage was delayed twice because of downpours that made the roads slick as glass. Haggard and completely out of sorts, Dru had arrived only two hours before the wedding and was left to hurriedly plan his scheme of abduction. But he had accomplished his purpose, even though he had spent the past few weeks telling himself this whole affair was a mistake. Now he faced a long trip home with this prissy minx and the recuperating Chinaman in tow. God-amighty, he needed to have his head examined for agreeing to this, he decided as he clattered down the alley.

Chapter 3

Muffled squawks erupted from the storage room adjacent to the chapel. Frowning, Hubert Carrington Frazier II strode over to investigate. When he spied the resident clergyman gagged and bound to a chair, he let out a cry of alarm that put the entire congregation of family and guests in arms.

Hubert charged toward the pastoral study and pounded on the door. He was met with silence. While he and his ushers kicked the portal open, Gwendolyn fell into a fit of hysterics. This long-awaited wedding had been transformed into a disaster, and there was no doubt in her mind who was responsible. Caleb Flemming had to be at the bottom of this, Gwen mused between wails of frustration. It was his way of retaliating against her for divorcing him while he wasn't around to contest. He was seeking restitution for being deprived of watching Tori grow up. Gwen just knew it!

But blast it, a woman had to do what she could do to get what she wanted from life. Long before Caleb had come upon the scene, Edgar Cassidy had courted her. But Gwen, silly fool that she was, had been infatuated by Caleb Flemming. Although he was dynamic and exciting, Gwen should never have married the man. He was an adventurer, a dreamer who chased rainbows, and Gwen had realized too late that she needed the finer things in

27

life to be content. And through it all Edgar had always been there, loving her from afar.

Although Gwen's family frowned on divorce, she considered it time and time again those first years of her marriage to Caleb. In fact, she had planned it all . . . the when, where, and how—every important detail. When Edgar made his rise to wealth in the railroad business, Gwen maneuvered Caleb out of the way and married Edgar. She thought she was well rid of her first husband, but it appeared he had found a way to torment Gwen and abduct Victoria. Damn the man!

Well, he wasn't going to get away with it, Gwendolyn told herself as she dabbed away the tears with her embroidered handkerchief. She would have Caleb's head for this bit of mischief.

Muttering vehemently, Hubert stepped over the discarded robe and charged out the back exit to see Dru's wagon careen around the corner. Although Hubert spouted several venomous threats, he gained nothing for his efforts. With his ushers and other members of the wedding party trotting along behind him, Hubert sailed through the church to fetch his carriage.

Dru rounded the corner on two wheels and thundered down Chicago's mud streets. The city was notorious for its puddles, and Dru swore he hit every water hole during his escape. And Tori tended to agree. She bounced uncomfortably in the wagon bed, half smothered by the canvas tarp that was draped over the top portion of her body and half covered with the mud that had flipped in all directions.

Hubert muttered furiously when he tripped over the uneven sidewalks during his mad dash to his coach. Taking up the reins, he led the rescue brigade that pursued his kidnapped bride.

"Damn . . ." Dru growled when he glanced behind him to see the entire wedding party galloping at his heels. He had hoped to sneak off undetected, but considering the kind of luck that had plagued him lately, he knew he

28

shouldn't be surprised to see Hubert giving chase. Dru urged the horses into their swiftest pace and veered around another sharp corner, hoping to lose Hubert and the wedding posse.

A pained groan erupted from Tori's lips when she slammed against the side of the wagon for the fifth time. She was sure her face had been smashed flat and her body bruised from the unfamiliar abuse to which it was being subjected. She had been whisked from her quiet, protected world into the arms of a brawny stranger to confront an uncertain fate.

It was one thing to be late for one's wedding and quite another to be abducted from it! Was she to be held for ransom—molested, murdered? Her mind whirled with grim speculation. Tori hadn't been all that keen on marrying Hubert but it stood to reason that she would have been safer with the intended groom than with this rough-edged scoundrel who obviously had evil designs on her. He was the kind of man Gwen had always warned Tori to avoid like the plague. According to Gwen, this sort of rugged, unscrupulous rapscallion gobbled women alive and seduced them for the mere challenge of it.

For fifteen minutes, Dru zigzagged down the streets, dodging mud holes and pedestrians. Since Chicago wasn't his usual stomping ground, he managed to lose himself, but not the wedding-party posse that was hot on his heels. Finally, he reached the outskirts of the bustling city, and the horses were able to stretch out into their stride. But the dirt path he wound up on was plagued with potholes and so severely washboarded that he bounced on his perch like a rubber ball. Still, he fared considerably better than Tori, whose stomach had leaped to her throat, very nearly strangling her. The fact that she was covered with a tarp like an Egyptian mummy made breathing virtually impossible. She was growing sicker by the second!

The horses Dru had rented from the stable were no match for the well-bred trotters who headed the wedding-party coaches. When the steeds found open road, they began to close the gap, and Dru began a string of fluent curses. He surveyed his surroundings and his mind raced to devise a plan of escape. If he didn't shake off his pursuers and quickly, he would face a necktie party—Chicago style! Gwen Cassidy would string him up, sure as hell!

The instant Dru spotted the bridge that spanned the creek ahead of him, a plan hatched in his mind, and not a second too soon! The instant he reached the bridge, he stamped on the brake, bringing the wagon to a skidding halt. Tori, unprepared for the hasty stop, smashed against the sideboards of the wagon and groaned miserably. She was going to be sick, she just knew it. She felt as if she had been riding a runaway carousel . . .

A startled gasp burst from her lips when an unseen hand groped across her body, touching previously unexplored territory. In less than a heartbeat, the canvas was yanked away and she was left to stare into those brilliant blue eyes that reminded her of chips of azure sky. Earlier, she had been intrigued by this man who had impersonated the parson, and again she found herself gazing in fascination at his incredibly virile physique and ruggedly handsome features. He was certainly a different person without his saintly demeanor and churchly robe. From saint to devil, Tori thought as Dru jerked her upright and then set her to her feet on the bridge.

"I hope the hell you can swim, Chicago," Dru muttered as he propelled the confused beauty toward the railing of the bridge.

Tori gave her head a negative shake and her eyes widened in alarm when she stared down at the water. Under protest, Tori was hoisted onto the railing, and her eyes fell to the rapidly flowing stream that had been filled to capacity during recent rains. Not only did Tori not know how to swim a lick, but she only just now realized she had a fear of heights. Sweet merciful heavens, she was going to drown and die of heart seizure all in the same moment!

Dru rolled his eyes and sighed in frustration. "Godamighty, Chicago, why don't you at least know how to do the simplest of things? But whether you can swim or not, you're taking the plunge."

Muffled squawks bubbled beneath the handkerchief Dru had stuffed in Tori's mouth. Fighting in earnest, she tried to hop down onto the bridge, but Dru was as strong as a bull. If he didn't want his captive to budge from her spot, then she wouldn't budge.

Grumbling at the comedy of errors and ridiculous antics he had been forced into in order to satisfy Caleb's whim, Dru steadied Tori on the railing. His gaze lifted over her silver-blond head to monitor the approach of the wedding-party posse.

Gwendolyn's shrill, hysterical screech could be heard in the distance, followed by Hubert's furious snarl. For a moment Hubert's fuming gaze clashed with Dru's. Dru broke into a gloating grin when recognition dawned in Hubert's eyes. Thus far, this was the only satisfaction Dru had enjoyed. Just knowing Hubert was irate did Dru a world of good.

The only one who wasn't scowling in outrage was Tori's stepfather, and Dru didn't have time to ask himself why. The man was the only calm individual in the bunch. In fact, he appeared more amused than outraged!

Wild-eyed, Tori peered up at Dru, who had fixed his attention on her. An ornery smile curved his lips as he wrapped his arm around her.

"Swimming lesson number one . . ." he declared as he bent his knees and sprang out from the railing with Tori clamped in his arms.

A muffled scream echoed in the afternoon air as Dru dragged Tori through the air to splash into the creek. Terror caused her overworked heart to skip several vital beats as she frantically fought to resurface. She would have clawed at Dru like a drowning cat if her hands hadn't been bound together. As it was, she was left to

31

flounder and pray the air in her collapsing lungs would sustain her until she reached the surface.

The instant her life passed before her and she swore she had breathed her last breath, a steely hand clamped around her tangled hair, dragging her head above the water. Tori had no time to dissolve into frightened tears as Dru grabbed her by the nape of the neck and paddled into the swift-moving current. After a wave of water slapped her in the face, Tori sucked in much-needed air through her flared nostrils. True, she hadn't known how to swim, but her legs automatically kicked to keep her afloat, even while the weight of her soggy wedding gown and heavy petticoats sought to tow her under like an anchor.

For what seemed forever, she felt the current and her abductor tugging at her. Valiantly, Tori battled her fear of drowning and swore that what was supposed to be the happiest day of her life had become positively the worst!

The desperation in Tori's eyes caused Dru to securely clench his arm around her waist, holding her body against him. He made sure her head remained above water most of the time, or often enough at least to prevent her from going down forevermore.

Courageous to the bitter end, Hubert Carrington Frazier II tore off his expensive jacket, executed a perfect swan dive, and gave chase. Several other gentlemen, whether to impress their wives or sweethearts or to save Tori from a fate worse than death, leaped into the stream to provide reinforcements. When Dru and his captive disappeared around the bend, the swimmers followed in pursuit.

The instant they were out of sight, Dru struggled to shore, ripped the hem off Tori's costly wedding gown, tied it to a piece of driftwood, and hurled it downstream. Grasping Tori's hand, Dru dragged her up the steep slope that was covered with underbrush and then shoved her facedown in the dirt. Tori's face became instant mud and her breath came out in a groan when the giant of a man

32

kerplopped on top of her. She couldn't have screamed if she'd wanted to. There was no breath left. Her lungs had been deflated when her petite body was mashed as flat as a pancake.

For an agonizing eternity, Dru kept her pinned down. After the flotilla of men swam by in pursuit of the white fabric that floated downstream, Dru leaped to his feet. Hoisting Tori upright, he threw her over his shoulder and raced off like a bat out of hell. Just as Dru had anticipated, the team of horses he had rented had become startled by the clatter of phaetons and broughams that rumbled over the bridge. His team of horses had thundered down the road to escape the commotion, but by the time Dru hauled Tori a quarter of a mile, the horses and his wagon stood waiting for him.

Sweeping Tori onto the seat, Dru plunked down beside her and charged down the road as fast as the team could go. Tori clenched her nails into Dru's arm to prevent being catapulted from the perch during their reckless flight down a road that barely measured up to minimal standards of what a road was supposed to be. More accurately, the path they traveled resembled a dragon's spine with its rocks and potholes. Tori didn't give a thought to leaping from the wagon while the landscape whizzed past her at such incredible speeds. She knew she would break her neck if she attempted to jump. And after very nearly drowning, she wasn't quite ready to risk another death-defying maneuver. Taking her chances with her daring captor seemed the least of several evils. And so there she sat, frozen to her perch, wondering what fiendish torment this gigantic renegade had in mind for her.

It was at that point that Tori again wondered if marrying Hubert and tolerating his two mistresses wouldn't have been safer, even if much duller, than this hair-raising escapade. Hubert would pay a king's ransom to get her back, wouldn't he? Of course he would, Tori tried to reassure herself. And even if he didn't, Edgar

33

would fork over the money because Gwen would demand it. Although Edgar was only her stepfather and her marriage to Hubert was nowhere near a love match, neither man would let her meet with disaster. Hubert's two mistresses probably couldn't care less that Tori had been abducted, but he had his family honor to uphold. Someone would come to her rescue, Tori assured herself. But then her shoulders sagged dispiritedly. This renegade, whoever the devil he was, had already eluded an entire wedding party. That thought left Tori speculating that she might have been a tad optimistic to think this wily varmint could be caught! Sweet merciful heavens, she was in serious trouble!

While Tori and Dru were racing cross-country, Hubert was growling furiously. He had finally swum close enough to realize the white object ahead of him was no more than the torn fabric from Tori's gown. Infuriated that he had been bamboozled, Hubert clambered ashore and stormed back to the bridge with his soggy ushers dripping along behind him.

When Hubert appeared empty-handed, Gwendolyn fainted in her husband's arms. Edgar stared downriver, fighting down a smile.

"He eluded us," Hubert reported bitterly. Shaking the snagging twigs and clinging moss from his trousers, Hubert stalked toward his carriage. "But I'll find that bastard. And when I do, he'll be publicly executed for this injustice. I'll see to that!"

"I think we should wait to see if the abductor sends us a ransom note," Edgar declared as he readjusted his limp wife in his arms. When Hubert opened his mouth to protest, Edgar held up a hand to forestall him. "No doubt the scoundrel saw his chance to make money by kidnapping Victoria. We will wait a few days for a note before we begin an all-out search."

Although Hubert didn't agree with the decision, he

clamped his mouth shut and plopped into his carriage. Furiously, he wracked his brain, trying to recall the name of the man he had tangled with the previous year. He hadn't forgotten the face, but the name was slow in coming. Simpson . . . Simon . . . It was something like that. Damn the man. This was probably his way of acquiring the money he had lost the previous year. Just what Hubert needed on his wedding day—a resentful man he had done business with who had an axe to grind!

Chapter 4

Darkness settled over the countryside, bathing the world in moonlight and shadows. Dru deemed it safe to pause and rest since there was no indication they were being followed. Now that he had his captive in tow, he couldn't employ the well-traveled roads, trains, or stages. Unless he missed his guess, the Cassidys and the Fraziers would have every police detective and bloodhound in Chicago combing the country in search of them.

Dru was dead-tired. For more weeks than he cared to count, he had battled the clock to reach Chicago in time. At long last he could catch his breath and relax. And when he returned to Virginia City, he was going to chew Caleb up one side and down the other for sending him on this insane mission.

Why Caleb would want anything to do with this overprotected little city slicker after all these years baffled Dru. Judging by what he had seen, Caleb and his ex-wife and daughter lived in two entirely different worlds. Little Miss Chicago would be completely out of her element in the raucous mining town. Hell, she couldn't even *swim* and seemed deathly afraid of heights. All she probably knew was how to garb herself in stylish clothes and attend parties, teas, and concerts. To Dru's way of thinking Caleb had allowed sentiment to rule his logic. This pampered minx would have been better off where she was!

This was a disastrous mistake! The blond-haired fairy princess in her muddy wedding gown had no business challenging the wilderness. She didn't know beans about surviving, and Dru was stuck with her for the duration of the journey. Even if he taught Tori everything he knew about life on the outposts of civilization, she was never going to fit in. Here he was—a no-frills kind of man— saddled with a sheltered and overprotected debutante. Caleb hadn't asked Dru for a favor; he had put a curse on him when he sent his ex-partner to retrieve this prissy bundle of fluff.

On that dismal thought, Dru tied Tori's hand to his left wrist so she couldn't escape him, then stretched out in the back of the wagon for some much-needed sleep.

Tori flinched at the feel of her captor's muscular body cuddled familiarly against hers. The unnerving feel of having a man lying beside her had her wriggling and flouncing like a fish out of water.

"Calm down, Chicago," Dru finally muttered as he draped a brawny arm over her to still her nervous squirming. "I'm only going to sleep beside you. If you were expecting something more, you'll be sorely disappointed. I'm about as tired as one man can get."

Mumbled sentences rattled beneath the gag that covered Tori's mouth. After a full minute of listening to her unintelligible comments, Dru tugged the handkerchief away to interpret her words.

"What the hell is wrong now, Chicago?" he questioned impatiently.

"I can't sleep on my left side," Tori insisted. "And with our hands tied together, I can't turn over and my arms are . . ."

Like a long-suffering man forced to deal with a dim-witted woman, Dru rolled his eyes and shook his head. Wearily, he pulled Tori over the top of him and twisted around so their heads were facing the back of the wagon, permitting Tori to lie on her right side with her left arm draped over his shoulder. Her right arm then became his pillow.

After wriggling for another few seconds, Tori grumbled uncomfortably. "This isn't going to work, either," she declared. "I'm accustomed to sleeping by myself!"

Dru muttered under his breath and propped up on his elbow to shove the handkerchief over her mouth. "Clam up, woman. This is as good as it's going to get."

The harsh tone of his voice assured Tori that she had pushed her captor to the limits of his patience. Obviously he was going to make no further effort to see that she slept comfortably.

When Dru slumped against her, Tori stared owlishly at the stars that twinkled overhead. She was caked with mud, bound and gagged, and forced to sleep beside this big galoot. God, this simply wasn't her day. Everything that could have possibly gone wrong had! Although she hadn't exactly anticipated her wedding night with relish, never in her worst nightmare had she imagined she would be spending what would have been her honeymoon with a perfect stranger.

Oh Lord, she prayed, *thank you for letting this day be over. And if You could see Your way clear to make tomorrow a little better, I'd really appreciate it.*

Depression drifted over her like a dense fog as she closed her eyes. She was sleeping with a man she didn't know in the back of a wagon. Those were firsts on both counts. Tori had never bedded down with a man—ever—and she had never slept without a roof over her head. If she managed to catch a wink of sleep, she would be surprised . . .

Victoria was not by any means a morning person. Gwendolyn had always insisted it was unfashionable for the very rich to rise before midday and Tori had become conditioned to late sleeping. When Dru nudged her at the crack of dawn, Tori was cranky, never having been expected to function at such an ungodly hour.

Dru's second nudge caused Tori to grumble into her gag, but he was persistent. "Get up, Chicago. We're burning daylight."

Heavy-lidded eyes glared back at her nemesis, and Dru inwardly groaned at Tori's exceptional beauty. Although her silver-blond hair was a mass of rattails, her face splotched with mud, and her white gown a dingy shade of brown, she had been blessed with elegantly carved features and a curvaceous body that no man could ignore. Dru appreciated natural beauty, and fulfilling his body's physical cravings had always been second nature to him. In every mining camp along the way, he had found satisfaction in the arms of the trollops who flocked to the gold fields. There had been dance-hall girls and paramours galore in Virginia City, and Dru had his favorites, but none of them came remotely close to matching Victoria's comeliness. Mother Nature had labored over this enchanting nymph. Tori's skin was fair, and as soft as satin. Her eyes were a fascinating shade of violet that changed in varying shades of light. And to make her even more distracting, she had a figure that would have stopped a stampede to the gold fields.

Although Dru admired Tori's beauty and regal poise, he resented all the opportunities she had been granted in life. Dru had forgone higher learning when necessity forced him to support his brothers. He had scratched and clawed to provide the essentials for his struggling family. In short, Tori was the symbol of elegant refinement, and Dru was the product of years of hard knocks, hard living, and firsthand experience.

Grumbling at the wanderings of his mind, Dru agilely rolled off the back of the wagon and pulled Tori down beside him not caring whether she was ready to get up or not. When Dru felt another wave of fascination rippling over him, he glanced away from the sleepy-eyed sprite. Already he was lecturing himself on keeping his distance from Caleb's daughter. She was a lovely creature, but she

40

came from a world Dru knew nothing about and didn't really care to. She would return to marry that dandy of a fiancé and Dru would never see her again. They had absolutely nothing in common. They looked at life from two different perspectives . . . But Godamighty, she was gorgeous by anybody's standards! He would do himself a great favor if he could just forget that . . .

Tori was becoming crankier by the second. The gag had left her mouth bone-dry and she had never been treated so disrespectfully in her life. She had just begun to realize she had a temper and now it was dangerously close to bursting loose. No one had ever crossed her before, except her mother, and Tori took quick offense to Dru's callous attitude and lack of consideration. She'd had nothing to eat or drink since the previous afternoon and she was certain she looked positively horrible—and felt the same. As tolerant and even-tempered as she had always been, this was simply too much! She lashed out in frustration at the man who kept her chained to him with her wedding veil.

"Ouch!" Dru jumped back when Tori kicked him squarely in the shins. "Cut that out or I'll turn you over my knee and throttle you."

Violet eyes flashed and muffled words filled the still morning air. Amused by her display of temper, Dru removed the gag. All her pent-up feelings came flooding out. Tori had experienced more emotion in the course of one day than she had in a lifetime and it had been bottled up inside her, waiting to explode. And explode it did!

"I have never in all my life been treated so abominably," she snapped, her amethyst eyes flashing fire. "I demand to know your intentions, sir! Your behavior is beneath contempt, and I expect your apology this instant."

Dru took one look at the rumpled beauty and burst out laughing. He didn't know ladies of quality were allowed to display their tempers, no matter what the situation. There were obviously a few cracks in Tori's sophisticated

41

veneer. All of Gwendolyn's strict discipline clearly hadn't squelched Tori's bold daring and fiery temper. It must have come from her mother's side of the family, Dru guessed. Caleb rarely lost his temper except when he was frustrated with "that woman," as he chose to call his ex-wife.

"How dare you laugh at me, you big ape," Tori spewed, amazed at her own audacity but enjoying this outlet of frustration. She had never raised her voice to anyone in all her life and now she was spouting like a whale. But it felt good to explode, even if this overt display of temper contradicted the strict rules Gwen had drilled into her head.

"My, my," Dru drawled. "What a nasty temper!"

His gaze instinctively worked its way over Tori's heaving breasts and the trim indentation of her waist. A waterfall of pearls was draped around her neck, partially concealing the plunging neckline of her gown and the generous display of bosom. Dru would have much preferred to feast upon her creamy flesh than have his view blocked by the thick strands of pearls and impulsively he removed the necklace.

"Give those back to me!" she sputtered in outrage, reaching out with her bound hands to snatch the pearls from his grasp.

A frown creased Dru's brow when Tori hugged the tarnished pearls to her breast as if they were a veritable treasure. After watching the sassy blonde fume for a moment, Dru broke into a taunting smile. "I didn't know ladies of quality were allowed to fly into snits. Isn't that sort of thing beneath the gentry?"

Tori did not appreciate his mocking tone. It rankled her to have this brawny giant in buckskin poking fun at her. It was obvious he wasn't a gentleman, because a gentleman would never purposely offend a lady. His resonant voice carried an unsophisticated drawl and his gaze wandered over her as if he were speculating on what lay beneath her soiled garb. Tori was not in the habit of being blatantly ogled. Her captor stared at her as if he were the rat and she was the cheese. He was certainly playing *his* part to the hilt, darn him. The thought provoked another gush of temper and heated words sprang to tongue before she could think to bite them back.

"I will not have some backwoods bumpkin taunting me," Tori snapped, her voice growing higher and wilder by the moment. "I have been dragged from my wedding. I very nearly drowned twice and I was forced to sleep with you. You are trying to starve me to death. If you expect me to behave like a lady, then you will have to behave like a gentleman—though I doubt you have the capacity, considering the deplorable way you have treated me thus far. And if you think . . ."

Dru stuffed the gag back in her mouth. Tori had hit an exposed nerve and she was trying his patience. She was a spoiled little snip who had placed herself on a pedestal to look down on the rest of God's less fortunate creatures. Dru had consented to this wild escapade because of Caleb's valued friendship, but he didn't have to tolerate a verbal lynching from this snippy chit!

"Look, Chicago, I don't like this any better than you do," he growled down into her sizzling glare that attempted to fry him to a crisp. "But I agreed to take you back to Montana so you could see your father, and that's exactly what I'm going to do, whether you or I want to travel together or not. We don't have to like each other. We only have to *tolerate* each other for the next few weeks."

Montana? So that was where her father was. But why would he want to see her now when he had ignored her for ten long years? Still grappling with the unexpected news, Tori allowed herself to be propelled to a tree and tethered like a horse. That in itself set her newfound temper to full bloom.

"There's a small settlement a mile down the road," Dru informed her. "I'll fetch some supplies and some

43

food." The crow's-feet that sprayed from the corners of his eyes deepened as a smile of ridicule spread across his sensual lips. "Heaven forbid that I should deprive this royal princess of a feast when she has never known the meaning of any form of deprivation."

After double-checking to ensure Tori couldn't tear herself loose from the tree without taking it with her, Dru dropped into a mocking bow. "I will take my leave now, Your Highness. But I do believe this cross-country jaunt is just what a haughty city slicker like you needs. After you discover how the other half lives, you can prance back to your stuffy fiancé and your rosy dream world." He looked her up and down in such an insulting manner that Tori bristled. "After I take that silver spoon out of your mouth and bring you down a notch or three, you might even be tolerable, Chicago. Maybe, but I doubt it . . ."

When Dru turned and sauntered away, Tori hurled a nasty rejoinder at him, but the gag caused a great deal of it to be lost in the mumbled translation. Dru knew by the tone of her voice that he had received a sound tongue-lashing, even if he couldn't decipher her words. And if looks could kill, he was sure he would have been drawn, quartered, and hanging in one of the slaughterhouses owned by Hubert Carrington Frazier II.

While Dru hopped onto the wagon seat, Tori's mutinous gaze followed him. Although she despised this rude heathen, there was something intriguing about him. Though she would never like him, this was a totally different experience than she'd ever had with a man. He didn't patronize her or cater to her the way Hubert and the other gentlemen in Chicago did. Being a lady of quality, men had handled Tori with kid gloves. But this uncultured bumpkin from Montana said exactly what he thought and he minced no words. It was obvious that tact was not among his scant virtues.

Against her will, Tori's assessing gaze wandered over Dru's lean hips and the broad expanse of his back. The

44

man had shoulders like a buffalo, and muscles bulged beneath his buckskin shirt. She had felt them the previous night when she had been forced to snuggle up beside him for warmth. He was swarthy and virile and rugged . . . and she wished she hadn't noticed! It was a waste of time to be physically attracted to a man she had her heart set on hating. And he clearly had no use for her at all.

Tori gave herself a mental slap for attaching any sort of romantic connotation to this harrowing experience. She had been abducted from her safe, secure world by a lower life form. There was nothing romantic about being in the custody of this varmint who probably hadn't even been *born*, but rather had simply cracked open his shell and slithered out from under a rock.

Just because this mountain of a man possessed a certain earthy sensuality and oozed potential vitality didn't mean he was Prince Charming. Just because his full lips quirked into a seductive smile and his baby-blue eyes danced with living fire didn't mean Tori had the slightest interest in him. They were cut from a different scrap of wood and they would do nothing more than share the same air for a time.

Tori prided herself on being reasonably sensible. She knew it was ridiculous to feel anything but contempt for this man who spoke so disrespectfully to her. Why, he didn't even call her by her name, for crying out loud! *Chicago*, he kept saying in that rich baritone voice of his. It was meant to be an insult, she reckoned. Well, she would give *him* a nickname! And she would call him a few other choice names when she got the chance, too. Let that big brute become the brunt of *her* intimidating remarks and see how *he* liked it!

45

Chapter 5

A curious frown knitted Tori's brow when Dru returned later with two horses, saddlebags, and bulky sacks of supplies strapped behind him. Without a word, he opened a can of beans, removed Tori's gag, and spoon-fed her. The meal did ward off the hunger pangs, but Tori was accustomed to lacy tableclothes, polished silverware, and succulent three-course meals. This was the poorest excuse for a breakfast she had consumed in all her twenty years. Her taste buds objected to the gooey substance and it was all she could do to swallow without gagging.

When Tori had choked down the distasteful beans, Dru grinned mischievously. It did his heart good to see this regal princess gulping down the kind of food that had sustained him during the difficult phase of his life. A person had to acquire a taste for cold beans, and Dru was initiating Tori. He would indoctrinate her into the real world, just as Caleb had requested. He was going to teach her to *survive*, instead of living in that fairy-tale world in Chicago.

"This stuff is horrible!" Tori croaked, and then shuddered when another glob of beans slid down her throat.

"Not too long ago, I lived on beans and stale bread," Dru reminisced before taking a bite of the plain fare. "I was down to my last handful of gold dust and there was no relief in sight. Life wasn't a bowl of cherries." A teasing grin crossed his face. "It was a can of beans. I sold everything of value to buy beans and I got by until times got better."

Her pretty face puckered in an offended frown. "And I suppose I am to suffer these disgusting meals just so I'll understand the hell you went through," she muttered sourly.

"You'll live, Chicago, just as I did. And when you go back to your safe little world in the big city, you'll appreciate a good thick steak and vegetables smothered in cream sauces." He dipped up a spoonful of beans and chewed. "But for now, you're going to eat to live, instead of living to eat. And I regret to report that you will have to miss all the grand social events of the season. We won't have much time for entertainment during our trek west."

Tori would have hurled an insulting comment, but she had yet to swallow the mushy beans that had finally come unglued from the roof of her mouth. When she sputtered at the repugnant taste that attacked her senses, Dru reached over to whack her between the shoulder blades.

"Come along, Chicago, you need to change clothes before we begin the long ride ahead of us."

Tori stared at him in stupefied astonishment when he retrieved a set of buckskins from the saddlebag and held them up for her inspection. "You expect me to wear those?" she scoffed.

He nodded his raven head affirmatively and broke into an ornery laugh.

"I won't!" Tori contested. "Ladies do not wear breeches!"

"Who the hell told you that?" he grunted.

"My mother."

"I should have known," Dru muttered. "The fact is, when necessity dictates, a woman will do what she must do." His blue eyes danced with deviltry. "Are you going to put them on or must I do it for you?"

48

The casual menace in his glance and his threatening tone provoked Tori's chin to jut out at a defiant angle. "I told you I'm not wearing them. First you'll have me looking like you, and the next thing I know, you'll want me to *act* like you." Her eyes raked his arresting physique, wishing she could find just one flaw. Unfortunately there were none as far as she could see. "I'd rather die than look like a Montana bumpkin."

A shocked gasp erupted from Tori's lips when Dru's calloused hand clamped around the bodice of her gown. His knuckles made unfamiliar contact with the swells of her breasts and shock waves undulated through Tori. To her indignation, Dru ripped the gown down the middle, exposing the lacy chemise beneath it. Tori turned every color in the rainbow as she attempted to cover herself from his leering gaze.

"Damn you, Montana!" she hissed furiously. She had never cursed in her life, and she had never *ever* allowed a man to see her in her unmentionables, either.

Dru threw back his head and cackled at the wild blush of color that rushed to Tori's cheeks. Lord, what an innocent she was. The way she was behaving, one would have thought it was the end of the world for a man to see a woman in her undergarments. Dru had seen far more than frilly chemises! He just wished he wasn't quite so aware of this particular female in this particularly enticing chemise that was so sheer, it revealed the rosy tips of her breasts. It took incredible self-control not to reach out and touch what his eyes beheld.

An unwanted tingle trickled down Dru's spine. He didn't appreciate that this bit of sophisticated fluff could arouse him without even trying. Caleb would have a conniption fit if his pure, chaste daughter wound up naked in Dru's arms and they . . .

Dru didn't dare finish the tantalizing thought. He was already experiencing an ache in his loins just visualizing how Tori would look in the altogether. Shaking himself free of the scintillating thought, he focused on her flashing eyes.

"Now, are you going to put these on or shall I do it for you, Chicago?" he asked her a second time. "The choice is yours, but I warn you, I'm running short on patience."

Begrudgingly, Tori let go of her ripped bodice long enough to snatch the garments from his outstretched hand. "I will manage on my own, thank you very much, Montana," she sneered, her voice thick with bitterness.

Dru crossed his arms over his broad chest and grinned in spite of himself. Tori was already beginning to emerge from her reserved shell. She might be a bona fide lady, but he'd bet she was learning things about herself that she hadn't known while puttering around in her fairyland castle—having her own way more often than not, no doubt. She probably never knew she had a temper, for one, and that she could stand up for herself when there was no one around to do it for her. Dru wasn't sure what possessed him to antagonize Tori, but he enjoyed razzing her. Maybe he was using Tori as his scapegoat, making her the brunt of all the frustration he'd experienced. Or maybe he was simply ridiculing a world he didn't understand . . .

His thoughts trailed off when Tori glanced suspiciously at him and then ducked under a tree limb. "It's not as if I've never seen a woman in the buff before," he called after her as she disappeared into the bushes. It wasn't a boast, only a statement of fact. "We are going to be living together for a month so you might as well get accustomed to seeing me naked, and vice versa. There ain't a helluva lot of private bathhouses out in the wilderness, Chicago. And you are going to have to become familiar with the phrase *make-do*."

"*Aren't*, not *ain't*," she corrected him as she peeled off her soiled wedding gown. "And we have seen enough of each other already." Hurriedly, Tori stepped into the doehide breeches that had obviously been tailored to fit someone even smaller than she was. The trousers hugged her hips like a glove and the shirtlaces strained across her

50

breasts, revealing more bosom than she preferred to expose to that lusty ape. "And you may well have gaped at every other female on the planet, but you'll not see any more of me than absolutely necessary!"

"My dear Chicago, I doubt you have anything I haven't already seen," he taunted unmercifully. "Besides, I already told you I wasn't interested in seducing you." That was an outright lie. Dru was definitely interested, but he would have preferred to die before he let that snippy minx know it. "I like my women experienced. You wouldn't know the first thing about pleasing a man, and I've got too much to teach you already without giving you lessons in passion."

No one had ever spoken so bluntly and disrespectfully to Tori in all her born days! For twenty years she had been protected from such uncouth degenerates and crude miscreants. Dru's mocking retorts set another fire beneath her temper, and she muttered several of the curses she had heard but had been told never to repeat.

It occurred to Tori that since Dru had untied her hands to allow her to change her clothes, she now had the perfect opportunity to make her escape. If she could dart through the bushes, Dru wouldn't have the slightest idea where to find her.

Giving way to that thought, Tori shot through the underbrush like a bullet and dived beneath a sprawling cedar bush. Growling irritably, Dru charged through the thicket, mentally kicking himself for taking this female for granted. But Tori was so inexperienced in deception that it was barely a minute before Dru grabbed her by the ankles and yanked her out from under the bush. While she sputtered furiously, he hoisted her to her feet.

"You can't escape me, Chicago, so don't waste my time and yours," he grumbled as he dragged her back to the horses. "You broke every tree limb you passed trying to hide from me. Even a blind man could have found you. Lord, woman, you have a lot to learn."

He and his colossal arrogance! she thought resentfully.

51

He was so cussed sure of himself and his abilities as a seasoned frontiersman. She ought to learn all he had to teach her and then beat him at his own game! Wouldn't that be the crowning glory if she could outfox this fox? She would know all *he* knew, plus all *she* knew. Then they would see who was the better man!

An amused grin crinkled Dru's bronzed features when he noticed that Tori was still wearing her tarnished pearls with her buckskins. Dru never claimed to know much about style, but the pearls and the doehide definitely clashed.

"Will you take those things off, Chicago?" When he reached out to rip them loose, Tori clamped her hands over the jewels.

"I don't care how bad they look with buckskins, I'm not taking them off . . . ever!" she insisted.

Amused by her streak of defiance, Dru smiled as he contemplated the strands of pearls. "Even though the gems don't suit your outfit, I suppose you could always tear them off and lay a path of pearls if you got into trouble. They would lead me to you."

The tender touch of his hand upon hers caused Tori's heart to flip-flop in her chest. It was much easier to deal with the goading bumpkin than the seductive rake she now encountered. But Tori wasn't going to succumb just because this rascal turned on the charm. "Believe me, Montana, the last thing I want, if I ever do manage to escape you, is to have you find me again," she assured him in no uncertain terms.

"Are you sure about that?" He stepped closer, eclipsing the sun and casting an ominous shadow over her. "I have been told that I am handy, and very entertaining to have around."

When his voice dropped to a low, provocative tone that sought to crumble her barriers of defense, Tori retreated a step. This wretched beast wasn't going to play up to her after he had insulted her every chance he got! And she most certainly wasn't going to be receptive to his disarming smiles and sensuous tone of voice.

"I thought you said you didn't want to waste daylight," she reminded him, flashing him a disapproving glare.

In wicked amusement, Dru watched the shapely blonde climb back inside her reserved shell. Which was just as well, he decided. She was off limits, even if he couldn't resist teasing and touching her.

When Dru ambled over to lead her horse toward her, Tori stared up at the long-legged steed in bleak silence. She had only just resolved to learn all there was to know about "roughing it" and she was facing her first challenge so soon. She had never been on the back of a horse and here Dru had already raised the stirrups so she could sit comfortably in the saddle. But she would need a ladder to reach the first step! And even if she did mount the huge creature without humiliating herself, she didn't know the first thing about steering a horse. The grooms at the stable tended the steeds and drove the carriages.

A muffled groan tumbled from Dru's lips as Tori gaped at the paint mare as if she were a creature from outer space. "Godamighty, don't tell me. Let me guess. Not only don't you know how to swim or eat anything except fancy Frenchified meals, but you can't ride, either. Hell's bells, Chicago, where have you been all your life?"

The intimidating question stabbed at Tori like a sharp-edged dagger. It cut her pride to shreds to realize how totally incompetent she was, how helpless she must appear to this brawny jack-of-all-trades.

Tears of frustration sprang to her eyes. She wasn't a crier, but then she never really had anything to cry about until now. Her abductor had preyed so heavily on her emotions that it thoroughly shattered her composure to have him ridicule her for the umpteenth time. The unwanted tears bled down her cheeks like an unleashed river, embarrassing her to no end and making it even more impossible to get herself in hand.

Dru muttered at the sobs that erupted from Tori's

53

buckskin-clad form. "Spare me the tears, Chicago," he snapped, giving her a sound shaking that caused her head to whip backward and the tangle of curls to ripple down her back like a waterfall of sun and moonbeams. All he succeeded in doing was wrenching more sobs out of her. "Stop that! You are not going to cry your way to Virginia City. Do you hear me?" His voice boomed like a cannon.

Tori wiped away the tears with the back of her hand and then reacquainted him with her look of contempt. "I hate you . . ." Her shattered voice trailed off, realizing she still didn't know the man's name. Until now he had only been a nightmare from which she'd been unable to awaken. Now that she despised the very real ground he walked on, she wanted to know exactly whom she detested. "Who are you anyway?"

Dru dropped into an exaggerated bow, similar to the kind Whong constantly executed. "Dru Sullivan at your service," he murmured in mock obedience.

"Well, Dru Sullivan, I cannot imagine why you feel inclined to drag me to Montana to see my father," she grumbled. "My father abandoned me more than ten years ago and he never answered a single one of my letters. If you think I will be grateful to you for carting me to a man who never wanted me around in the first place, you are sorely mistaken. And if you think I'm going to climb up on that horse and ride like a man, your biceps are obviously a great deal larger than your brain!"

The insult bounced off without leaving a mark, but the comment about Caleb left Dru frowning. He knew full well that Caleb had written to his daughter regularly, and that she was the one who had never answered . . . unless the letters had never arrived. Unless he missed his guess, Gwendolyn had intercepted all the mail to drive a wedge between father and daughter. That was a rotten thing for "that woman" to do. Dru spitefully hoped Gwen was miserable right now, wondering what had become of her daughter. She deserved to fry in her own grease if she had indeed deceived Tori into thinking her father wanted nothing to do with her!

"You are the one who is sorely mistaken," Dru contradicted as he scooped Tori into his arms and deposited her atop the paint mare. "Your father and I prospected together for seven years, and I can attest that he wrote letters to you, letters you never answered. I'd bet my right arm your mother didn't want you to correspond with your father. You probably have her to thank for your father's complete absence in your life. Not that you cared," he added scornfully. "While you were tripping the light fantastic at all the grand balls and attending all those uppity concerts and lectures, your father was struggling to survive."

"Damn you," Tori growled, becoming aware that there were moments when profanity had its place. And *this* was definitely the time and the place. If Dru didn't stop mocking her, she swore she was going to clobber him and then consign him to the fiery pits of hell with condeming curses.

Two black brows jacknifed as Dru swung up behind her. "Godamighty, Chicago, you really are beginning to sound like me. My lack of culture has already begun to rub off on you."

His lack of culture wasn't what concerned her most at the moment! It was the feel of his virile body plastered against hers that really rattled her. His inner thighs hugged her hips and his muscular chest was meshed against her back. And to make matters worse, his brawny arms encircled her to take up the reins. Tori could feel him breathing. Every ounce of air she inhaled was clogged with his masculine scent. Suddenly she was aware of the vast difference between his rock-hard body and her own soft one. Her heart fluttered in her chest and she squirmed, discomforted by the effect his nearness had on her.

"What the blazes do you think you're doing?" she crowed, her voice two octaves higher than normal.

"I'm going to teach you how to ride," he informed her,

fighting down the unexpected tremor of pleasure that sitting so close to this shapely nymph aroused. "And by dusk you'll probably have blisters on your bottom from so many hours in the saddle. But you'll be an experienced rider before you know it."

Tori flushed beet-red. Her bottom was none of his business, and she'd cut out her tongue long before she confessed to a blistered backside! This rake, who seemed so casual about nudity and sex, would probably insist on inspecting her derrière and applying some home remedy to the blisters! Hell would be encased in glaciers before she permitted him to see her posterior!

"Grasp the reins like this . . ." Dru instructed as he wrapped his hand over hers. "Keep the tension loose and touch the mare's neck lightly when you want her to change direction." He demonstrated. "A horse is what you make of it. If you respect its power, strength, and contrariness, you'll never be surprised when it suddenly decides to throw you. Treat it with kindness, and it will respond accordingly. Abuse it, and it will turn on you every chance it gets."

"Does that advice also apply to men?" Tori smirked, finding there was also a place for sarcasm in this world. Until now she had had little reason to employ it. But there was something intimidating and unnerving about this muscular giant whose body was enflaming hers. She found herself striking out to devastate him, just as his mere presence and close contact devastated *her*.

A peal of laughter rang deep in Dru's chest and Tori felt the vibrations ricochet through her. Dru's laughter was appealing. It was a warm, wholesome sound that made her even more aware of the man and his moods than she wanted to be.

"You really don't know anything about men, do you, Chicago?" His big hand lifted to comb his fingers through the thick silver-gold strands that fluttered across his line of vision.

"My name is Victoria," she declared. "Not Chicago. I

would prefer that you employ my given name if you must speak to me at all."

"You don't, do you, Chicago?" he persisted, flagrantly disregarding her request.

Her shoulders lifted in a shrug as Dru maneuvered the paint mare right, left, and then backed her up. "I know men keep mistresses to pleasure themselves, even though they marry for position and prestige. In Hubert's case, he kept two paramours. And I have been told that a wife's duty is to submit to her husband when he wishes to produce heirs. What else is there to know about men except that they must be tolerated with all their limitations and accepted for what they are?"

Dru stared at the back of her blond head. "That's what you think marriage is all about?" he asked.

"It is in my world," Tori replied, taking the reins to practice what Dru had taught her.

"Well, it sure as hell ain't in mine," Dru snorted.

"Sure as hell *isn't* in yours," she corrected him. "*Ain't* isn't a word, Montana."

"Look, Chicago, you talk your way and I'll talk mine," he muttered crossly. "I have no aspirations of being a highfalutin gentleman. And if I ever decide to take a wife, I intend to take my pleasures at home, not in some other bed, the way your fiancé obviously plans to do."

Tori's lashes fluttered up as her head swiveled on her shoulders to peer into Dru's craggy face. "*All* the time?" she wanted to know, her tone bewildered.

"Hell yes, *all* the time." Godamighty, this chit had a distorted view of marriage. Ten to one, she didn't know beans about love, either. She didn't know anything that really mattered. Thanks to Gwen, Tori had grown up in a vacuum. That woman ought to be whipped for doing her daughter such a disservice!

Tori was thoughtful for a moment. "What's it like for a man and a woman to sleep together?" she questioned, startling both herself and Dru. Tori had never before broached that delicate subject with anyone. Why she

57

picked this rough-edged frontiersman to enlighten her was anybody's guess. Perhaps it was because Dru had assured her he wasn't interested in bedding her. Knowing he didn't want her in that way put her mind at ease. Perhaps.

Dru rolled his eyes in dismay. He hadn't expected to teach Tori about the birds and bees; only about the necessities of surviving in the wild.

"You know what I mean." Tori blushed, but she pursued the mysterious subject. "Is there any satisfaction in it . . . other than making babies?"

Dru expelled his breath in a rush. What a long trip home this was destined to be with this babe-in-arms. "If you tell me you haven't even been kissed yet, I'll . . ."

"Twice," Tori announced, and quite proudly. She twisted in the saddle to study Dru, whose shoulders were shaking in silent amusement. "But I must confess there wasn't much to it. If I was supposed to hear bells ringing or feel something, I didn't. Was I supposed to?"

Dru told himself a half second too late that he shouldn't have peered into those luminous violet eyes or stared at those cupid's-bow lips. It was a crucial mistake. He looked at this naive imp and he wanted her in ways that would shock and frighten her. His brain warned him to keep his distance, but his male body roused to the feel of Tori's shapely form in his arms. He knew he shouldn't tamper with desire, not with this innocent maid. But Lord, she had so much to learn, and he suddenly found himself wanting to teach her what she had been missing in life.

"If you didn't feel anything, Chicago, it was because you've never *really* been kissed . . ."

The husky sound of his voice and the way he was staring at her sent goose bumps across her skin. Her gaze focused on his baby-blue eyes that were surrounded with black velvet lashes. Tori suddenly found herself wanting to feel his sensual lips on hers, to compare experiences.

As if Dru had read her secret thoughts, his head moved

deliberately toward hers. Tori waited with bated breath, wondering if she would be repulsed or if she would be mildly pleasured. The abrasiveness of his unshaven face caused her to flinch, but the light whisper of his full lips on hers contradicted the rough texture of his beard. For a long moment, he nibbled at her lips before his tongue glided into her mouth to explore the soft recesses.

Tori gasped at the unexpected tremors that rippled through her. Dru had leaned her back against his arm, tilting her face to his. The instant she relaxed against him, his kiss deepened and his free arm glided up her thigh to swirl across her belly. Tori jerked upright so quickly that she nearly threw herself off the mare. His intimate touch caused her heart to leapfrog, and breathing was impossible.

This was not at all what she expected from this rough-edged bumpkin. Very quickly, Tori realized how dangerous Dru Sullivan really was. He had made her aware of him as a man, a man who could awake her slumbering passions. Tori hadn't anticipated such a volatile reaction to Dru. Indeed, she wished she had felt nothing at all!

"I think perhaps I should concentrate on my riding," Tori bleated, her voice unsteady.

"And I think I'd better climb onto my own horse," Dru rasped, his tone thick with unappeased desire.

With masculine grace, he drew his legs beneath him and hopped onto the steed that trotted along beside them. Dru cursed under his breath when Tori's wide-eyed gaze fell to the bulge in his skintight breeches. There was no sense pretending she hadn't affected him. It couldn't have been more obvious, and it was high time she learned about male anatomy!

"Can you ride in . . . that condition?" Tori covered her mouth, cursed her runaway tongue, and blushed ten shades of red. Sweet merciful heavens! What possessed her to pose such an intimate question? Her feminine curiosity was outdistancing her brain!

The embarrassment that stained her cheeks provoked

Dru to chuckle. "Riding ain't gonna be easy," he admitted as he nudged his steed. "But I'll survive."

"*Isn't* going to be easy," Tori unthinkingly corrected.

"Godamighty, Chicago, lay off, will you?" Dru snapped more gruffly than he intended. "I haven't been educated at the finest schools money can buy. If I want lessons in English, I'll—"

"Grammar," she specified, and then slammed her mouth shut when Dru glared her into silence.

"Grammar," he amended tersely. "My 'grammar' isn't important out here. It's what I know about people and wild creatures that matters most. When you can ride like hell to avoid disaster and shoot from the hip while your horse is at full gallop, you'll be worth your salt in the lawless West. And until you can, I ain't . . . am not taking lessons in proper grammar."

"I'm sorry. I didn't mean to offend you," Tori murmured, feeling the sting of unexpected tears at his sharp words.

For some unexplainable reason, she was so vulnerable to this man that one harsh word or look from him crushed her. And why on earth was she heckling him? For spite, she supposed. But all it earned her was more biting insults. Her emotions were in a tailspin. The sensations that tormented her were beyond the realm of her understanding.

But it was really his fault that she ribbed him, she consoled herself self-righteously. He automatically put her on guard with his intimidating size, and his goading remarks, not to mention how much he'd rattled her with those sizzling kisses and exploring caresses.

"Godamighty, Chicago, don't start with those damned tears again," Dru growled as he settled himself, quite uncomfortably, in the saddle. "I didn't know you had so much water in you. If you're going to spring a leak every time I scold you, I'll have to buy a canoe to float to Montana. Now quit being so blasted sensitive."

"You probably bleed ice water, callous heathen that

you are," she grumbled half aloud and wiped away the infuriating tears. "As soon as you teach me to use a pistol, I'm going to shoot you and find out."

Dru eased his steed over beside hers and reached out to cup her quaking chin. Gently, he raised her misty gaze to meet his disarming smile, amazing Tori with his quicksilver change of moods. "You really are something, Chicago," he murmured, his eyes glued to her petal-soft lips.

Impulsively, he bent to kiss away her frustration and then decided he was only making matters worse. With each passing minute his fascination for this sheltered bluestocking was increasing by leaps and bound. He found himself wanting to teach her everything there was to know about life.

That prancing dandy she intended to marry wasn't good enough for Tori. She deserved more than a man who kept two mistresses. She needed to be loved and loved often, not because of what she was in the world of high society, but just for herself. Tori was a wealth of unexplored promise waiting to blossom. When she came into her own, Hubert would be no match for her. Dru would see to that! He was going to have the last laugh on Hubert Carrington Frazier II.

Tori hadn't meant to respond to Dru's tender kiss, but she did. It just sort of came naturally—like breathing. He was many things, few of which she approved of, but he definitely knew how to kiss. Why, he had probably forgotten more about kissing than she would ever learn in a lifetime. His kisses in no way resembled the hasty pecks Hubert had bestowed on her. Tori was already becoming addicted to those full moist lips that courted her with intimate promises.

Tori had leaned toward Dru, and when he abruptly withdrew, she very nearly tumbled from the saddle. Chuckling at her blush, Dru pushed her upright on the mare and playfully flicked the tip of her upturned nose.

"You catch on quick, Chicago," he complimented with

a roguish wink. "With a little more practice . . . you could be one helluva . . . horsewoman . . ."

Tori's eyes flashed as she realized she had fallen prey to his prank, that he had led her to believe he intended to say one thing before he said something else. She felt like a naive little mouse being toyed with by a gigantic jungle cat. "You're a cussed damned helluva nuisance, Montana," she sniped. "And if the truth be known, I'd rather kiss a snake."

"I'll round one up," he volunteered with a devilish grin, amused at her attempt to curse. She needed more practice in that department, too.

Tori's back stiffened as she took up the reins exactly as Dru had taught her. Touching her knees to the paint's flanks, she trotted off, her body bouncing ungracefully in the saddle. "One snake around here is one too many," she muttered. "You stay on your side of the road and I'll stay on mine."

A rakish smile pursed Dru's lips as he watched Tori bobble down the road. If she knew how appetizing she looked in her form-fitting garb that exposed the generous swell of her breasts, if she were aware of the tantalizing effect she had on him, she would have enjoyed a great deal of satisfaction. But Dru was determined to maintain the upper hand in his dealings with this sassy minx!

When Tori bolstered her self-confidence, she would be a force to be reckoned with, Dru predicted. Already she was showing signs of shedding her indifference to life in general and to him in particular. She was no longer the melancholy bride he had encountered on the front steps of the church. Dru was willing to bet Hubert Carrington Frazier II wouldn't even recognize his fiancée when he finally got her back. Tori really was going to be something else when she got a little experience under her belt. Her spirit had been stifled while she was under Gwen's rule, but she was undergoing a rapid metamorphosis.

Good for her, Dru mused as he watched Tori study the

way he moved in rhythm with his steed and attempted to emulate his riding style. There would be nothing easy about this cross-country journey across swollen rivers and rugged Indian country. This wasn't a Sunday picnic, that was for sure! And while Tori was learning to adapt, Dru had better start reminding himself whose daughter he was toting to Montana. If he buckled to the quiet whisperings of his male desires, Tori might wind up learning far more than he originally intended. The thought caused conflicting emotions to rage through Dru's body. He wanted her. He was all too aware of that. He just had to convince himself that he would seriously complicate matters if he yielded to his desires. And judging by the aftereffects of their kisses, he was going to have his work cut out for him if he was going to forget how much she aroused him when she wasn't even trying!

Chapter 6

Tori muffled a groan when Dru finally stopped to rest and she was allowed to slide from the saddle. Her muscles screamed with each step and her backside was definitely blistered, just as Dru had predicted. Damn him for being right.

It was with great care that Tori ambled to the stream and knelt to wash her face. She swore her legs would be permanently bowed after so many hours in the saddle.

Dru admired Tori's shapely backside while he stood as posted lookout. He found his betraying gaze mapping Tori's tantalizing figure each time she looked the other way. Godamighty, it was unnatural to spend so much time dwelling on a woman who was off limits to him! He was so cussed aware of that blond-haired chit, it was scary! If he didn't watch his step he would be doing something crazy like grabbing her to him and devouring her.

The taste of her innocent kisses still lingered on his lips, and even a refreshing sip of water hadn't washed it away. Caleb would kill Dru where he stood if he knew what thoughts were buzzing through his ex-partner's mind. Dru had been weeks without a woman, thanks to this frantic dash to Chicago. Every glance he stole at Tori was an agonizing reminder of his celibacy, and Dru was definitely feeling the strain of doing without.

Muttering at his wayward thoughts, Dru stalked back to fish a can of beans from his sack. Tori spied the can in his hand and pulled a face.

"Not beans again!" she groaned. "We had the same disgusting thing for breakfast and lunch. I've already eaten a hill of beans."

"Take what you can get, Chicago," Dru grunted, refusing to punish himself by glancing at the disheveled beauty.

"Your lack of imagination baffles me," Tori mocked, accepting the can Dru thrust at her. "If you're such a whiz at surviving in the wilds, why don't you hunt game for our meals—or at least teach me to shoot so *I* can!"

"Wild game means cooking. I'm not building a campfire to alert anyone to our presence, especially not the posse your family probably sent to track us," he explained. "And I wouldn't dare put a weapon in your hands. You'd probably get excited and shoot me instead of the wild game."

"Don't you credit me with having a smidgen of common sense?" she hurled indignantly.

"Not a lot, no," he replied in all honesty.

Having been slapped with the insult, Tori stamped over to retrieve his Winchester rifle from its sling in the saddle. She was determined to prove she was capable of handling the weapon. How hard could it be, after all?

The speed with which she snatched it up caused the loaded rifle to explode. To Dru's stupefied horror, the can of beans in his hand flipped up in the air and he reflexively dived for cover. Tori, who was unprepared for the fierce kick of the weapon, wound up flat on her back. The jarring motion caused the hair trigger on the repeating rifle to fire when she carelessly clutched at it. A spray of buckshot whizzed past Dru's head, relieving him of his Stetson and peppering it with bullet holes.

"Godamighty, Chicago!" Dru roared as he rolled out of

the weapon's path and circled behind the stunned blonde. "You are living proof that a weapon in the hands of the ignorant is disastrous. Gimme that!"

When Dru tried to yank the rifle from her quaking hands, her finger slid over the trigger and the weapon exploded again. Muttering in colorful profanity, Dru stormed over to replace the Winchester in its sling.

"You've had enough target practice for one night," he muttered crossly. "Now we have to ride a few more miles. You probably sent a signal to every creature in the county."

When Tori was slow to respond to Dru's command to aim herself toward her horse, he stalked over to hoist her off the ground. When he forcefully stuffed her back into the saddle, an agonized groan tumbled from her lips as her backside complained about being reunited with the saddle.

"Sorry!" Tori mumbled, unable to meet Dru's gaze after she had very nearly blown him to smithereens.

"You and me both," he snorted in disdain. "You damned near blew my head off."

"I said I was sorry!" she repeated, her voice becoming louder with each syllable she rapped out.

"Sorry don't heal the dead . . . which is exactly what I would have been if your aim had been two inches lower!" he snapped back at her.

"*Doesn't* heal the dead," she corrected him, and then compressed her lips when his head swiveled on his shoulders to flash her a silencing glare.

"Don't, doesn't, what the hell difference does it make when I'm riddled with buckshot?" He gave her a black look.

When Dru stomped off, madder than a hornet, Tori burst into an impish grin. The situation wasn't the least bit funny, but Dru's display of temper was. He was not always as cool, calm, and collected as he led her to believe. It did her heart good to see that the mighty Dru

67

Sullivan had a few cracks in his composure. He was human after all. For a while there, Tori had begun to wonder.

Although Dru did take time out to offer Tori basic instruction in handling his Winchester, the monotony of riding day after day began to wear on her nerves. Tori had eaten so many cans of beans that she was beginning to have nightmares about them. Her taste buds had been destroyed, she was sure of it. A steady diet of beans had spoiled her appetite and it was all she could do to choke down the boring fare.

To compound her frustrations, a storm rumbled toward them and heavy gray clouds piled atop each other like doubled fists, theatening to pummel them with rain. The rumble of thunder shook the ground and Tori involuntarily ducked away, expecting to be struck by a lightning bolt any second. Dru, however, didn't bat an eye at the possibility of remaining in the saddle during a downpour.

Since the night Tori had very nearly blown his head off, he had become distant and remote, taking every inconvenience in stride and sparing her no more of his time than necessary. Tori had tried very hard to adapt to the standards Dru set for her. Although she felt terribly inadequate compared to Dru's talents in the wild and their relationship was strained, she was looking forward to being reunited with her father. Tori couldn't comprehend why her mother had purposely deprived her of communicating with her father all these years. And after what Dru had told her about Caleb, she was anxious to hear his side of the story.

When Tori didn't receive any letters from Caleb, she had withdrawn into herself and tried to eat herself into oblivion. She had become as plump as a baking hen and so shy and reserved that Gwen and Edgar had bundled her off to boarding school, hoping association with other young ladies would snap her out of her depression. Eventually it did, and Tori had changed from a clumsy caterpillar into a graceful butterfly that men began to notice. But Tori had transferred her frustrations over being forgotten by her father to an avoidance of all those of the male persuasion. And Gwen, fearing her daughter might be overpowered by zealous men before she was given in marriage, packed her off to an elite school for women. Now that Tori glanced back through the window of time, she realized she hadn't had much of a life, even though her family *was* fabulously wealthy.

A dispirited sigh escaped her lips as she plodded cross-country beside Dru. He thought she had been lounging in a bed of roses, but she knew her life truly had been dull and uneventful. She had progressed from a thin, unhappy child to a chubby, resentful girl to a young woman who had been educated to the limits of her intelligence. All she knew was what she had read in the vast load of books that had been thrust at her. Now here she was, completely out of her element, relying solely on a man who would have preferred not to have her underfoot. Not that Tori blamed him, mind you. But as the days progressed, she was becoming increasingly fascinated with the darkly handsome rake. He was the first man she had ever come to know so well. She didn't understand what made him tick, but she was learning as much about him as she knew about herself.

There was an aura of masculinity and vitality about Dru that appealed to Tori. He was totally unlike any man she had ever met. Dru admitted he had no aspirations of being a gentleman and he didn't cater to her the way other men did. Tori was expected to take care of herself.

The peal of thunder yanked Tori from her silent reverie. When the first gust of wind that preceded the storm slapped her in the face, she squirmed uneasily in the saddle. She would have preferred to climb under her horse, but Dru kept right on riding.

"Did you know thunder is caused by expanding air

heated by lightning?" she rattled, shooting nervous glances at the ominous clouds that loomed overhead. "The hot air collides with the cooler air which sets up gigantic sound waves that produce the roar of thunder."

Dru stared incredulously at the human encyclopedia who was nervously rattling off everything she had ever learned about storms. "I'm fascinated," he replied, his tone suggesting he was nothing of the kind.

Lightning zigzagged across the sky, and Tori felt herself growing more apprehensive by the second. "Even though lightning and thunder occur simultaneously, we hear the sound after we see the flash of light." Thunder cracked above them, emphasizing the point she was making in her science lesson. "In fact, you can determine the distance between yourself and the storm by counting the number of seconds between lightning flashes and crashes of thunder. It's five seconds for every mile . . ."

Dru had no time to test the scientific theory of the difference between the speed of sound and light that Tori was spouting. A lightning bolt shot from the sky, striking a lone tree a hundred yards in front of them. Thunder boomed simultaneously. The storm was definitely upon them, and Tori's mare reared in fright. Tori, having not yet polished her skills as an equestrienne, was unable to remain in the saddle. A terrified shriek gushed from her lips as she somersaulted backward over the mare's rump. The ground came up to her at incredible speed, knocking the breath out of her. She lay there, facedown, stunned. Huge raindrops splattered over her and the sky opened up to hurl torrents of rain. Tori was drenched before she could pull her knees beneath her and stagger to her feet.

A steely hand clamped around her elbow, jerking her upright. Her head snapped back as Dru yanked her toward the canopy of trees beside the road.

"Now what, oh great weather wizard?" Dru questioned sarcastically. Muttering, he watched their horses charge off in every direction at once. Damn, it would take him an hour to round up their mounts. "Are you

70

predicting a quarter- or half-inch hailstones with this storm?"

His ridicule kindled her temper again. "Half-inch," she growled just as sarcastically, glaring at him before she surveyed the low-scraping clouds. "And severe wind gusts, I expect."

And sure enough, she was right—much to Dru's dismay. Hailstones pattered against the leaves of the overhanging limbs, causing a shower of rain and vegetation to beat down on them. Swearing colorfully, Dru shoved Tori beneath a sprawling cedar bush for extra protection and then plopped down on top of her.

Tori's breath was forced out in a rush. "Get off me, you big gorilla," she chirped. "You must weigh at least two hundred pounds!"

"Two hundred and thirty," he corrected with a smug grin. "Ha! Gotcha on that one, little Miss Know-it-all."

"I was not trying to flaunt my knowledge. Storms make me nervous, and I was only trying to make conversation to distract myself," Tori grumbled in defense. "Will you get off me! You're squishing me flat."

Dru eased off beside her and grinned down at her smudged face. "In case you're thinking of reciting the reproductive procedure of these cedar bushes, don't bother, Miss Bookworm. I don't give a flying *twig*."

His constant taunts set Tori's teeth on edge. The man derived wicked satisfaction in goading her. "Fine. Just remain an ignorant bumpkin. Why should I care?" she sniffed. "I'd prefer to study storms and trees than to become stagnant of mind like you, Montana."

The insult struck like a poison arrow. "I wouldn't trade my life for yours for all the gold in the Montana mountains," he snorted. "And if it wasn't for me, you would have been dead by now."

Lightning struck a distant tree and a limb dropped to the ground, sizzling and smoldering. It had nothing on Tori. "If it weren't for you, Montana, I wouldn't be here at all. Stop behaving as if you're doing me some

71

stupendous favor," she sassed him. "I certainly didn't ask for this. In fact, I could have lived out my whole life without meeting you and I'm sure I would have been much happier!"

The wind howled, the rain splattered, and Dru muttered under his breath. Chalk one up for the feisty, quick-witted little Miss Know-it-all, he thought resentfully. She had proven she was knowledgeable about weather conditions and, what's more, she had quickly put him in his place with her cutting remarks.

"At least I'm trying to apply what I've learned," Tori went on as she squirmed to find a more comfortable position. "But stubborn as you are, you are satisfied to wallow in your own little world without understanding it."

Dru puffed up with so much indignation, he nearly split a seam. "Before we reach Montana, you'll be thanking me for knowing as much as I do. Because of me, you'll survive to be reunited with your father."

"And I have discovered that I want to do more than merely survive," she declared, having just come to that conclusion after days of contemplation and considerable searching of her soul. "I want to live life to its fullest, knowing and understanding all. You can poke fun at me if you wish, but one of these days I'll be a better man than you are, Montana. And just see if I *ain't*."

Her jibe at his poor grammar struck another well-aimed blow to his masculine pride. He felt a strong need to put this saucy bluestocking in her rightful place.

"Will you now?" he smirked, his blue eyes drifting over the clinging garments that outlined her appetizing figure. "Then perhaps I should give you a few lessons in love since you have your heart set on broadening all your horizons."

His cool lips came forcefully down on hers, exerting his male superiority and his expertise. His hand stole around her hips, bringing her into intimate contact with the hard contours of his thighs.

At first Tori had been too startled by his amorous assault to protest. And later, she was still too stunned to voice a complaint. His hot, explosive kisses sent shock waves undulating through her body, standing her nerves on end. Crosscurrents of sensation bombarded her. Lightning bolts may have been sizzling overhead, but there was another brand of electricity leaping back and forth between his muscular body and hers. Tori was instantly and totally aware of the man who lay beside her—chest to chest, hip to hip. She could feel him absorbing her will and her energy. He had been an emotionally draining man during their verbal sparring matches, but this form of battle was by far the worst!

Her naive body reacted to the breath-stealing kisses and bold caresses that investigated the curve of her hips and the trim indentation of her waist. Tori compared herself to the tree that had been lightning-struck. Her entire body shuddered and smoldered when Dru engulfed her in his powerful arms. She didn't want to respond to this devastating male, but it was impossible not to.

Dru was a most exasperating man who clearly resented her formal education and her wealth. But Tori knew she was no match for this half-civilized renegade. His heart-shattering kisses and masterful caresses sent wild tingles of pleasure channeling into every part of her being. The touch of his hands made her body glow in a most phenomenal way. He was so much of a man that he made her feel more like a woman than she had ever felt in her twenty years of existence.

Tori hadn't meant to wrap her arms around his neck, to explore the whipcord muscles on his back, but her hands were there, moving of their own accord. Utilizing the techniques Dru employed on her, Tori teased his full lips. Then her darting tongue enflamed him and her innocent movements caused his passions to rebel against their confines. Suddenly Dru found himself wondering if he were winning or losing this tender battle with Tori. Although he knew more about passion than she would ever learn from that weasel Frazier, Dru questioned his ability to pull away and compose himself. His self-control suddenly evaporated. When this lavender-eyed blonde kissed him back, he melted into a pool of bubbling desire.

With a maddening groan, Dru slid his hand under her derrière and pulled her luscious body beneath his. His hot, greedy kisses devoured her lips and he was oblivious to the rumbling thunder and driving rain. As his roaming hands investigated the curvaceous terrain of her body, he nudged her legs apart with his knees. He shifted to let her bear half his weight, letting her feel his ardent need for her.

Dru was amazed at his own abandon. He was like a starving man devouring a long-awaited feast. He must have kissed and caressed Tori a dozen times, but he still felt shaky and ravenous. Even the imprint of her pliant body beneath his wasn't enough to satisfy him. He couldn't get close enough to the fire that burned him inside and out. He craved so much more and resented the soggy garments that separated them, resented the fierce, uncontrollable attraction he felt for this innocent beauty.

His questing hands tunneled beneath the buckhide garments to map the velvety plane of her belly and then glided upward to caress the soft, full mounds of her breasts. Hungrily, his lips descended to trace the creamy swells that he had exposed from beneath the leather lacings that crisscrossed the deep slit in the front of her shirt. He took the bud in his mouth, cherishing the taste of her on his lips, relishing the feel of her delectable body lying intimately against his. His free hand skied down her ribs to delve beneath the band of her breeches, drawing a ragged moan from Tori's lips.

While his tongue teased the dusky peaks, his fingertips languidly explored the silky texture of her hips and caressed the ultrasensitive flesh of her inner thighs, causing Tori to instinctively arch toward his seeking hands. He could feel her innocent body yielding to the unfamiliar pleasure of a man's touch, feel her quivering uncontrollably beneath his ardent fondling. Lord, he wanted her! His entire body shook at the tantalizing thought of burying himself in her exquisite body to ease the torment of being so close to this luscious beauty and yet so far away.

"Godamighty!" Dru growled, jerking away from Tori as if he were lying on live coals.

His frustrated gaze poured over the bewitching temptress who lay beneath the cedar bush. Her lips were swollen from his demanding kisses. Her buckskin shirt gaped from the intrusion of his hands upon her breasts. Her violet eyes had turned deep purple in the shadows, glowing with the awakened passion he had stirred in her. Her damp silver-blond hair sprayed wildly about her, snagging in the limbs of the cedar. Dru ached for her!

Inhaling a shuddering breath, Dru struggled to clamp down on the primal desires that were still running rampant. Lord, he should say something to break this unnerving spell. Frantically, he fought the overwhelming need to pounce on this gorgeous beauty before she scraped herself off the ground and slapped him for taking outrageous liberties with her.

"I've always wondered about these cedar bushes," he croaked, floundering for any topic of conversation to divert his attention.

"What?" Tori braced herself on wobbly elbows and stared at him as if he had tree branches sprouting from his ears.

With a trembling hand, Dru reached over to untangle her silky hair from the snagging limbs. "Evergreens," he said in a tone that still rattled with unappeased desire. "Fascinating foliage, don't you think, Chicago?"

Tori studied this raw, muscular package of masculinity for a long moment, astounded by the side effects of his ardent embrace. She had felt his hands and lips migrating over her body and she had craved more of his skillful touch. As much as she hated to admit it, Dru had a startling effect on her. It was incredible the way she responded to the feel of his steel-honed body meshed against hers.

Thoughtfully, Tori levered up on one elbow, pondering this handsome giant with a sense of wonder and blatant curiosity. "You could have made love to me just now and I'm not sure I could have prevented it or even wanted to," she admitted honestly. Her gaze drifted over his chiseled features, marveling at the lingering sensations that still tormented her. "Why didn't you, Montana?"

The point-blank question and her admission set Dru back on his heels. He stared at the cedar bush above her head. "Don't ask me that," he muttered irritably.

"My inquiring mind wants to know," she countered. "Why? There was no one around to stop you."

He scowled as he shoved branches out of his way to gain his feet. "I better fetch the horses."

As he stamped off, Tori sat up cross-legged to stare bemusedly after him. Why had he stopped what he was doing? *She* couldn't have. She had experienced sensations she never realized existed. The feel of his masculine body lying upon hers had been wildly exciting. She hadn't been able to think straight. She had only reacted to the feel of his masterful hands gliding beneath her shirt to tease the taut peaks of her breasts. He had made her want more than his hands and lips upon her quivering flesh. She had wanted to share the secrets of intimacy with him, to explore the mysterious dimension of desire.

Tori heaved a tremulous sigh and retied the lacings on her shirt. It must have been her lack of experience that repelled him, she reckoned. Dru had declared at the onset of this journey that he liked women who were skilled in the art of lovemaking. It was obvious to Tori that Dru aroused her far more than she aroused him. She was merely someone to trifle with until he could get his hands on an experienced woman. But he had no fascination for virgins who didn't know the first thing about passion.

Tori supposed she should be thankful that her virtue remained intact. After all, she was an engaged woman. Hubert didn't think twice about leaping into bed with his mistresses, but he would have thrown a conniption fit if Tori came to him less than pure.

Baffled by her fiery reaction to Dru and her meandering thoughts, Tori slumped back to survey the scalelike leaves of the cedar bush. A wistful smile pursed her lips as she brushed her fingers over the damp leaves. This is what she would like to find in life, she mused. An evergreen love—affection that was as fresh and new from beginning to end. She wanted a love that never faded from one season of life to the next, one that flourished after drenching storms, one that was tried and true and everlasting . . .

Tori expelled a dispirited sigh. Her mother had warned her not to become a dreamer who looked for things that weren't really there. She had to be content with her lot in life. She would eventually return to Chicago to marry stuffy old Hubert with his scads of money. She had been raised and groomed to become the proper wife of a young aristocrat who would eventually assume complete control of his father's business. She would be incredibly wealthy and she would want for nothing except . . .

Impulsively, Tori broke off a branch of cedar and tucked it into her pocket. She reckoned she would never know Dru intimately, but she wished these lingering feelings he stirred in her could be the beginning of something warm and everlasting.

Ah well, Tori reminded herself, dreams were for fools. Chasing rainbows was for those who had nothing at all. Tori had everything a woman could possibly want, so why didn't she feel contented?

The crackle of twigs jostled her from her contemplations. She glanced up to see Dru towering over her, grasping the reins to their runaway horses and wearing a black scowl. Without a word, he thrust an open can of beans at her.

Tori stared at her dinner as if he were offering her a five-day-old-dead fish. "I'm not eating that again," she protested.

"Fine, starve to death," he snorted disdainfully. "See if I care."

Tori was on her feet in a single bound. "You don't. We have already established that I mean nothing to you, nothing at all," she hurled in a bitter tone. "Now give me your knife!"

Dru did a double take, and a suspicious frown plowed his brows. "For what purpose? If you're thinking of stabbing me, you can't have it."

"That was my second option." Her violet eyes flashed as she thrust out an arm. "The knife, Montana," she demanded.

Warily, Dru pulled the dagger from its sheath on his belt and handed it to her. His brain hadn't switched gears as rapidly as hers had. He was still mulling over her earlier comment about not caring for her. Why the devil had she said that? And what did *she* care if *he* cared anyway . . . ?

When Tori stomped off, shoving branches out of her way, his thoughts scattered. He watched the fuming blonde pick up a fallen limb and whittle one end into a sharp point as she wove through the timber. With her task complete, she pivoted to toss his knife back at his feet.

With her head held high—a gesture of defiance that Dru had begun to recognize at a glance—Tori marched toward the river with her makeshift spear in hand. Curiously, Dru followed a few paces behind her to determine what she intended to do.

Amusement danced in his eyes as he watched Tori wade into the river and stand in midstream like a warrior poised for battle. When a fish swam by, she stabbed at it with her improvised spear. To Dru's amazement, the blow struck its mark and Tori triumphantly pulled her

78

supper from the channel. Beginner's luck, he thought to himself. She couldn't repeat the procedure with the same success, never in a million years.

Tori was so proud of herself that a smile burst out all over her exquisite features. But on her way back to shore, she stepped in a hole and went in over her head. Panic set in. Tori thrashed to reach the surface. Before she went down for the third time, a hand clamped onto the nape of her shirt and dragged her to shallow water.

"If you can't swim, don't wade out so far next time," Dru growled. "You and your bright ideas. You almost drowned."

In dismay, Tori watched her fish and the spear drift down the river. Her eyes fell on the can of beans Dru was still holding in his left hand.

"Supper," he grunted, thrusting the can at her. "It ain't a feast, but it don't swim and it don't walk away before you can eat it."

"Isn't and it *doesn't*," she muttered in correction. "I wish you would stop slaughtering the English language!"

Dru flung her a withering glance and then turned around and stalked off. In bleak resignation, Tori plunked down in the wet grass to choke down her unappetizing meal. Beans! Lord, what she wouldn't give for a thick juicy steak now! Why, she would even promise not to antagonize that blue-eyed rake for twenty-four solid hours if she could only sink her teeth into something besides these gooey damned beans!

Chapter 7

When Tori made her way back to the horses, she spied the garments Dru had draped over the branches to dry. Part of her winced at the thought of seeing Dru in all his unclothed glory, and the curious side of her nature yearned to feast upon the hard-muscled flesh she had felt beneath his form-fitting garments. It was positively sinful of her to crouch down in the bushes and scan the surroundings, hoping to catch a glimpse of Dru, but that was exactly what Tori did.

Her assessing gaze roamed over a pair of bare feet and well-formed thighs that were revealed from beneath the lower limbs of the bush in which she was hiding. *You are truly disgusting*, Tori scolded herself harshly. But even her lecture didn't stop her from pulling down another clump of limbs in hopes of seeing more of Dru.

A hot blush blossomed on her cheeks when she was granted a view of this muscular giant from the waist down. The male statues she had observed in museums were meager substitutes for this awesome package of masculinity! Dru Sullivan put Greek gods to shame.

Continuing her firsthand lesson in anatomy, Tori separated a higher clump of branches to gawk at the broad expanse of Dru's hair-matted chest and the bulging muscles that encased his ribs and arms. Sweet merciful heavens! Tori never dreamed the male of the species could look so utterly breathtaking. It made her feel hot and shaky just staring at his striking physique. To touch that hair-roughened flesh, to explore every square inch of that sinewy body would be . . .

A disappointed frown puckered her brow when Dru wandered off into the thicket. Tori impatiently waited for him to reappear, and while she did, she committed the arousing visual picture to memory, savoring the forbidden sight of rippling muscle and bronzed flesh. Hubert Carrington Frazier II would never measure up to Dru Sullivan, not in any arena, Tori was sure. He was the kind of man who intrigued a woman, even when she would have preferred not to notice. But who could overlook a man who was teeming with dynamic vitality, devilish charm, and earthy sensuality . . . ?

A shocked shriek erupted from Tori's lips when an unidentified hand clamped around her boot, jerking her backward. Mortified that Dru had sneaked around to catch her peeping on him, Tori came up fighting. But it wasn't Dru, come to tease her unmercifully for such unladylike conduct. Instead, Tori confronted a toothless, whisker-faced vagabond who had seen the lower half of her body protruding from the bushes. Before Tori could claw at the homely face that was frozen in a lusty grin, the varmint dropped down on top of her. The bloodcurdling scream that leaped to her lips died beneath the most repulsive kiss imaginable. Whiskey and tobacco invaded her senses, and Tori fought to unseat the scavenger whose hands were roaming everywhere at once. But worm and wriggle though she did, she couldn't escape the disgusting creature who had every intention of mauling her for the mere sport of it.

When his hand slid between her thighs and clamped on the fastenings on her breeches, Tori kicked and bucked for all she was worth. Nauseating fear curdled her stomach and she fought wildly. It shocked her to realize that this overpowering brute could take her, and she was unable to send up a cry of alarm to summon Dru, wherever he was! Knowing if there was any saving to be done that she was going to have to do it herself, Tori sank in her nails and teeth and twisted sideways . . .

And suddenly, it was as if her lusty captor had sprouted wings. His bulky body flew through the air to collide with a tree. Disbelieving eyes fluttered up to see Dru's massive body draped in a feed sack. His muted growl pierced the late-afternoon air. Before her stood six feet five inches and two hundred thirty pounds of raw fury. The murderous look on his face and the deadly gleam in his sky-blue eyes were enough to scare the living daylights out of anybody!

Tori lay sprawled on the ground, grasping her ripped shirt and gasping for breath. Never in her life had she seen a man beat another man to a pulp. Dru had pounced on the intruder like a starved dog on a bone, all meaty fists and snarling growls. If Tori's assailant had had teeth to begin with, she was certain Dru would have knocked every last one of them out. He hit the scraggly scavenger with enough force to fell a gorilla, and if that wasn't enough, Dru laid into him again and again, even after his opponent didn't have the strength to fight back.

The dazed man slammed back against the tree and slithered downward when his wobbly legs folded up beneath him. And still Dru continued to hammer at him like a carpenter driving nails. Pained grunts and gasps came from bloody lips before Dru delivered a brain-scrambling blow that sent the scavenger toppling sideways to sprawl lifelessly on the ground.

When Tori bounded to her feet, he caught her by the arm and spun her around, forcing her to stare at the disgusting man on the ground. Muttering, Dru shook her and pointed a lean finger at the unconscious heathen.

"See what happens when you don't pay attention to your surroundings, Chicago?" he snapped brusquely. "Take a good look at him. The forests are thick with scavengers and thieves just like him. You always have to sleep with one eye open. You never let yourself believe

83

you are completely alone in the wilds, and you listen for sounds of approaching danger with one ear, no matter what else you're doing. And don't you ever forget that!"

What Tori needed after her near brush with disaster was a comforting shoulder to lean on, not a lecture on her stupidity. Dru's rough handling sprung the trap on her temper and she retaliated without thinking.

"Well, Mr. Know-all-and-see-all, you weren't doing such an expert job of paying attention, either," she hurled sarcastically. "You were oblivious to the fact that I was . . ." Her face flushed purple.

One thick brow climbed to a mocking angle while he regarded the blush that stained her cheeks. "That you slinked under the bushes to get a peek at me while I was stark-bone naked," he finished for her.

Her face turned crimson red and Dru grinned devilishly. "I suppose your inquiring mind wanted to know what a man looked like without his clothes on. Well, Chicago, is your feminine curiosity appeased or shall I drop my feed sack so you can take another gander at close range, in case you missed something the first time?"

Tori had never been so embarrassed in all her life! Sweet merciful heavens, the man obviously had eyes like an eagle. And curse him for parading around in front of her when he knew she was peeping at him! That low-down good-for-nothing . . . !

As tears of humiliation welled up in her eyes, Dru scowled under his breath. "Godamighty, Chicago, will you stop that! We've had enough rain for one day. There's no need for you to flood the place. So you got caught peeking. You're not the first woman to gawk at a naked man."

Exasperated beyond words, Tori yanked herself loose from his grasp and stamped away. She wanted to snap back at him, but she was so frustrated, she was afraid her tangled thoughts would fly off her tongue without making any sense.

"By the way, Chicago," Dru drawled, striking a suggestive pose. "Did you like what you saw?"

And sure enough, a raft of jumbled curses and muted hisses spewed from her lips, making her sound like a babbling idiot. Tori wheeled to punish him with a scathing glower. Furiously, she struggled to put her angry thoughts into proper order and cut this tormenting rake down a notch. "I suppose you would have looked the other way if *I* had been standing naked in the clearing," she sneered, daring him to deny it. And he had the audacity to do just that!

"Of course I would have," he declared with noble hauteur. "It ain't polite to gawk."

Tori was downright furious. Her emotions had been put through a meat grinder. She had stared at Dru's handsome, virile physique until the tantalizing image was branded on her mind. She had been mauled by a lusty brute and then forced to swallow another dose of Dru's taunting ridicule. Later, she would question the sense of what she did to even the score with this infuriating man, but at that moment, Tori was too upset to think straight.

To Dru's utter disbelief Tori started ripping off her clothes. She was so furious, she didn't seem to care if he saw her naked! Even if he had bedded more women than she would ever meet in her lifetime, he would stare at her and prove her right!

Dru's eyes bulged from their sockets like a naive schoolboy. He couldn't believe she dared to peel off her clothes. He hadn't meant to drink in the tantalizing sight, but there wasn't a man on the planet who could have turned his back after he had visualized how she would look since the day he'd met her. Even though he willed himself to spin about, his feet were nailed to the ground. He couldn't look away, not when absolute perfection stood before him. Her alabaster skin glowed in the waning light. The dusky peaks of her breasts invited his touch. The trim curve of her hips left him gulping for breath. This angry but enchanting beauty was what

85

dreams were made of, and Dru ached to . . .

"It *ain't* polite to gawk, Montana." She flung his words back at him, picked up her clothes, and stalked off to the bushes to dress.

Muttering to himself, Dru pivoted to stare at the lifeless vagabond who had attacked Tori. Dru had been overcome with murderous fury when he witnessed that creature mauling Tori. He couldn't tolerate the thought of another man touching her. In the short course of the afternoon, Tori had clearly learned a great deal about men. He had nearly seduced her for passion's sake. She had gaped at him to satisfy her feminine curiosity, and she had come within a hairbreadth of being raped. Lord, after all that, he wouldn't be surprised if she developed a strong aversion to men!

Grumbling, Dru dug into the unconscious man's pocket, but he found nothing of value and no identification. Spying the mule that had been tethered in the bushes, Dru strode over to retrieve the rope and tied the scalawag to the tree. This done, Dru took the mule—and the supplies strapped to it—for compensation and ambled back to the horses.

Tori was sitting Indian-style beneath a cedar tree, staring pensively at the spiny twig that she twirled in her fingertips. She had shrugged on her damp clothes and her head was downcast. When Dru walked up, she didn't even acknowledge his presence.

Silently, Dru rummaged through the saddlebags to determine what the vagabond carried with him. "Beans," he announced, fishing out a can for Tori's inspection.

"Goodie, goodie," she sniffed sarcastically, but she didn't look up. After she had calmed down, she realized what an idiotic fool she had made of herself by stripping naked in front of Dru. Now she felt terribly uneasy in his presence. For a long, awkward moment she peered at the sprig of evergreen. "I'm sorry for what I did. I behaved outrageously." Her quiet voice wobbled with mortification. "Peeping at you was sinfully wicked and disrobing

86

in front of you was . . ." Her face blossomed with color. "I'm deeply ashamed."

"And incredibly lovely," he complimented unexpectedly.

Her tangled blond head jerked up to meet his rakish smile, and she blushed all over again. "And since you're such a connoisseur of women, I suppose I should be flattered."

Dru knew better than to antagonize her on such a delicate subject, but he was too apprehensive about where this conversation would lead not to rib her. They were already terribly aware of each other and that was dangerous, considering the amount of time they were forced to spend alone together. "Yes, you should be flattered, Chicago," he drawled, his gaze drifting over her, mentally peeling away the soggy garments to admire her curvaceous figure. "I've seen my fair share of females, but you're better endowed than most."

Tori's back stiffened like a ramrod. "Damn you, Montana," she spluttered, unsure why the remark made her so irate. It couldn't possibly have been that the jealous green-eyed monster was nipping at her pride! Why should she be the least bit envious of any woman who had succumbed to this rake? Dru probably had so many notches on his bedpost that it resembled a totem pole. Why should she care? He meant nothing to her, absolutely nothing at all. In fact, she despised him for a hundred good reasons!

Stomping around like a mad bull, Tori snatched up her quilt and marched off to bed down for the night. She detested Dru's male arrogance, she really did.

His callous remark couldn't have hurt her any worse than if he had struck her. Dru didn't want her and neither did Hubert, not really. Hubert had two concubines to appease him and he didn't really need Tori in his bed. Her mother hadn't wanted her all that much, either. To Gwen, her daughter was a doll to dress and drag around to social gatherings. Her father hadn't seen her in ten years. And Dru felt only an obligation to a friend. Nobody really wanted her, Tori realized, giving way to a bad case of self-pity. She meant nothing to anyone.

Brushing away the tears, Tori snuggled deep into her blanket. She felt alone and unwanted . . .

It was depressing to realize how vulnerable she was to Dru. His taunts destroyed her. His masterful kisses and caresses devastated her. This whimsical fascination for Dru Sullivan was a dead-end street. They came from two entirely different worlds. She didn't fit in his, he didn't want her there, and he scorned her lack of . . .

A long shadow fell over Tori. Her thick, moist lashes fluttered up to see Dru towering over her. He had donned his clothes and was staring somberly down at her. Oh, why wouldn't he go away and let her have a good cry? She was sure she would feel a hundred times better after wallowing in tears and self-pity for a couple of hours.

"You thought I didn't make love to you because I didn't really want you, because you mean nothing to me. But you're wrong on both counts, Chicago." His voice was low and husky, and the expression that clouded his craggy features indicated he resented making the admission, resented his physical attraction to her. "I have a great deal of respect for you. I haven't been easy on you because I want you to be competent and self-sufficient. Caleb means a great deal to me. He has become the father I lost so long ago in an Indian massacre in Kansas. Caleb and I are friends. If you were anyone else, I wouldn't have stopped . . ."

He had done it again. He'd said the wrong thing. Tori was pleased to know she had some sort of effect on this hard-hearted galoot, but she was still frustrated to no end. "Well, maybe I'd like to be somebody else," she spouted bitterly. "I'm tired of being treated like a child, protected as if I didn't have the sense God gave a duck. And if I decide I want to give myself to a man, then the choice is mine. No one is going to make my decisions for me from now on!"

88

The burst of independence brought a smile to Dru's lips. Tori could change moods like the wind—from gentle breeze to raging tempest. One of these days she was going to be a full-fledged cyclone. And if Hubert Carrington Frazier II thought he could exert any control over his wife, he was going to be in for one helluva surprise. Tori would blow the rigid caste of high society wide open.

It wasn't only Tori's delicious body that stirred Dru. In fact, it would have been better if that was all it was. The spark of fire in her lavender eyes touched something deep inside him. She was like a butterfly straining against her cocoon, determined to break free of her confining shell and prove to the world that she was a free woman.

With masculine grace, Dru squatted down on his haunches to comb his fingers through the silver-gold strands that lay about her like a shiny cape. This child-woman fascinated him in ways no other women ever had. Tori had many sides to her, and he had gotten to know her better than any other woman. She was bright and quick-witted and she was adapting well to a life without luxuries.

"I like you, Chicago," he admitted as he traced the delicate features of her face. "You're beginning to show a great deal of spunk. But considering the situation, the best you and I can hope for is to be friends." A long sigh tripped from his lips. "If things were different . . ."

"Yes, I know, you'd probably seduce me for the mere sport of it," she flung in a spiteful tone. "Well, maybe I don't want to be a naive virgin anymore—some sacrificial lamb to be led into a marriage to a man who already has two women in his harem." Good grief, what was she saying? Her innermost feelings were spewing out like a geyser. "And maybe I want to know what a woman experiences when she loves a man. Maybe I don't want to be treated like a royal princess. I *want* to be like everybody else for once in my life!"

"You shouldn't say such things," Dru snapped. "You're only making this more difficult for me. I am

89

trying to be a gentleman where you're concerned and it ain't easy, believe you me!"

"Oh, go soak your head in the river, Montana," Tori flared. "And quit trying to be noble and tactful. It's out of character. Stick with something more familiar—like intimidating sarcasm. You don't want me because I don't know the first thing about satisfying a man so don't pretend otherwise. I almost wish that scoundrel had had his way with me so at long last I would know what all this mysterious business is all about."

Dru peered at Tori as if she had sprouted antlers. "You're talking crazy, Chicago!"

"And quit calling me that," she blared at him.

Dru stared long and hard at the young woman who glared up at him. Day by day, her true nature was beginning to emerge. Tori was learning to use her temper to blow off steam instead of holding in her anger. With each new conflict she confronted, her determination proportionately increased. And when she was irritated, those violet eyes flashed like lightning bolts. What a delightful little bundle of femininity she had become! It was a shame she was off limits because he might even find himself falling . . . Dru smothered the ridiculous thought on the spot. Love was out of the question. Tori belonged to another man. And Dru had no need of any more commitments in his life than he already had. He enjoyed his freedom and didn't want to be tied down. He was thirty years old and too set in his ways to buckle to the responsibilities that love entailed.

A faint smile pursed Dru's lips as he rose to full stature. "Go to sleep, wind-child, before your ranting and raving brews up another storm."

As he ambled away, Tori slammed her fist into the ground. He had called her a child. Darn it all, she was a woman! But nobody had bothered to notice. Like an ignoramus, she had stripped naked in front of Dru and even that hadn't driven home the point! Blast it, what did it take to make a man like Dru Sullivan notice her and want her the way he wanted other females? Respect her, did he? Big deal! What she could use around here was a little less respect!

Tori was so exasperated by the maelstrom of her conflicting emotions, Dru was making her feel insane. She was attracted to him, and he had admitted he was mildly attracted to her. His fiery kisses and caresses made her want to discover the sensual world of passion, but he showed no interest in introducing her to the mysterious dimension of desire.

Since she had met this ruggedly handsome rogue, she was left wanting things she couldn't comprehend. Dru was the devil's own temptation—a torment. If there was another woman nearby, he certainly would have bedded her without batting an eyelash. But Tori was forced to sit here and wonder what she had been missing until she mildewed in her soggy clothes. Dru wasn't doing her any favors by keeping his distance. He was driving her stark raving mad and she was saying, doing, and thinking things she never believed possible!

Part Two

The height of farce it is, I ween,
  To be so perfumed and anointed,
And when one's appetite's most keen,
  To have it thus most disappointed.
                    —Martial, *The Epigrams*

Chapter 8

When Dru pulled his steed to a halt overlooking an obscure farmhouse that was nestled in the hills, Tori peered curiously at him. Did he actually intend to make contact with other human beings? Hope rose inside her, speculating on the possibility of enjoying a meal the main course of which didn't consist of beans.

Dru bent his gaze to Tori, marveling at the mass of hair that sparkled with silver-blond highlights and her elegant features that now carried the amber tint of sunshine. "We'll stay the night here, if you promise not to divulge who you are," he bargained with her.

The temptation of mingling with other people and sinking her teeth into real food was too great to resist. The truth was, Tori was anxious to see her father and she was in no hurry to return to Chicago and to Hubert—not when she was so fascinated with this complex, blue-eyed rake of many moods. If Dru was offering to break the monotony of the trip, Tori was prepared to promise him anything.

"For a decent meal, I'd even be nice to you for the entire evening," Tori vowed faithfully.

For a long moment Dru scrutinized the shapely minx. When he was certain she meant what she said, he nudged his steed down the slope. Before they reached the farm, a brawny man in homespun clothes ambled out of the barn to survey his unexpected guests.

Dru pasted on a pleasant smile as he swung from the saddle. "My sister and I were hoping you could put us up for the night in your barn."

Olin Steep's assessing gaze flooded over Dru's stubbled face and then flitted to the blonde who still sat atop her pony. The expectation on Tori's lovely face provoked him to smile and nod agreeably.

"We'll gladly pay for the chance to sleep with a roof over our heads," Dru added as he reached up to lift Tori from the saddle. "I've been back East to fetch my little sister from school. Ma and Pa are sure anxious to have her home after she's been away in the big city so long."

Sister? Ma and Pa? Tori struggled to stifle the grin that threatened to curve the corners of her mouth upward.

Olin dragged his straw hat from his salt-and-pepper hair and raked his blunt fingers through the tousled strands. "We've got a room at the back of the barn for travelers," he informed Dru. "But we don't charge for putting up guests." The hint of a smile found his lips. "The fact is, we like the company. I'll tell Margaret to set a couple of extra plates for supper."

Dru fished into his pocket to retrieve a gold nugget. "We appreciate your generosity, but I'd feel much better if we paid for our room and board. Ma and Pa would insist."

Olin hesitated momentarily, but then accepted the money Dru offered him. "I'll show you where you can put your gear."

Grabbing the saddlebags, Dru and Tori followed Olin through the rows of stalls to the rustic room that contained a table, two chairs, and an overhead loft with two straw pallets. Their accommodations were a far cry from the luxuries Tori had known, but after sleeping on the ground and surviving on beans, Tori considered the crude quarters as elegant as a palace.

After the introductions were made, Olin pivoted toward the door. "I'll send my daughter Angela down

96

with some soap and towels so you can freshen up," he offered. "Dinner should be ready in an hour."

When Olin exited, Tori climbed into the loft to inspect the straw ticking that would serve as her bed. Lord, it was glorious to lie down on something besides the damp ground! Ah, this was heaven.

An amused smile pursed Dru's lips as he watched Tori stretch out on the pallet and sigh contentedly. If nothing else, this trek west had taught this spoiled miss to appreciate the simplicities of life. After roughing it for two weeks, she considered a straw pallet as comfortable as her own special cloud in heaven!

The creak of the door brought Dru's head around. His gaze fell to the trim redhead who breezed inside carrying a pitcher, soap, and towels. One eyebrow climbed to a surprised angle when Angela raked him up and down, making no attempt to disguise her interest. As luck would have it, Tori had just raised her head over the railing to watch Dru and Angela appraise each other. For the life of her, Tori couldn't imagine why she was stung by the slightest bit of jealousy when she intercepted their glances. Angela, who appeared to be only a few years older than Tori, made no bones about the fact that she liked what she saw and would have no aversion to seeing more.

Feeling like an overlooked stick of furniture, Tori sat up on the pallet to watch Angela work her wiles on her male guest. As Dru swaggered across the room, Angela batted her eyes, and Tori swore the woman's lashes would fly off her face. And if that wasn't enough, the redhead's tone of voice was so syrupy that it could have been poured over a stack of pancakes.

"Daddy said we had company," Angela gushed at Dru, setting the pitcher and basin on the table. "But he neglected to say how handsome you are."

Tori rolled her eyes at Angela's coquettish flirtations.

"Why thank you, ma'am," Dru drawled, countering with a roguish smile. "Olin also neglected to say what a lovely daughter he had."

"Call me Angela," she cooed with another melting smile and a flurry of eyelash's batting.

Tori was becoming more annoyed by the second. Swinging down, she bounded to the floor to interrupt this sickeningly sweet scene of male conquest and female surrender. "If you'll kindly tell me where I can fetch some water, I'll retrieve it while you and my brother get better acquainted," Tori volunteered.

One tapered finger indicated the general direction of the well, but Angela was too entranced to take her eyes off the magnificent man who towered over her. Snatching up the bucket by the door, Tori stalked out.

"He didn't say how handsome you were," Tori mimicked, and then batted her lashes at the barn at large. Her voice dropped one octave. "He didn't say what a lovely daughter he had." If Tori had to endure too many of these sticky sweet conversations between Dru and Angela, she swore she'd develop a toothache! And although Tori told herself she couldn't care less if Angela and Dru were groping at each other, she found herself hurrying to draw water and hot-foot it back to the barn.

And when she did, she wished she had tarried longer at the well, for she saw that Angela had sidled up to Dru, brushing provocatively against his chest, tracing his full lips with her forefinger.

Sweet merciful heavens, the chit certainly didn't waste time! And Dru, cad that he was, was lapping up all her attention like a thirsty pup. Why, before the night was out, Tori predicted these two would be . . . The thought had her silently fuming.

Disappointment clouded Angela's brow when Tori struggled across the room, slopping water as she went, spoiling the mood of the moment. "Well, I'll let you freshen up before supper," the redhead muttered, then with a provocative sway in her hips, sashayed toward the door, paused to toss Dru a most seductive smile, and batted her lashes for the umpteenth time. "See you later . . ."

"Thanks for the warning," Tori smirked, only to have Dru clear his throat to drown out her snide remark.

Dru focused on the shapely redhead who blew him a kiss before making her theatrical exit, then glanced at Tori, who moved toward the table in stiff, agitated jerks. "The young woman seems to be lonely for a man's attention," he commented. "Her husband was killed during the second year of the war."

"And since you are oozing with charm, I'm sure you can comfort the poor grieving widow," Tori sniffed caustically.

"I'm sure I can," Dru said just to get Tori's goat. And he did . . .

"Is that all women are to you? Conquests?" she hurled nastily. "You don't give a whit about the personality attached to a female body, do you, Montana? All that concerns you is seizing and conquering."

"I could have sworn I was *Angela's* conquest," Dru parried as he dug into his saddlebag to fetch his razor. "And if I didn't know better, I'd swear you're jealous, Chicago."

"Don't be ridiculous," Tori scoffed. "I couldn't care less what you and Angela do. I'm just thankful to have a roof over my head and the chance to feast on a meal that doesn't come from a tin can. As far as I'm concerned, you and the widow can tumble around on the straw ticks to your heart's content. Just give me fair warning so I can make myself scarce while you're practicing your hot and heavy breathing."

With her face and hands scrubbed to a shine, Tori sashayed toward the door in the same provocative manner Angela had employed. After batting her lashes, Tori blew Dru a kiss. "I'll be in the kitchen, helping Margaret with supper if you need me . . . *dahling* . . ." she cooed for dramatic effect and then breezed out the door.

A deep skirl of laughter bubbled in Dru's chest as Tori treated him to an exaggerated sway of her curvy hips and a throaty voice that poked fun at Angela's tactics. Still snickering, Dru lathered his face and shaved off the stubble.

It was a shame that violet-eyed sprite didn't realize it was best that Dru looked elsewhere for physical satisfaction. She was too busy being annoyed with him for attracting female attention. He needed a distraction, Dru assured himself. He had become far too aware of Tori. If she were to keep her innocence, Dru was going to have to devote a few hours to the shapely widow.

Angela didn't possess Tori's keen wit and natural beauty, but Dru had been weeks without a woman. And riding beside the world's greatest temptation was playing havoc with his emotions. Tonight Dru was going to relieve the tension. He was actually doing Tori a favor, even if she didn't see it that way! Tori might not thank him, but Caleb certainly would.

Tori took an instant liking to Margaret Steep. Although the woman's list of chores appeared endless, she had accepted her tasks and carried them out without complaint. After learning that Tori had supposedly been away at school in the East, Margaret bombarded her with questions about the latest fashions and the life Tori had enjoyed during her studies.

It was fortunate that Tori volunteered to assist with the meal because Angela was so enamored of Dru that she was following in his shadow while he helped Olin with the last-minute chores. Each time Tori glanced out the window, she saw Angela making some sort of physical contact with Dru—a hand on his arm, her body brushing lightly against his . . .

"Angela seems to be quite taken with your brother," Margaret observed, following Tori's gaze through the

100

window. "Most of the travelers who come through here aren't worth having around, just tumbleweeds and such." She set the heaping bowl of potatoes on the table and turned back to fetch the fried chicken and gravy. "Olin usually warns Angela away from strangers. But your brother impressed him."

Before Tori could spitefully announce that Dru wasn't that good a catch, the threesome sailed through the door. And while Angela gushed and bubbled and flirted with Dru, Tori wolfed down the succulent dinner—in which there was not a single bean!

When the meal was over, Angela offered to show Dru around the farm and neglected helping her mother clear the table. Tori rolled up her sleeves to wash dishes. She couldn't remember the last time she had her hands in dishwater and she cursed herself for speculating on what Dru was doing with *his* hands. Not that she cared, mind you. She was only curious.

Quit behaving like a betrayed lover, Tori silently scolded herself as she scrubbed the plates with enough vigor to peel off the finish. *Dru means nothing to you, nor you to him. He is no more than a traveling companion.*

Clinging to that sensible thought, Tori completed her chore, thanked Margaret kindly for the scrumptious meal, and ambled back to the barn. Her footsteps faltered when merry giggles wafted their way from around the side of the stables. Tori muttered under her breath when she heard Dru's rich baritone voice drop to a husky tone that could send goosebumps dancing across a woman's flesh.

Why was she allowing Dru's tête-à-tête to get under her skin? She didn't give a whit what he and Angela were doing. But the words had an empty ring to them, and Tori had difficulty convincing herself that she didn't wish she were in Angela's shoes. Dru's masterful kisses and tantalizing caresses had awakened something in her, but he wanted nothing to do with her now! The instant another female crossed Dru's path, his roving eyes

101

wandered and lust overcame him. He only viewed Tori as a bothersome child who had a great deal to learn, a responsibility he had undertaken because of his friendship with Caleb.

Men were all alike, Tori thought cynically. Grumbling at the male of the species in general and Dru in particular, Tori stomped through the row of stalls to reach her quarters. Hubert kept his mistresses and Dru took lovers anytime and any place he pleased. Men didn't know the meaning of fidelity. From all Tori had seen, her stepfather was the only loyal male on the Continent, and why Edgar had been faithful to Gwen when she could be such a shrew at times, baffled Tori. Occasionally, Tori found herself thinking Edgar was an exceptionally good sport, and she wondered why she had worked up such a dislike of him all these years. He had taken her in and treated her like a princess. He had even drawn up a will that entitled her to his fortune. Edgar had been generous and devoted. It was a shame Tori hadn't realized he was the one friend she really had. And it was even more of a shame that Dru wasn't more like her stepfather.

Ah, well, Tori mused as she sprawled on the pallet. Dru would never notice her. She had stripped in front of him and even that hadn't rattled him. There was no hope for it. Tori simply wasn't woman enough to lure a man like Dru Sullivan so she might as well give up this silly infatuation. Dru already had her crying like a baby when he ridiculed her. It would never do to let him break her heart. That would be infinitely worse!

Chapter 9

Angela leaned back in the circle of Dru's arms and flashed him an inviting smile. "I know a quiet little place by the river where you and I could lie beneath the stars and . . ." Her voice trailed off, letting him form his own conclusions about what else they could do.

Dru stared down into hazel eyes that flickered suggestively. He was all set to accept the invitation when Tori's image flashed through his mind. Frustrated, Dru asked himself why he was hesitating for even a second when opportunity was staring him in the face. Angela was offering to appease needs that had lain dormant for more weeks than he cared to count. She was reasonably pretty and obviously experienced and he couldn't think of one good reason to decline the offer.

"I had better check on my sister," Dru heard himself say and wondered why the devil he had. Godamighty, he hadn't planned to spare that violet-eyed elf another thought tonight!

An exaggerated pout puckered Angela's lips and she yanked herself loose to glower at Dru. "I should think your sister could take care of herself for a few hours. If there was a man hereabouts to occupy her, she wouldn't be worrying about you, you can bank on that!"

"Tori doesn't flaunt herself around men," Dru snapped, surprising himself and Angela.

"And you think I do?" Angela asked. "Well, as far as I'm concerned, you can crawl back to your bed and entertain your little sister. Good night, Mr. Sullivan!"

When Angela stomped off in a huff, Dru swore under his breath. He'd had the chance to ease his needs and he had rejected the offer. Growling at his foolishness, Dru stormed through the barn, glaring at every milk cow, mule, and horse along the way. He had been frustrated before, but now it was infinitely worse. He had denied himself the pleasures of passion and he wasn't even sure why. What did he care what Tori thought of him? They had no hold on each other. She was just baggage he was carting west for Caleb. If he wanted to dally with a farmer's daughter he could . . . and he would have if Tori's beguiling features hadn't kept cropping up in his mind's eye each time he looked at Angela.

The slamming door caused Tori to crane her neck over the railing. She noticed the black scowl plastered on Dru's craggy features. "What's the matter, Montana?" she taunted. "Did Angela turn you down? The woman has better taste than I thought."

Dru shucked his shirt, tossed it over the back of the chair, and stomped up the ladder. "She was more than willing," he informed the smug blonde.

Tori sat up cross-legged, her pretty features furrowing in a mutinous frown. "I see. And I assume the only reason you are here is to rout me out so the two of you can—"

"I'm here to get some sleep," Dru bit off. "And if you'll clam up, Chicago, I intend to do just that."

In bewilderment, Tori watched Dru flop his bedroll over the straw tick and flounce down upon it. "You turned Angela down?" Her incredulous tone indicated she didn't believe him for a second. "Come now, Montana. I may be naive, but I'm not stupid."

Dru's hand snaked out to grab a fistful of her long hair and yank her to him. His face was a scant few inches from hers. Shock waves shot through Tori's body and she cursed her spontaneous reaction to this philandering rake.

"I'm in no mood for your taunts, minx," he growled, his breath hot against her flushed cheeks.

Her tongue flicked out to moisten her bone-dry lips. Tori told herself she didn't want to feel his sensuous mouth on hers, but she did. And she was too innocent of men to understand why Dru was in such a snit. Frustrated passion was gnawing at him, but Tori didn't know that. All she knew was that this virile, swarthy giant was too close for comfort. He did incredible things to her blood pressure and heartbeat, causing both of them to leap through her body.

Flashes of the night not so long ago tormented Tori. With vivid clarity she remembered the feel of Dru's masculine contours molded familiarly to hers, recalled the sizzling sensations that had come dangerously close to burning out of control. She found herself wanting to relive those tantalizing moments, to discover where the fiery sensations would lead.

"I didn't seduce Angela because she wasn't you," Dru breathed, his voice ragged with desire. "Haven't you figured it out yet, Little Miss Innocent? I wanted you, not her. She would have been no more than a meager substitute."

Tori winced at his gruff tone and gulped over the lump that collected in her throat. Helplessly, she stared into those spellbinding sky-blue eyes, feeling her willpower buckle. "I thought you said you wanted someone who had the experience to please you," she said.

Dru's fierce grasp on her long silver-blond hair eased slightly and he heaved a deep sigh. "I said I *wished* you were someone else," he clarified. His thick black lashes swept up and his gaze locked with rippling violet. "The truth is, I want you, Chicago. I did then and I do now. And unless you want to lose your innocence to me, I suggest you crawl back on your pallet and let well enough alone."

105

Tori was stung again by the incredible cravings that had nagged at her since Dru had awakened her slumbering passions. When she was this close to him, she wanted him in the most unexplainable ways. But he had made it clear that he didn't want to overstep the boundaries he had set for himself concerning her.

"For a kiss, I'll go back where I belong and I'll even climb down to snuff the lantern," she bartered.

His dark brows climbed into an arch. Tori constantly surprised him. She was changing minute by minute, shedding her inhibitions to reveal the vivacious spirit her mother had fought so hard to stifle.

"You think I'll stop after one kiss?" he chortled, focusing his unblinking attention on her cupid's-bow lips.

"If you could turn down a tumble in the grass with Angela, I'm sure you have more than enough self-control to limit me to one kiss," she replied before flashing him a saucy grin. "I'll take what I can get."

A low growl rattled in Dru's chest. Tori was trying some of Angela's flirtatious techniques out on him, and the effect was devastating. He had only to look at her and he wanted her in all the wild, breathless ways he had ever wanted a woman—and more . . .

His mouth slanted over hers, drinking in the sweet nectar of her kiss, teaching her scintillating techniques and letting her practice them on him. Involuntarily, her arms wound around his neck and she surrendered to the spark of passion that leaped from her body to his and then back again.

It was a scorching kiss that left her questioning her ability to settle for so little when she hungered for so much more. She was tempting fate, she knew. But ignoring these compelling sensations was like willing the sun not to shine while it hung in the midday sky. As always when Dru kissed her with such expertise, her brain melted. She was left quivering with forbidden needs, yearning for that which she wanted to accept from only one man. Dru could turn her wrong side out, exposing emotions that Tori had never before confronted. He made her feel wild and reckless and every inch a woman who wanted to share the passion of her man.

Lost to the wild tremors that wracked her body, Tori gave in to the urge to brush her inquisitive hands over the dark matting of hair that covered his chest. Brazenly, her caresses wandered across his lean belly, skimming the scar caused by a bullet from years past. She memorized the feel of his whipcord muscles, the hard tendons and masculine contours. She marveled at the warm pleasure that throbbed in her own body while she was touching him.

Her adventurous caresses ebbed and flooded, mapping the taut planes and rock-hard terrain of his bronzed body. Tori was intrigued by the vast differences between a man and woman. Dru was sinewy muscle and potential strength—the very essence of masculinity—and his magnificent body invited her curious touch.

A muffled groan rattled in Dru's throat when Tori dared to touch him so boldly. Her exploring caresses left him a mass of raw emotion. Suddenly, his own hands were trespassing on unchartered territory, aching to discover every delicious secret of her feminine body, to teach her the sweet mysteries of intimacy. His lips devoured hers as if she were a long-awaited treat. His caresses wandered to circle the roseate buds of her breasts. Then, like a swift-moving tide, his hands swept beneath her buckhide breeches to make tantalizing contact with her curvaceous hips and silky thighs, marveling at the luxurious texture of her skin.

Dru heard Tori's quick intake of breath when he intimately fondled her, but he had held himself at bay too long to be content with merely a kiss and caress. He yearned to know her as no other man had. He longed to discover what aroused her, to trace each sensitive point on her body and bring her to life. He ached to appease the

107

insane craving that had gnawed at him since he had first laid eyes on this gorgeous pixie.

Tori's senses were flooded with Dru's masculine aroma, the feel of his steel-honed body brushing suggestively against hers. Tingles ricocheted through her when his tongue flicked at the taut peaks of her breasts, when his knowing fingers glided between her thighs to tease and arouse her by maddening degrees. His intimate touch left her breathless, created monstrous cravings that demanded fulfillment.

The world teetered precariously and Tori found herself living only to feel Dru's muscular body joined to hers, to experience the ultimate pleasures his skillful caresses promised. She would have sacrificed her last breath if he would only ease the needs that mushroomed inside her.

"I want you . . ." Tori rasped, her voice thick with passion.

Through the cloudy haze that fogged his brain, Dru heard her quiet words. He knew how to make a woman beg for his touch. He was an experienced lover. And yet, in the back of his mind, the voice of reason whispered to him, scolding him for daring so much with this innocent elf. It was sweet torture to caress her shapely body, to leave her breathless with longing. He could have taken her, and she would have welcomed him.

As much as Dru disliked Hubert Frazier, he couldn't forget that Tori had been promised to another man. And as much as Dru wanted this violet-eyed sprite, he couldn't quite forget she was Caleb's daughter.

There were times in a man's life when he had to forgo his own personal wants and needs. Integrity prevented Dru from yielding to temptation, even when Tori was warm and willing. She was too inexperienced and vulnerable.

God, he hated being honorable where this lovely nymph was concerned! He hungered to ease his male desires, but he wouldn't. He couldn't, not if he hoped to live with his conscience and face Caleb again. Tori wasn't just one of the many females he'd seduced and discarded along the way. She was the first real lady he'd ever known. He wanted her, but he knew by robbing her of her innocence, he would only complicate her life.

When Dru finally found the will to drag his lips away from hers, Tori blinked owlishly. Her entire body throbbed with intense pleasure and her heart thundered around her chest like a runaway stallion.

"Snuff the lantern, Chicago," he commanded, his voice hoarse with enflamed desire. "There's already enough heat in this loft to catch the barn on fire."

Rolling onto limp, shaky legs, Tori wobbled the ladder to douse the lantern, then fumbled back to her pallet, guided by the shaft of moonlight that sprayed through the opening in the loft. To her surprise, Dru had dragged her pallet beside his. She peered questioningly at him.

"I'm not going to make love to you," he told her as he drew her down beside him. "God knows I want to, but I'll settle for holding you. If I dare to do more than I already have, we'll both probably live to regret it."

Tori flashed him an impish smile, trying to make light of the situation. "Spoilsport. If I can't have you, is it all right if I pretend we're doing more than just . . . sleeping together?"

Dru wasn't sure he could handle this flirtatious gamin. *She* might have been teasing, but *he* was dead serious and they were treading on dangerous ground. It had taken all his willpower to pull away when he did. And even now, his body was warring with his common sense.

Propping himself on an elbow, Dru peered down into sparkling lavender eyes. "I've already imagined making love to you a dozen times," he told her frankly. "You're lucky I've turned out to be such a gentleman."

Tori drew the quilt over her shoulder and presented her back to him. "To tell the truth, Montana, there have been times lately when I wish you weren't so confounded honorable."

A rueful smile hovered on his lips as he uplifted a silver-gold strand and let it trickle from his fingertips. Lord, she was making this difficult! Dru knew damned well that this little dove was testing her wings, using him to experiment with passion. She was learning to flirt, discovering the meaning of desire. They set fires in each other, and God, it was hard not to give in to the burning passion that sizzled inside him.

Heaving a frustrated sigh, Dru curled his arm around Tori and willed himself to go to sleep, even though that was the very last thing he wanted to do. This tempting minx was putting a severe strain on his noble intentions. Each time he touched her, he dared more than the time before. He wondered how long he could restrain himself before he threw caution to the wind and followed his lusty desires. Godamighty, wanting this lovely sprite already occupied his thoughts to the extent that he could barely contemplate anything else!

Tori silently sighed at the feel of Dru's arm sliding around her waist. She knew it was dangerous folly to imagine how it would feel to lie naked in his powerful arms, to discover all the wondrous pleasures that had been unleashed when they kissed and touched. For Tori it would have been a voyage into paradise, but she was smart enough to know she would be just another of his many women. He wasn't the kind of man who played for keeps. He had agreed to accompany her to Montana because of Caleb, but that was the only pledge Dru planned to uphold. The only reason Dru wanted her at all was because he had made up his mind he couldn't have her, her being Caleb Flemming's daughter and all. If not for that, she was certain she would have become just a smile and a moment to him, like so many females before her.

She supposed she should be flattered that Dru respected her innocence enough to restrain himself. But it was frustrating to find herself so attracted to a man who would have preferred to have no obligation to her at all.

While Tori was assuring herself that despite the fierce attraction, she was better off not becoming intimately involved with Dru, Dru himself was cursing himself up one side and down the other for rejecting Angela Steep. He could have been sleeping like a baby now, his needs appeased. But hell no, he had settled for several soul-shattering kisses and bone-melting caresses that kept him on a slow, tormented burn.

If Dru could have snapped his fingers, he would have wished himself back to Virginia City. The cross-country trek with this gorgeous bundle of temptation was driving him mad with wanting.

"Help!"

Pinkerton detectives Tom Bates and William Fogg pricked their ears to the cry for assistance that rattled through the trees. Urging their steeds into a faster clip, they wove through the forest in search of the source of the sound. Tom frowned curiously when he spied the whisker-faced vagabond tied to a tree.

"I'm sure glad to see you fellas," the man said hoarsely. He had been screaming at the top of his lungs at regular intervals for the past two days.

"What happened?" William questioned, swinging down to free the captive.

"I was just minding my own business when a giant of a man jumped me," he lied through his teeth. "The big brute knocked me silly, tied me to this tree, and stole my mule."

William shot a glance at Tom, who was frowning suspiciously. "Did this man have a blond-haired woman with him?"

The scoundrel eyed the detectives warily. "How'd you know that?"

"We've been tracking him," Tom declared, shifting uncomfortably on the saddle that felt as if it had become his Siamese twin.

111

"Well, he was here" came the muttered reply. "I don't know where he went, but I hope to God I never meet up with that big ape again. He almost broke my jaw with a whalloping right cross."

Swinging onto his mount, William looked speculatively at Tom. "Now what?"

Tom's shoulder lifted in a shrug. "We keep searching. Frazier said not to come back until we apprehend the kidnapper."

The two detectives pointed themselves west, searching for signs and clues that would lead them to Dru Sullivan and Hubert Frazier's missing fiancée. Tom prided himself in following through with the Pinkerton Detective Agency's guarantee: We always get our man. But Tom was beginning to think the manhunt might take a while. This was the first clue they had picked up in over two weeks! They weren't chasing a fool who left a path that was easy to follow! In fact, their investigation had been hit and miss and they were fortunate to have stumbled onto this scavenger who had crossed paths with Victoria's abductor.

Chapter 10

Dru gazed pensively down at the community that lay at the junction of the Des Moines and Raccoon rivers and then peered into Tori's weary face. Dru had pushed hard to put distance between himself and the posse he expected Frazier to send in search of his lost fiancée.

Although Tori hadn't voiced one word of complaint, with the exception of grumbling about the steady diet of beans, her strained countenance indicated that the tedious journey was taking its toll on her. There were dark circles under her eyes, confirming to Dru that he had pushed her to the limits of her stamina. He wanted Tori to become adept in her surroundings, and she had listened to each and every instruction he offered. She had responded like a trooper, attempting to prove she could match him stride for stride. A lesser woman would have whined and wailed, but Tori had accepted every challenge Dru thrust upon her. Yet, being unaccustomed to such rigorous travel, Tori needed a break.

"I've decided we're going to spend the night in Des Moines," Dru announced.

Tori let out a squeal of delight and reached over to hug him. Remembering herself and the invisible wall Dru had kept between them since the night in Steep's barn, she resettled in her saddle. "Excuse me," she murmured sheepishly.

It was only a brief contact, but Tori's feminine scent clung to Dru like hypnotic cologne. He could feel the imprint of her supple body against his, and he cursed his fierce reaction to her careless touch. His body absorbed her scent and her touch like the parched ground soaking up a long-awaited rain. For countless days, Dru had cautiously kept his distance, battling this ill-fated attraction. But it was there, lurking just beneath the surface and it took so little to trigger his emotions.

Clamping a firm grip on himself, Dru stared into the distance. He should have dragged Whong along with him, even if the poor man could barely hold his head up. Dru definitely needed a buffer between him and this striking beauty.

Dru was becoming attached to her, even though he constantly reminded himself that she had a fiancé awaiting her in Chicago. Gwendolyn would never permit her daughter to remain out west. Tori would be whisked out of his life, and if Dru were smart, he would remember that Tori was no more than a temporary distraction . . .

His thoughts dispersed when they neared the outskirts of Des Moines. Tori was like an excited child who had come back to life after being promised the prospect of mingling with civilization again. He suspected Tori was accustomed to being surrounded by admirers and that she was growing tired of solitude. Dru, on the other hand, preferred his sprawling ranch to life in town, preferred privacy to socializing.

Tori didn't even turn up her nose at the crude hotel into which they walked. Dru could detect the relief that overcame her as she toyed with the possibility of taking a bath in a tub and sleeping on a feather bed. A radiant smile blossomed on her tanned features. It made him wish he could be the reason for that dazzling smile. But he reminded himself that he had been nothing but a constant frustration to Tori, forcing her to adapt and live by his rules, pushing her to the limits of her abilities.

The moment the innkeeper laid the key on the desk

and turned the guest book around for Dru to scribble his signature, Tori latched onto it and bounded up the steps two at a time. Dru's measuring gaze wandered over her tight-fitting garb, silently admiring her beauty and her spirit. If Gwen could have seen the way her prim and proper daughter leaped up the steps, she would have fainted dead away, Dru predicted.

"I think the lady would also like a bath," Dru murmured, distracted. "Please see that she has the tub filled."

The innkeeper grinned at Dru's unblinking stare. "Newlyweds, I'd guess," he tittered before he summoned the servants to fetch water for the tub. "She's a mighty pretty little lady."

Dru flinched. Newlyweds? "Yes, we are, as a matter of fact," he lied through his smile. "And you're right. She is indeed a pretty lady."

When Dru swaggered through the door, Tori was stretched on the feather bed like a kitten lounging in the spring sunshine. A stream of silver-gold hair trailed out beside her and Dru was stung by the impulsive urge to rip off his clothes and join her . . .

Godamighty, there he went again! At least a hundred times he had lectured himself against entertaining those lusty ideas. Tori was off limits, he reminded himself fiercely.

To Dru's relief a rotund maid waddled inside. She was followed by a brigade of three teenage boys who floundered when they caught a glimpse of the shapely blonde lounging on the bed. Three pair of admiring eyes roamed over Tori's tantalizing figure, even though she was oblivious to the attention she was receiving. The boys were gaping at her as if she were lying there stark naked. And Dru should know, after all—he had been staring at her the same way when she wasn't watching.

Dru wasn't sure why he felt so possessive, but he moved in front of Tori like a shield, blocking the boys' view. He focused his glare on each young face. Having been caught gawking, the lads dropped their gazes and scuttled over to dump the water in the tub.

Still unaware that she had attracted so much attention, Tori sighed and twisted this way and that, leaving Dru scowling at the provocative picture she presented. Godamighty, that vixen didn't know how incredibly seductive she was lying there. She was doing impossible things to his body, not to mention the dramatic effect she had on the young boys who kept stealing glances at her when they thought Dru wasn't looking.

When the foursome filed out, Tori noticed the frown that was stamped on Dru's craggy features. Curious, she sat up on the edge of the bed. "What's wrong?" she asked innocently.

"Nothin'," he grumbled in a sour tone. "Just take your damned bath while I fetch you something decent to wear to dinner."

He turned and walked out, leaving Tori staring bemusedly after him. Shrugging off his foul mood, she concentrated on the long-awaited bath. Ah, this was paradise! She would never ever again consider bathing anything less than a luxury.

Oblivious to time, Tori soaked to her heart's content. She could relax and enjoy the first privacy she'd had in almost three weeks. Humming a light tune, she washed her hair and scrubbed away the layers of dirt that clung to her skin. A contented smile hovered on her lips as she submerged in her tub to rinse the soap from her hair. Resurfacing, she blindly groped for the towel to wipe the bubbles from her eyes, but the fluffy fabric flew into her hand as if it had sprouted wings.

Blinking, she peered up at the massive form that loomed over her. "Godamighty, Montana, you shouldn't sneak up on a person," she sputtered, attempting to cover herself.

Dru stood frozen to the spot, wishing he hadn't waltzed in without announcing himself. The picture of Tori's luscious body had lingered in his mind since the day she

116

had thrown her outrageous tantrum and stripped naked to prove her point. But this was even worse!

"Watch it, Chicago, you're beginning to sound like me," Dru chastised her, trying to do the honorable thing by looking the other way and failing miserably.

"I am, aren't I?" she replied, aware that she had resorted to using one of his favorite expressions and also aware that, for the first time, she had Dru's undivided attention.

It thrilled her to note that she was having an effect on him. At last he had noticed she was a woman! His ravishing gaze flattered her beyond words. She supposed she should have squealed in indignation stranded like this in a bathtub with a man ogling. But this wasn't just any man. This was Dru Sullivan, who had the self-control of a granite mountain. He had been ignoring her since they left the Steeps' farm and any sort of reaction from him was welcomed.

"Aren't you what?" Dru mumbled as his gaze worked its way over creamy, bare flesh dancing with water droplets that reminded him of diamond chips.

Soft laughter bubbled from Tori's lips. It boosted her feminine pride to realize she had distracted Dru. "I'm beginning to sound like you," she prompted him, and then broke into a teasing grin. "See anything you like, Montana?"

Dru scowled at having his own words tossed back in his face. Tori could have sworn she noticed a faint blush beneath his deep tan. She had finally gotten his goat.

"You're turning into a shameless tease," he admonished, forcing himself to turn his back like he should have done in the first place.

An impish grin pursed her lips. Tori found wicked delight in rattling Dru. He had certainly rattled *her* on numerous occasions. "Am I? Perhaps I was a trollop in another lifetime and my true personality is just beginning to emerge."

Dru gnashed his teeth. He was letting her get to him.

Even when he turned his back, the vision of satiny flesh sparkling with water droplets emblazoned itself on his brain . . .

He heard the splash, but he didn't dare look back, even though his hungry eyes were begging him to swivel his head around.

Clearing his throat, Dru indicated the package on the end of the bed. "I could only guess at your size. I hope the gown and slippers fit," he said lamely.

Wrapped in her towel, Tori approached the bed. She opened the package to find a lavender gown that was adorned with dainty ruffles and lace. It wasn't as elaborate as the custom-made gowns her mother had tailored for her by the best seamstress in Chicago, but it was exquisite nonetheless.

"Thank you, Dru. It's lovely," she murmured appreciatively.

"It ain't much compared to your lavish wardrobe," he contradicted with a snort. "*Isn't,*" he corrected himself before Tori did it for him.

The remark triggered her temper. It annoyed her that she couldn't appreciate his gift without him spoiling the moment. "Confound it, Montana, do you think all I care about is expensive clothes and elegant parties?"

Dru cringed as she stamped around in front of him, wearing nothing but that skimpy towel that barely concealed what his eyes were eager to devour. "Well, isn't it?"

"No, it certainly is not," she contested. "Sometimes you can be a narrow-minded dolt!"

"Thank you very much for the insult!"

"You're very welcome."

While Dru was still growling and scowling, Tori snatched up the petticoats and gown and sailed behind the dressing screen. After she heard the splatter of water and was assured that Dru's magnificent male body was reasonably concealed by bubbles, she sailed toward the door.

118

"I'm going to have a look around town while you bathe," she announced.

"Stay out of trouble, Chicago."

"Why should I? It's the only time I'll ever get to have any fun," she said airily. "Honestly, Montana, sometimes you can be as dull and stuffy as Hubert Carrington Frazier II."

On the wings of that barb, she sailed out the door as Dru hurled the sponge at her. Godamighty, didn't she have any idea how difficult it was to keep his distance, to be polite and respectful? This was an unfamiliar role for Dru and he wasn't adapting to it well at all. With each passing second he was wishing he had never met Tori. She was turning him inside out.

That minx wanted fun, did she? Well, he would show her a good time—within his strict limitations, that is. Tori was probably bored and was anxious for a diversion, he speculated. Resolving to accommodate the shapely sprite, Dru hurriedly shaved and dressed. Garbed in the new clothes he'd bought, Dru checked his appearance in the mirror and then breezed out the door. Dull and stuffy, indeed! Tori was going to find out just how entertaining he could be. Dru vowed to be the best companion Tori ever had. He'd make her retract that degrading comment about his being as exciting as Hubert!

A large crowd had gathered at the edge of town, and Tori's curiosity got the best of her. Following the flow of traffic, she ambled down the street to view the county fair that was in progress. Carefree laughter filled the air and lighthearted music lifted Tori's spirits. Delighted with the diversion, she wandered past the row of booths to inspect the crafts and then paused to watch the horses that raced around the track encircling the fair grounds.

Things were going splendidly and Tori was having a marvelous time until a young man, who had obviously been drinking his share of whiskey, swaggered up to drape his arm over her shoulder.

"Where have you been all my life, honey?" he drawled, and then smiled drunkenly. "You must have just flown down from heaven."

Tori attempted to shrug off his arm without making a scene, but the wiry-haired baboon was persistent with his amorous assault.

"Ah, come on, honey. Let's you and me dance," he slurred out.

"No thank you," she declined, finally removing his limp arm from her sleeve with a heavy jerk.

The drunkard tugged on her elbow, knocking her off balance. But Tori had no intention of going anywhere with the clumsy oaf. He could barely stand on his own feet and she feared he would be trouncing all over hers if she dared to dance with him. When he roughly yanked Tori to him, she employed the technique she had seen Dru use on the vagabond in the forest. She doubled her fist and delivered a "right cross" that sent her overzealous suitor staggering backward. Liquor had slowed his reflexes, and the unexpected punch in the nose sent him spinning like a top.

The bystanders snickered when Tori punched him a good one, removing the last vestige of his dignity. With his lips twisted in a snarl, he propelled himself toward Tori like a charging bull. Two burly arms sought to entrap her and Tori lifted her knee, catching him in the private part of his anatomy. When he doubled over, her fist swung upward to collide with his chin.

The drunken brute went down and he didn't get up again.

Tori rubbed her stinging knuckles and fluffed the sleeve he had crushed, then, after straightening the gown he had twisted around her, she spun around to march away. There, grinning in wry amusement, was Dru, looking positively dashing in a white linen shirt that gapped to reveal the thick matting of hair on his chest.

120

Black breeches hugged his muscular thighs like a second set of skin. Tori felt the fierce stirring of arousal.

Ignoring the tantalizing effect this dashing rake had on her, Tori slanted him a disdainful frown. "Thanks for pitching in, Montana," she smarted off.

"Why should I have?" he questioned, falling into step beside her. "You were doing fine without me. It gave you a chance to practice what you learned. I'm impressed."

She *had* done superbly without him, she realized with a start. Well, imagine that! She didn't need a bodyguard! Her self-confidence elevated a notch when she discovered she was capable of meeting disaster head-on. Maybe she wasn't as removed from her element as she had been the first week of their journey.

"I was pretty darned good, wasn't I?" she commented with a proud smile.

"You're learning, Chicago." A teasing grin hovered on his lips as he curled his hand beneath her dainty chin. "I noticed the boxing champion of Iowa was accepting challengers this evening. Shall I sign you up for a bout?"

Violet eyes twinkled up at him and Dru very nearly folded up at the knees. When Tori smiled in that special way of hers, it was absolutely devastating. It was like being blinded by the sun.

She giggled recklessly. "After I get a decent meal under my belt, perhaps I'll consider it."

Dru dropped into one of Whong's exaggerated bows and then offered her his arm. "May I have the pleasure of your company at dinner, my dear?"

Tori studied Dru for a pensive moment. What had come over him? Why was he showering her with all this attention? Well, whatever the reason, Tori liked this new facet of their relationship. He was flirtatious and flattering, and Tori instantly responded to the kindness he bestowed on her.

Her hand slid around his elbow and she graced him with another dazzling smile. "I would be honored to join you, sir," she replied. "But don't cross me. My boxing

121

instructor says I pack quite a wallop."

Spellbound, Dru escorted Tori to the finest restaurant Des Moines had to offer. He was beginning to see why Gwen had kept Tori under lock and key all these years. The delightful nymph was an incredible temptation, and when she shed her inhibitions, she was like a breath of springtime. Her blithe, carefree mood was contagious. Lord, she made him feel like a schoolboy again—a silly, gushy schoolboy on his first date.

Tori absorbed her food and wine in ravenous gulps. Each time her glass went dry, she refilled it. The liquor loosened her and she found herself relating bits and pieces of her life to Dru. When she had exhausted the telling of her experiences under Gwen's strict rule and confided her annoyance with the constant chaperones who had hounded her from the age of ten, she eased back in her chair. Luminous lavender eyes roamed unhindered over Dru's chiseled features. Tori preferred Dru's rugged features to the refined, classical features of the gentlemen she had known. Dru was handsome in his own unique way, so magnificently built, so overpowering . . .

Tori gave herself a mental slap and straightened in her chair. She wondered if Dru had the foggiest notion where her thoughts had strayed. Apparently not, for he simply sat there, staring at her with a meditative look that she couldn't decipher. "Tell me about yourself, Montana," she requested.

His broad shoulders lifted in a casual shrug as he studied the contents of his whiskey glass. "There isn't all that much to tell," he murmured before taking another sip. "My parents were killed by renegade Indians and I sought any job I could find to earn money. I took any kind of work I could get my hands on, no matter how difficult or demeaning. After a few years of odd jobs, I went west to the gold fields in hopes of making more

122

money to send back home to my four brothers in Kansas."

"Four brothers?" Hazy eyes blinked in astonishment.

He nodded affirmatively. "John-Henry is two years younger than I am. He's twenty-eight and the father of two active boys. Jerry-Jeff turned twenty-six last month. Jimmy-Pete is twenty-four, and he married a feisty redhead last year. Billy-Bob is the baby of the family and he'll be twenty-two in three months," he reported.

Tori was amazed. The Sullivans must have had a difficult job raising that passel of boys. The tragedy must have devastated the family. The fact that each one of the boys went by two names set Tori to wondering what they called their oldest brother. Somehow, she couldn't imagine referring to Dru as anything but Montana.

"Most of my education came from firsthand experience," Dru commented, unable to keep the smidgen of resentment from seeping into his voice. "I had just turned fifteen when disaster struck my parents and I felt responsible for keeping our family together. None of my brothers had much time for schooling while we worked our farm. I left John-Henry in charge while I struck out to find work to support us. I came up through the ranks of life the hard way, taking my knocks and learning to survive by my wits and strength. There were times when all that kept me going was the thought of my brothers struggling on what money I could send to them and what little they could obtain from the crops. It has been a long haul for all of us."

"And I lived with the sad, humiliating belief that my own father didn't want me," Tori sighed. "Even though Edgar showered me with gifts, my mother kept me imprisoned in a sheltered world. My only escape was books. I'm not sure which is worse, drowning in a vacuum or scratching and clawing to get by."

"I suppose the grass always looks greener on the other side of the fence," Dru murmured, and then downed another drink. "Looking for something better than we have is the curse of life." He refilled his glass and lifted his hand. "To better days."

"To evergreens," Tori toasted, clinking her glass against his.

Dru didn't have the faintest idea what she meant, but he drank to it nonetheless.

"To the wind," Dru chuckled. "May it blow us to Montana."

"To three sheets to the wind," Tori countered with a giddy giggle.

Dru polished off the remainder of his drink, and then pushed to his feet. "Come dance with me at the county fair," he requested in a slurred voice. "I've never danced with a debutante before."

"I'd love that." Tori peered up at the towering giant and wished this night could last forever. She was having the time of her life!

Leaning on each other for support, Tori and Dru wove their way out of the restaurant and down the street. En route, Dru taught her the words to several rollicking drinking tunes that would have had Gwen gasping in horror. But Tori didn't bat an eyelash at the off-color songs. Dru was showering her with attention, and she was relishing every marvelous moment of it.

"I didn't mean to call you dull and stuffy," Tori apologized over her thick tongue. "You are anything but. The truth is you're incredibly appealing . . ." Tori hiccupped and giggled. "'Scuse me. And you have the most magnificent body, even if I had to peek through the bushes to see it."

Tori's brash remark caused Dru to burst out laughing. The last of her inhibitions had flown off in the wind and she was walking on air, saying and doing anything that came to mind.

But when they reached the county fair and Dru took Tori in his arms to twirl her around the dance area, her playfulness evaporated. The world shrank to fill the space Dru occupied. Suddenly Tori was no longer aware of the other couples who whirled beside them, only of the muscular giant who held her in his powerful arms. Dru was light and agile on his feet and the feel of his lithe body brushing against hers reminded her of other times and other places, of forbidden pleasures. Tori felt her body catch fire when flashes from the past blazed through her mind.

"Where did you learn to dance so splendidly?" she questioned, fighting down the waves of pleasure that crested upon her. They were only dancing, for heaven's sake. If she didn't get herself in hand, she was going to be imagining doing something else with this irresistible rogue.

"In the California and Nevada gold fields," he murmured sluggishly, and then broke into a grin that melted Tori into puddles. "At that time there weren't many women in the camps. We had to take turns being girls. And what about you?"

"I learned in the ballroom, with the private tutor my stepfather hired to instruct me," she responded.

When the music ended, an attractive young man ambled forward to take Dru's place, but he refused to give Tori up to anyone. For this one night, Dru intended to fully enjoy the violet-eyed beauty's company, to delude himself in whimsical dreams. Tomorrow he would shrug on his sensible clothes and continue the difficult journey west. But tonight . . . tonight he and Tori had discovered their own private fairyland of castles in the air.

Chapter 11

The spiked punch flowed freely at the fairgrounds. Dru and Tori drank their fill and sampled the refreshments that had been placed on makeshift tables. Torches burned in the night and music rang through the air on which Tori found herself walking. It had been a glorious night, and she swore she would never forget the pleasures she had enjoyed with Dru as her attentive escort. They drank and danced until the musicians finally put their instruments away and went home for the night. Tori hated to see the evening come to the end. It was the first time she had ever been alone with a man without a chaperone monitoring her every move. The fact that it was this particular man who was courting her made all the difference.

"I've never had so much fun," Tori declared with a slur that indicated she'd drunk a tad too much liquor.

A silly smile dangled on the corner of Dru's mouth when Tori let go of his arm to perform several complicated dance steps in the hall of the hotel. Graceful though she was, Tori was showing the effects of her drinking spree. When she executed a pirouette, she trounced on the hem of her gown and had to wave her arms like a windmill to maintain her balance. Although Dru's reflexes weren't what they should have been, he did manage to catch Tori's arm before she slammed into the wall.

"You've definitely had enough dancing and drinking for one night, Chicago," he scolded, in a voice containing too much laughter to sound gruff. "I'm putting you to bed."

"I don't want to go to bed." Tori's bewitching features puckered at the distasteful suggestion. "I want to sing and dance all night long." She tap-danced across their room, accompanying herself with one of the outrageous mining ditties Dru had taught her and now wished he hadn't.

"Ssh . . . shh . . . You'll wake the whole damned hotel," Dru muttered. Lord, the world had tipped sideways, he thought as he glanced around the room. Either the floor or his brain was warped. He wished he was sober enough to know which.

"I don't care who hears me." Tori spun about and then staggered to keep her balance. Wide lavender eyes blinked owlishy when the full impact of the evening hit her. "For the first time in my life I don't have to answer to anyone. My mother and stepfather and chaperones aren't here to tell me I'm supposed to care if I'm disruptive, to scold me that I'm not exhibiting behavior becoming a lady."

Tori pulled the pins from her hair and shook out the long, silky tendrils, letting them tumble over her shoulders in disarray. She felt free—like a bird that had just escaped its cage and had come to full grips with its limitless freedom. With a bubbly giggle that smoothed every last wrinkle from her soul, Tori bounded into Dru's arms. And before Dru could decide whether he wanted her there, Tori squeezed the stuffing out of him. While Dru stood there in a daze, Tori launched herself out of his arms to gaze through the open window that framed a distant world of stars.

"Did you know the evening star isn't a star at all?" she murmured sluggishly.

"Do tell." Dru chortled as his gaze mapped Tori's

tempting form, more interested in her shapely curves than twinkling stars.

"It's the planet Venus that was so named in honor of the Roman goddess of love and beauty," she informed him.

On impulse, she eased a hip over the sill to stare at the starlit sky and to dance across the balcony that encircled the front and east side of the hotel.

"What in tarnation . . . ?" Dru strode across the room to see Tori step out of her slippers and pull herself onto the wooden railing. Lifting her hampering skirts, she danced a jig, spouting another of the off-color jingles Dru had taught her.

His heart stalled in his chest when Tori paused at the corner of the balcony rail and lifted her arms as if she were about to launch herself through the air. In record time, Dru scrambled through the window to save her from her own drunken daring.

Smiling impishly, Tori glanced down to see Dru approaching her. "I can fly," she declared with great conviction.

"Come down from there, Chicago," Dru demanded, growing more apprehensive by the second. If he made a grab for her, he would probably send her plunging to her death when she tried to scamper away from his outstretched hands. "You're going to break your neck."

"Nonsense," Tori protested.

Dru wasn't sure what this tipsy elf thought she was doing, but she was scaring the living daylights out of him, that was for sure. Jeezus, she was teeter-tottering on the railing, and Dru's heart kept skipping beats each time she looked as if she were about to fall!

The instant Tori gazed across the glittering horizon, Dru pounced. Like a starving snake, his arm hooked around her waist, dragging her into his arms, only to hear her grumbling in disapproval.

"Godamighty, Chicago. You scared the hell out of me. If you have the inclination to dance, at least do it on

129

the floor."

Dru stuffed Tori through the window, and the moment her feet touched the floor, she floated around like a ballerina. Peeling off his shirt, Dru sprawled out on the bed to watch Tori's amusing antics.

Lord, he was tired. It had been a long two weeks. What he needed was a good night's sleep instead of watching a ballet performance. Well, he actually wanted more than sleep, he amended as he settled back to study Tori, who twirled and leaped across the room as if it were a stage.

Heaving a weary sigh, Dru fluffed the pillow and pulled it under his head. Mesmerized, he watched Tori execute several unfamiliar dance steps. She was poetry in motion. Even the liquor she had consumed didn't detract from her sylphlike grace. She knew every dance maneuver imaginable, and Dru was spellbound by her movements, by the way the moonbeams streamed through the window to spotlight her.

My, the room was like a furnace, Tori mused as she whirled on tiptoes. She paused to shed her petticoats and then performed several more graceful leaps and turns that she had been taught in the privacy of her stepfather's ballroom but had never been permitted to perform in public.

Dru pulled the frilly petticoats away from his head after Tori recklessly flung them at him. Amusement glistened in his eyes as he studied the intoxicated minx. Gwen might have clipped this debutante's wings once upon a time, but now there was no holding Tori back. She was vibrant and reckless, living every moment to its fullest . . .

His thoughts scattered when Tori pulled off her gown and tossed it toward the bed. Again the garment fluttered over Dru's head and again he brushed it away. His gaze flooded over the skimpy chemise that swooped low on her breasts and barely concealed the curve of her hip. Lord, if she didn't stop clowning around, he was going to have a seizure! Tori's scant attire and her seductive movements were doing impossible things to Dru's body and playing havoc with his common sense. It was difficult enough not to visualize the sensual delights he could have been enjoying with Tori if she wasn't Caleb's daughter and Hubert's fiancée. Damn, why did he have to be cooped up with the one woman he couldn't have when he wanted her to obsession?

"Don't you dare take that off!" Dru croaked when Tori paused to shove the strap of her chemise from her shoulder.

A deliciously wicked smile tugged at her lips. "I'm going to run naked through the streets," she taunted him. "And not even you are going to stop me."

"Lady Godiva, you are not!" Dru growled, tormented by his wayward thoughts and Tori's daring shenanigans.

"Prude," she teased as she sauntered toward the bed. "Tonight I'm my own chaperone and I'll do as I please wherever and however I wish."

When she bent over him, the chemise gapped, and Dru's eyes wandered freely over the luscious swells of her breasts. He ached to touch what his gaze devoured, but he willfully restrained himself. "I've warned you about wading in over your head, Chicago," he chirped, his voice rattling with restrained desire. "We're both going to drown."

A curious frown knitted her brow when Dru shrank away from her. "You're afraid of me," she realized, and said so.

"I am not," Dru protested, dragging his betraying eyes back to her enchanting face.

"No? Then why are you looking at me as if you expect me to attack you any second?"

Her tapered fingers drifted over the broad expanse of his chest, marveling at the power and strength beneath her inquiring hand. Only once before had Tori dared to touch him so familiarly. Now temptation and too much liquor were getting the best of her. This magnificent creature fascinated her. She longed to recapture those

131

brief, sensual moments when Dru had kissed and caressed her. She yearned to know where these compelling feelings led, to rediscover the muscular planes and whipcord muscles that tensed beneath her light, inquisitive touch.

Dru caught her straying hand and struggled to inhale a breath. "Don't do that. You've become too damned daring for your own good."

"You really *are* afraid of me." She chortled, her eyes twinkling with mischief.

His gaze locked with hers, but there was no laughter in those sky-blue pools. "No, Chicago," he contradicted in a low, rumbling purr. "I'm afraid of *me*, afraid I'll succumb to the spell you've cast upon me."

The burning desire in his gaze set sparks in Tori's blood. Her senses were overflowing with the sight and feel of this handsome rogue. His masculine fragrance teased her nostrils and the lingering taste of his kisses beckoned her to explore fully the sensations that teased her naive body.

Ever so slowly, Tori moved toward him, captivated by needs that bubbled to the surface. She wanted to feel his sinewy arms around her, to be swept up in the sensual fantasies that had hounded her since the first time Dru had kissed the breath out of her.

Men had catered to her and pampered her, but no one had ever truly loved her or needed her for any of the right reasons. And maybe Dru didn't, either. But that didn't seem so important just now because Tori needed and wanted him to teach her things she didn't know—the intimate pleasures shared by a man and a woman. For once she yearned to follow her heart's desire and unveil the mysteries of passion.

Dru groaned in torment when Tori's petal-soft lips whispered over his. He could list a zillion reasons why he should pull away, but his traitorous body rebelled against logic. He had held himself at bay, fighting the fierce attraction to this stunning nymph far too long. Now she

132

was too close, too tempting, and his self-control crumbled like the walls of Jericho.

Dru gave way to his hungry craving, and his greedy lips rolled over Tori's. She, in turn, surrendered to the tidal waves of pleasure that splashed over her. Uncontrollable urgency buffeted her. Her hands swam over his bare flesh, adoring the feel of his rock-hard muscles, drowning in the wild flurry of rapture that consumed her. She couldn't get close enough to the fire that burned through her, leaving her trembling with monstrous needs.

Desire unfurled inside her, opening like a fragile blossom that sought the heat of the sun. She reveled in the feel of his masterful hands gliding over her innocent body, setting fires in their wake. It seemed Dru had sprouted an extra pair of hands and they were everywhere at once, discovering every inch of her flesh, sensitizing her skin. Tori shamelessly arched toward his intimate caresses, needing his touch as much as she needed air to breathe.

His moist lips abandoned hers to ski over the slope of her shoulder and her heart fluttered wildly in response. When his tongue encircled the throbbing peaks of her breasts, a soft sigh of pleasure spilled forth and her lashes swept down to block out all except the sensuous ecstasy of his touch, to marvel at the incredible sensations that riveted her body.

A quiver of excitement raced through her nerves as his caresses trekked across her stomach to swirl over the sensitive flesh of her thighs. Not once, but over and over again, his hands wove a titillating path over her belly and then encircled the tips of her breasts. His touch was like the rolling surf that caressed the seashore, erasing all that had come before, intensifying the pleasures of this long-awaited moment.

Dru raised his head to peer down at the luscious package of femininity he had unveiled. God, she was beautiful, every silky inch of her! Moonlight sprinkled over her satiny flesh and glistened in the wild spray of silver-blond hair that streamed across the pillow. Her kiss-swollen lips trembled with awakened desire.

He hadn't meant for this to happen . . . Dru stumbled on that noble thought. *Liar,* he scolded himself. If he hadn't wanted Tori to wind up in his arms, why hadn't he rented a separate room for the night? He was every kind of fool if he let himself believe he hadn't wanted her in his bed . . .

"Teach me to please you," Tori murmured, jolting Dru from his musings. "I want you to want me . . ."

He couldn't want her more than he already did! Dru was already prepared to swim across shark-infested waters to have her. His body cried out for satisfaction, demanding an end to these weeks of noble restraint.

When her exploring hand drifted over his chest to follow the furring of hair to his belly, Dru forgot how to breathe. Tori needed no instruction. She instinctively knew how to set his passions ablaze. As her hand trailed over the band of his breeches, Dru's heart rammed against his ribs, threatening to stick there. His massive body shuddered uncontrollably when her fingertips glided over the buttons of his trousers and then pushed them out of her way to explore his muscled hips.

Tori had never been so bold in all her life. But passion and liquor had a fierce grip on her, and she longed to know this virile man by touch. She yearned to journey through the dark, sensual corridors of desire and discover the elusive universe of passion. Intense feelings consumed her, compelling her to satisfy this sweet tormenting hunger that gnawed at the core of her being.

The moment they were flesh to flesh, Tori gave herself up to the windswept sensations that bombarded her. Her adventurous hands roamed and investigated, marveling at the arousing tingles that tumbled over her. Dru's rumbling moan encouraged her to continue her daring explorations. She wanted to devastate him as thoroughly as he devastated her with his skillful touch. She yearned to return the wondrous pleasure that had engulfed her, to intensify it.

Dru had become a prisoner of his own desires, a captive of his own savage passions. He could feel Tori's supple body moving suggestively against his, and he went hot all over. He tried to tell himself to be gentle with her, that she was totally unprepared for his ardent love-making. But she was a banquet and he was starved for a feast. He longed to devour her.

Over and over again he warned himself that he would destroy the splendorous moment if he didn't proceed at a cautious pace. Although Tori was a dozen kinds of passion seeking release and twenty years of pent-up emotions trying to escape, she was completely innocent of men. If he rushed her over the hurdle of initiation, she would be deprived of the ecstasy of lovemaking. It was important to him that her voyage from maidenhood to womanhood be one that stole softly across her mind in the days to come.

Ever so gently, Dru guided her thighs apart. He didn't want to frighten her, only to reveal the wondrous sensations that a man and woman shared when they were close. As he lowered himself to her, he felt Tori tense beneath him. Displaying more patience and tenderness than he ever thought he possessed, he withdrew to allow her to adjust to the feel of a man's body moving familiarly against hers. Carefully, he came to her, whispering his need, assuring her that she pleased him with her innocent touch.

The stabbing pain speared through the cloudy haze of pleasure, and Tori felt as if she were being swallowed alive. Dru was absorbing her strength, and the instinctive need to struggle overwhelmed her.

"Tori . . ." The sound of her name tripping from his lips was like a hypnotic incantation. Tori surrendered to his spell when his sinewy body settled exactly upon hers. The gentle cadence of his lovemaking left her trembling with needs that arose from nowhere to engulf her. Her body began to move of its own accord, matching his penetrating thrusts, seeking sweet, satisfying release, enjoying lovemaking in its purest, wildest form.

Gentleness fell away when Tori ardently responded to him. Desire raised its unruly head and strained against its captivity. The crescendo built into forceful, riveting sensations, flooding from her silky body to his and back again. They were one—a beating, breathing entity unto each other, a living puzzle that defied rhyme and reason.

Dru crushed her to him when convulsive shudders seized his body and soul. Her wild, sweet love blew the stars around and sent the clouds scattering in all directions. She was passion's tempest—a whirlwind of emotions that begged for release. She caused waves to ripple across Dru's soul, and then she calmed the stormy sea of emotion that had devastated him, leaving him bobbing in tranquility.

Tangled lashes swept up to study the craggy features that were framed by moonlight. Tori felt so incredibly content and yet stunned by the turmoil of emotions she had experienced. Her married friends and her mother had hinted that lovemaking was a service a wife provided for her husband only on rare occasions when there was no other way around it. But this wasn't anything like what she had been told it would be. Loving Dru had been glorious—a splendor that was almost beyond bearing, life's ultimate pleasure!

"Surely lovemaking isn't always like this," Tori rasped, her eyes wide with wonder.

For more than a decade Dru had taken pleasure where he found it, appeasing his needs and then going his own way. But Tori made lovemaking a fascinating new experience that surpassed his previous relationships with women. It made Dru wonder what he'd been doing the past few years. Whatever it was, it sure as hell wasn't what he had been doing with this innocent minx!

Dru had never tied himself down to any woman—only to his family and his dreams of a prospering ranch in the

136

mountain valleys of Montana. He was always uncomfortable with the lingering feelings that hadn't faded when the loving was over.

"You ask too many questions, Chicago," he hedged, dropping a quick kiss to her cupid's-bow lips.

Tori pulled a face at his evasive remark. "How am I supposed to learn anything if you won't tell me?" Her gaze dropped self-consciously, wondering if he was trying to be tactful. Perhaps he hadn't enjoyed the same magical pleasures that had consumed her. Maybe he was trying not to hurt her feelings. That was it, of course, Tori told herself dispiritedly. She hadn't known how to satisfy an experienced lover like Dru, even when she had given herself to him, body and soul.

"You're still wishing you were with someone else, aren't you?" she queried in a deflated tone.

Her wounded expression tugged on his heartstrings. "No," he confessed in a hoarse whisper. "Only that you *were* someone else."

To Tori the comment sounded as if he was rephrasing what she had just said. With a frustrated shriek, she wriggled away to curl up in a tight ball. "I hate you, Montana," she choked out, embarrassed, humiliated, and tormented to no end.

Dru braced himself above her, waiting for her to look up at him, refusing to move away until she did. "I do wish you were someone else. I've told you that before. I wish you were someone I could walk away from without looking back." His breath came out in a rush. "You're engaged, for God's sake! You're Caleb's daughter. I betrayed the trust of a long-time friend. Now what the hell am I going to tell your father when I deliver you to his doorstep?" Hollow laughter tripped from his lips. "Shall I say, 'Here she is, Caleb, and by the way, she and I are lovers. Hope you don't mind.'" His blue eyes drilled into her. "But Caleb *will* mind, you know. And he will be positively furious that I took such liberties."

"And it's all my fault," Tori muttered at him. "I

137

practically begged you to seduce me, and when you didn't, I seduced you. Be sure to tell him that. It's the truth after all."

Dru knew he should have backed away. He and Tori had dared too much already, and they had seriously complicated their relationship. But seeing her lying there, knowing she was hounded by her own feelings of guilt, tore him to shreds. She was all woman, the stuff dreams were made of. He couldn't let her walk away thinking she didn't have the ability to satisfy a man. Dru couldn't destroy her sexuality or let her live with thoughts that she was totally reponsible for what had happened. He was as much to blame as she was.

What was done was done. To hell with Caleb and that prissy Hubert Frazier. Hubert certainly deserved no consideration after their conflict the previous year.

Distracted, Dru traced the delicate line of Tori's jaw. Oh, he'd hate himself in the morning and the day after the day after, he predicted. And Caleb would sure enough kill him for tampering with his daughter. But none of that mattered when he peered down at Tori's bewitching face. Nothing mattered except the undefinable feelings that she aroused in him. What was between them was rare and special. And for this one night, there were no external influences to consider.

"Lovemaking was never like this for me," he admitted huskily. "And I know I'll have hell to pay. But for now, little minx, I'm going to show you all the ways you arouse and pleasure me . . ."

The instant he touched her, Tori surrendered in total abandon. She didn't care about tomorrow or repercussions, either. Nothing made any difference when she was in Dru's powerful arms. He chased the world and sane thought away, and Tori came to realize that her initiation into passion was only the stepping stone that led to a universe of wild, wondrous desire. Dru's caresses worshipped her. His reverent kisses drifted over her quaking flesh, causing torrents of ecstasy to tumble upon her. She matched him touch for touch, returning kiss for kiss, reveling in the explosive realm of passion that defied time and created a world with its own unique design.

It was a wild coming together that was filled with delicious sensations. Dru made her feel wanted and loved, even if he didn't want the complications of their reckless night together. Tori chose to block out the past and the future, to live in her splendorous dreams. For this night she had escaped all the confines of her sheltered life to experience the miraculous sensations of lovemaking.

In the aftermath of passion, Tori drifted off into a peaceful sleep that took up where reality left off. Pensively, Dru studied Tori's exquisite features. His forefinger trailed over her moist lips, contemplating the crosscurrents of emotions that hounded him. What was he going to do about this tempting vixen? He had thought after making love to her twice that his fascination would ebb. But that hadn't been the case. Tori had delighted him with her untutored caresses and instinctive responses. He had given part of himself away when he taught her the meaning of passion. He had taken her innocence, and even his feelings of guilt didn't diminish his desire for her.

Godamighty, what was he going to do about this ill-fated attraction? And worse, what was he going to do about this unquenchable need to love her again and again, all through the night?

The tantalizing thought sent tingles skitting down his spine. Impulsively, Dru glided his hand over the curve of her hip, coaxing her from sleep. There was only one thing to do about this eternal fire that refused to burn itself out. Dru's lips slanted over hers and he fed the constant flame until it billowed and consumed him . . .

Chapter 12

Although Tori awoke with a nagging headache, nothing could overshadow the silky web of pleasure that engulfed her. The previous night had been a wondrous dream of images and sensations. Dru had come to her in the night, whispering his need for her and she had responded without hesitation.

Tori had awakened to the knowledge that she was in love for the first time in her life. She had expected that was what had been tormenting her the past week, but now she was sure of it. After her lengthy engagement to Hubert Carrington Frazier II, Tori knew what love *wasn't*. And knowing that she harbored tender emotions for Dru, Tori had let go with her whole heart.

Overwhelmed by exhilaration, Tori reached out to map the craggy features of Dru's face that were soft in repose. Lovingly, her hand drifted past his high cheekbones and square jaw to investigate the swarthy muscles of his chest and ribs. Touching him aroused her. Remembering the wild, breathless moments of splendor put a blush of color on her face. Lord-a-mercy, the things she had done. Her, the inhibited aristocrat who had always behaved with reserved dignity in every situation!

Thick black lashes fluttered up to see the face of an angel poised above him. In unguarded appreciation, Dru assessed the shapely nymph whose glorious mane of hair

141

reminded him of a waterfall of sunbeams and moonfire.

Dru had expected to wake regretting their night together. But he had no regrets in discovering the subdued passions beneath Tori's shell of sophistication. She had been bred and schooled to be a proper lady, but once her reserved cocoon fell away . . . Lord, it was staggering to speculate on the potential this saucy beauty possessed.

Dru strangled the thought. They had no future together, not when he was a rough-edged westerner and she an eastern aristocrat. Edgar and Gwendolyn Cassidy had too much power and influence not to ensure that Tori returned to her own world. And Dru knew he would ultimately make trouble for her and her dandy of a fiancée. The bastard. Hubert didn't deserve Tori. She was more woman than Hubert was man. And if Hubert took offense, that was just too bad. Dru would have the last laugh on that shrewd but shallow oaf because he had been the first to discover Tori's charms.

Like a rousing lion, Dru levered himself up to curl a brawny arm around Tori. She melted against him, hiding not one smidgen of the affection she felt for him.

"Did you sleep well?" she murmured against his sensuous lips.

A peal of roguish laughter echoed in his chest. "I hardly slept at all, if you recall," he purred seductively.

Tori returned his suggestive grin. "Forgive me for disturbing your sleep." Her tone wasn't the least bit sympathetic.

"It wasn't my sleep you disturbed, minx," he whispered before stealing a kiss. "It was my self-control."

Her leg slid suggestively between his, and Dru was shocked to realize how easily she aroused him, how quickly she had become a skilled seductress. "If you don't stop what you're doing, we'll be here the rest of the day," Dru choked out.

Heaving a disappointed sigh, Tori retreated, "Ah, yes,

how could I have forgotten we are burning daylight."

As she sashayed across the room wrapped in the sheet, Dru clamped onto the end of the fabric and twisted her around like a top, granting himself one last glimpse of her perfection.

His hungry eyes said it all. He still wanted her. Tori's heart swelled with pleasure. Dru didn't love her. She knew that as surely as she knew her own name. But he still desired her. It was a start. And perhaps by the time they reached Montana, he wouldn't want her to return home. Oh, she knew she was clinging to impossible dreams. Dru wasn't the marrying kind. If he were, he would have settled down long before now. But Tori wasn't giving up hope, not yet. If she were forced to return to Chicago to face a dull future, at least she would have a few treasured memories of this one special man.

Tori wanted him to want her for herself. She had seen enough manipulation by both her mother and Hubert to last her a lifetime. A man like Dru would never be content if he were forced to marry her for the sake of propriety . . .

Her thoughts scattered when Dru, wearing nothing but a rakish grin, unfolded himself from the bed and swaggered toward her. She looked at him, and she felt warm and bubbly inside. Tori could have spent the day admiring his well-sculptured physique. Well, most of the day, she amended with a wicked smile. She had discovered there were better things to do than just look at this powerful package of masculinity!

Dru caught her to him, drawing her silky body full-length against his. Mercy, what was the matter with him? He couldn't get enough of her. They needed to dress and aim themselves west, but Dru had no inclination to set foot out of this secluded paradise. The tantalizing memories were still too fresh in his mind and they kept luring him back to Tori's arms.

Without preamble, his mouth came down on hers in a ravishing kiss that stole the breath from her lungs. He molded her into his muscular contours and devoured her. It was a long moment before he found the will to let her go. And even when he did, he felt like a pile of smoldering coals.

"Get dressed, Chicago. You're making me crazy running around here like that," he ordered gruffly.

Tori flung him a flirtatious glance before stepping into her buckskin breeches. Dru's legs threatened to fold up like an accordion as his eyes roamed over her full breasts and the tiny indentation of her waist. It was a good thing she wasn't riding topless or Dru would find himself slamming into trees. Lord! The visual flashes that would be hounding him from this day forward would be enough to drive a sane man mad. Tori cast a potent spell with her saucy behavior and scanty attire. It would be best if he pretended the events of the previous night never happened, but Dru seriously doubted if he could forget the experience anytime soon.

Batting down his eagerness to take her in his arms again, Dru gathered their gear and ambled out the door. By the time he watched the graceful sway of her hips as she sauntered down the hall, Dru was begging for a cold bath, and it wasn't even Saturday night! Damn, how was he going to keep his mind on their surroundings instead of this appetizing minx? She filled up his senses and his world until he couldn't entertain a single thought that didn't have her name attached to it.

Hubert Carrington Frazier II stalked through the door of the Cassidys' sprawling mansion. His face was twisted in a scowl, and it had been for two weeks. He had been in a towering rage since the day of his wedding. It hadn't taken him long to recall where he had met the scoundrel who had abducted Victoria. Hubert had cursed vehemently each time he speculated on what that rough-edged heathen was doing while he was alone with Victoria. Over and over again, Hubert had mulled over

144

the incident of the previous year concerning Dru Sullivan. They had gone several rounds, and when Hubert tried to intimidate the cocky cowboy, he had wound up with a swollen jaw that had taken weeks to heal. But Hubert had been too furious by then to give Sullivan the high price he demanded for his cattle. Hubert had been vindictive enough to pull a few strings and ensure that Dru found no better prices anywhere else, either. Dru had been forced to accept the only offer in town, but it seemed the scoundrel had evened the score and gone one better!

After Tori's abduction, Hubert had contacted the stage and railroads and had sent out an all-points bulletin, even though Edgar insisted they wait for a ransom note. Hubert had also hired two Pinkerton detectives to track Sullivan and haul him back in shackles. But Sullivan had proved to be an elusive and experienced frontiersman. The detectives had yet to return from their mission, and the only clue they had turned up was the scavenger Dru had tied to a tree in Iowa.

Hubert wasn't accustomed to being crossed. He had always had things his way because he had the money to buy favors and privileges. The fact that a pesky bumpkin had kidnapped Chicago's most sought-after debutante and Hubert's coveted fiancée infuriated him. Hubert swore he would ruin Dru financially when he caught up with him. Damn, it would help if only he could remember where that bastard called home!

His frustrated thoughts scattered when Gwendolyn Cassidy swept into the foyer to greet him. "Have your detectives found any sign of them yet?" she questioned anxiously.

Hubert heaved an annoyed sigh. "I checked every train and stage depot in the surrounding area and no one recalls seeing them. All I have learned is that they are traveling cross-country. Sullivan is utilizing his expertise in the back country to elude the detectives. Despite Edgar's speculations, I think Sullivan has taken Tori just to get back at me."

"Oh, God! Victoria is being dragged around like a slave by that uncivilized heathen!" She very nearly swooned. "I swear my ex-husband is somehow connected with this." Her pretty features puckered in a mutinous frown. "I should have known Caleb would somehow find a way to torment me."

"Your ex-husband?" Hubert blinked in bewilderment. "I thought you said he was dead."

Gwendolyn muttered at her carelessness. That was the story she had given the Fraziers and the other members of their elite social circle. She thought it would be in her best interests to let the rest of the world think Caleb had perished in the gold fields chasing a foolish dream, even if, in truth, *she* had been the one who insisted he go in the first place. Gwendolyn had never allowed Victoria to mention Caleb in public. Privately she had ensured her daughter bore ill feelings toward Caleb and forced her to accept Edgar in Caleb's stead.

"Well, he *was* dead . . ." she stammered, her mind racing. "That is, I received that news several years ago. But it seems the report of his death was just a mistake. He is alive and well and living in Montana and he—"

"That's it! Montana! That was where Sullivan came from!" Hubert blurted out. He hadn't bothered to remember that detail because he hadn't planned on crossing paths with that big brute ever again. Unfortunately, Hubert hadn't been granted his wish. The sneaky bastard had turned up the day of the wedding to whisk Victoria off to that godforsaken territory in the Northwest, no doubt. And if that miserable scoundrel had laid a hand on Victoria, Hubert swore to see Sullivan tortured within an inch of his life and then publicly executed. A guillotine would be a nice touch, he thought spitefully.

"Where is Edgar?" Hubert demanded in an impatient tone.

"He went to make arrangements for our journey

146

west," Gwen reported. "I was afraid Caleb was somehow mixed up in this and I insisted that we travel to Montana to confront him face-to-face."

"I'm going with you," Hubert declared.

Gwendolyn wasn't sure that was such a good idea. Any connection between Tori's fiancé and Caleb could cause problems for Gwen herself. If Caleb blurted out his side of the story, Gwendolyn's friendship with the Fraziers might be jeopardized. It had táken her three years to become accepted by the crème de la crème of Chicago society, and she wasn't about to have her reputation spoiled by any vicious gossip Caleb revealed to Hubert. In her opinion, social position was of paramount importance and she refused to let anything stand in the way of her greatest aspiration in life.

And if Hubert decided to withdraw his marriage proposal, the Cassidys would be scandalized! To Gwen that would be a fate worse than death. Losing her important position with the potentates and dignitaries of Chicago horrified her.

"Don't you think it best to remain in Chicago to monitor the progress of the detectives?" Gwen remarked, hoping Hubert would take the hint and stay home, for her sake.

"I'm going with you," Hubert repeated before he pivoted on his heels and stormed toward the door to gather his belongings for the trip. "And if we find Victoria before the Pinkertons do, I'm not paying them a cent! They should have caught up with Sullivan long before now!"

Gwendolyn stamped her foot in frustration. Confound it, Caleb was giving her hell. He would rue the day he interfered with her life and with Victoria's. The Cassidys and Fraziers had been making plans to ensure Hubert was elected to a political office in the next election. Tori would have taken her rightful place beside him. But all the rumors and speculation surrounding Victoria's abduction were already damaging the reputation of both families. The Fraziers were already one of the most influential families in the city. It would have been a feather in Gwen's bonnet to be related to them by marriage. And if Caleb spoiled her rise to one of the most envied positions in Chicago, Gwendolyn swore she would have his head!

Damn it all, she should never have married Caleb in the first place. It had been a disastrous mistake. But she had tired of Edgar's mild manners and had gone off in search of spice and variety. Gwen had become infatuated by Caleb's dynamic, adventurous spirit. After their whirlwind wedding, she realized that passion wasn't what it was cracked up to be, and that what she needed was wealth and stability to make her happy. She had been a fool to wed a man who had yet to establish himself in society. But luckily for Gwen, Edgar had never given up hope that she would come back to him. So devoted and faithful was he that he had waited until she was free and had generously forgiven her for becoming bewitched by a man with far more charm and personality but far less money than Edgar possessed.

They had both been fools, Gwen reminded herself as she flounced in her chair to sip her tea. Edgar was a fool for loving her so completely, and she was an idiot for marrying Caleb, who hadn't been able to give her all the things she hadn't realized she wanted and needed until it was almost too late. Gwen would have dissolved the marriage to Caleb years earlier if her father hadn't thrown such a tantrum when she approached him with the idea. But once her father was no longer there to protest a divorce in the family, Gwen had suggested that Caleb go west to seek his fortune and then had quickly dissolved the marriage that had lasted ten years longer than it should have.

Too irritated to sit another moment, Gwen bounded to her feet to pace the parlor. She dreaded the confrontation with Caleb. And occasionally she spared Tori a thought, wondering how she was faring in a world that was foreign

148

to her. But mostly Gwen worried about herself and the repercussions her scheming lies might have on her reputation and position in Chicago. Besides, Victoria had never quite turned out the way Gwen had anticipated. She went through the motions of being an aristocrat because she was forced to do so, but she hadn't taken to the role Gwen expected her to play. The girl was Gwen's cross to bear, and no matter how much she fussed and scolded, Tori had never really been content.

But somehow Gwen would come out of this unpleasant situation with her dignity and reputation intact! No one was going to undermine her ascent to the pinnacle of society. And even if Hubert did accompany them west, Gwen would ensure that he didn't learn more about her first marriage than she wanted him to know!

Chapter 13

Just as Dru expected, the long hours in the saddle were torment. Each time Tori flashed him a dazzling smile, he entertained thoughts of waylaying their journey to appease his lusty needs. But he did manage to contain himself until they cuddled into their pallet beneath a canopy of stars each night. Dru still wasn't getting much sleep, but it didn't seem to matter—nothing mattered except discovering all there was to know about this appetizing nymph. Watching Tori blossom into a full-fledged woman fascinated him. She had become a most imaginative and skillful lover. Dru felt a certain sense of pride in knowing that he had taught this lovely goddess about passion.

Lost to his dreamy thoughts, Dru stretched out to peer at the stars that seemed so close, he could have reached out to touch them. He couldn't help but wonder what was running through Hubert's mind now. Dru hoped that weasel was pulling out his hair in frustration. It served him right. There was no telling how many cattlemen Hubert had swindled out of a fair price. The agony Hubert was suffering because of the loss of his fiancée was fair compensation for the exasperation Dru had endured the previous fall . . .

A pained grunt erupted from his lips when Tori plopped down on his belly. Suddenly, Hubert Carrington

151

Frazier II was the farthest thing from Dru's mind. Tori had an uncanny knack of distracting him.

When his hands glided possessively over her thigh and wandered under her shirt to caress her breasts, Tori grabbed his wrists and held him at bay.

"Beast," she teased playfully. "Is that all you ever think about?"

"When you're around, yes," he admitted with a rakish leer.

Tori giggled in impish delight. "Good. I was hoping I wasn't the only one around here who had a one-track mind."

"Why is that, Chicago?" he questioned before he pulled her down on top of him to devour her with a ravishing kiss. "Because I'm your first experiment with passion?"

"No, because I love you . . ." Tori bit her lips and sat up on his belly.

Damn, she hadn't meant to say that. She didn't want Dru to feel any obligation to her or pity her because she was harboring a one-sided love. She knew she was only the time he was killing during his trek west. She hoped he would come to feel something special for her, to care for her to the same intense degree she cared for him. But blurting out her feelings wasn't the proper way to handle a confirmed bachelor like Dru. She imagined he would back away if his freedom was threatened in any manner.

When Dru simply stared up at her and then frowned, Tori's heart twisted in her chest. His silence was all the response she needed to know that all he felt for her was lusty desire. Tori vaulted to her feet and kicked herself every step of the way as she jogged to the river. If she had destroyed the fragile bond between them with words Dru didn't want to hear, she would never forgive herself!

Tugging at her clothes, Tori hurriedly undressed and waded into the river to wash away the dirt from the long day's ride. Damn, if only she could swim, she would stretch out and glide across the channel, letting the current take her where it would.

"You're wrong, you know." Dru's hushed voice drifted over the water.

"About what?" Tori asked in feigned innocence.

"You know what." Stuffing his hands in his pockets, Dru ambled down to the water's edge, silently assessing the mermaid who was surrounded by a pool of silver. When Tori moved toward the middle of the stream, Dru frowned disapprovingly. "I told you not to wade out so deep until I teach you how to swim."

When Tori shrugged carelessly and ignored his warning, Dru peeled off his shirt and walked toward her. His somber gaze never left hers as he approached, sending silver ripples undulating around him. "You don't, you know, Chicago."

"I thought we just had this conversation. I can't swim, so what!" she muttered resentfully. When he reached for her, Tori dodged his outstretched hand.

"That wasn't what I meant." His voice was ruefully tender, but it wobbled with the hint of frustration.

Damn, he wasn't handling this encounter well at all! He kept hopping from one topic of conversation to the other like a frog because he felt awkward and ill at ease. And as quick-witted as Tori was, she couldn't keep up with his meaning when he jumped from one subject to the other.

Heaving a sigh, Dru tried again. "You don't love me, Chicago. You might think you do, but you don't. You are infatuated with passion because I'm the first man you've known intimately. Passion is new and exciting to you. But that's all it is—a fascination that will fade in time, and it has more to do with discovering the dimensions of desire than with *me*."

For ten years Tori had listened to her mother tell her what to do and how to behave while she was doing it. And then along came Dru Sullivan who taught her what to do in the wilds and told her what to wear while she was doing it. Now this infuriating man who could never love her back had the audacity to interpret what he *thought* she was *thinking!* Since he couldn't return her confession, he chose to cancel hers. He hadn't solved the problem, he simply declared that the problem of her loving him didn't exist. Men! Their brains had been frozen at the age of sixteen! He had reduced her affection for him to an equation of lust and carelessly shrugged off her innermost feelings.

"Fine, you're right," she patronized for the sake of argument. "Now leave me be. I've decided to teach myself how to swim like a Godamighty fish!"

Amusement bubbled to the surface. Tori still couldn't cuss with authority. She never put the right curse words together. Her grammar might have been excellent, but profanity wasn't her true medium and never would be.

Frustrated to no end that Dru was chuckling at her, for whatever the reason, Tori inhaled a deep breath and dove into the water. She was determined to sink or swim— anything to avoid this particular conversation . . .

Calmly, Dru reached down to grab a handful of hair and dragged her to the surface. "We need to talk, Chicago. You can learn to swim later."

"I have nothing to say," she grumbled, slapping at his hand.

"Well, I've just begun talking," he insisted.

"What a shame. I'm already through listening."

Dru paused to pull Tori's resisting body against his and stared down into her enchanting features. Moonfire sparkled down on this naive angel like a spotlight from heaven. Gently, he brushed away the water droplets that danced like diamonds on her cheeks.

"All those technical and scientific textbooks you've been reading the past few years are fine and dandy. But they can't teach you everything you need to know . . ." he began in a quiet tone. "In many areas, you're still a novice and you must analyze what you feel before attaching words to emotions."

Here it comes, Tori mused bitterly. This must be what was called "letting a woman down gently." He'd probably done this sort of thing a hundred times before and she was in for an overrehearsed farewell soliloquy. Dru had the knack of saying the wrong thing. Tori predicted that, before he was through, he would manage to dent her pride and she would be furious with him.

Ah, what a fine line there was between love and hate. When a woman was vulnerable to a man, she could love him one minute and despise him the next. Vulnerability left no room for indifference when the heart hung in the balance. Dru could cut her to shreds with sarcasm or heal her with tenderness. This one man had the power to make her feel whole and alive or to leave her feeling hurt or betrayed. Bearing that in mind, Tori vowed to remain rational and calm during the upcoming sermon. But she doubted she could. She loved him, and that made her emotional and sentimental. From what she'd heard, it was difficult to be reasonable and in love. It was a contradiction in terms.

"You haven't been around enough to know what you want in a man. You are still a naive little girl with stars in her eyes," Dru declared with great conviction. "You are trying to see things in me that you want to see, even if they aren't really there."

Three sentences and she'd already heard enough! But when Tori tried to pull away, Dru held her fast.

"We found ourselves alone together and that was the first time in your life you've been really and truly alone with a man. We have put ourselves in situations that tempted fate. You're only testing your wings, Chicago. I'm just an experiment and you got a little carried away, that's all. What happened was a perfectly natural response between a man and woman who are forced to band together to meet obstacles." His massive chest rose

155

and fell in a deep sigh. He waited, hoping she would meet his level gaze. She didn't. "Don't you understand, Chicago? I could have been *any* man. If I had sent one of my brothers to fetch you, you would have fancied yourself in love. But Caleb sent me because . . ."

Dru's voice trailed off when the full impact of what he'd said struck him between the ears like a doubled fist. Godamighty, it had certainly taken him long enough to figure out that he had walked into a trap! Lord, he was dense! Curse that Caleb's deviousness! He probably knew what would happen when Tori and he were alone together. Caleb knew Dru wouldn't be able to travel by any usual mode of transportation without risking being apprehended. And that meant Dru and Tori would be imprisoned in privacy, sleeping side by side for nights on end.

Dru gnashed his teeth, knowing he'd been *had*. "I just wanted to see my little girl," Caleb had said. That was all? *My eye!* Dru thought sourly. Unless Dru missed his guess, Caleb had anticipated something like this would happen. Naturally, Caleb would insist Dru do the right thing by Tori. And if Dru did, Caleb would have the last laugh on Gwendolyn. That scamp! Caleb had had more than one reason for not traveling to Chicago to fetch Tori himself! And now Dru was honorbound to accept the responsibility of what he had done. He was going to have to pay the full price for their nights of reckless passion. If Dru didn't do it now, Caleb would see to it that his ex-partner did later.

And now that he and Tori had been intimate, could he truly send her back to Hubert? Considering what a vindictive man Hubert was, Dru wondered if that weasel would take his fury out on Tori, who had become an innocent victim. The thought made Dru's skin crawl. This naive beauty realized she had been maneuvered by her mother, but Caleb had also lowered himself to the tactic to have his revenge on Gwen. And in his own way,

156

Dru had used Tori to satisfy his vendetta against Hubert . . .

"If you're quite finished, I'd like to get out of the river before I shrivel up like a prune," Tori muttered, dragging Dru from his contemplations. "You have made your point. Now let me go."

Dru was between a rock and a hard spot. If he didn't marry Tori, Caleb would probably be breathing down his neck, even if that sneaky rat had shoved Dru into this unforeseen trap. And secondly, Hubert and the Cassidys would find a way to punish Tori for what had happened between her and her captor. And if he *did* marry her, Hubert and Gwen would still be outraged. But no matter what, Tori was destined to be caught in the middle. Well, hell, he was as obligated as one man could get, Dru thought in frustration. He might as well get this over with.

"I've thought it over and I want you to marry me," he blurted out.

Tori's jaw dropped off its hinges. She stared at Dru as if he had moss growing on his head. "You're a lunatic," she crowed when she gained control of her voice. "First you list all the reasons why I can't possibly love you and then you propose. You have obviously been out in the sun too long. The heat fried your brain."

She had every reason in the world to think he was unstable, Dru reckoned. But there was simply no other way. Whether Dru wanted a wife or not, it looked as though he was going to get one. Lord, wouldn't Hubert and Gwen be hopping up and down in indignation when they found out? It would almost be worth it, just to annoy those two selfish individuals.

"I'm perfectly sane," Dru insisted. "We'll get married in Council Bluffs."

When Dru released Tori's hand, she rushed to the riverbank to jump into her clothes. Anger, bitterness, and frustration warred to master her emotions. She knew why Dru had suddenly decided to marry her. It had nothing to do with love, only with an obligation he thought he owed to her after he had taken her virtue. He had obviously decided marriage was the noble and honorable thing to do.

Well, as much as Tori would have delighted in becoming his wife, she couldn't—not unless Dru was offering his love, and he wasn't doing that. If he cared for her, he could have said so when he had the chance. But he didn't and he hadn't. She had been forced to comply with Hubert's proposal because Gwen had accepted for her and set the date. But Tori didn't have to accept Dru's proposal. She wasn't escaping one prison to march into another one. And it would be a prison of torment if Dru didn't truly want her in his life. She would become another of his obligations. The thought crushed her pride as flat as a pancake.

"There isn't going to be a marriage," Tori proclaimed as she flounced on her pallet. "I'm going to run away to join a convent."

"No, you aren't, Chicago," Dru growled, towering over her. "You said you loved me and we're going to get married. I'll even buy you the best gown to be found in Council Bluffs."

He'd done it again. He had said the wrong thing and with it, had set fuse to her temper. Dru still perceived her as an empty-headed debutante who was so vain and fashion-conscious that he could tempt her with a fancy new dress to right any wrong! Damn him, he couldn't have hurt her more if he had slapped her in the face.

"A new gown?" she parroted furiously. "How generous of you!"

Dru, it seemed, had developed a serious case of foot-in-mouth disease since he crossed paths with this she-devil. Somehow he always managed to set her off. For crying out loud, Dru thought with an exasperated sigh. He and Tori were either loving or fighting. There was never an

158

in between.

Tori presented her back and cursed into the blanket she had rolled up to form a makeshift pillow. "I've decided you were right. I don't love you, and because I don't, I'm not going to marry you. I can't bear the thought of being another of your responsibilities."

"If you don't say yes, I'll tell Caleb what happened in Des Moines and he'll insist," Dru threatened, for lack of a better tactic of dealing with her.

Tori twisted around to glare flaming arrows at the looming giant. "You wouldn't dare."

"I'd do it in a minute," he assured her with casual menace.

For a long moment, Tori glowered at him, mentally selecting his most vulnerable spot and picturing herself kicking him black and blue. Tori was declaring her independence here and now. It was time for her to take command of her life and live it as she saw fit.

But there was no sense butting heads with this billy goat of a man on this issue, she reckoned. Tori would do the only thing she could possibly do in this situation—lie and deceive him into thinking she had accepted his terms.

"Very well, I'll marry you," she announced before she pulled the quilt over her shoulder.

"I'm glad that's settled," he said in relief.

It *was* settled all right, to *her* satisfaction not *his*. However, Dru didn't need to know that just yet. He'd find out soon enough. But one thing was certain. Tori was never ever going to make the mistake of blurting out her inner feelings to this big baboon or anyone else ever again. He didn't want her love and he didn't need it and he wasn't going to have it, either! Tori was going to be long gone, come dawn. She was going to find her own way to Montana to visit her father. And who knew? After their reunion, she might even ride off into parts unknown. But no matter what, she was going to do

159

exactly as she pleased for the first time in her life because after all, it was her life. Everyone she knew seemed to have forgotten that highly significant detail!

From this day forward, Tori wasn't going to give a whit what anyone else said! Victoria Flemming Cassidy had a mind of her own and she was going to start using it. She had been pushed around, knocked down and stepped on for the very last time. This was her independence day and tomorrow would be the first day of her new life—one over which she alone had control. And if Dru Sullivan didn't like it, well, that was just too God-amighty bad!

Part Three

The sweetest flower that blows
  I give you as we part.
For you it is a rose
  For me it is my heart.
                    —Frederick Peterson

Chapter 14

When Dru woke to find Tori and both horses gone, his furious roar sent the birds fluttering from their perches in the overhanging branches. On the flattened grass where Tori's pallet had been the previous night was a wildflower that still sparkled with morning dew. With a muted curse, Dru crushed the fragile blossom and flung it away. Damn that little witch. She had deceived him into thinking she had accepted her fate. But it had been only a ploy. She had sneaked off while he had his guard down.

Muttering several curses, Dru stomped over to the mule he had confiscated from the scavenger who had attacked Tori. Studying the tracks and broken limbs, Dru pulled onto the swaybacked mule and trotted off. Damnation, did Tori think she was ready to venture alone into the wilderness? She wasn't, he silently fumed. She was going to get herself into trouble, sure as hell!

A muddled frown creased Dru's brow when he saw the tracks led back into the forest to the east. Tori had learned a thing or two about eluding an experienced tracker. Clearly, she no longer broke every single limb in her path and so it was difficult to pursue her. Dru suspected she was heading back in the direction she had come. At least all the signs supported that theory . . . until the tracks vanished into thin air.

After circling the clump of trees, Dru finally spotted tracks that now headed northwest. Damn her, she had become clever! She had obviously tried to lead him off in the wrong direction. But wherever she was, she still had to contend with unexpected dangers. Dru had given her a few lessons in handling a pistol and knife the past few days, but Tori had only progressed far enough not to shoot herself in the foot while loading his Winchester and Colt. Her weaponery skills were meager at best.

Cursing Tori with every plodding step the mule took, Dru followed the trail northwest throughout the day. But he saw neither hide nor hair of her. Although Dru was mad as hell, he was more concerned about Tori's welfare. He wasn't accustomed to caring about a woman. But he was frightened for Tori, and he hadn't been frightened of anything in years! Lord, that lavender-eyed minx constantly preyed on his emotions. How was he supposed to think straight when he was worried sick about her? When he caught up with her . . . *if* he caught up with her and she was still alive, he was going to strangle her for her reckless daring!

Godamighty, what had happened to that naive, incompetent innocent he had kidnapped from Chicago? She had changed like the wind. Her mother and that miserable excuse for a fiancé wouldn't recognize Tori. She dressed like a hoyden, adapted to her new surroundings, challenged Dru on every front, and she had turned lovemaking into a . . .

Dru compressed his lips. He wasn't going to sidetrack himself by thinking about that right now, he told himself firmly. He had enough on his mind without becoming entangled in lingering memories. The first thing he had to do was find that elusive sprite. Then he would decide what he wanted to do most—choke the life out of her or clutch her to him and forget the torment that was hounding him every step of the way!

*   *   *

164

Tori paused briefly to rest after riding well into the night. During her solitude she decided she would trek west into Nebraska to find a job that would earn her enough money to pay passage to Montana to see her father. Tori didn't have a cent to her name and it had been impossible to dig into Dru's pocket while he slept to confiscate enough money to sustain her for the next few weeks. With her credentials, she could easily obtain a position as a teacher in a frontier school. Although the teaching profession was still considered a man's occupation in the East, westerners had accepted the idea of female instructors. And besides, westerners were desperate to see that their children were granted a good education. Tori wasn't qualified to do much else, but she had gained a wealth of knowledge from books and she could share it with children. At least she would feel needed for once in her life . . .

"Well, look what we got here, boys."

Tori nearly leaped out of her skin when a gravelly voice erupted from the darkness. She had been very cautious and observant until her weary mind began to wander. To her dismay, three bearded men in tattered clothes clomped through the underbrush to surround her. Tori wracked her brain, trying to remember everything Dru had told her about turning situations to her advantage. Since the odds numbered three to one, Tori carefully considered her options and the consequences of each. Well, as she saw it, there was naught else to do but pretend she welcomed the company and the lust that was revealed in those leering smiles.

When one of the men swaggered toward her, Tori forced a smile and allowed her gaze to drift over his shadowed form. She found nothing appealing about the stocky galoot, but it was important that she pretend she did!

"Whatcha doin' out 'ere all by yerself, honey?" Cal Reynolds questioned, his eyes raking Tori.

Tori was reasonably certain that English was not this

165

big oaf's native language, he so butchered it with his colloquial accent. He spoke just like he looked— uncultured, illiterate and half-civilized.

Conjuring up a flirtatious smile, Tori reached out to trail her forefinger over the collar of his stained jacket. "I'm lookin' fer a man. Do you know where I kin find one?" she inquired in English this uncouth scalawag could understand.

His roguish grin revealed teeth that Tori could swear were yellow, even in the moonlight!

"No need to look any farther, sweetlin'," he cooed.

Tori fought down the urge to gag. *Sweetling?* What did he think she was? A stick of sugar cane? Repulsed though she was, Tori hooked her arm around Cal's elbow and leaned as close as she dared without inviting the fleas that probably infested this mangy varmint to leap from him to her. "Kin you git rid of yer friends, honey? Fer what I got in mind, we don't need 'em around . . ."

Another face-splitting grin appeared and a roguish chuckle tumbled from Cal's lips. "Jack, why don't you and Marty take a stroll down by the creek fer a bit. Me an' the lady want some privacy."

Grumbling, the other two cretins lumbered off to do as they were told, hoping they would be next in line to pleasure themselves with the shapely tart they had happened onto.

Tori had already made a mental note of the dagger that hung on Cal's belt and the Colts in the holsters that were draped on each hip. When his arms stole around her, Tori's hands slid over his hips in what was meant to feel like a caress. But that was hardly what Tori had in mind. She wanted the pistols and dagger and nothing else from this foul-smelling hooligan who had obviously never taken a bath of his own free will. She imagined that getting rained on was as close as he came to cleanliness.

Cal grunted in surprise when he felt the point of his own knife settling between his ribs. He glanced down into glittering eyes and a menacing sneer.

166

"Make one false move, *sweetling*, and I'll cut off everything that protrudes from your body," Tori growled in venomous threat.

Standing as rigid as stone, Cal waited for Tori to relieve him of his pistols. When she had confiscated the weapons, she stepped back and smiled in satisfaction . . . until she asked herself what she was supposed to do next. Shoot him down? Tie him up? Turn and run for her life? Damn, what would Dru have done in this situation? He probably wouldn't have stumbled into it in the first place, she decided. Dru usually met trouble halfway instead of letting it sneak up on him . . .

A sharp gasp gushed from her lips when an unseen arm snaked across her breasts and she was jerked back against a rock-hard chest. Tori had so many weapons in her hands that none of them were of any use to her.

When Cal tried to turn tail and dart away, the click of a trigger shattered the silence and froze him in his tracks. "You move and you're a dead man." The ominous tone in which the threat was conveyed was enough to send an angry lion retreating to its den.

Damn, right out of the frying pan and into the fire, thought Tori. She would have known that voice anywhere. Blast it, how had Dru tracked her? She had purposely tried to lead him astray before she reversed her route. But no matter how hard she tried to lose him, here he was. The man had a nose like a bloodhound and the eyes of an eagle, it seemed.

Cal glanced frantically around him, calculating a method of escape. "If I was you, mister, I'd git out of 'ere in a 'urry. I got two friends roamin' 'round here." A smug grin stretched across his whiskered face. "Fer all you know they may be trainin' their rifles on yer back at this very moment."

"No, they aren't," Dru counted with a deadly smile that caused Cal to swallow with a gulp. "They never knew what hit them." He gestured with the barrel of his pistol that was draped over Tori's shoulder. "Lay

167

down, friend . . ."

"*Lie* down," Tori automatically corrected him and then winced when Dru growled in her ear.

Dru was already as annoyed with Tori as he could be for eluding him. Having her correct his grammar in the middle of this tense situation had him itching to shake her until her teeth rattled.

Cal did as he was told. His nemesis seemed too short-tempered to challenge. And if the feisty chit ever got one of her weapons turned around the right way, someone was going to accidentally get shot or stabbed, and Cal certainly didn't want it to be him!

Slowly, Dru backed toward the horses, keeping a watchful eye on Cal. Roughly, he snatched the weapons from Tori's hands and stuffed them into his belt. After he threw her over the saddle like a feed sack, he swung up behind her. Leading the other horses and mule, Dru took off like a house afire.

Tori was thankful she hadn't taken time to eat. If she had, her meal would have come back up after she was forced to ride jackknifed over the saddle while the steed thundered off at a full gallop. Blood rushed to her head and she swore her skull would explode.

Dru didn't slow his breakneck speed until the horses began to labor. And then for pure spite, he kept his horse at a trot to make Tori's ride as uncomfortable as possible. Dru was intent on punishing her for leaving him to ride that swaybacked mule that had to be slapped continuously on the rump to keep it moving.

"I think I'm going to be sick," Tori gulped as the saddle horn rammed into her ribs for the hundredth time.

"Tell somebody who cares," Dru snorted derisively.

"You don't have to be cruel," Tori muttered. "All I did was run away. I'm nothing but a responsibility to you anyway, one you don't really want. You should have thanked me for leaving you."

Dru gnashed his teeth. "That was a damnfool thing to

do. You could have gotten yourself raped—or even killed."

"Then I would have been off your hands forever," she shot back.

"Pipe down, Chicago," he snapped brusquely. "I'm too goddamned mad to argue with you right now!"

"The Lord will get you for taking His name in vain," Tori warned him.

"He already has," Dru sniffed bitterly. "He let me get mixed up with you, didn't He?"

Tori slammed her mouth shut. It was obvious that Dru was in a full-blown snit. She couldn't imagine why he was so upset. She had tried to do him and herself a favor, but the muleheaded man couldn't see that.

For what seemed forever, Tori was forced to view the world from her upside-down position on the horse. The trek to Council Bluffs wasn't the least bit enjoyable. Every time Tori squirmed to find a more comfortable position, Dru whacked her on the derrière, just as he had done to the contrary mule he had been forced to ride for two frustrating days.

Chapter 15

Whong was delighted to see Dru again, but he was startled by the wild-haired young woman who was kicking and screaming while the muscular giant dragged her through the hotel-room door. When Dru had clamped a firm hand on Tori to make her stand still, Whong bowed obediently and murmured a greeting.

"Mr. Surrivan, I'm so grad you're back," he murmured, casting an apprehensive glance toward Tori.

Tori stopped struggling to frown curiously at the Chinaman who stood only two inches taller than she did. To her surprise, he bowed over her as well.

"It is a preasure to make your acquaintance, Miss Fremming."

A mocking grin tugged at the corner of Dru's lips. "Well, Chicago? Aren't you going to correct Whong's English? He constantly substitutes *r*'s for *l*'s."

Tori flashed Dru a smoldering glare. "He has an excuse. *You* don't," she sniped, jerking free from Dru's viselike grip.

Dru glowered back. "And not all of us were granted the privilege of a lengthy formal education," he countered sourly.

"Are we going soon, Mr. Surrivan?" Whong questioned curiously. "I have made the purchases for our trip home, just as you requested." This said, he bowed again.

Tori rolled her eyes at Whong's subservient manner. It annoyed her that the devoted Chinaman was treating Dru as if he were a king. He was a dirty rotten rat after all!

"We just fought a war to free the slaves," she announced, glancing scornfully at Dru. "You do remember the war, don't you, Montana? It was in all the papers. The obscure territory from which you hail does have a newspaper, doesn't it?"

Dru looked as if he would have liked to hit her. "Don't test my temper," he threatened in a low growl.

In a bit of a snit herself, Tori dropped into an exaggerated bow. "Forgive me, Your Excellency, I did not mean to offend you," she said, her tone implying that was exactly what she intended to do.

"Cut that out," Dru snapped, yanking her upright.

"You've dragged me around like a captured criminal for two days," Tori grumbled, violet eyes flashing. "I thought this was the way you expected your servants to behave."

"He saved my rife twice," Whong felt compelled to say, growing more aware of the friction between Dru and Tori with each passing second. "I am indebted . . ." Hurriedly, he pulled his handkerchief from his pocket, sneezed into it, and then blew his nose. "I'm obrigated to Mr. Surrivan."

"He saved your life and he ruined mine," Tori declared, flinging Dru a mutinous frown. "I'm not indebted to him."

Deciding it best to leave before a full-fledged war broke out, Whong doubled over at the waist and backed toward the door. "I fetch your dinner now, Mr. Surrivan."

"Don't bring any beans," Tori called as Whong scuttled into the hall.

Whong poked his head back inside and frowned at the sassy young woman whose wild blond hair looked as if it had been styled during a cyclone. Tentatively, he glanced at Dru who was exchanging frigid glares with Tori.

"No beans, Whong." Dru's tone dripped icicles. "The

172

lady has an aversion to them. Bring this royal duchess the finest steak to be had in town so she can celebrate before our wedding ceremony."

Whong braced himself against the doorjamb at Dru's announcement. "Your wedding?" he squeaked, his eyes round as dinner plates.

Tori's glare was meant to maim and mutilate, but she managed to restrain herself until after Whong took his final bow and went on his errand. "We aren't really going through with this, are we?" she growled in question. "Why do you need a wife when you've got Whong bowing over you every other minute and waiting on you hand and foot?"

Dru stared at the defiant snip long and hard. "You know perfectly well why we have to get married."

There it was again—his exaggerated sense of obligation. Tori wanted to be loved for what she was. This crazy idea of marriage had more to do with what Dru thought he was obliged to do than what he wanted to do. Tori wasn't a fool. She knew Dru didn't need a wife any more than he needed a devoted servant like Whong. Dru Sullivan was self-sufficient, and what he wanted from a woman he could get anywhere with no more than one of his devastating smiles as invitation. Angela Steep's instant attraction lent testimony to that fact.

"Quit trying to be so confounded noble," she bit off. "I seduced you, remember? You have no obligation to me. I have decided to find a job to support myself and to live out my life on the outposts of civilization."

"Doing what, for God's sake? Correcting everybody's grammar?" he smirked. "Face it, Chicago, you fit into the life of the West like a daisy in a patch of dandelions."

"I'm learning to adapt!" she all but yelled at him.

"You attract too many men," he snorted gruffly. "You need someone to take care of you. After the two near brushes with catastrophe you had in Iowa, I would think you would have learned your lesson."

Deliberately, he moved toward her, leaving her no

direction to retreat. His eyes roamed over her curvaceous figure, not missing even one minute detail. "You said you love me." His voice was low with caressing huskiness. "And we are very good together . . ."

How he could switch moods so quickly baffled Tori. She refused to be seduced into changing her mind about this ridiculous marriage which was only intended to salvage her reputation—and that meant as much to her as a hill of beans.

"Well, I carefully considered what you said and you were right. I don't love you," she declared, dodging his intended kiss. "It was a silly romantic notion. I mistook passion for love, that's all."

Although her comments were meant to erect a wall between them, it didn't halt Dru. Whether she loved him or not, she was still going to marry him. He had made up his mind and he wasn't changing it. He had no choice, and neither did Tori.

"I want us to be the way we were in Des Moines," he murmured as his hand lifted to trace her silky cheek. "I'm not sure what that is, Chicago, but it's good and you can't deny it."

Tori felt herself buckling beneath his husky tone and the seductive flicker in those baby-blue eyes. But just in the nick of time, her temper came to her rescue and saved her from humiliating surrender.

"What we had was lust," she said tersely. "You were my first experiment with passion. And you were right about my trying to read more into it. But there was nothing but passion for passion's sake. I would have experienced the same reaction with any man."

Dru could have strangled her for that remark. It infuriated him to visualize this saucy minx in another man's arms. And damnit, she hadn't been around enough to know that what they shared was as good as it got. And for some unknown reason, Dru had become so possessive of her that he had no intention of letting her experiment to find that out for herself.

"We are still getting married, Chicago, even if I have to bind, gag, and carry you to the altar," he muttered in warning.

Damn her, he had never proposed to another woman in all his life. And the one time he did, even if it was only out of obligation, she rejected him. Women! They were so infuriating at times. Especially Tori, Dru thought to himself. She changed day by day, minute by minute. And don't forget fickle! he added bitterly. One day she claimed she loved him and overnight she shrugged him off like a worn shirt. She had become so unpredictable that he never knew what she was going to say or do until she said or did it. All he had intended was to teach Tori to survive in the wilds. But somehow, while he was trying to mold her in his own image, he had created a monster! The shy, reserved debutante he had whisked away from Chicago had become a feisty, independent hellion who defied him for the pure sport of it!

"If you insist on going through with this, I'll make your life hell," Tori threatened.

"You already have," he scowled. "I wish I was home sick in bed."

"*Were* home," she sniped in correction. "Subjunctive mood."

"No, *bad* mood," he qualified. "And you're the one who put me in it . . ." His voice evaporated when Whong struggled through the door with a heaping tray of food, bringing quick death to their argument.

"No beans," Whong declared with a smile, gesturing toward the overloaded tray.

Tori decided to forgo the argument to appease her appetite. It had always been her habit to feed her frustrations. And feed them she did, until she very nearly popped from overeating. The juicy steak and potatoes were a feast.

While Tori gobbled her meal, she ignored Dru and quizzed Whong about his trip to America and his Gypsy life-style of migrating from one gold camp to another.

175

Whong, she found out, had worked in a San Francisco laundry that his cousin owned for almost a year before he struck out to open his private business in obscure gold fields. In broken English, Whong explained how Dru had intervened when drunken miners tried to cheat him out of his salary by claiming his work was below standard. When he refused to let the incident drop uncontested, the miners had dragged him to the street to whip him. According to Whong, Chinamen were treated as second-class citizens and that he was not the only one who had been subjected to cruel treatment by miners. But Dru had arrived upon the scene to shoot the whip out of one of the scoundrel's hands before he laid it to Whong's back a second time. The scar that slashed across Whong's shoulder blades was a constant reminder of the fact that Dru had spared his life.

"Mr. Surrivan is a very fine man," Whong said in closing. "You very rucky to have him as your husband."

"Ah yes, rucky me," Tori sniffed sarcastically. "As for myself, I think I would have preferred the lashing."

Tori's biting sarcasm was not well received. Dru gritted his teeth and put a stranglehold on his silverware, wishing it was Tori's swanlike neck. Damn that Caleb. This was all his fault, Dru silently seethed. If Dru had stayed home where he belonged, he wouldn't have become entangled with this misfit who no longer had a place in Chicago and probably would never truly fit into Virginia City, either.

After finishing off their meal, Dru ordered Tori to change into her gown while he and Whong stood guard outside the door. When she had bathed and changed, Dru shucked his garments and sorted through the luggage he had left in Whong's care. After locating garments befitting a groom, he ambled into the hall to greet his belligerent bride.

Begrudging admiration filled Tori's eyes when she surveyed the black tailored jacket and breeches Dru had donned. Although he was an impossible man who had no

176

use for love in his well-organized life, he could turn any woman's head when he fastened himself into the fancy trappings of a gentleman. He cut a striking figure with his midnight hair, sky-blue eyes, and muscular physique. And beneath that civilized veneer was a forceful, dynamic individual who had stolen her innocence and her heart, though she would never again make the mistake of admitting it aloud. Dru could have been everything she had ever dreamed of finding in a husband. He had only two unforgivable flaws—he didn't love her and he didn't need her love to make his life complete. The man had a tender spot in his heart for lost dogs, unfortunate Chinamen, hopeless causes, and he had a fierce obligation to his friends and family. He had more than enough to satisy him, and Tori would never mean anything to him, even if she did become his wife.

Tori, on the other hand, had spent her life in a sheltered world where she had been told what to do and when to do it. Now that her newfound independence was bursting out all over, she didn't want to be dictated to or overprotected. And knowing what a domineering man Dru was, they were bound to clash.

This marriage wasn't going to work, Tori speculated while she was hustled down the hall, bookended by Whong and Dru. Sooner or later the love she felt for Dru would wither and die because he couldn't return it. They would wind up hating each other, and even the passion that sparked between them wouldn't be enough to salvage their marriage. Unless Dru could offer his heart as part of the bargain, the marriage was doomed from the beginning. Tori had very nearly walked into a loveless marriage with Hubert and she didn't want to march into a second one with her one-sided love . . .

Before Tori knew it, she found herself standing beside Dru while the justice of the peace rattled off the vows that he had obviously repeated a hundred times before. The ceremony was relatively quick and painless, except for the instant when she had refused to repeat the vows

177

and Dru had very nearly twisted off her arm.

When Whong bowed and extended his congratulations, Tori forced a smile. But appearing polite and civil was the best she could do, considering her predicament. She wasn't the least bit happy, not when she found herself at the bottom of Dru's long list of noble obligations.

The remainder of the day was spent purchasing Tori's new wardrobe for their wagon trip across the Oregon and Bozeman Trail that led to Virginia City. Tori selected her garments carefully, and it galled her to no end that Dru was forced to pay for everything she now owned. Another of his responsibilities to the wife he felt obliged to marry, she mused dispiritedly.

"Will you quit looking at all the prices and buy what appeals to you," Dru grumbled when Tori studied a blue satin gown, checked its cost, and promptly replaced it on the rack. "I'm not as wealthy as your stepfather, but I'm hardly a pauper."

"Until I can find a job to pay for my wardrobe, I'm not spending any more of your money than absolutely necessary," Tori told him in no uncertain terms.

"A job?" Dru hooted incredulously.

"You don't think I plan to hang around your house the rest of my life, do you?" she snapped in question. "You have Whong to attend to the menial chores. Why do you need me around?"

A seductive smile dangled on one corner of his mouth. "Whong can't satisfy all my needs, Chicago."

The remark didn't sit well, and it put Tori in an instant huff. Dru had just confirmed her belief that she would be no more than a mistress who was to remain at his beck and call when lust got the best of him.

Tori snatched up four of the most expensive gowns to be had in the shop and slammed them down on the counter. Damn him! He was going to pay through the nose for that comment. And while she was at it, Tori scooped up three flimsy negligees that had obviously been designed with a trollop in mind. If that was to be her role in life, she might as well look the part! Double damn him!!

An amused smile pursed Dru's lips as he watched Tori stomp around the shop, gathering paraphernalia. His statement had gotten the hoped-for results. He had managed to make Tori angry enough to be spiteful. She hadn't intended to spend much money until he purposely agitated her. She was mad as hell, but at least she had purchased garments she would have selected if it had been her money that paid for them.

When Dru curled his arm around her elbow to escort her to the street, Tori jerked away as if she had been stung by a wasp. "You needn't touch me until dark when I'm expected to satisfy your lusts," she hissed poisonously.

Dru allowed her to storm ahead of him. Lord, she really had become a human cyclone! She was compensating for all the years she had held her temper in check. Dru had maneuvered her into doing exactly what he wanted her to do, but he knew he would pay dearly for it. She would spite him at every turn, he predicted.

Blast it, why was she making this marriage so difficult? As intelligent as she was, she should have been able to see that neither of them had any choice in the matter. Why couldn't she simply make the best of the situation and try to be pleasant? Godamighty, she had resigned herself to a loveless marriage to Hubert, but she set her feet when she was forced to marry Dru. What was the big deal anyway? They were attracted to each other, and some marriages didn't even have that going for them, for heaven's sake. He would see to it that she wanted for nothing. She could be near her father for the first time in a decade. And if she missed the culture of the city, he would take her to the theater in Virginia City occasionally. Jeezus, it wasn't as if he were sentencing her to a life in prison! Things could

179

have been worse. Tori could have married Hubert-the-weasel-Frazier who kept two mistresses at his beck and call. Lord, surely she didn't think he was as bad as Hubert . . . did she? She did, Dru decided when Tori glowered at him as if he were a varmint that had just slinked out from under a woodpile.

Chapter 16

The war had begun. Tori was polite but remote while Whong was underfoot. But when she was alone with Dru, she chose to pretend he didn't exist. Although they shared the same space, Tori didn't even pay Dru the courtesy of glancing in his direction when he spoke to her.

The only amusement she found was in watching Whong apply a variety of home remedies to treat his sneezing spasms and stuffy nose. He had mixed up a variety of herbs and other ingredients and swallowed them down, hoping to soothe his suffering. But nothing seemed to help. Whong sputtered constantly and apologized all over himself for exposing the Sullivans to every affliction known to man. He brewed honeysuckle tea, to which he added lemon juice and honey, and then sipped the concoction throughout the day. At night he soaked wool in olive oil, camphor, and vinegar and applied the warm compress to his chest. Alternately, he sipped on a cup of anise seeds, boiled water, and honey. Then he chased that antidote with a dose of boiled horseradish root which had been soaking in honey.

Tori had been able to avoid intimacy with Dru since Whong shared the hotel suite with them. For that she was grateful. It would have been difficult to pretend Dru had no effect on her if she surrendered to the sensations he so easily aroused in her. Tori had spent the proceeding days telling herself she really didn't love that blue-eyed gorilla. It was purely a physical attraction that would fade in time. And once they reached Virginia City she would feel absolutely nothing for him. She would plead with her father to take her in because her hasty marriage had turned sour. Caleb would surely do as she requested. If he wanted to see her after all these years of separation, he wouldn't refuse her request, Tori assured herself confidently.

After the wagon had been ferried across the Missouri River, the threesome had climbed upon the seat and aimed themselves west. With Whong acting as a buffer, Tori relaxed enough to enjoy the scenery and the brief stops at Fort Kearney, Plum Creek Station, and Fort Cottonwood, Nebraska. The traffic on the Oregon Trail had increased, and the threesome found themselves amid a wagon train of settlers who were headed west.

For the first time in weeks, Tori was allowed to associate with other women. But each time one of the men in the group paused to pass the time of day with her, Dru appeared out of nowhere to wrap a possessive arm around her. Tori was miffed by Dru's peculiar behavior. He had spent the past few weeks teaching her to take care of herself and yet he always seemed to be around when she confronted a man, no matter how harmless the encounter. Didn't he have any faith in his abilities as an instructor? Dru didn't really want her, she knew, but he didn't want anyone else to have her, either. And again Tori found herself marveling at the idiosyncrasies of men in general and Dru Sullivan in particular. The man was a walking contradiction.

When Tori ambled down to the North Platte River, which they had been following northwest, Dru was one step behind her, warning her of the river's notorious quicksand. He stood as posted lookout while she bathed, while she visited with the other travelers. In short, he treated her like a witless child, and Tori came dangerously close to losing her temper with him a dozen times a day. If not for Whong, Tori would have clanked the big ox over the head with the butt of his rifle and shoved him into the quicksand that he constantly warned her about.

As if Dru wasn't enough strain on her disposition, the journey itself became more tedious with each passing day. Sightings of roaming Indians were an ever-constant threat. The tribes, through whose land the trail crossed, had agreed to let travelers pass, but the road was plagued with renegades who didn't respect the treaties. And as they progressed up the shallow Platte River, the country grew sandier and more arid. Sagebrush, with its narrow gray leaves glowing like silver when the hot wind burned its undersides, dotted the landscape. Its shriveled appearance reminded Tori of her relationship with Dru. She had wanted evergreen and she wound up with sagebrush. Such was life, she supposed. She was left wanting what she knew she could never have—Dru's everlasting love.

During the westward trek, the rolling hills began to take on fantastic shapes that left Tori marveling at Mother Nature's handiwork. The slender spire of Chimney Rock and the domed rock formation of Scotts Bluff broke the horizon, but there were very few trees except the fuzzy cottonwoods that were nestled beside the river. Although her love life was in miserable shape, Tori had gained a firsthand lesson in geography, and she took solace in the fact that she had the opportunity to view the places she had only read about.

When the procession of wagons paused to rest and replenish their supplies at Fort Laramie, Wyoming, Tori was grateful for the break in what had become monotony. The weary travelers lingered for two days beside the walled fort, taking time out to celebrate their progress west. The affair was a far cry from the grand balls she had attended in Chicago, but Tori delighted to hear the sounds of banjos, tambourines, harmonicas and fiddles

183

filling the air. The soldiers flooded from the fort to join in the festivities, but each time Tori was asked to dance, Dru was there to monitor her partner's behavior. Tori had somehow acquired another chaperone, just like the ones that followed her around Chicago.

The instant Dru stomped over to insist that one of the officers was not observing a respectable distance while dancing, Tori lost what was left of her temper. Dru hadn't even asked her to dance, but he refused to let her relax enough to enjoy herself in the arms of another man. Flashing him a murderous glare, Tori stormed back to the wagon to pout in private.

"You're making a spectacle of yourself, Chicago," Dru declared as he strode up behind her.

"Well, you started it," Tori muttered resentfully. "You hover around me like my fairy godmother, except you don't grant wishes, only curses!"

"Your dance partner wasn't behaving himself," Dru countered.

If Tori's rigid stance was indicative of her disposition, she was silently seething, he speculated. He was right; she was.

"Godamighty, Montana," she spewed at him. "What could the man possibly have done in front of a prairie full of people?"

"He was thinking," Dru snapped harshly, "and would you like me to tell you of *what?*"

Tori rolled her eyes in disbelief. Now Dru considered himself a mind reader! "The lieutenant wasn't doing whatever you seem to think he was thinking of doing," she parried in a sarcastic tone. "Stop treating me like a child. I'm a grown woman and I have learned to take care of myself!"

The distant torchlights displayed the heaving swells of her breasts, which were dangerously close to spilling from the scoop-necked bodice of her gown. Dru was vividly aware, as was every soldier at the fort, that Tori was every inch a woman. He hadn't touched Tori since their wedding, which ironically was the only time he should have. He wasn't quite sure why he had allowed her to give him cold shoulders that dripped icicles. He should have demanded his husbandly rights. Perhaps he wanted to prove to himself that this lavender-eyed minx had no magical hold on him, that he wasn't bound to her as tightly as he was beginning to think he was. Or maybe he feared she would reject his advances to punish him for forcing her into a marriage she hadn't wanted. Dru suspected a wife's method of retaliation when she was peeved with her husband would be to withhold intimate favors. But he had outfoxed her by refusing to give her the chance to deny him.

Tori was in a full-fledged snit, and she itched to strike out at Dru, to hurt him as she was hurting. She wanted him to share the company that misery loved so well. "Well, maybe I was thinking about the same thing that nice-looking lieutenant was," she hurled spitefully. "You claimed I would feel the same about any man who took me to bed, so maybe I wanted to test that theory." Let him stuff that in his pipe and smoke it!

He was smoking all right. It was rolling out his ears. Roughly, Dru yanked Tori to him, mashing her heaving breasts against his chest, which was swelled with so much indignation that he very nearly popped the buttons on his shirt.

"You are my wife and you will remain faithful to me, just as I will remain loyal to you," he boomed like an exploding cannon.

"Your wife? My eye!" Tori sneered, squirming in vain for freedom. "All I am is a possession you think you need to protect. You feel the same way about the two horses and mule that are trailing behind our wagon. You feed them, shod them, and watch over them, but you have no particular affection for any of them, either."

"If you'd start behaving like a wife instead of contrary nag, maybe I could tell the difference." Let her chew on that possibility for a while and see how she liked it!

185

Tori reacted instinctively to the insult. She cocked her arm and struck like a rattlesnake, leaving her handprint on Dru's bronzed cheek. And to her outrage, he slapped her back. The beast! He was treating her like his misbehaving horses. She hated him!

Dru cursed a blue streak when he realized what he had done. Tori had made him so furious that he had reacted without thinking. God, he could kick himself for laying a hand on her, and if he could have contorted his body to become the donor and recipient of a hard kick in the seat of the pants he most certainly would have.

"I'm sorry, Chicago," he murmured apologetically. Gently, he reached out to smooth his fingertips over her face, but Tori knocked his hand away before he could touch her.

Tears sprang to her eyes and her cheek pulsated in rhythm with her heart. She was so frustrated she wanted to scream and probably would have if the place hadn't been crawling with soldiers and travelers.

"I despise you, Montana," Tori burst out on a sob.

When Tori wheeled around to stomp off, Dru snagged her arm and spun her to face him. Holding her in place when she would have broke and run, Dru reached up to reroute the tears and brush his hand over the welt he regretted leaving on her satiny cheek. Although Tori told herself not to buckle beneath his tenderness, she felt her traitorous body respond when his sensuous lips whispered over hers in the slightest breath of a kiss. Lord, there was no hope for it. She had valiantly tried to talk herself into loathing this rake who had the sensitivity of a rock. But she still loved him, flaws and all. And God only knew why she did. He hadn't given her any reason to love him—unless overprotectiveness and possessiveness counted for something . . .

"Forgive me, Chicago," Dru whispered as he pressed her reluctant body to his. "I didn't mean to hurt you and I swear I'll never strike you again, no matter how angry you make me. I'm truly sorry . . ."

186

Dru melted the wall of bitterness around her heart with his softly uttered apology and his masterful kisses. He made her forget why she was so furious with him, why it was so important to cling to her feminine pride. She wanted him and he wanted her, physically at least. Why should she expect more from a man who had always taken women for granted and who had loved them with his body but never with his heart?

She expected too much, she supposed. After all, it wasn't as if her life had been rewarding and fulfilling up to this point. It was time she learned to settle for what she could have instead of making herself miserable by wanting what she could never acquire.

Love was only a bedazzled state of mind, an elusive dream, Tori told herself sensibly. She wanted more than she could ever possibly get from Dru. She had to be satisfied to settle for the physical pleasure he was offering and be content with her lot because this was probably as good as it was ever going to get.

His magnificent body wasn't such a bad bargain, Tori mused as she involuntarily surrendered to his breath-stealing kiss. At least the man she had married appealed to her. Things could have been worse. He could have been Hubert who, in Tori's opinion, didn't have enough appeal to attract one mistress, much less two. But Dru Sullivan oozed with magnetic charm. He was wild and sensual and he knew how to make a woman thankful she was a woman, even if he refused to offer his love.

But Tori, although she knew she couldn't find the will to resist Dru, intended to ensure that he didn't mock her lack of self-control when the loving was over. She would, at least, go down fighting, and clinging to her dignity.

"If you're going to seduce me for your own satisfaction, be quick about it," she demanded, her voice not as steady as she had hoped. "For fun, I had planned to manicure my nails this evening."

Dru jerked back as if he had been snakebit. "You little witch," he growled sourly.

Tori managed a taunting smile for his benefit. "The first few times we made love, I was merely curious," she said to get his dander up. And that she did, for Dru scowled poisonously. "Now that the mystery is gone, I'm certain my role as your lover and wife will be bound by duty, by nothing more than a sense of obligation. I'm sure you can understand that."

At that moment, Dru could have cheerfully choked her. She was challenging his prowess, his ability to enflame her. Tori was far too clever to simply reject him the way less imaginative women might have done when they were infuriated with their husbands. Oh no, this sassy vixen went directly for the throat! Well, they would see which one of them was more affected by their lovemaking. The first few times may well have been the simple appeasement of curiosity on her part. Tori still had a lot to learn, and tonight she was going to explore every dimension of passion, he promised himself.

To Tori's dismay, Dru didn't stomp off in a snit. He smiled roguishly into her defiant face. Then his hand slid over hers, and he had to resist the urge to break every bone in her fingers. "Very well, you will perform your wifely duties, Chicago, and I'll try not to take up too much of your time. I should hate for you to neglect your nails."

Reluctantly, Tori allowed Dru to lead her to the river's edge. Even in the moonlight she could see the wry grin that lifted one corner of his sensuous mouth. She couldn't imagine what he thought he could prove. But then, she didn't know how naive and inexperienced she really was. But Tori was about to find out!

Chapter 17

Tensely, Tori stood on the riverbank while Dru positioned himself behind her. His left hand settled on her waist and then glided up and down her ribs, setting off a chain reaction of unwanted sensations. Forbidden desire instantly uncoiled inside her. His full lips whispered over the trim column of her throat while his right hand nimbly loosed the stays on the back of her satin gown. As the dress sagged, he greeted every inch of exposed flesh with worshipping kisses and skillful caresses.

Tori fought down the moan of pleasure that threatened to escape her lips. She didn't want Dru to know how much he stirred her, how she adored the feel of his hands and lips migrating over her sensitive skin. But she did enjoy his practiced touch. He knew just how and where to touch her.

When his hand flowed over her shoulder to push the gown away, Tori melted into a pool of liquid desire. The night air did nothing to cool the white-hot flames that leaped over her flesh. Her body was alive with anticipation. She was a prisoner of her own hungry desires.

The gasp she sought to smother burst free when his slow, tormenting caresses wandered over her chemise to trace the inner curve of her breasts. Tori bit her lips when his fingertips trailed over the throbbing peaks and then slid beneath the fabric to make tantalizing contact with her bare skin.

All the while his caresses explored and sensitized, his moist lips traced a titillating path along her shoulder. Tori ached to feel his mouth upon hers, to return the intense pleasure that undulated through her. But Dru deprived her and tormented with his teasing caresses and butterfly kisses. Tori's knees folded up when his hands swirled over her belly and drifted over her inner thigh. Over and over again, his caresses ascended and descended, leaving her quaking with unappeased needs that burned in the very core of her being.

Dru paused to shuck his shirt and then brushed his hair-matted chest against her bare back. When he took up where he had left off with maddening caresses that breezed over the taut peaks of her breasts, Tori swore she would melt.

"You're exquisite, Chicago," he murmured against the sensitive point beneath her ear. "Touching you pleases me." His hand dipped beneath the hem of her chemise to trace the shapely curve of her hip, and Tori's brain broke down. "I could make a meal of you . . ."

He bent her backward then to let his lips follow the path of his adventurous hands. Tori struggled to inhale a breath, but his greedy mouth suckled at the tips of her breasts and trailed over her belly and her heart stalled in her chest.

Sweet mercy, Dru had proven himself to be a tender, skilled lover in the past, but suddenly he seemed to have incredible imagination and patience. His techniques were soul-shattering. His kisses showered her trembling flesh with unrivaled pleasure and created monstrous cravings that Tori wondered if even he could satisfy . . .

Tori choked on her breath when his knowing fingers found her womanly softness. When his kisses trailed over her shoulder to tease the silky flesh of her spine, her pulse leaped, depriving her of oxygen. And then, ever so slowly, he peeled away the last of her undergarments and shed his breeches. Lifting her into his arms, he walked into the river. But all the water in the Platte couldn't extinguish the fires he had kindled within her. Tori was a mass of quivers, her body so hungry for his that she swore she'd die before he appeased the intense ache he had aroused in her.

"Your duty, Chicago?" His deep baritone voice held an underlying taunt. He left her adrift on the water while he performed his sweet seductive magic on her luscious body. "Your obligation? No, love," he contradicted. "It will never be as simple as that between you and I . . ."

"*Me*. Between you and *me*," she corrected him in a strangled chirp.

This was one time Dru didn't take offense to being corrected. He merely smiled. "You can teach me to speak proper English later. But tonight I'm going to teach you the language of love . . ."

While Tori was adrift on a shimmering river of silver, Dru spun a web of scintillating pleasure upon her. His hands and lips were everywhere at once, doing delicious things to her body, causing her mind to whirl furiously. His wandering hands glided the full length of her, lingering on her inner thighs and then ascending to repeat the same erotic procedure all over again. His tongue flicked at the throbbing buds before his lips skimmed over the valley between her breasts and Tori swore she was drowning in the most enticing sensations ever created.

One hand kept her lightly suspended in the water and the other one explored and aroused her to the limits of her sanity. Tori could no more control the moan of pleasure that trickled from her lips than she could fly to the moon. Dru had captured her in his spell and had hypnotized her so completely that she couldn't think past the delicious moment.

When he finally lifted his raven head, his shadowed gaze locked with hers. "Does this feel like duty, sweet witch?" he purred in question. "Have I taken from you without giving in return?"

Tori's voice had long ago collapsed in her throat and she could do nothing except shake her head in response.

"This marriage of ours was never meant to be one in name only." His full mouth descended to play softly against her lips. "This fire between us is very real. We feed off each other's passions. We did the first time we made wild sweet love and we still do now, even though there are obstacles between us. And before the night is out, I'll hear you say you want me to come to you, that you want me in all the wild ways I want you . . ."

Oh no, he wouldn't, Tori assured herself shakily. She couldn't have formulated a sentence if her life depended on it!

To prove his seductive threat, his hands and lips scaled the rose-tipped crest of her breast and skied down her belly to her thighs, teasing her with intimate promises of ecstasy to come. Tori's body went boneless and convulsive shudders rocked her soul. Dru's lovemaking was devastating. He was teaching her things about passion that she never dreamed existed. At last she realized how childish and naive she had been to mock his ability to devastate her with desire. He left her dizzy, lightheaded, and quaking with ravenous needs that screamed for fulfillment. He spun her nerves into tangled twine and turned muscle into mush.

"Dru . . . please . . ." she gasped, wondering where she had found the breath to speak.

Slowly, he carried her from the river and laid her in the sand, where ripples of water lapped against the shore.

"Please what, Chicago?" he whispered against her parted lips. "Please stop? Please go away and leave you alone? Tell me what you want . . ."

Damn him! He was tormenting her to no end. "Make love to me . . ." she choked on a ragged breath. "I want you . . ."

"In time," he murmured as he levered up beside her to

stare down into her moonlit features. He took her trembling hand and brushed it over the dark matting of hair on his chest and belly. "I want your loving touch. Show me how much pleasure I gave you. Return it . . ."

Tori was like a victim of a trance, lured by his deep, resonant voice, tempted by the feel of his rock-hard flesh beneath her hands. She had touched him before, but not as boldly as she did now. She investigated every whipcord muscle, each taut tendon, until he relaxed beneath her worshipping caresses. Her senses were filled with the taste, feel, and scent of him.

Her hands and lips flooded over him like the gliding surf that tumbled lazily ashore. Touching him provided pleasure in itself. And when her hand folded about him, dragging a groan from his lips, Tori discovered that she could devastate him as thoroughly as he devastated her.

Employing her entire body, she caressed him, and Dru strangled on his breath. He had allowed no other woman such bold privileges, and he wondered if he could endure the sweet torment of Tori's imaginative caresses. He had always been in control of lovemaking and now he wished he hadn't been so generous with Tori. She instinctively knew how to arouse him by maddening degrees, to make him shudder with frustrated passion. He felt as if he had been besieged by an earthquake that had set off volcanic eruptions. She had transformed him into a quivering mass of barely restrained passion, and desire burned him alive.

Tori marveled at the power she suddenly held over this strong, magnificent creature. He reminded her of a great, powerful jungle cat whose masculine grace wasted not one ounce of unnecessary energy. There was a wild nobility about Dru that had intrigued her from the beginning. And yet there was a subtle gentleness about him that fascinated her. Dru was a complex man who had learned how to do everything in this world but how to fall in love. Tori wished she could be the one to tame his restless heart, to make him care as deeply for her as she did for him. She longed for an affection that the cold winds of insult and the scorching heat of sarcasm couldn't destroy.

How could she make Dru understand that there was more to marriage than belonging, more than physical pleasure? How could she touch his soul and make him realize that she wanted to share his life, his hopes, his dreams, as well as his bed?

Her kiss and caress expressed the emotions that transcended desires of the flesh. She conveyed her love for him in the way her body moved suggestively against his, the way she kissed him with an affection that requested more than the joining of one body to another. She longed to be not only flesh to flesh with him, but soul to soul—one heart beating for another for all seasons—like the long-enduring ever-constant life of the evergreen . . .

Dru could endure no more of the maddening pleasure of having and having not. Tori's loving touch drove him wild with desire. He ached to crush her to him, to hold her, and to go on holding her luscious body to his until the fiery blaze of passion had run its course. Like a rousing tiger, he rolled above her, his eyes burning with such fierce, uncontrollable need that he trembled with the overwhelming want of her.

Tori had the power to move him as no other woman before her ever had. She could shatter his self-control and turn him into a human torch. Tori made him want things that he had never considered in any of his previous relationships with women. She made him question his own theories on passion. So quickly had he become possessive of her. Watching other men hold her in their arms annoyed him. Knowing other men wanted her the same way he did incensed him. He was jealous and he couldn't help it. *Couldn't*, mind you. Tori was like a wildfire in his blood, a living breathing part of him that time and determination hadn't been able to erase. No one quenched his needs the way she did. He wanted her as hungrily tonight as he had the first time. Nothing had changed except that his need for her had become an impossible addiction . . .

Dru whirled with passion when Tori arched to meet his driving thrusts. When she dug her nails into his back and gave herself up to the explosive sensations that burst within her, Dru shuddered with ineffable pleasure. Gentleness evaporated in the storm of mindless passion that engulfed them. Dru was a man possessed. Violet eyes beckoned to him. Even with his eyes closed he could see Tori's elegant face amid the tempest of swirling passion. He felt himself reaching upward to grasp that one elusive sensation that evaded him, and then suddenly he was there, beyond the sun, drifting in a world where time dangled in space. He was at peace and he was gliding across the heavens with an angel in his arms.

A quiet groan tripped from his lips when the darkness split asunder and twinkling beams of light pierced his mind's eye. It was like watching a pitcher of stars tumbling down onto the black velvet sky. Ever so slowly, Dru descended from his fantastic flight around the universe. His body was numb with ecstasy. He swore that if someone lit a fire under him, he would simply lie there and burn to a crisp before he could gather the strength to move.

A tremulous sigh escaped Tori's lips as she snuggled in the circle of Dru's sinewy arms. Well, so much for needling Dru with remarks about lovemaking being a wife's duty, she mused disparagingly. He knew perfectly well how his kisses and caresses affected her . . .

"Mr. Surrivan? Yoo-hoo!" Whong's concerned voice wafted its way across the river, shattering the spell.

Muttering, Dru bounded to his feet to fetch their clothes.

"Mr. Surrivan? Are you out here?" Whong called.

Frantically, Tori and Dru dived into their clothes while the crackle of twigs heralded the Chinaman's approach. Wearing a black scowl, Dru slipped from the clump of cottonwood trees to startle Whong. The little man leaped back, his wide eyes focused on Dru's shadowed face.

"*What*, for God's sake?" Dru growled, annoyed by the untimely interruption.

Whong dropped into a bow. "The commander of the fort wishes to speak with you," he reported. "I said we were headed toward Virginia City and he says there has been trouble with the Sioux in the Brack Hirrs."

"*Black Hills,*" Dru corrected, and then rolled his eyes in disbelief. Lord, now Tori had him doing it!

"That's what I said, the Brack Hirrs," Whong declared. "The commander suggests another route to Virginia City that wirr avoid trouble."

Godamighty, just what he needed, Dru thought disgustedly. He would have to leave the wagon behind and climb atop the horses to take the obscure paths through the foothills of the Bighorn Mountains to the Absaroko Range, traveling by night if he hoped to avoid confrontation with the Sioux and Crow.

Muttering, Dru strided off with Whong, leaving Tori to make her own way back to the wagon. This she did with a heavy heart. Tori was beginning to wonder if she would be better off if she were captured by the Sioux. But, she reckoned, every form of refuge had its price. Being captured might solve one set of problems, but she supposed it would only create another. And no matter where she was, she wouldn't be able to get over Dru.

Damnit all, enduring a one-sided love was nothing short of hell. Why did she have to care so deeply for that infuriating man? She was every kind of fool. And where was she supposed to go from here? she asked herself. He knew she would buckle each time he reached for her. Resisting him was next to impossible. Lord, if only she could hold out until they reached Montana and she could seek sanctuary with her father.

Clinging to that encouraging thought, Tori ambled back to the wagon to fetch her nightgown, and snuggled onto her pallet. Exhaustion lured her into a sleep that was tormented by warm, arousing dreams.

A tender smile pursed Dru's lips when he returned from his conference to find Tori nestled on her bedroll. Sometimes this saucy minx had him cursing in frustration and sometimes . . .

Dru heaved a heavy sigh. What the blazes was the matter with him? He should have been well satisfied after their night of splendor. But he never seemed able to get enough of her. Sharing her uninhibited brand of passion was pure, sweet ecstasy, but he wanted to touch her heart and soul as well. Tori had tied his emotions in knots and left him wanting her every waking hour of every day. If he and Tori didn't come to some sort of understanding and soon, Dru swore he would be a raving lunatic. One minute she was hurling biting insults at him and the next minute she was taking him on the most arousing voyage through star worlds far, far away. How was a man supposed to remain on an even keel when this sweet, tormenting witch kept his emotions in turmoil?

Too tired to delve any more into his dilemma, Dru stretched on the pallet beside Tori. And somewhere in the night, he cuddled up against her, as if he belonged there. It felt right and natural to keep a possessive arm around her while he slept. But when dawn spilled over the horizon, Tori slapped his arm away and declared she was not his pillow and that there were enough wide-open spaces in Wyoming; that he had no need to crowd onto her spot.

And suddenly they were right back where they started. He was having to fight his way through her barriers of defense, just to touch her as he longed to do. Godamighty, Dru thought with an exasperated growl. That woman was sure enough making him crazy!

Relief settled on Tom Bates's features when he spied Dru Sullivan's signature on the hotel guest ledger in

Council Bluffs. Finally, another clue! When Tom quizzed the proprietor, the man broke into a smile of recognition.

"Mr. Sullivan was a right nice fellow," the hotel owner declared. "He and his new bride spent one night here before they climbed into their wagon and started up the trail."

"Bride?" William Fogg croaked, bug-eyed.

The innkeeper nodded affirmatively. "And what a beauty she was, too," he remarked enthusiastically. "I remember commenting to Mr. Sullivan about what a pretty wife he had."

After kindly thanking the proprietor for the startling information, Tom and William moseyed outside.

"I dread telling Frazier that his fiancée married her captor," Tom muttered.

William's shoulders sagged tiredly. "Thank God we can inform him by telegram," he mumbled. "I don't relish telling him, either. He was so fired up when he demanded we take this case that I thought he was going to go up in smoke!"

Grimly, the detectives trudged toward the telegraph office to relay the latest information before aiming themselves northwest. But as luck would have it, Hubert and the Cassidys had already left Chicago to confront Caleb Flemming and Hubert didn't receive the news about his fiancée.

Silently fuming, Tyrone Webster plunked down at his desk in the back room of the Queen High Saloon. A dark scowl puckered his bony features as he chewed on the tip of his cigar and reflected on his most recent confrontation with the stubborn Caleb Flemming. Tyrone was running short of patience with the obstinate owner of Virginia City's most prosperous hotel and restaurant.

"I don't suppose Flemming accepted your offer to buy him out," Duke Kendrick smirked at his fuming employer.

"No, he didn't," Tyrone muttered irritably. "And I think it's about time to use one of our scare maneuvers on him, especially since Dru Sullivan is not in town."

Tyrone's gaze shifted to the two other gunslingers who bookended Duke Kendrick. Although Sam Rother and Clark Russel were short on brains, they followed orders to the letter. Duke Kendrick, however, was the most cocky and temperamental of the three hired henchmen who worked for Tyrone, and he saved the more grisly duties for Duke who never batted an eyelash at dropping his victims in their tracks.

Tyrone's narrowed eyes swung back to Sam Rother, who was chewing vigorously on the wad of tobacco that bulged in his unshaven jaw. "Sam, I want you to follow Caleb Flemming. The first chance you get . . ."

"I know what to do," Sam grunted in offended dignity. "I ain't so dense that you have to spell it out for me, Boss." He pushed himself out of his chair and lumbered toward the back door of the office. "I'll see to it that Caleb thinks twice before he refuses one of yer offers."

When the door whined shut, Tyrone fixed his eyes on Clark Russel. "You take some of the men from my ranch and pay the Sullivans' cattle herd a visit," he ordered.

"Rustlin'?" Clark questioned. "Sure thing, Boss. Them Sullivans got too damned many cattle to take care of anyway. Me an' the boys will relieve 'em of some stock."

Before Clark reached for the doorknob, Tyrone swiveled in his chair to fire another order. "And if any of Dru Sullivan's younger brothers get in your way, shoot 'em. That should make Dru more agreeable to my offer to buy his ranch."

A devilish smile quirked Clark's lips as he nodded in compliance. "You don't have to worry about nothin', Boss. Them cattle will be long gone and I'll take care of any Sullivan who gits in my way." That said, Clark moseyed out the door.

"And what about me, Webster?" Duke demanded,

199

refusing to call the lean and lanky owner of the Queen High Saloon, "Boss."

Tyrone gnashed his teeth, well aware of Duke's defiance and his refusal to acknowledge the mastermind of their local theft ring as his superior. Stifling his annoyance, Tyrone focused on the problem at hand. "Two of the prospectors that I grubstaked haven't paid me my share of the gold they dug from their claims." His meaningful stare riveted on the steely-eyed gunslinger. "I've warned Barnes and Emmerson once already . . ." He let the remark hang in the air, allowing Duke Kendrick to form his own conclusions about what was to be done with the contrary prospectors.

Duke unfolded himself casually from his chair and swaggered toward the back door. "I get half of the gold they're withholding for disposing of them."

"Half!" Tyrone snorted. "Our deal has always been a third and you damned well know it."

"My price for killing just went up," Duke growled malevolently. His curled fingers hovered over his well-worn Colts when Tyrone looked as if he were about to voice another protest.

Swearing under his breath, Tyrone slouched back in his chair and glared at the gunslinger. "All right, you can have half," he muttered begrudgingly. "But just make sure those two weasels don't live to point an accusing finger. I'm having enough trouble pressuring Flemming and the Sullivans without inviting more difficulty."

A diabolical smile spread across Duke's lips. "There won't be any survivors, Webster. I always hit my mark. Too bad you can't say the same for those two dim-witted morons you hired."

When Duke sauntered into the alley, Tyrone chomped on his cigar. Damn that Duke Kendrick. He was so cussed cocky that Tyrone could barely tolerate him. But unfortunately, he was far more competent than Sam and Clark. Tyrone just had to grit his teeth and endure Duke's arrogance . . .

His peeved frown transformed into a satanic grin when he turned his thoughts to Caleb Flemming and the Sullivan brothers. Very soon, Caleb and the Sullivans would realize they couldn't hold onto their property without risking their lives. They, like the other men with whom Tyrone had dealt, would realize it was safer to sell out and move on. Caleb Flemming and the Sullivan brothers would accept Tyrone's offer sooner or later. Either that or he would sic Duke on them. As Duke said, he wasn't in the habit of leaving survivors . . .

Chapter 18

Tori's admiration for Dru's talents in the wilderness grew by leaps and bounds with each passing day. They had trekked northwest through the empty sagebrush desert, skirted past the pine-clad ridges and towering peaks of the Bighorn, into the spectacular valleys of Yellowstone toward the Absaroko Range. Dru's sixth sense alerted him to danger before it was upon them. Twice he spotted Sioux hunting parties and managed to elude disaster. And although Whong sneezed and sniffled his way through Wyoming toward Montana, Dru never ridiculed the devoted little man who worshipped the ground he walked on.

Tori found herself marveling at the change of scenery. They had left the plains behind to travel up the valleys and hills near Wind River. There was something exhilarating about the country through which they passed. It was wild and rugged and yet challenging and it inspired Tori. She knew why her father had been captivated by the wide-open spaces and why her mother would never fit into life in the West. Gwen never had adapted well to open spaces and inconveniences. Tori herself might not fit in, but Gwen would have had a far worse time of it. Tori was sure of that.

The grandeur of the mountains and the rolling meadows that were carpeted with rich blue gamma, bunce, and bluestem grasses got into Tori's blood. Among the way they had met men who sought beaver in the fast-moving streams of the high country and optimists who were headed toward Bannack, Virginia City, and Last Chance Gulch. They were men blinded by visions of gold for the taking, as well as sodbusters who were anxious to turn the range land into wheat fields.

Tori sighed appreciatively at the horizon, which was broken by butte formations, wide river valleys, and jagged, isolated mountain ranges that were capped with fir, cedars, and ponderosa pines. This was a brawny, bold land that catered to free-spirited men and women who loved challenges and thrilled to the Chinook winds that followed the storms, warming the rugged land like a breath of spring. The western region of the territory was protected from the harsh arctic winds by the looming mountains, and the white-capped peaks added a splash of grandeur that Tori found irresistible.

Somehow this magnificent land seemed to fit the memories Tori held of her father—big, robust, and bold. Caleb . . . Ah, it had been forever since Tori had seen her father. The closer they came to Virginia City, the more anxious Tori became. She concentrated her thoughts on Caleb and averted them from Dru as much as possible.

Tori loved Dru, but wounded pride refused to release the words she had once offered to him. Dru hadn't wanted her confession because he wasn't interested in an emotional commitment. Tori just had to adapt to the limitations of this marriage and make the best of it until she could have it annulled.

"We'll stop here for the night," Dru announced, jostling Tori from her contemplations.

"Whatever you say, Mr. Surrivan," Whong murmured obediently. With an effort, the Chinaman slid from his mount and scurried about to prepare their camp beside the clear ultramarine waters of the Yellowstone River.

Tori sat atop her horse, marveling at Mother Nature's

handiwork. The river was lined with trees and vegetation of every imaginable shade of scarlet, yellow, and green. The warm spring that fed the river was so transparent that Tori could see all the way to the bottom. She wished she knew how to swim, just so she could float across the sparkling water and enjoy a few moments of solitude in this mountain paradise.

"While Whong makes camp, I'll teach you how to swim," Dru volunteered, watching Tori peer at the inviting river as if it were a long-awaited feast.

Tori hadn't meant to look so thrilled with the prospect, but she couldn't help herself. The thought of gliding across the sparkling river was too great a temptation.

Nudging his steed, Dru aimed himself south. "Come downstream where we will have some privacy," he insisted.

While Whong built a small campfire and boiled his concoction of water, roots, and honey, Tori followed Dru. Although relations between husband and wife hadn't been all that good of late, Tori decided to forgo her irritation for the moment. She had waited weeks for Dru to teach her the skills of swimming. And this was the perfect place for lessons.

When Dru stepped from the stirrup and peeled off his shirt, Tori frowned. Maybe this wasn't such a good idea after all, she thought to herself. Swimming naked in the river invited intimacy and she had resolved never to give in to Dru again. She had shamelessly surrendered that night beside Fort Laramie, and it was difficult to restrain her emotions when Dru made wild, sweet love to her . . .

"I thought you were anxious to learn to swim," Dru remarked when Tori remained glued to her saddle, chewing indecisively on her lip.

"I am," she mumbled, eyeing him warily. "But I'm wondering if that is all you have in mind."

Dru shrugged with pretended carelessness. Of course it wasn't all he had in mind, but he wasn't about to let his suspicious wife know that. When he shucked the rest of his clothes and dove into the river with masculine grace, Tori stood on the bank, unwillingly admiring the brawny giant who was poetry in motion and perfection in the flesh. It was going to be difficult not to reach out and touch him as she longed to do.

"Lord, this feels good," Dru taunted as he backstroked across the channel. "It's like a miracle bath that relieves all aches and pains."

Tori buckled to temptation. She wanted to learn to swim as expertly as Dru. Refusing to allow him to watch her disrobe, she ducked behind the underbrush and then waded into the water while Dru's back was turned. When he glided toward her, she wondered why she'd bothered with modesty. The water was crystal clear and there was nothing left to the imagination. He could see her bare flesh as clearly as she could see his well-sculptured body. Water droplets danced in his midnight hair and sparkled on his tanned skin, making her even more aware of him than she already was.

"The first thing you have to learn is to hold your breath and submerge without panicking," Dru insisted as he pulled his feet beneath him and stood up on the sandy riverbed. "Don't let the river intimidate you. Let it caress you."

Sweet mercy, the man couldn't even give swimming instructions without employing romantic terms, thought Tori. He was making it doubly difficult for her to concentrate on developing her skills.

"Take a deep breath and let yourself sink into the river as if it were a puffy cloud," Dru instructed his reluctant student.

Inhaling as much air as her lungs could hold, Tori did as she was told. But when she sank down, Dru was there smiling at her under the water. Tori tried not to panic when she was surrounded by gallons of water, but when Dru leaned forward to place a kiss to her lips, she shot to the surface to give him the evil eye.

"I thought this was going to be a swimming

lesson, nothing more," she muttered, flinging him an accusing glare.

"It is," Dru defended, reaching over to reroute the stream of water that trickled over her forehead. "I was only trying to distract you from fretting over being engulfed by water."

His very presence was distraction aplenty, Tori mused. Although she was staring skeptically at him, Dru gestured for her to inhale another breath and dive into the depths. Copying his movements, Tori placed her hands together in front of her, tucked her head between her arms, and dove into the river.

Dru had indeed selected the perfect location for swimming instructions. The water was so clear that Tori had no horrifying visions of sinking into murky depths, never to be seen or heard from again. There was something intriguing about gliding through the river, kicking her feet as Dru was doing while he swam just ahead of her. The fact that she was allowed to survey his muscular body while she was doing it provided enough preoccupation for her fear of water to ebb.

"Now, cup your hands like so and use them to pull the water toward you," Dru instructed. He positioned himself behind Tori to demonstrate the arm motions while she was simultaneously kicking her feet.

"Good," he congratulated her when she did exactly as he told her.

It was the first compliment she could remember receiving when Dru instructed her at anything. "You mean I actually did something right?" she smirked.

"You do a great many things superbly." His voice dropped to a husky tone as he murmured against the sensitive point beneath her ear.

Tori darted away when his sensuous lips migrated down her neck, sending a fleet of goosebumps cruising across her skin. He was trying to transform this swimming lesson into a seduction and Tori wanted no part of it. He would touch her and she would melt and then she would curse herself for giving in to him like a witless moron. Tori hadn't forgiven him for rushing her into a marriage he hadn't wanted. It killed her to be another of his zillion obligations.

"Let's get back to the swimming lesson, shall we?" she chirped, her voice disturbed by the unwanted effect this nude giant had on her.

Dru heaved a frustrated sigh. He was getting nowhere fast with this stubborn minx. He had hoped to call a truce, but Tori was still armed for battle. For the past ten days she had avoided him, clinging to Whong for protection against privacy with her husband. She considered ten days a long time for Dru to go without touching her—even though she was unaware that wanting her was his obsession. But as contrary as Tori had become of late, she refused to place herself in any situation that might lead to intimacy.

Resigning himself to a battle lost, Dru settled for doing nothing more than admiring Tori while he taught her to swim. He would need a chisel to crack her defenses!

"Now that you know you won't drown when your face is under water, lower your head and combine the motions of your hands and feet to propel you across the top of the water." Dru sprang out to demonstrate.

Tori watched him cut through the water like a ship, employing the power of his arms and legs. Inhaling a breath, she stretched out to copy his graceful movements. At first she had difficulty timing the strokes of her arms while she raised her head to catch a breath. But with Dru holding her around the waist, she finally caught on to the motions involved in swimming.

"Try doing the same thing, only in reverse," Dru suggested, rolling her onto her back. "Reach above your head and pull the water to your waist and then push it away."

While Dru marveled at her exquisite figure, Tori concentrated on the back stroke. She had gained confidence in her ability to swim rather than flounder

208

and drown. Avoiding deep water, Tori paddled backward and then rolled over to practice the first stroke Dru had taught her.

A faint smile brimmed his lips while he watched the enchanting mermaid skim the surface. Jeezus, she was bewitching, he mused as his hungry eyes absorbed her appetizing form. He had to admit Tori was quick in learning her skills. She had made tremendous progress. Dru well remembered the three times Tori had found herself in water over her head. She had panicked at the prospect of drowning. But now she was self-assured and was gliding across the river, perfecting the motions he had taught her.

While Tori swam back and forth across the channel, Dru walked ashore to retrieve the horses. After unsaddling them, he urged them into the river. Climbing atop his horse, Dru executed a graceful dive and then commanded that Tori do the same.

Having a marvelous time, Tori employed her mare as a springboard and plunged into the clear depths. Ah, what simple pleasures she had been missing all these years! Gliding through the river was like entering another world. Tori almost wished she had been born a fish. What a peaceful existence the fishes lived. There were no men to torment their thoughts and emotions, no one-sided loves to plague their souls . . .

Dru caught Tori to him and grabbed her horse's tail. "Let your mare propel you," he suggested. "Just keep to her side so she doesn't kick you while she's swimming."

Whacking the mare on the rump, Dru watched the steed take her mistress across the river. Tori's carefree laughter wafted across the water, and Dru smiled ruefully. How he wished he could be the reason for the radiant smile that captured Tori's enchanting features. But, he was more the cause of her skeptical and disdainful frowns. Ah well, this was far better than the silence he had endured from her the past week, he supposed.

For the time being, Tori set aside her irritation with Dru and relished every moment in the river. Still tittering in pleasure, Tori grabbed the mare's mane and looped her arms over the steed's sturdy neck to float backward. While the mare treaded back and forth across the channel, Tori drifted beside her, sighing in satisfaction.

The smile that pursed her lips faded when her gaze locked with Dru's. It was like plunging a dagger into her heart. Oh, how she wished there were more to their marriage than obligation. Her swim in the Yellowstone could have been heaven if he truly cared for her . . .

Tori clamped down on that whimsical thought. Dru had already offered her all he had to give, she reminded herself. His love was an elusive dream that would never coincide with reality.

A curious frown plowed Dru's brow when he saw the sparkle vanish from Tori's amethyst eyes. "What's the matter, Chicago?" he wanted to know.

Immediately, she pasted on an artificial smile. "Nothing," she lied. "I'm thoroughly enjoying myself."

To some extent, Dru speculated. But each time she glanced in his direction, he detected the hint of sadness. It reminded him of that naive beauty he had met on the cathedral steps in Illinois. Even then, Dru had longed to erase that rueful expression. And now he would give anything to replace that look with the one he'd seen on her face that night in Des Moines and the entire week that followed. Dru hadn't realized what a special time they had enjoyed together until it had gone. It had become just another phase through which Tori had passed during her metamorphosis. But if Dru could have had his wish, he would have turned back the hands of time to relive those precious days when he and this violet-eyed pixie had been so closely connected.

When Dru turned to lead his steed from the river and dress, Tori sighed in disappointment. She would have

210

preferred to spend another hour swimming and frolicking in the water. But at least now she could enjoy a swim each time they paused for the night, she assured herself. And with a little more practice, she wouldn't have to depend on Dru to come to her rescue if she waded in over her head.

After Tori had stepped into her buckskins, she followed Dru back to camp to see Whong huddled over the tiny fire he had built. The Chinaman's head was draped with a towel and he was inhaling the vapors of honey and only God knew what wild herbs he had rounded up to brew for his stuffy nose. An amused grin settled on Tori's features as she surveyed Whong. The man was completely preoccupied with vaporizing his nostrils.

Thoughtfully, Dru glanced at the rocky hillside behind Whong. "I suggest you move camp closer to the river. There are such things as rock slides, you know."

Whong pulled the towel from his head to stare at the craggy peaks that abounded with loose pebbles and boulders. "Yes, Mr. Surrivan," he replied, bowing from his knees. "As soon as I comprete my treatment, I wirr move our suppries."

"And keep an eye on Tori while I scout the area," Dru commanded as he stepped into the stirrup. He tossed her a smile. "Tonight, if I can find game, we'll dine on something besides beans."

A frown knitted Tori's brow as she watched Dru circle the jutting hill. She could almost swear Dru was trying to get back into her good graces. First it had been the swimming lesson and now he had tempted her with the prospect of dining on meat instead of beans. No doubt, lust was getting the best of him again and he was playing up to her in hopes of gaining the favors of her flesh.

Tori's shoulders slumped dejectedly. She had the feeling a long tormenting night was in store for her. She would have to be on her guard and marshal her defenses. If Dru touched her, she would never be able to resist him.

211

Damn, why was it so hard for her to disguise the love she felt for this man?

Dru could switch his emotions off and on. He had seduced her without feeling emotionally attached to her. Unfortunately, Tori hadn't mastered that skill. And by damned, she wasn't giving in to him tonight or any other night just because he was being nice to her, she promised herself stubbornly.

On that determined thought, Tori ambled off to gather wood for the campfire while Whong completed his ministrations. The smell of honey filled the evening air, mingling with the fragrance of pine and cedar. Tori forced herself to concentrate on the panorama of the mountains instead of the perplexing man who kept her emotions in turmoil. If only she could hold out for another week, they would be in Virginia City and she could take refuge with her father! And then maybe she could forget that blue-eyed rake.

With the kindling placed inside the ring of stones and the larger logs stacked on the riverbank, Tori strode over to Whong to fetch the tinderbox. Tori stifled a giggle when Whong rocked back on his heels, laid back his head, and inhaled a deep breath. The smell of boiled honey hung over the Chinaman like a fog, and it was a wonder to Tori that he could breathe at all. She was beginning to think his experimental antidotes were the *cause* of his sneezing and congestion . . .

Tori's senses came to life when she heard pebbles trickling down from the ledge above them. The low growl of an unseen beast broke the silence. Her apprehensive gaze lifted to scan the timbered ridge, searching for the source of the sound. Horror flashed in her eyes when she spied the monstrous grizzly that had appeared from the canopy of trees above them.

Whong bounded to his feet and whirled toward the

hill. A shocked gasp burst from his lips when he spied the huge creature that towered over them. The shaggy, eight-foot-tall beast turned his hairy head and stared down at him and Tori with dark, beady eyes. The aroma of honey had lured him from his den and he had come to investigate.

Suddenly Whong was babbling in rapid Chinese and he scurried toward the horses, gesturing for Tori to follow him. Tori shot toward her mare without realizing she had moved from her spot.

A vicious growl echoed through the air as the grizzly reared up on his hind legs and swung a huge paw in threat. When he dropped down on all fours, his front feet collided with the loose boulders that lined the ledge. Falling rock pelleted Whong and Tori as they attempted to mount their unsaddled horses. But being an inexperienced rider, Tori was unaware that it was difficult to control a frightened steed that wanted nothing to do with growling grizzlies, either! The mare's shrill whinny split the air, and she pranced sideways, straining against the rope that confined her to the tree.

Whong experienced the same difficulty when he tried to swing onto his nervous steed. He found himself wedged between the braying mule and his skittish horse. A grunt gushed from his lips when the two animals collided, squishing him between them.

Braving a glance at the grizzly, Tori tried desperately to swing onto the wild-eyed mare. Before she could pull herself up, the grizzly lumbered down the steep slope, sending a debris of dirt and rock rolling beneath his feet.

A scream of terror erupted from Tori's lips when the bear caused an avalanche of dirt and rock to tumble down the slope, followed by the grizzly that had lost his footing in the loose rock. Another blood-curdling shriek escaped her lips when Whong was kicked by the frantic mule. The Chinaman staggered backward, his arms flailing wildly about him. He wheeled to regain his balance just as a

213

flood of dirt and rock poured off the ledge, wedging him between the two boulders where he stood.

In horror, Tori watched Whong buckle beneath the debris that tumbled down the last thirty feet of the mountain. And suddenly there was a pile of earth and stone and a cloud of dust where Whong had been standing the previous moment. Screeching Whong's name, Tori dashed toward him, but she came to a skidding halt as the grizzly rolled to his feet. When the snarling bear reared up again, blocking her path, Tori wheeled to dash to safety.

The horses and mules strained against their ropes and finally broke their halters in their frantic attempt to escape. Desperately, Tori lunged to clutch at the first horse that shot past her, but it was impossible to latch on to any of the animals when they raced past her at a dead run.

Tori found herself facing the grizzly alone, counting the deadly, curved claws of his paws and painfully aware of the sharp fangs that protruded from his curled lips. When the ominous creature took a swipe at her with a monstrous paw, Tori dove to the ground and rolled under the cedar bush. Her heart was pounding against her ribs like a sledgehammer, threatening to beat her to death before the grizzly did. Her breath came in short, ragged gasps, very nearly strangling her.

She was going to be mauled by this thousand-pound monster. She knew that as surely as she knew the sun rose in the east. She was going to die an agonizing death and she wouldn't have the chance to see her father or Dru ever again. She and Whong would become two of the many ghosts who roamed the rugged mountains of Yellowstone, howling with the wind . . .

Another terrified scream tripped from her lips when the grizzly whacked at the limbs, shredding them. Frantic, she wriggled backward and then darted toward another nearby bush. The beast's harsh growl rang in Tori's ears as she ran as fast as her legs would carry her.

She asked herself why she was prolonging the inevitable by attempting to flee. She knew she didn't stand a chance against this dangerous creature, but the self-preservation instinct is strong, and it put wings on her feet. Tori ran for her life, knowing her minutes were numbered, knowing she was doomed to endure a bloody, horrifying death . . .

Chapter 19

Dru's heart slammed against his chest as he thundered through the river valley. He had heard Tori's terrified scream reverberating through the trees, heard the pounding of horses' hooves, the rumble of falling rock. His breath lodged in his throat when he galloped back to the site where Whong had made camp and found nothing but a pile of dirt and stone on top of the Chinaman's small campfire.

In a single bound, Dru was off his horse. His astute gaze darted across the pile of rocks, searching for a sign that Whong and Tori had been buried beneath the rubble. Frantically, Dru stumbled over the mound until he spied Whong's pigtail protruding from the debris. Dru clawed at the rocks and dirt to uncover the head that was attached to the queue. Whong was draped facedown between two boulders. A knot the size of an egg swelled upon the back of his dusty head.

In desperation, Dru hooked his arm around the Chinaman's waist to hoist him from the debris. From all indication, Whong was still alive, though thoroughly bruised and battered. The fact that Whong had wedged himself between the two boulders had saved his life. A pocket of air had been trapped beneath him, and the huge boulders had protected him from the blows of bone-crushing stones.

After Dru had laid Whong in the grass he dashed to the river to scoop up a hatful of water. When Dru dumped the water on Whong, he sputtered and choked and sneezed. Groggily, his dark eyes fluttered up to see Dru's concerned face hovering over him.

"You saved my rife *three* times," Whong wheezed, attempting to prop himself on a wobbly elbow.

"Where's Tori?" Dru questioned urgently.

The question brought Whong straight up. He glanced wildly around him. Horrified, he began to rattle in a flurry of Chinese.

"Damnit, in English!" Dru growled. "What happened to Tori?"

"A grizzry set off the rock sride," Whong hurriedly reported before breaking into several sentences in his native tongue. At Dru's sharp command, Whong translated in broken English. "We tried to mount the horses, but I was kicked backward. Mrs. Surrivan tried to save me, but the bear went after her. I don't know what happened after I was buried!"

Leaving Whong to babble in Chinese and nurse the knot on his head, Dru vaulted to his feet. Quickly, he scanned the area, searching for clues to Tori's whereabouts. With his heart drumming, Dru surveyed the broken cedar limbs and finally found bear tracks leading toward the river.

Knowing Tori had faced perilous danger rattled Dru. For a man who was usually cool and calm in the face of adversity, Dru suddenly couldn't live up to his reputation. It was an entirely different matter when it was that blond-haired sprite who confronted catastrophe. Just thinking she might be wounded—or dead—left his soul to bleed. Knowing if she was alive, she would be terrified, scared the living daylights out of Dru.

Feeling as if he were moving in slow motion, Dru jogged along the riverbank with his Winchester clutched in his fist. After running a quarter of a mile, his gaze circled the towering peaks that lined the river. His body tensed when he spied the bear poised on a ledge some two hundred yards away. There was no sign of Tori, but vengeance drove Dru toward the snarling beast. With every step he took, he envisioned Tori's mangled body lying beneath those sharp claws and deadly fangs.

With fiend-ridden haste, Dru scrambled up the rocks, weaving around boulders until he was within rifle range of the monstrous creature. When he heard Tori's whimper, his heart stalled in his chest. Crouching down, Dru took careful aim. As the grizzly pushed up on his hind legs to swat at the boulder that protected Tori, Dru fired. A vicious growl rang through the air when the bullet lodged in the grizzly's leg. He dropped down on all fours to charge at his challenger.

Staring down the barrel, Dru waited until he could aim at the bear's most vulnerable spot. When the grizzly was no more than twenty feet away, Dru squeezed the trigger. The bear stumbled forward and snarled, but he kept coming. Tensely, Dru squinted down the sight of his rifle and took his last shot. This time the grizzly dropped in his tracks.

Dru was on his feet in a flash, circling past the shaggy bear that blocked his path. There, tucked inside a narrow niche of stone that was protected by a boulder sat Tori. Her wide violet eyes were flooded with tears and her cheeks were stained with dirt. The shoulder of her shirt had been shredded by a near brush with deadly claws.

When Tori realized it was Dru who was looming over her instead of the growling grizzly, she bounded from her niche and flew into his arms, wailing like a frightened child. She knew Dru loathed tears, but she was too terrified to compose herself. She just wanted him to hold her and go on holding her until she regained control of her shattered emotions.

"It's okay now," Dru soothed as he cuddled her quaking body in his protective arms.

It wasn't okay. Tori was a mass of quivers. Flashes of the bear's relentless pursuit of her still shot across her mind. Even after Dru ordered her to inhale a steadying breath, she couldn't stop shaking. Her legs felt like rubber.

"Whong!" Tori finally managed to choke out through the gasping sobs. "He was buried alive!"

"I pulled him from the rubble," Dru informed her as he brushed a kiss across her puckered brow. "He'll be fine."

Her shaky body slumped against his, and another flood of tears gushed from her eyes. Dru scooped her up in his arms gently and sidestepped down the slope toward the river. When he set Tori in the grass, she curled herself in a tight ball and bled another bucket of tears.

Dru retrieved his handkerchief, dipped it in the water, and then smoothed it across Tori's flushed cheeks. A faint smile touched his lips as he wiped away the shimmering tears that trickled from the corners of her violet eyes. Her moist lashes swept up to peer at him, and Dru fell into those shimmering depths.

Suddenly the obstacles between them fell away. Having come so close to death, Tori's ordeal had made her vividly aware of how precious each moment was. Her senses had come to life in the face of adversity, and even now the masculine fragrance of Dru's cologne seemed to hover over her like a fog. The sight of him was a treasure, and she found herself memorizing every craggy feature, the touch of his hand, the appealing way his doehide shirt strained across his massive chest.

The impulse to feel his sensuous lips playing softly on hers was strong. Tori wanted to replace the nightmare with a sweet dream, to communicate this love that was bottled up inside her. Her trembling hand lifted to sketch the crow's-feet that sprayed from his sky-blue eyes, the smile lines that bracketed his mouth. She studied him as if he were a priceless portrait that had been stashed from her sight for years.

Her forefinger drifted over his lips to swirl over the dark matting of hair that peeked from the lacings of his

220

shirt. Stubborn pride bowed down to the needs that lurked just beneath the surface. Tori wanted his kiss as much as she had wanted to escape the grizzly. She was willing to accept whatever Dru could offer. She longed to be one with him, to feel passion instead of fear, to feel wanted instead of threatened.

"Make the world go away . . ." she whispered brokenly.

When her petal-soft lips parted in invitation, Dru braced his arms on either side of her and followed her to the ground. He bent his dark head to take her mouth under his, savoring the sweet taste of her. All the pent-up emotion that had sustained him during his frantic search transformed into hungry passion. Dru had to force himself to be gentle. He yearned to devour her, to absorb her delicious body into his. But he knew Tori needed a tender touch, not ravishing passion, after what she'd been through. Dru promised himself he would kiss and caress away each lingering fear that hounded her, to cherish her.

And cherish her he did. His hands worshipped her exquisite body as he removed her garments. Adoringly, he massaged away her tension, replacing fear with warm, tingling pleasure. He spread kisses as soft and light as a butterfly's velvet wings over her cheeks and throat. He offered caresses as gentle as a breeze. He murmured comforting words that drowned out the memories of the growling grizzly and tore all thought from her mind.

As the sun bowed its head behind the craggy peaks and darkness slid down the slopes, Dru made love to Tori as if there were no tomorrow. And Tori was fully aware of the fact that for her, there almost hadn't been. She responded to Dru's masterful touch, reveling in the feel of his powerful body brushing intimately against hers. She rediscovered every muscular inch of his flesh, showering him with a love that refused to die, one that had always been his for the taking. Tori gave herself up to the wild, soul-shattering sensations, feeding on them,

221

marveling at them as if they were more precious than gold.

Dru couldn't still his roaming hands for even a moment. While Tori caressed him, he cradled her in his arms, assuring himself that she was alive and well when she could have so easily perished. Her hands and lips wandered everywhere, tasting and touching him. She filled up his senses until his emotions were overflowing with the sight, taste, and feel of her pliant body molded tightly to his.

Greedily, his lips suckled at the throbbing peaks of her breasts while his fingertips swirled over her abdomen, sensitizing every silky inch of flesh he touched. His kisses skimmed down her ribs as he whispered his need for her, letting her hear his words as well as feel them vibrating on her skin. His fingertips flooded over her hips and thighs in an all-consuming caress that branded her as his own. He memorized the feel of her satiny skin beneath his inquiring hands, savored the taste of her on his lips.

His intimate fondling left Tori gasping for air. Her trembling body surged toward his, starved for more than his kisses and caresses, aching to fulfill the wild needs and the splendor she had discovered in his arms. She was prepared to sacrifice her last breath to feel his steel-honed body molded to hers, to soar past the stars into a universe of fiery splendor.

Dru braced himself above Tori, staring down into those luminous eyes that were alive with passion. He could never remember feeling this way about a woman— so incredibly hungry, so fiercely possessive, so bedeviled. He peered down at her and his body shuddered with indescribable need.

Trembling with barely restrained desire, he came to her, letting the gentleness he had displayed earlier buckle to the hot-blooded passions that boiled inside him. His body cried out for hers as if she were a part of him that had been missing for days on end. He was mindless to all except the ardent cravings that undulated through every fiber of his being. But Tori didn't seem to care that he was consumed by impatience; she was engulfed by an urgency that equaled his fervent passion. She met each deep, demanding thrust, clinging to him in wild abandon.

Their desire for each other was uncontrollable. Dru quivered with the maddening needs she instilled in him. The tumultuous emotions that riveted his body screamed out for sweet release. He could feel himself letting go with his body, mind, and soul, feel himself drowning in a sea of bubbly sensations. He gave himself up to the splendorous moment that defied description, clinging as tightly to her as she was clinging to him. His masculine strength became hers. He could feel his energy flowing from his taut body to hers and back again. His soul forged to hers, needing more than physical satisfaction, craving the sublime pleasure that transcended reality . . .

Like an avalanche, the sensations that had piled atop him came tumbling down, pelleting him with convulsive tremors that shook his body and rocked his soul. Desperately, Dru clutched Tori to him, shuddering against her. Streams of ecstasy drenched him, numbing him to all except the rapture of loving this blond-haired nymph.

After what seemed forever, Dru managed a few sane thoughts, but he still couldn't muster the will to move away. Having come so close to losing Tori, Dru wanted to savor each treasured second of their time together.

Languidly, Tori's fingertips migrated over the tendons of Dru's back and then drifted over the scar on his ribs. She hadn't meant to invite his caresses or to succumb to her wanton desires. But the thought of never seeing or holding him again had overwhelmed her while she made her frantic dash to safety with the grizzly on her heels. All the while that she had crouched in the narrow space between the boulders, Dru's handsome face hovered above her. She had wanted to live to see him again. Her love for him had been her salvation . . .

"Feeling better, Chicago?" Dru whispered against the alabaster column of her throat. "*I certainly am.*" He expelled a sigh. "I was—"

Dru had managed to do it again—say the wrong thing, that is. Tori took immediate offense to his carelessly worded remark. It sounded as if Dru had made love to her because he believed passion was the soothing balm that healed all wounds. Whong had his remedies for what ailed him and Dru obviously had his!

Maybe Tori had left the impression that she wanted nothing more than a moment's distraction after her frightening ordeal. But she felt far more than distracted and she wanted Dru to experience more than simple satisfaction. Damnit, why had he said anything at all? She would have been more content if he would have held her without making conversation.

As far as Tori was concerned, Dru would never say the right thing at the right moment, at least not until he whispered those three little words that said it all. But she had the sinking feeling the phrase—*I love you*—wasn't in his vocabulary.

Before Dru could complete his sentence, Tori shoved him away and sat up. "Is that all there is with you? Feeling better? Is your only concern feeding your lust of appetite?"

Dru frowned at the harsh tone of her voice and the fuming glare she leveled at him. "I was scared as hell, if you want to know," he snapped back at her. "I thought I'd lost you and I—"

"Ah, such a great loss," Tori interrupted him with a sarcastic smirk. "If I had perished, I would have been one less responsibility for you to keep track of. I can't imagine that you would have minded all that much."

"Not have minded?" he parroted. "What kind of stupid remark is that? You know I . . ." His voice trailed off and he floundered over the words that had involuntarily darted to the tip of his tongue.

"What is it I know, Montana?" she prodded, peering into the chiseled face that was submerged in shadows. "That lovemaking is second nature to you and that, being your wife, you expect me to provide passion when the mood strikes you? Or did you nobly make love to me just now because you thought I needed the distraction after the grizzly came within a hairbreadth of ripping me to shreds?"

"Why is it that you have to dissect everything?" Dru muttered in frustration. "We wanted each other just now because we arouse each other. Why can't you just accept what is between us and enjoy it?"

"I can't because I . . ."

Tori clamped down on her tongue and exhaled an annoyed breath. She had promised herself never to confess her love again to this infuriating man. No matter what she said or did, she couldn't make him love her. There was no sense beating her head against a wall, no sense expecting Dru to fall in love with her. He was satisfied with passion for passion's sake, and he wanted nothing more because he obviously wasn't accustomed to commitments to women—even if the woman happened to be his wife.

"Because what?" Dru quizzed her. His index finger tracked over her soft lips while he studied her from beneath a veil of thick lashes. "What is it you want from me, Chicago? My heart?"

He tipped her head back and a curious smile hovered on his lips. "If I gave you my heart, would you wear it as a prize around your neck like your pearls?"

Tori ran her fingertips over the strand of pearls that encircled her throat. "It would be a nice addition to my necklace, don't you think?" she taunted for pure spite.

"Would that be all you wanted with my heart, minx?" he queried, staring deeply into her amethyst eyes to search out the secrets of her soul. "Tell me, what does a woman like you want with a man like me? Would you cherish my affection or flaunt it?"

225

The big oaf! Didn't he know how precious his love was to her? Why did he have to have such a distorted view of love and passion? Why did he think of women only in terms of pleasure and possession? Probably because he had never had anything except brief, shallow affairs with women, Tori diagnosed. He knew nothing else and he behaved accordingly.

"And what would *you* do with my heart if I gave it to you?" she questioned his question.

"That depends on what *you* did with *mine*," he countered with a cryptic smile that infuriated her to no end.

Dru was a hopeless cause! He had braved every danger known to man and tested his skills to the very limits. But he was a coward when it came to affairs of the heart. This conversation was going nowhere, and so was this ill-fated marriage of theirs. Dru was far more wary of being hurt than she was, for crying out loud! And she was the one who had been burned once already, not him!

"For starters I'd throw your heart in the river to determine if it sank like the rock it is," Tori muttered before grabbing her discarded clothes.

"And then what?" he continued in a serious tone.

Agitated by his persistence, Tori squirmed into her buckskins and stepped away. The man was blind and stupid if he didn't realize she would cherish the gift of his love, now and forevermore. And he *was* blind, deaf and stupid, she decided. She had told him how she felt once before and he had scoffed at her confession. She wasn't about to give this skeptical rake the opportunity to do it again.

"I'd fry your heart and eat it for supper instead of the can of beans I'm about to ingest," she grumbled as she stalked away. Tori paused to glance back at the sleek, muscular giant who lounged stark-bone naked on the riverbank. "There is no sense speculating on what I would do with your heart if I had possession of it," she shouted. "Let's face it, Montana. You don't have one.

226

You are too cynical of women to trust their intentions. And if you have to ask what I would do with your love, then you haven't bothered to get to know me these past several weeks!"

"I'm not as cold and uncaring as you think," he called after her. "I don't trust what I don't understand. I'm cautious by nature and suspicious by habit."

Tori wheeled about to glare at him. "And just why is that? Do you think I would be unfaithful to you, that I wouldn't return your affection if you offered it?"

"Would you?" he asked quietly.

The fact that he had to ask infuriated her. "You are absolutely impossible!" she exploded like a keg of blasting powder.

"What the hell did I say wrong now?" he grumbled in frustration.

"What did you say *right* . . . ever?" Tori spumed.

"What is it that you really want from me?" Dru demanded to know. "Can't you just say it flat out without talking in circles and mocking my questions?"

"Smart as you are, figure it out all by yourself," Tori hurled at him. "And if you can't, then it isn't worth the trouble for me to explain it to you!"

What did he take her for anyway? A gamin who toyed with men for the sport of it and then carelessly discarded them? If he did, he was obviously laboring under the ridiculous notion that all women were gold diggers and adventuresses who had no regard for a man's feelings.

"You are the one who is impossible," Dru growled as he stuffed his leg into his breeches and fastened them around his waist. "I asked a simple question and you refuse to answer. I need to know if you want this marriage of ours to last or not."

Tori threw up her hands in a gesture of futility and stamped off. Muttering under his breath, Dru yanked on his shirt. He didn't know what he felt for that feisty minx. Relief that she was alive? Most certainly. Satisfaction with the fiery passion they evoked in each other? Most definitely. But blast it, the way Tori had behaved the past week, Dru wasn't sure what she expected from him—to be loved or to be left alone.

Their complicated relationship was as tangled as jungle vines. Sometimes he let himself believe that she did care for him in her own weird way. And sometimes he swore her greatest pleasure in life came from annoying him. This was the strangest dalliance he'd ever had with a woman, that was for sure! Tori never made any specific demands on him, and because she hadn't, Dru wasn't sure where he stood or if she cared enough to bother.

Weeks ago, she said she loved him. He hadn't believed her, which was a good thing because the fickle sprite had retracted her confession soon after. If she had meant what she said, she would have been more persistent and certainly more loving than she had been of late, wouldn't she?

Godamighty, if he and Tori didn't get their true feelings for each other out in the open and soon, there would be too many external influences pushing and pulling on them. But try as he might, Dru couldn't figure Tori out. He honestly believed she was better satisfied hating him than she would ever be loving him. He seemed to bring out the worst in that gorgeous pixie and they couldn't even have a conversation these days without it evolving into a shouting match!

After rounding up the horses and the mule, Dru ambled back to camp. He found Whong fussing over Tori and sympathizing about her ordeal with the grizzly. She seemed perfectly content with Whong's company, and Dru was in no mood to find himself dragged into another argument. Everything he said set Tori off. He looked at her wrong, and it put her in a snit. She seemed quite comfortable and satisfied hating him.

Keeping to himself, Dru sank down cross-legged to munch on beans. The rabbit he'd shot for supper had been absconded by some unidentified varmint and the incident with the bear had spoiled everyone's appetite. Sullenly, Dru ate his beans and didn't say a word.

After, Dru stared for two hours into the small campfire that provided warmth from the evening chill—coming from the high elevations as well as Tori's cold shoulder that dripped icicles. Over and over, he contemplated his argument with Tori. He wondered what he was going to do if he *did* fall in love with that sassy minx. He also wondered if he already had and he was just too damned stubborn to admit it for fear of having his feelings trampled on. Tori had become proficient at concealing her emotions, and Dru was never quite sure what she was thinking. Godamighty, how he wished he could read that woman's complicated mind. If she did love him as she once said she did, she had the most peculiar way of showing it!

Chapter 20

"How much longer do we have to tolerate these deplorable conditions?" Gwen groused as she struggled in vain to bat away the swarm of pesky insects that had descended upon her.

"The worst part of the trip is yet to come," Edgar told his grumbling wife. "If you wish to remain at Fort Laramie while Hubert and I continue on, I will . . ."

"Remain here on this remote outpost of civilization?" Gwen squawked in horror. "I will do nothing of the kind, Edgar. How dare you even voice such a distasteful suggestion!"

"The commander indicated there have been Indian uprisings in the area," Edgar reported grimly. "It would be safer if you . . ."

"I'm not staying behind and that is that!" Gwen muttered in irritation. "You tell that bumpkin commander to muster a military escort for us. The reason for the cavalry being located in the godforsaken place is to protect and guide travelers through these savages' stomping grounds. Why the government hasn't confined those heathens to a reservation is beyond me. They shouldn't be allowed to run around loose!"

"I don't imagine the Sioux and Crow would take kindly to the idea of being herded onto reservations," Edgar replied. "After all, this is their land, not the government's, even if politicians behave as if it is. And I did request an escort from the commander, but he maintains that—"

Gwendolyn cut him off with an indignant snort. "You don't *request* anything of these bumpkins, Edgar. You *demand*. Assert your weight and threaten the man's position. You've got all sorts of important contacts in the government. Offer the commander a bribe—anything. Just get us out of this disgusting camp before I shrivel up like a dried weed!" Gwen smacked the mosquito that had landed on Edgar's forehead. "This blistering wind and these infuriating insects are ruining my skin. I'm sick to death of living like a barbarian. Do something!"

Heaving a weary sigh that was indicative of a man who was forced to call upon his long-suffering patience to deal with a shrewish woman, Edgar pivoted on his heels to confront the commander of the post. The journey hadn't been easy, but Gwen had made no attempt to adapt without the luxuries to which she had grown so accustomed, and she refused to settle for less. They had traveled in the Cassidys' private railroad cars to Council Bluffs and had purchased an enclosed carriage and supply wagon to make the next leg of the journey to Fort Laramie. But still Gwen moaned and groaned about the conditions. As devoted as Edgar was to his wife, he was beginning to wonder if Caleb hadn't gotten the best end of this arrangement. Caleb had his freedom to live life as he pleased. But Edgar had Gwendolyn. Ten years earlier, Edgar had been prepared to do anything to take his childhood sweetheart as his wife. Now he was beginning to wonder if he hadn't gotten exactly what he deserved for being so taken with the comely blonde. Gwen was making a difficult journey over sparcely populated country positively unbearable!

While Edgar marched off to secure an army escort to accompany them northwest, Gwen complained about living like a victim of the Stone Age. Hubert, who had adapted to the situation no better than Gwen, sat brooding in his seat. His fury against Dru Sullivan had festered the past three weeks into a mutinous hatred. He could almost see Dru laughing in that taunting way of his—just as the varmint had done after he had knocked Hubert off his feet with a meaty fist the previous year. That bastard was going to pay for the insults and degradations Hubert had suffered, he vowed stormily. It was bad enough that Hubert had to muck about like a commoner during this trek west. But having Dru spirit Victoria away had Hubert cursing a blue streak. He would bankrupt Dru Sullivan, he swore he would! That scoundrel would sacrifice all his worldly possessions and compensate for the hell Hubert had been through. And shortly after Hubert ruined Dru financially, he intended to drag the blackguard onto the gallows and have him publicly executed before tossing his body to a pack of starving wolves!

Chomping on that vindictive thought, Hubert whacked the oversized mosquito that was trying to make a meal of him. Damned pesky insects. And damn Dru Sullivan to hell and back!

Home at last! Dru paused on the ridge overlooking Virginia City. The bustling town hugged the hillside that was draped in the purple shadows of the towering precipices of the mountain ranges. Virginia City, which had originally been named Varina in honor of Jefferson Davis's wife, was the hubbub of fourteen miles of crowded, feverish mining activity. Millions of dollars of gold had already been taken from the area. Thankfully, Dru and Caleb had found their generous share and had put it to good use. Now there were fortunes to be made in providing goods and services for the fourteen thousand miners who milled around the area of Alder Gulch near Stinking Creek and Last Chance Gulch. Banking, freighting, and merchandising were doing booming businesses in the region, and dozens of saloons had been erected to quench the miners' thirsts. The "light ladies" who followed the "heavy gold" had set up cribs and parlor houses and were making a killing off love-starved men.

There had been a great deal of lawlessness and turbulence the past two years, but the Vigilante Committee, of which Dru was a charter member, had sent twenty-two of the toughest undesirables to their graves and brought the rowdy town under control. There still were, and always would be, a few diehards like Tyrone Webster who were out to bleed miners and citizens dry in every devious way imaginable. But for the most part, Virginia City had been tamed after the notorious Plummer gang had been duly hanged for their numerous crimes the previous year. Although the town had its faults, Dru was content to be a part of the history-making activity in the new territory and to own a ranch that lay in the spectacular valleys.

Heaving a thankful sigh, Dru's eyes made another thorough sweep of the timber-clad mountains and bustling city. Dru felt as if he had been gone forever. During that time, his emotions had been put through a meat grinder, thanks to that female cyclone he had felt obliged to marry. Just wait until he got Caleb alone, Dru thought resentfully. He had a few choice words to say to that sneaky old goat!

Dru's eyes were magnetically drawn back to the beauty in buckskins. Extended hours in the sun had tanned Tori's complexion to a warm brown blush and highlighted the silver-blond tendrils of her hair. Her indoctrination into the wilds was complete. She had become proficient at riding, reasonably capable with a revolver and rifle. She had learned to confront danger in various forms and she had emerged from her shell.

That was what Caleb had wanted, for Dru to ensure she could adapt to life in the rowdy gold town in the mountains. Only Dru hadn't counted on becoming quite so attached to his saucy little protegée. They had endured a great many ordeals together, made too many memories that were slow in fading. Dru had awakened to the sight of violet eyes shimmering in the sunlight and he had fallen asleep at night with a need that he hadn't been able to appease since their rendezvous beside the Yellowstone River.

Casting his frustrated deliberations aside, Dru nudged his steed down the slope. He could detect the expression of anticipation in Tori's eyes. She was anxious to catch up on lost time with her father. Knowing how she felt about being forced into marriage, Dru predicted she would employ the long separation from Caleb as an excuse to remain with him indefinitely. Dru could feel himself losing Tori bit by excruciating bit, and it left an unfamiliar emptiness gnawing at his belly. Godamighty, he had grown so accustomed to having that feisty sprite around that he couldn't imagine a day without her in it.

He'd adapt soon enough, Dru told himself confidently. He would have a zillion chores to occupy him. Why, he probably wouldn't even miss her. *Famous last words* came the quiet, mocking voice from somewhere deep inside him.

Dru stubbornly chose to ignore the soft murmurings of his heart.

Caleb paced around the parlor of his home that was attached to the lobby of the hotel. Grumbling, he massaged his left arm that he'd cradled in a sling for eight days. Damn, it had been a long, hectic three months and now Caleb regretted sending Dru off on the tedious journey to Chicago. Tyrone Webster, greedy, vengeful scoundrel that he was, had resorted to violent tactics to convince Caleb to sell the hotel and restaurant that was making money hand over fist.

With Dru out of town, Tyrone had ordered his band of cutthroats out of hiding, and they had gone on the rampage. After the Plummer gang had been rounded up and hanged the previous year, crime had declined. But for every outlaw hanged in the gold mining towns, it seemed two more worthless cretins appeared to replace him. Gold lured bandits and gamblers like cats on the trail of fresh milk, and Tyrone had become impatient to have his hands on every productive business in town.

Being the avaricious scalawag he was, Tyrone had forced one saloon owner to sell out to him ten months earlier. The man who previously owned the town's most frequented tavern was prone to gamble when he had a mite too much to drink. Rumor had it that Tyrone had cheated at poker and won the saloon from its proprietor, who now worked as a janitor at the establishment he had once owned. Of course, no one had been able to prove that Tyrone had cheated, and those who spread the rumor had found themselves assaulted in dark alleys.

But owning the saloon and the blacksmith shop wasn't enough to satisfy Tyrone Webster. He had visions of taking the whole town under his management and raising prices on everything that could possibly be sold to prospectors. Tyrone had even cast his greedy eyes on the Sullivan Ranch, which had become the most prosperous cattle business in the territory. No doubt Tyrone viewed the spacious stone-and-timber home, which was the headquarters for the five brothers, as the perfect meeting place for his gang of thieves, who preyed on the stage, unsuspecting miners, and other passersby.

Two weeks earlier, Tyrone had paid Caleb a call, offering to raise the price for the sale of the hotel and restaurant. Caleb had insisted that he had rejected the other four offers and that there wasn't enough gold in the hills to buy his establishments. Tyrone had lost his temper and issued a few threats which Caleb countered by tossing several accusations and insisting that Dru would take charge of the town's Vigilante Committee the instant he returned.

It had been a stupid thing to say, Caleb thought in retrospect. Two nights later, an unidentified assassin had taken shots at Caleb when he rode toward the Sullivan Ranch. One bullet had caught him in the shoulder and sent him tumbling from his horse. And while Caleb was being patched up by the physician, Caleb learned that Billy-Bob Sullivan had also been bushwhacked. The youngest Sullivan had happened onto a group of thieves who were in the process of rustling Bar S cattle, and Billy-Bob had attempted to take them on single-handed.

Sure as hell, Dru would be chewing Caleb up one side and down the other when he returned to Montana. Dru hadn't wanted to go to Chicago in the first place. But Caleb had manipulated him and provided extra incentive by informing Dru that Tori was about to marry his archrival from Chicago. He hadn't turned down the chance to even the score with that swindling cattle buyer who had practically robbed Dru blind when he drove his herd to the stock yards in Illinois . . .

Caleb glanced up when a quiet rap rattled the door. Cautiously, he reached for his revolver. Caleb had become wary of late. As much as he hated to admit it, Tyrone's death threats had gotten to him. The sneaky bastard always made certain there were no witnesses to accuse him of crimes, but those who crossed Tyrone invariably suffered for their defiance.

"Come in," Caleb called before ducking behind his desk for protection, should he find himself in need of it.

The door eased open and Tori glanced around the seemingly empty room. Finally, a bushy head appeared from the edge of the desk.

"Oh, my . . ." Bewildered, Caleb rose to full stature, his wide brown eyes focused on the enchanting young woman who was garbed in buckskins and whose tangled blond hair tumbled over her shoulders like a shimmering cascade. "Tori . . . ?"

Caleb marveled at the incredible transformation his little girl had undergone. Even more than before, he resented the years Gwen had deprived him of being with his daughter. That woman! Caleb cursed her vehemently.

237

He would never forgive Gwen for keeping Tori from him.

"Papa?" Tori's violet eyes flooded over the tall, stocky figure of a man whose left arm was cradled in a sling.

The miles and years that had separated them were etched on Caleb's weather-beaten features. He looked at least twenty years older than the portrait Tori had carried in her mind. All the repressed memories swamped her like a gigantic tidal wave. She remembered how lively and rambunctious her father had been with her, how he made her giggle with irrepressible laughter and teased her about her childish antics. Gwen had always scolded Caleb for rolling and tumbling with Tori on the carpet as if she were a rough and rowdy little boy. But Tori adored all the attention she had received from her father. And when Caleb disappeared from Tori's life, she had turned her frustrations inward and climbed into a shell that had not burst open until she met Dru Sullivan.

Huge, shimmering tears welled up in Tori's eyes as she darted into her father's outstretched arms. Even Caleb's eyes misted with sentiment while he squeezed the stuffing out of his long-lost but never-forgotten daughter. He had feared Tori would resent being snatched from her secure world in high society and toted into the wilds. But she didn't seem the least bit disappointed to be in Montana . . . in her father's arms . . .

Finally, Caleb set Tori away from him to survey the shapely woman who was bleeding a river of tears. "Let me look at you, baby," he insisted. His loving gaze ran the full length of her comely figure, marveling at the dazzling beauty who possessed her mother's fair complexion and elegant features. "My, you're all grown up!"

His gaze landed on the string of pearls that still encircled Tori's neck. A look of recognition flickered in his eyes. "Did you put those on just to remind me of years past?"

"I never take them off," Tori assured him. "Each one is a precious memory." Muffling a sniff, she quoted

Robert Roger's poem that she had read during her studies and had memorized.

> "'The hours I spent with thee,
>   dear heart,
> Are a string of pearls to
>   me;
> I count them over, every one
>   apart,
> My rosary, my rosary.'"

Tori's gaze slid to Dru, wishing she could tell him that the words of the poem applied to him as well as her father. But Tori knew Dru didn't care that her string of pearls carried a double sentimental value these days.

The pleased smile that pursed Caleb's lips wilted into disappointment when he noticed the wedding band that encircled her finger. Damn, it was apparent that Dru had been unable to reach Chicago in time to stop the ceremony. Confound "that woman," she had purposely neglected to inform Caleb until it was too late for him to halt the marriage.

"You have a very fine daughter, Mr. Fremming," Whong complimented. He blew his nose into his handkerchief and then bowed respectfully. "I'm sure you are very proud of Tori. And Mr. Surrivan and I are preased that we could deriver her to you."

Caleb's hazy gaze lifted above Tori's head to smile at the short Chinaman and the towering giant who lingered in the open door. Dru was studying the sling on Caleb's arm with curiosity. Then his gaze shifted to Tori momentarily before it drifted back to Caleb's satisfied expression.

"Thank you for bringing my little girl to me," Caleb murmured with emotion. He dabbed his eyes with his kerchief and grinned wryly. "I guess I'll have to stop calling her my little girl . . ." Caleb gave her another affectionate squeeze. "She's all grown up and even more lovely than I imagined she would be."

Thus far, Dru had said nothing. He merely leaned casually against the doorjamb. His keen blue eyes darted from Caleb's wounded arm to his leathery face and then to Tori's enchanting features.

"Dru? Are you all right?" Caleb questioned after a moment.

Hell no, he wasn't all right! There were several troubled thoughts simultaneously buzzing through his mind, and he didn't like the implications of any of them!

"What happened to your arm?" he demanded, gesturing toward the sling.

"Our mutual friend Webster and his henchmen have been on the rampage," Caleb grumbled, soured by the topic of conversation. "The last time Tyrone tried to buy me out, I flatly refused his offer and he had some of his thugs ambush me. But of course, I can't prove who was responsible."

Tori silently seethed at the news. She made herself a mental note to seek out this Webster character and issue a few threats of her own after he had assaulted her beloved father. Tori had traveled halfway across the country to be reunited with him and she would not have some ruthless scoundrel trying to remove Caleb from her life permanently! The very idea!

Caleb shifted uneasily from one foot to the other. He dreaded informing Dru of his youngest brother's collision with disaster. Dru felt responsible for his family, especially Billy-Bob who still lived with Dru. The boy had nearly bled to death before John-Henry found him lying in a crumpled heap in the meadow. Billy-Bob had been bedridden for two weeks and was lucky to be alive at all.

"There has been a lot of rustling going on lately, too," he reported, watching a black scowl swallow Dru's rugged features. "Billy-Bob happened on a gang of thieves, but he'll be back on his feet in another week."

Dru felt as if someone had doubled a fist and punched

him in the midsection. "How bad was he hit?"

Caleb's expression was grim. "He took a slug in the ribs, but Doc said he was young and healthy and he would recover."

Without a word, Dru spun on his heels and stalked through the corridor that led to the hotel lobby. He was spurred by the murderous desire to confront Tyrone, who would have the perfect alibi, just like he always did. Although Dru was anxious to see for himself that Billy-Bob was alive and recuperating from his near brush with catastrophe, he itched to confront Webster. Giving way to the temptation, Dru made a beeline toward the Queen High Saloon. After he eased his frustration with Webster, Dru would bound into the saddle and ride to the ranch, he promised himself.

When Dru sailed out the door like a flying carpet, Tori stared after him, her heart dangling around her knees. Dru hadn't even bothered to say good-bye or to ask her if she wanted to go with him. She would have rejected the offer, of course, but the least he could have done was asked! Although she had every intention of staying with Caleb, it hurt to know Dru didn't care what she planned to do. Obviously, he was relieved to dump her in her father's lap and put some distance between them after having her underfoot for almost six weeks.

"I expect it was a rough trip," Caleb speculated as he led Tori toward the sofa and urged her down beside him. "You probably didn't want to see me again, but . . . well . . . I was afraid you despised me and I wanted the chance to tell my side of the story before you began your new life with your husband."

"I wrote to you often," Tori sighed as she laid her head on her father's broad shoulder. When Caleb's mouth dropped open, she peeked up at him through thick, moist lashes. "It seems Mother withheld both the mail going out and coming in. Dru assured me that you had tried to correspond with me and that I never replied. All these years I thought you were happy to have me out of

241

your life."

"Why that devious . . ." Caleb burst into a string of indecipherable epithets to Gwen's name and he didn't let up for a full minute.

Tori reached up to smooth the agitated frown from her father's ruddy face. "None of that matters now, Papa. I'm glad you sent for me. Seeing you again makes up for the misunderstandings and the long journey."

Caleb let out his breath in a rush. "Even if you were forced to sacrifice the luxuries of Edgar's ritzy palace in Chicago to visit me?"

"The trip has been an enlightening experience," Tori confessed. "But Dru taught me to survive when I found myself out of my element. And I'm not the least bit sorry I came."

Caleb couldn't help himself. He gave Tori another heart-felt squeeze that squashed her nose against his shoulder. "Lord, it's good to have you here, baby. I regret every moment I've spent away from you and we're going to make up for all those years of separation."

Tori settled back against the sofa to quiz Caleb on his ordeal with Tyrone Webster and on every facet of his life since the day he left home. Although she was frustrated by her rocky relationship with Dru, she was delighted to be with her father, and she relished every moment she spent with him. He cleared up all the vindictive untruths Gwendolyn had fed Tori. Even though Tori tried to be forgiving and objective, she found herself siding with Caleb and sorely resenting the lies her mother had told her the past ten years. In her estimation, Gwen had treated Caleb abominably.

Caleb was having his sweet revenge at last as he told Tori how much he had despaired over the surprise divorce and the lack of communication between himself and his daughter. Gwen had kept Tori a prisoner in a web of carefully concocted lies that made Gwen look the victim instead of Caleb.

Even though there was trouble brewing in Virginia

242

City and expected complications in the form of the Cassidys trekking west from Chicago, Caleb was a contented man. He had been reunited with his daughter. And what a lovely young lady she had become! Damn, if only Dru could have abducted Tori before she married that weasel Hubert Carrington Frazier II, Caleb would have been absolutely delighted!

Purposely, Caleb avoided the subject of Tori's wedding. It wasn't a topic that appealed to him. And if Caleb had his way, Tori would remain with him instead of her stuffy, social-minded mother and her wealthy stepfather. As for Hubert Frazier, Caleb didn't want to think about him just now. The very thought curdled his stomach. When Caleb had met the young upstart ten years earlier, Hubert was a skinny, spoiled pipsqueak who threw tantrums when he didn't get his way. According to Dru, Hubert hadn't changed all that much in the last decade. Now he was a full-grown spoiled pipsqueak who threw vindictive tantrums and tried to cheat everyone every chance he got. It was a shame Caleb hadn't thought to have Dru abduct Tori the previous year when he trailed cattle to Chicago. If he had, perhaps Tori wouldn't have wound up married to that boorish aristocrat!

Tyrone Webster jerked his head up when Dru Sullivan burst through the door without announcing himself. The vicious snarl that puckered Dru's tanned face caused Tyrone to grimace apprehensively. Dru hadn't come at a good time. Tyrone was without reinforcements to support him. Stumbling on that thought, Tyrone grabbed for his pistol, but Dru, lightning quick with his Colt, had already drawn and aimed before Tyrone fumbled to retrieve his revolver.

With his pistol trained on Tyrone's chest, Dru stormed across the office, reached over the desk, and jerked Tyrone out of his chair. "My little brother had damned well better be alive and well or you're a dead man," Dru growled into Tyrone's face.

Tyrone sputtered to catch his breath while Dru twisted his shirt around his neck. In desperation, he reached up to unclench Dru's fingers from the collar of his expensive silk shirt and choked on his last ounce of air.

"You have no right to threaten me," he chirped. "I had nothing to do with your brother's accident."

"Accident?" Dru scoffed caustically. "There are no accidents in Virginia City—only the ambushes and bushwhackings that you instigate."

Straightening his costly shirt and jacket, Tyrone drew himself up proudly, even though he darted glances at Dru's Colt at irregular intervals. "You and Flemming are always quick to accuse me of wrongdoing simply because you have taken a dislike to me. And if that federal marshal ever shows up, I intend to press charges against both of you for defamation of character and unwarranted threats of retaliation."

A menacing smile bracketed Dru's mouth while he breathed down Tyrone's skinny neck. Dru couldn't imagine why he had suffered this conniving blackguard to live so long. The world would have been a far better place without Webster in it.

"You have no character to defame," Dru replied with a smirk. "And I wouldn't be the least bit surprised to learn that you're the reason the marshal hasn't shown up yet. It's to your advantage that he doesn't, considering how you browbeat and ambush your competition."

"I take offense at your accusations!" Tyrone blustered. His feral features shriveled into a sour frown.

"And I take offense at having my brother shot down when your cutthroats tried to steal our cattle," Dru countered in an ominous tone. "If there are other incidents, if one of my family or Caleb suffers another 'accident' because of you, I will make certain you aren't around to cause anyone trouble ever again."

A taunting smile curled Tyrone's thin lips. "Do you

intend to call out the Vigilante Committee? You know perfectly well that the territorial governor, Sidney Edgerton, frowns on taking the law into one's own hands. He'd have you put away."

A slow smile rippled across Dru's bronzed features. "And what a pity that you wouldn't be around to see me punished. You'd still be just as dead . . ." Dru looked the scrawny scoundrel up and down, disliking everything about him. "I'll give you the benefit of the doubt for the last time, Webster. If my brother and I have to take on your brigand of thieves, we will. But you have my guarantee that you'll be the first man cut down. I always did believe in starting at the top and working my way down when it came to weeding out the undesirables in the territory." Piercing blue eyes bombarded Tyrone. "You've been duly warned."

With that, Dru backed toward the door, his pistol still trained on Tyrone's heaving chest. When the door eased shut behind Dru, Tyrone collapsed in his chair to rake a shaky hand through his hair. Damn. Dru Sullivan was back and Tyrone would have to be more cautious with his activities. That swarthy giant was a threat. Tyrone had no intention of backing off, but he would be more discreet in the future. And one of these days he would devise a way to get the upper hand. He coveted Dru's influence and power in the territory. The Bar S Ranch had become a landmark. Tyrone hungered to take control of the vast acres Dru owned, to assume command of Flemming's hotel and restaurant. Tyrone wanted it all—the wealth, the prestige, and the power. And by damned, one day he would see his dream come true. Even Dru Sulllivan wasn't going to stand in his way!

Chapter 21

Trail-weary, Tom Bates swung from his saddle and scooped up a hat full of water from the Platte River to cool his sunburned face. He and William Fogg had made a little progress the past week. After reaching Des Moines, Sullivan had become less discreet in his cross-country journey with Hubert Frazier's fiancée in tow. Will and Tom had been met with nods of recognition each time they described Dru and Victoria. The agents had interrogated scads of citizens along the way, all of whom had nothing but kind words to say about the brawny giant and his enchanting wife.

According to reports, the couple was now traveling with a Chinaman named Whong. Tom didn't have the foggiest notion why Sullivan had coerced Victoria into marriage. He could only speculate that it was Sullivan's vengeful way of retaliating against Frazier, with whom he had clashed the previous year. But Tom suspected Hubert was cursing a blue streak each time he received a telegram from the Pinkerton detectives.

"Well, shall we go see what the commander of Fort Laramie has to say?" Will questioned, peering thoughtfully at the walled fort in the distance. "I only hope to God, Sullivan hasn't headed to California or some such place. I'm already tired of trailing a fugitive of whom everyone speaks so highly." He shook his head and raked his fingers through his thick brown hair. "Damned if I can figure this Sullivan fellow out."

Tom heartily agreed with his associate on all points. He couldn't figure out Sullivan's motive, either, and the man wasn't easy to track down. And if the past few weeks was any indication, this manhunt was far from over. Tom also found himself wondering what Frazier intended to do if the Pinkerton agents did locate Sullivan. Since he had married Victoria Flemming Cassidy, she couldn't testify against him in court. If Sullivan had subdued Victoria and she was too afraid to speak out against her captor, it was Hubert's word against Sullivan's. The marriage had thrown a wrench in Hubert's plan of retaliation.

Ah well, Tom mused as he led his weary steed toward the fort. It wasn't his concern. His duty was to catch up with Sullivan. Frazier would have to decide what was to be done. But Tom had the inescapable feeling, Hubert's troubles would be far from over once he learned where Sullivan had taken Victoria.

"It's about time you got back," Billy-Bob sniffed, and then grimaced when he pushed himself up against the headboard and strained his wound. "I could have bled to death while you were lollygagging about all over creation."

Relief washed over Dru's strained features when he assessed Billy-Bob. It was obvious his baby brother was mending nicely or he wouldn't have been lying there complaining. One glance around the recently cleaned room indicated that Caleb had sent a regiment of hotel maids to tidy up the house and Billy-Bob's room in particular. The basket of food beside the bed also suggested that Caleb had been catering Billy-Bob's meals from the restaurant. All that his baby brother lacked was a full-time nurse to shower him with attention. But he rather suspected his other brothers and their wives paid regular visits to the invalid.

"You look healthy enough to me," Dru observed as he pulled off his Stetson and tossed it aside. "I'm the one who needs sympathy. You've been treated like a king while I've been living on the barest of necessities and tramping from here to kingdom come."

"I certainly hope Caleb's daughter was worth your long trip and my getting blasted out of the saddle by rustlers," Billy-Bob snorted indignantly.

The faintest hint of a smile pursed Dru's lips. Carefully, he eased down on the edge of the bed. "When you get a look at Chica—Victoria," he quickly corrected himself, "I think you'll know why Caleb was so anxious to see her. She'll be the toast of Virginia City."

Billy-Bob immediately perked up. "She's that pretty?"

Dru nodded his tousled raven head. "In a sophisticated sort of way," he replied in the blandest tone he could muster.

Billy-Bob was a sucker for a pretty face. Women fascinated him, and he had just arrived at the age of testing his prowess with them. Ten to one, Tori would have a devoted admirer in Billy-Bob, Dru wagered.

"She's even prettier than the dance-hall girls at Webster's Queen High Saloon?" Billy-Bob questioned excitedly.

There was nothing wrong with Billy-Bob, Dru diagnosed. After threatening Tyrone, Dru had stopped by the physician's office on his way out of town before riding to the ranch. According to Doc Brenner, Billy-Bob was on the road to recovery. Serious though his wound had been, Brenner thought it was time for Billy-Bob to climb out of bed and begin functioning like a normal human again.

Billy-Bob, however, enjoyed being coddled and pampered, being the baby of the family and all. Although Dru's other three brothers treated Billy-Bob like a child, the eldest son had employed the same tactic on Billy that he had utilized on Tori. Dru never did anything for Tori

249

that she couldn't do for herself. It might have appeared to be a cruel technique at times, but it had taught both Tori and Billy-Bob self-reliance. Obviously, Dru's kid brother had suffered a setback while Dru was away from the ranch. The youngest Sullivan was soaking up sympathy like a sponge.

"You can decide how Victoria measures up to the calico queens day after tomorrow when we ride into town," Dru announced with an air of nonchalance. "And tomorrow you can begin your chores. This place looks like hell. I didn't expect you to let things go just because I left the territory."

Billy-Bob's face fell. "Chores?" He was looking sicker by the second. "Go into town?" he croaked. "But I'm just barely off my deathbed!"

It was apparent that the youngest of the Sullivan brood wasn't ready to give up being waited on hand and foot. He rather liked all the pity and attention he'd gotten from his brothers and Caleb.

"So you got shot. Big deal," Dru sniffed unsympathetically.

When Billy-Bob gaped at him as if he had sprouted devil's horns, Dru inwardly grimaced and reminded himself there were times when a man had to be cruel to be kind. This was one of those times. Dru had profited from his experiences with Tori. He had been tough and demanding, and she had responded by meeting his expectations. Dru had refused to let her settle for being less than she could be. Tori had once been shy and reserved, but now she was confident and competent. The same was true with Dru's baby brother, he reckoned. Treat the kid like a baby and he'll respond in like manner.

"You're not the first man to take a bullet. I've got a scar on my rib from the bullet I took from a greedy miner who tried to jump my claim near Silver City," he reminded his brother. "But I recovered and I didn't have a slew of nurses doting over me. There's work to be done around here and you can't do it while you're lounging around here like a helpless invalid."

"I could have died," Billy-Bob bellowed, color flushing his handsome face.

"But you didn't," Dru countered. "Now get into your breeches and meet me downstairs. We have business to discuss."

In stupefied astonishment, Billy-Bob watched his oldest brother mosey out the door. He'd show that callous brute, Billy-Bob vowed stormily. He'd dress and walk downstairs and collapse in a lifeless heap. Then Dru would be sorry, just see if he wasn't!

Yanking back the sheet, Billy-Bob snatched up his breeches and muttered at Dru with every breath he took. But he got himself dressed without realizing he'd been *had.*

When the door slammed shut, Dru pivoted to find three somber faces riveted on him. My, news certainly traveled fast, thought Dru. Whong must have circled past the other Sullivan ranch houses to announce their return.

"A mite hard on the kid, weren't you?" John-Henry muttered, eyeing his brother disdainfully.

"Yeah, he's only a boy," Jerry-Jeff grumbled.

"And he was hurt pretty bad, after all," Jimmy-Pete chimed in.

"And thanks to the three of you, he's been lying abed when he should have been strengthening his endurance," Dru shot back at his three overprotective brothers. "Godamighty, he's almost twenty-two years old and it's time you started treating him like a man instead of a thumb-sucking infant!" He started down the stairs with a string of lookalikes trailing behind him. "I want to know everything that's happened while I was gone."

"Billy-Bob got shot all to hell," John-Henry snorted sarcastically. "Seems like you forgot that already."

"I most certainly have not." He wheeled on his brothers. "And the first one of you who makes over him when he comes downstairs to join us is going to taste my beefy fist. You got that?"

"Damn, Andy-Joe, you're a mite touchy since you got back from Chicago," Jerry-Jeff observed with a condescending frown. "You wanna talk about it?"

"No," Dru scowled before he pivoted to storm down the rest of the steps. He was dead tired and concerned about Billy-Bob, even if he didn't allow his brothers to know it. And to make matters worse, a pair of violet eyes kept appearing in front of him.

"What's bothering you?" Jimmy-Pete taunted. "Are you carrying a torch for Caleb's daughter or something?"

"That's probably it," John-Henry snickered. "He got all gushy over that little princess Caleb sent him to haul back to Montana. Big brother probably has a crush on . . . what's-her-name?"

"Lay off," Dru muttered, flashing his ornery brothers the evil eye. "It's been a long two months. And remember what I said about Billy-Bob." He leveled each brother a meaningful glare. "The first one to pamper him is going to be sprawled on the floor like a misplaced doormat."

The threesome studied their oldest brother in silent speculation. My, what a snit Andy-Joe was in. Something was gnawing at his disposition, that was for sure. But none of the Sullivan brothers thought it wise to push him too far in his present frame of mind. Dru didn't even bother to greet them before he started chewing them up one side and down the other, and his mood was black as pitch! But whatever was frustrating him, Dru was, as always, keeping his own counsel.

Adorned in one of the many elegant gowns Caleb had purchased for her, Tori sailed through the hotel lobby on her secret mission. After Caleb had gone into detail about his ongoing battle with that Tyrone Webster character, Tori decided to confront the scoundrel. It was ridiculous to her that no one had even sought Webster out after Dru's brother and Caleb were shot. It incensed her that

252

the big bully was running around loose, threatening everyone upon whose property he had cast his greedy eyes.

Now that Tori was brimming with confidence, she planned to see justice served. The fact that her frustrations with Dru had her spoiling for a fight made her even more bold and contrary. In her opinion, Webster deserved to be slapped with a counterthreat. That shrewd brute wasn't going to push her or her father around. *Nobody* was! Tori was her own woman and she was taking the matter into her own hands to protect the father she hadn't seen in ten years.

When Caleb had shown Tori the skull and crossbones Tyrone's thugs had carved on the hotel-room doors to frighten off customers, she had been outraged. And when she spied the bloodstains Tyrone's henchmen had planted on the sheets of the beds, she had very nearly gone through the ceiling. Webster was beneath contempt!

Caleb had also conveyed his speculations that the scalawag who ran Webster's blacksmith barn was casually quizzing travelers about their destinations and then alerting Webster's road agents of the individuals worth robbing. According to Caleb, Webster also grubstaked prospectors by offering to sell them necessary supplies and then demanding half the gold they mined from the Montana gulches. Webster was mining the miners in every conceivable way to make himself rich. He not only wanted to become a household word in Virginia City but he wanted to own the town, as well as the Bar S Ranch that possessed the water rights to thousands of acres of grazing land.

Although law and order had just come to Montana Territory, Tori had her own ideas about how to handle Webster. Caleb informed her that the Sullivan brothers were the core of the Virginia City Vigilante Committee who had once dealt severely with the offenders of justice. But the territorial government had frowned on overt acts of quick and expedient justice. Governor

Edgerton insisted on trials and concrete evidence of wrongdoing. And until Webster made a careless mistake, he would remain a menace that society couldn't punish unless he was proven guilty. Yet, there were ways to handle men like Webster. Tori had seen her stepfather employ several successful tactics while he organized his railroad company. Tori was intent on utilizing some of those techniques to bring Webster down a notch . . . or three.

The piano music in the Queen High Saloon died into silence when Tori breezed through the door like a whirlwind. Laughter faded into hushed murmurs and all eyes fell on the sophisticated young woman who had invaded territory that was reserved for men and hurdy-gurdy girls. When wolfish whistles bombarded Tori from all directions, she squared her shoulders and met each rakish leer with a defiant stare.

"I wish to speak with Mr. Webster," she announced to the saloon at large.

Several thumbs hitched toward the closed door at the rear of the saloon. Bowing her neck, Tori marched forward like the cavalry responding to a blowing bugle. Without knocking, she barged into the elaborately decorated office to find Tyrone lounging in his tufted chair and three guard dragons draped in their seats. She didn't bat an eyelash when Colts automatically flew from the gunslingers' holsters and silver barrels pointed at her chest.

Four pair of eyes focused on the comely blonde who had burst into the office as if she owned the place. After recovering from the initial shock, the men replaced their revolvers and stared curiously at their unexpected guest.

Tori's assessing gaze flicked over the local toughs who were armed to the teeth and garbed in tight breeches, silk shirts, and leather vests. Paid for by some poor unsuspecting miner no doubt, Tori mused bitterly.

Sam Rother, who sat in the chair to her left, reminded Tori of a pig with his upturned snout, oversized nostrils, and beady little eyes that were set too close together. His pointed ears jutted out from the sides of his face and his sagging jowls were also reminiscent of a hog. His sandy-blond hair could have used a good washing and, judging by the offensive aroma that emanated from him, he could use instruction in personal hygiene.

Clark Russel, who sat beside Sam and apparently shared the same pungent fragrance of a barnyard, reminded Tori of a horse, with his long, angular face, round eyes, and oversized front teeth. His ears were mashed against the sides of his head and his carrot-red hair grew toward the crown of his head like a mane.

Tori inwardly flinched when her assessing gaze shifted to Duke Kendrick, who sat to her right. He was sly-looking, and there was a cold deadly glint in his dark eyes. His lips were thin, but his mouth was wide. His nose sprawled in the middle of his face and flattened above his flared nostrils. Reddish-brown hair capped his square face and his stout body seemed much too large to fit his head.

After studying the three henchmen, Tori focused her full attention on Tyrone Webster, who was seated behind his desk. Snapping lavender eyes drilled into the chestnut-haired man who was garbed in a red velvet jacket and gold brocade vest. The huge desk concealed Webster's torso from the waist down. Although Tyrone's tastes were clearly expensive, he reminded Tori of a scarecrow who was draped with ill-fitting clothes. His physique left much to be desired. Mother Nature had skimped on her handiwork when she carved Tyrone's face and figure. His complexion was the color of ochre and his features were dug out instead of etched in his face the way Dru's were. The man's hair jutted out in all directions, even though he had slicked it down with wax. He had a beak that a toucan would envy, and an unbecoming goatee cupped his chin. The word *homely* had been invented to describe Tyrone Webster. Tori instantly decided Tyrone would have made the perfect villain for the western dime novels she had read. He was long and lean and ugly and the slit that she presumed to be his mouth naturally turned down at the corners.

In Tori's estimation, Tyrone's appearance was without redeeming virtue and, to compensate, he had channeled his energies into making himself wealthy, just so other folks would envy and fear him.

Shrugging off her wandering thoughts, Tori concentrated on her purpose for barging into this den of iniquity. She had a few choice words to convey to this homely weasel who had surrounded himself with gunslingers to make him feel like a king in command of an intimidating army.

Tori drew herself up, met Tyrone's leering gaze, and squelched the urge to slap him silly for what he was thinking. "Mr. Webster, I presume."

Tyrone removed the cigar from his lips and blessed Tori with what she assumed to be his attempt at a dazzling smile, though it clearly lacked sincerity. His hawkish gaze flooded over Tori's trim-fitting pink satin gown, dwelling overly long on her bosom. "I'm at the disadvantage, my dear," he drawled in a tone that did more to repulse than seduce. "I don't believe I've had the pleasure."

"Nor do you now," Tori countered airily. "I am Caleb Flemming's daughter, and I do not appreciate your dastardly tactics of trying to strong-arm my father into selling his business interests."

Her brash remark set all four men back on their heels. Tyrone looked incredulous, and his three henchmen were thunderstruck.

"You and your gang of cretins will find yourself behind bars if you issue more threats to my father and to other upstanding citizens. I have already telegraphed our family lawyer in Chicago and he is, at this very moment, arranging to organize an investigation and send the proper authorities to monitor your suspicious activities. If my father is injured again, you will be the prime

256

suspect of an investigation headed by Pinkerton National Detective Agency." Tori paused to allow the men to digest her words and then plunged on. "If something should happen to my father, I will inherit his worldly possessions, and I can assure you that I would give the property away before I sold out to you and your thugs."

Tyrone's bony face fell like an avalanche. This soliloquy had the same overtones as the one delivered by Dru Sullivan. Dru and this firebrand could have been related, considering the way they rattled off threats.

Webster's narrow hazel eyes drilled into Tori. "You presume too much, young lady," he growled at her. "I wasn't anywhere near the road where your father was shot on the evening in question."

A taunting smile hovered on Tori's lips as she looked down her nose at the cocky scoundrel. "And how do you know where and when my father was shot, Mr. Webster? My father didn't tell you, now did he?"

His plain features puckered in a scowl. This snippy chit was as sharp as a tack! "I know everything that goes on in this town, my dear." He made the endearment sound like a curse and that was exactly how he meant it.

"I have no doubt that you do since you are the one who instigates all the trouble to be found here," she parried with a ridiculing smirk, just like the one Dru had used on her on occasion.

When Duke Kendrick moved his itchy trigger finger toward his pistol, Tori scoffed at the silent threat. "Do, by all means, shoot me down," she challenged the shifty-eyed miscreant. "That is your method of dealing with those who dare to challenge you, isn't it? But bear in mind that I took the precaution of announcing my destination and my purpose to several businessmen in town before I entered this pirate's den. If I don't come out alive, you'll be swinging from ropes in a half hour, perhaps sooner."

A wordless growl resounded in Tyrone's chest. He didn't know if this sassy firebrand was bluffing or not, but he wasn't taking any chances until he knew more about her. When Tori had first sailed into the room, Tyrone had been overcome with lust, but it didn't take him long to recognize trouble. This spitfire was trouble, and Tyrone promised himself to deal with her in his own way and in his own time. No one, especially not a woman, crossed him and lived to brag about it. As pretty as this she-cat was, she would have to be dealt with or she would have the entire town up in arms to back her daredevil crusade.

Tossing her head, Tori singled out each face before she propelled herself toward the door. "Good day, Mr. Webster. I'll ask Papa to save the scraps from the restaurant to throw to your pack of guard dogs." Leaning casually on the door, Tori glanced back at the four puckered faces that glared at her. Sam and Clark had blank, brainless looks in their eyes; it was easy to understand why they let their Colts do their talking for them.

Duke Kendrick was another matter entirely. Again, Tori noted the ominous look in his eyes. But any of the four men looked as if they were capable of firing shots at Caleb and Dru's youngest brother. And of the foursome, the burly galoot, Duke Kendrick, looked the type who would not only shoot to kill, but that he would derive pleasure from it.

Well, she had made enough of an impression on Tyrone and his henchmen, she decided. They could chew on the threats she had issued and see how they liked it for a change.

When Tori swept out the same way she came in—like a misdirected cyclone—Tyrone bit into the end of his cigar and cursed fluently. He didn't appreciate being outsmarted by a feisty woman. Females, in his opinion, had been placed on earth for no other purpose than to feed men's lustful appetites. That blond-haired hellion obviously didn't know her place and she wouldn't have stayed in it even if she did! And it was even more apparent that

258

Virginia City wasn't big enough for the both of them. One of them was going to have to go. Tyrone was staying put.

"That snippy little tart is bound to cause us trouble," Tyrone predicted. "And what is worse is that she saw the four of us together." He had always been cautious and insisted that his henchmen employ the back door when they entered and exited so there would be no connection between them. But Tori had blown their secrecy wide open!

"Give me fifteen minutes with that uppity little bitch and I'll change her tune," Duke Kendrick requested as he cracked his knuckles. His dark, beady eyes riveted on the door through which Tori had exited.

"That's exactly what she expects us to do," Tyrone muttered, puffing on his cigar until he had surrounded himself with a cloud of smoke.

"Well, we can't let her go around town spouting accusations," Duke growled. "You know what happened to the Plummer gang when the Sullivans and the rest of the citizens decided to weed them out."

"I remember," Tyrone snorted. A mutinous frown swallowed his homely features. "But we are far more discreet. There are no witnesses to point accusing fingers at us. Speculation doesn't stand up in the territorial courts."

"Well then, what are we gonna do about that rabble-rouser?" Duke demanded to know. "She needs to be brought down a notch." A diabolical grin stretched across his lips, thinking he would like to be the one to bring that saucy minx down in more ways than one.

Tyrone eased back in his chair to stare thoughtfully after Tori. He could think of a dozen things he'd like to do to that violet-eyed firebrand himself. The picture forming in his mind provoked him to burst into a sinister smile. "Give me a little time, Duke. I'll think of a way to take care of that spitfire . . ."

Duke and the other two gunslingers exchanged glances, knowing they would all have their chance to

259

retaliate against the insults Tori flung at them.

"I wonder how brave the lady would be if her life really was in danger. It could very well be that her bark is worse than her bite . . . And even if she does try to make good with her threats, it would be weeks before Pinkerton's detectives could reach town. Why, there's no telling what might become of Caleb Flemming and his daughter in that space of time . . ." After taking a long draw on his cigar, Tyrone glanced at Duke. "Go check the telegraph office to see if the lady really did send off a message to Chicago. I'd like to know if she's bluffing, at least on that count."

While Tori was feeling quite satisfied with herself, Tyrone was mentally plotting to dispose of his biggest headache—a five-foot-two-inch blonde who had taken up a crusade to rid Virginia City of its social menace. Tori had barged into Tyrone's office, spoiling for a fight, and she had put herself on a collision course with disaster, without Dru or Caleb knowing it!

Part Four

An' all us other children,
  When the supper things
    is done,
We set around the kitchen
  fire an' has the mostest
    fun
A-listenin' to the witch tales
  'at Annie tells about
An' the gobble-un 'at gits
  you
    Ef you
      Don't
        Watch
          Out!
                    —James Whitcomb Riley

Chapter 22

Bookended by Dru and Whong, Billy-Bob sat in the carriage, anxiously waiting to get a look at the dazzling young beauty whom his oldest brother had described. Having never met a woman he didn't love at first sight, Billy was primed and ready to court Caleb's daughter.

To the rest of the family's surprise, Billy-Bob had dressed and ventured downstairs as Dru had demanded three days earlier. Billy-Bob and his brothers had briefed Dru on the events that had taken place during his absence and explained the circumstances surrounding the ambush that had laid Billy-Bob up for a few weeks. A line shack had been set afire and fifty head of cattle had been stolen. The three brothers had attempted to check Webster's herd for the missing livestock, but Tyrone's band of desperadoes refused to allow the Sullivans near the stock pens. Outnumbered five to one, the Sullivans had been forced to retreat.

Since Webster was selling beef to the other restaurant owners in Virginia City, Bannack, and Last Chance Gulch, the Sullivan brothers suspected their stock had already been butchered to dispose of the evidence. Webster had undoubtedly turned a tidy profit with the stolen cattle since beef on the hoof was bringing one hundred dollars a head in the gold camps and mining towns. As usual, Tyrone had covered his tracks carefully and had offered to buy Caleb out with money stolen from Sullivan livestock.

Although Dru had every intention of dealing with Webster, his mind was on Tori as he rode toward town. Behind the carriage that transported Billy-Bob, Dru, and Whong rode the other three Sullivans who had come to pay their respects to Caleb's daughter. Dru had hoped his preoccupation with the pressing matters at hand would distract him from his stormy relationship with Tori. But she still crossed his mind at least two dozen times a day.

Even though his brothers were anxious to lay eyes on the comely blonde, Dru was apprehensive about retesting his reaction to her. And to compound his frustrations, he kept picturing Tori standing beside her father. Flashes from the past had an unsettling effect on Dru. Intuition told him that Caleb was asking for more trouble when he sent Dru to fetch Tori. He couldn't help but wonder if Caleb had any idea that . . .

"How do I look?" Billy-Bob questioned, straightening his cravat. "I've never met a real lady before."

"You rook very handsome, Birry-Bob," Whong assured him.

"I'm still a mite pale," Billy fretted, pinching color into his pale cheeks. "She'll probably think I've never worked a day in my life."

"Godamighty," Dru grumbled crankily. "If I'd known this jaunt into town was going to throw you into a tizzy, I would have left you at home."

When the procession paused in front of the Flemming restaurant, Dru climbed down and reflexively reached up to assist his injured brother down. Catching himself in the nick of time, Dru stepped back to permit Billy-Bob to ease down of his own accord. Although Jerry-Jeff flung him a disapproving frown, Dru shrugged him off with deliberate nonchalance.

"I still think you're rushing him," John-Henry muttered, falling into step beside Dru.

"When I want your opinion I'll ask for it," Dru bit off.

"I swear to God, you'd have the kid in diapers if you thought he'd wear them. You've got two young ones of your own. If you want to spoil somebody rotten, concentrate on them."

John-Henry compressed his lips to prevent lashing out at his brother. Since Dru had become the head of the family, he thought the only opinions that mattered were his own. The Sullivans owed their good fortune and promising future to Dru, but he had carried the lion's share of the responsibility so long that he had difficulty accepting advice from his younger brothers, even when they were all grown up. Maybe Dru was handling Billy-Bob correctly and maybe he wasn't. But the Sullivans were accustomed to doting over their baby brother, and it was difficult to change what came naturally.

"If Billy-Bob suffers a relapse, I'll hold it over your head for the rest of your life," John-Henry threatened.

"I concede that you have a special knack for handling animals," Dru replied glibly. "That's why you are in charge of breaking and training the horses. But you don't have a lick of sense when it comes to recognizing what is best for two-legged creatures. Billy-Bob will be exactly what you perceive him to be. If you three keep mothering him, he will always be a baby."

"Since when did you get so all-fired smart?" Jimmy-Pete sniffed sarcastically.

"Just bite your tongue and let me handle Billy-Bob my own way," Dru demanded.

"You always handle everything your own way," Jerry-Jeff grumbled resentfully.

"But you better take a good look at all of us, big brother," John-Henry insisted. "We have all grown up and some of us have families of our own. Just because you've taken care of us all these years doesn't mean you have to push and prod us into doing what you think we should be doing *when* you think we should be doing it."

Dru allowed John-Henry to have the last word because he remembered a similar conversation between himself and Tori. She had pointed out that he was too domineering, and maybe he was. Perhaps it was time to take a long look at his brothers.

Before Dru could pursue that thought, he strode into the restaurant to find Caleb and Tori ambling down the corridor that led from the hotel lobby into the adjoining restaurant. His gaze feasted on the beauty who looked as poised and sophisticated as she had been the first day Dru laid eyes on her. Gone were the wild tangles that lay around her shoulders. Her silver-blond hair had been swept up into a neat bun atop her head, and enticing curls dangled around her temples and forehead. The emerald-green gown she wore was befitting a queen and the ever-present strands of pearls complemented her stunning attire. She reminded Dru of a princess from a fairy tale. Caleb had wasted no time in bestowing lavish gifts on Tori. An emerald ring encircled her finger, making the wedding band Dru had purchased for her appear plain in comparison.

Dru idly wondered if Tori had informed her father of her marriage or if she had allowed Caleb to assume she had wed Hubert Frazier. Dru suspected his new wife had avoided the subject, just as he had neglected to make the announcement to his brothers.

"My God, she's absolutely gorgeous . . ." Billy-Bob croaked. His eyes wandered over Tori's voluptuous figure in masculine admiration. "She's the prettiest thing I've seen in my whole life . . ."

Dru rolled his eyes skyward, requesting divine patience to carry him through the evening. He could tell it was love at first sight for his youngest brother. Sure as hell, Billy would be heartbroken when he learned that Tori already had a husband.

Dru supposed he should have made the announcement to his family, but he had procrastinated, knowing they would razz him unmercifully. For years they had teased him about being a dedicated bachelor. And knowing his ornery brothers, he predicted he'd be subjected to taunts

266

that would try the patience of a saint, which he wasn't. Hell, he wasn't even within shouting distance of sainthood and never had been.

Tori missed a step when she spied the troop of men who swarmed around the front entrance of the restaurant. The Sullivan brothers reminded her of the towering precipices of the mountains that loomed over Virginia City. Not one of the muscular brothers stood under six feet tall and the family resemblance was astonishing! They were all carbon copies of Dru—midnight hair, baby-blue eyes, and built like buffaloes! They made poor Whong look like a midget in comparison. The little Chinaman never had to worry about having a heat stroke from standing in the sun because these towering giants would eclipse any harmful light that might have fallen on him!

Flabbergasted, Tori gaped at the five dashingly attractive men until Billy-Bob weaved through the maze of tables to pump her hand as if he were drawing water from a well. Although Billy-Bob still possessed boyish features, Tori predicted he would soon be every bit as devastating as his four brothers. It was also apparent that the youngest Sullivan was mending nicely, judging by the way he zipped across the dining room to squeeze her hand.

"I'm pleased to meet you, ma'am," Billy-Bob gushed, all eyes and a bright smile that stretched from ear to ear. "Dru said you were pretty, but I never dreamed anyone could be so beautiful . . ."

An amused chuckle rumbled in Caleb's chest. Fatherly pride put a grin on his lips. It was delightful to see Billy-Bob up and around after his near brush with death. And it was exhilarating to be on hand to see what a dramatic effect Tori had on men. She had been proposed to four times since she had arrived in Virginia City!

"I'm in love. Marry me," Billy-Bob breathed, half jesting, half serious.

Five times, Caleb quickly amended before Tori

responded to the proposal, just as she had to the other four.

"I'm flattered, but I already have a husband."

Billy-Bob stared down at her left hand. He looked as if someone had hit him with a sledgehammer. "Just my luck that I have finally met the light and love of my life and she's already taken."

"Victoria, this is Billy-Bob Sullivan." Caleb made the formal introduction.

Flashing a radiant smile, Tori curtsied politely.

"Now I know why you were gone more than two months," John-Henry murmured to Dru. His eyebrows lifted suggestively. "I bet it was hell reminding yourself that the lady was married."

Dru didn't respond. He was too busy telling himself the gnawing in the pit of his belly was the result of skipping lunch. But it wasn't and he damned well knew it.

"Well, don't just stand there." Jimmy-Pete gave Dru a nudge with his elbow. "Introduce us, big brother. Damn, she is gorgeous . . ."

Hesitantly, Dru threaded his way around the tables with his brothers following in his footsteps. His gaze flooded over Tori's captivating figure. He was stung by the forbidden memories and tormented by the rapt attention she was receiving, not only from his brothers but also from the other male patrons in the restaurant. Godamighty, he was jealous of his own brothers, he realized. Damn, why couldn't he have been an only child!

When Tori glanced past Billy-Bob, her heart somersaulted around her chest. Blast it, why did she have to react so fiercely to the mere sight of this handsome rake? Dru walked in and the world shrank to fill the space he occupied. For three days Tori had tried to forget the past six weeks existed, that Dru was just a man she had met along the way. But nothing had helped to quell the longings. She peered up at him and she wanted him with all her heart and soul. Love was a cruel curse, Tori decided as she tried to still her thundering heart. She had to stop yearning for a man she could never have.

From beneath a fan of thick black lashes, Dru stared down at the exquisite beauty who was poised in front of him. Damnit, she was only a woman, Dru told himself. She meant nothing special to him, nor he to her. He had married this curvaceous sprite because necessity and obligation dictated. Tori had no magical hold on him and he had no right to be jealous because his brothers were ogling her . . .

Jerry-Jeff gouged him in the ribs, jostling him from his silent reverie. Dru managed a faint smile of greeting. "Victoria, I would like you to meet the rest of my brothers. This is John-Henry, Jerry-Jeff, and Jimmy-Pete."

Again Tori's gaze flicked from one ruggedly handsome face to the other, marveling at the striking resemblance. It still amazed her that they all had hair as black as a raven's wing, eyes like chips of azure blue sky, and muscular physiques that could turn a woman's head and hold her attention. Never had Tori seen so many overwhelming packages of masculinity congregated in the same place. The impact was ovewhelming!

"And this, my dear brothers is Tori Flemming Sullivan, your new sister-in-law," Dru announced, never taking his eyes off her spellbinding features.

Dru watched Tori's cheeks flame when five pair of incredulous eyes riveted on her, Caleb's included. The only one who didn't gasp in astonishment was Whong, who had been told to keep his mouth shut until Dru chose to make the announcement. Dru had intended to be tactful about informing his brothers and Caleb of the marriage that had taken place en route. But after watching his brothers drool over her, Dru decided to drop the bomb in their laps.

Caleb stared at the wedding band on Tori's finger and then glanced in bewilderment at Dru who had yet to take his eyes off Tori. All this time he had been laboring under the erroneous notion that Tori had wed Hubert. Oh, this was ripe! Gwen would be in a furious snit when she received the news. Caleb was delighted. His scheme had been as effective as he had hoped.

"Well, I'll be damned," Caleb chuckled, bursting into a smile that rivaled the brilliance of the sun.

"You probably will before this is all over," Dru murmured cryptically.

A bubble of laughter echoed in Caleb's chest. Dru had enjoyed the ultimate revenge on Hubert after their confrontation the previous year, and Caleb had his spiteful vengeance on that devious woman who had deprived him of his daughter's affection. My, things had turned out splendidly!

"Married?" the Sullivan brothers crowed in unison.

"I don't believe it," John-Henry declared. "I never thought Andy-Joe would find himself a wife who would put up with him, not after he's loved and left so many . . . Argh!" A pained grunt erupted from his lips when Dru trounced on his foot, silently warning him to mind his tongue.

"Andy-Joe?" Tori peered amusedly at Dru. She was annoyed with him for blurting out the announcement, but learning his name eased the sting of embarrassment and put a wry smile on her lips.

"Andrew-Joseph," John-Henry scolded, clucking his tongue and giving his eldest brother the evil eye. "Shame on you for waiting so long to tell us about the grand event." His assessing gaze slid over Tori's arresting figure before he winked playfully at Dru. "My, my, we'll have to throw a party to celebrate this monumental occasion."

"You always did have all the luck in the family," Billy-Bob grumbled acrimoniously. "I got shot to pieces and you got married."

"Wonders never cease," Jerry-Jeff snickered playfully.

"Ain't love grand," Jimmy-Pete tittered.

"*Isn't,*" Dru automatically corrected his younger brother. "Isn't it though."

Tori's heart sank like an anchor when Dru's baby-blue eyes drilled into her. It was apparent that Dru intended to leave the impression that he and his new wife were deliriously happy. Fat chance of that, thought Tori. This was all an act staged for the Sullivans' benefit. Dru didn't love her. That was as obvious as a wart on the end of one's nose. Dru wanted his brothers and Caleb to think the match was made in heaven. Dru and Tori would be forced to play the role of the loving couple in the family's presence. It would be a simple task on her part, she knew. But Dru would have to call upon his theatrical abilities to pretend he felt something special for the wife he had been obliged to marry.

Dru cast his grinning brothers a pointed glance. "No pranks," he commanded sternly.

John-Henry suddenly looked so innocent, Dru expected him to sprout wings and a halo any second. "Us? Play practical jokes on you, the same way you and the rest of my dear brothers did on Elizabeth and me when we got married?"

"What sort of pranks?" Tori questioned warily.

"Nothing too serious," John-Henry scoffed caustically. "Andy-Joe and the others did insignificant little things like stuff a frog in the pillowcase and short-sheet the bed." His eyes narrowed on Dru, who had suddenly taken an interest in the toes of his boots. "And then, of course, there was the howling ghost they rigged up to fly out of the closet . . ." His mouth curved into a devilish grin that made his sky-blue eyes twinkle. "But the other boys and I wouldn't think of doing anything like that to our big brother when he got married. We aren't that spiteful and childish. After all, we're grown men now."

The double jibe caused Dru to wince. If his brothers dreamed up an excuse to leave town early, Dru would expect they planned to stop at his ranch house to leave a few surprises for the new bride and groom. They would never bypass the opportunity to play a practical joke on him. Dru made a mental note to be prepared for anything

271

when he returned to the ranch.

"Dinner is on the house," Caleb announced as he gestured toward the large table in the back corner of the dining hall. "I'll tell the cooks to put the best steaks on the fire—Sullivan prime beef, of course."

While Caleb scuttled off to order their meal, Dru curled his hand around Tori's elbow and propelled her toward the table. "Miss me, Chicago?" he murmured against her ear.

All eyes were upon her. Tori could feel them. "Were you gone?" she murmured so quietly that only Dru could hear her. But for the benefit of the Sullivan brothers, she reached up to adoringly pat his bronzed cheek. "You know I did, my love. I thought you had abandoned me . . ."

Her voice trailed off when she saw Duke Kendrick rise from his chair in the opposite corner. Her body tensed when Duke's gaze raked over her with mocking disdain. This was the third time today she had seen that scalawag hanging around her. If she didn't know better, she would have sworn he was following her. Why? Tori shuddered to guess. More than likely, Duke was acting under Tyrone Webster's orders. If Duke could have gotten her alone, he probably intended to dispose of her . . . permanently.

Dru caught the silent exchange and frowned suspiciously. "Have you had trouble with Duke?" he queried as he pulled out a chair for Tori.

She shrugged off his inquiry and blessed him with a blinding smile for appearance sake. "You didn't tell me you had such handsome brothers, Andy-Joe," she chided lightly.

Dru studied Tori for a long pensive moment. He'd bet his right arm Tori had clashed with Duke. But little Miss Independent was intent on fighting her own battles these days to prove that she could take care of herself.

"My wife has been after Andy-Joe for years to settle down," John-Henry remarked, and then shook his head in amazement. "I still can't believe my big brother got married." His appreciative gaze flooded over Tori in silent appraisal. "But I can certainly see why he did . . ."

Dru had gotten married, Tori mused, but he hadn't settled down. And if John-Henry had known Dru wed Tori to salvage her reputation, he wouldn't have been carrying on about the wedding. In fact, he wouldn't have brought up the subject at all!

"Thank you for the compliment." A becoming blush stained Tori's cheeks when John-Henry gave her the onceover twice. "You are very generous with your flattery." Her fingertips slid over Dru's in a gesture of affection, even though she would have preferred to break all twenty-seven bones in his hand. "But I'm the lucky one. Dru swept me off my feet." He also picked me up and tossed me in the back of a wagon and dragged me away from my first wedding, Tori silently tacked on.

Dru curled his hand around Tori's and brought it to his lips to press a kiss to her wrist. "I'm the fortunate one," he contradicted in a low, husky voice that sent unwanted goosebumps stampeding across Tori's skin.

"Don't that beat all," Jerry-Jeff snickered, watching Dru fawn over his lovely wife.

"*Doesn't,*" Dru automatically corrected.

"Since when did you become a grammar instructor?" Jerry-Jeff grumbled. "Now, I can't even talk to suit you."

Dru forgot all about his brothers when he stared into thickly fringed violet eyes that rippled like wildflowers on a mountain meadow. He had hoped the three-day separation would put his thoughts back in proper perspective. It hadn't. He wanted Tori as much as he ever had. More, he amended as the light touch of his hand became an absent caress. She was like a fire in his blood that had never burned itself out.

He kept telling himself he would have to give up this captivating blonde when her mother came to fetch her home. But letting go of her was inconceivable. He had grown accustomed to watching out for her, accustomed to wanting her. Their three-day separation had been hard

273

on his emotions. Getting over Tori when she returned to Chicago would take a long time, Dru predicted deflatedly. She wouldn't want to stay with him, he knew that. Why would she? When Tori had the chance to go back where she belonged, she would jump at it.

Tori forced herself to look away before Dru deciphered the unrequited love in her gaze. What he didn't want was a clinging female to strangle him. All he wanted was for Tori to play a convincing charade for the Sullivans' benefit.

To Tori's relief, Jerry-Jeff, who had a special knack of telling stories, began to relate anecdotes of childhood pranks. He claimed Andy-Joe was responsible for getting the whole brood of boys in trouble. Tori realized how much she'd missed by being an only child when she listened to the rollicking tales and pranks the Sullivans had pulled during their youth. She became increasingly aware of the close-knit family into which she had married . . . at least temporarily. Dru was devoted and loyal to his brothers and they to him, even if they did razz each other constantly. The playful camaraderie between them was something Tori had never experienced.

According to Jimmy-Pete, who was not to be outdone by his brother, told the story of how Dru had gone out into the world to seek his fortune and had struck it rich in Alder Gulch. He had strategically purchased land that contained valuable water supplies and had thereby been allowed to graze the federal lands that were worthless without the springs and creeks that lay on Dru's property.

The Sullivan cattle herd that had been driven up from Texas was allowed to graze the mountain meadows, and the livestock sales and gold mine he and Caleb shared, had permitted Dru to purchase even more land. Through careful planning, Dru had acquired enough property to generously dole out land to each of his brothers, and they had all toiled and worked to build their own homes on separate corners of their vast cattle empire. It was as if the Sullivans owned their own private country beside the Montana gold fields. Now the thousands of prospectors who flooded the area were the chief consumers of the beef and horses the Sullivans raised.

If not for Dru's self-sacrificing generosity, his brothers would not have enjoyed such prosperity. Dru had scratched and clawed to make a place for himself and his younger brothers. Tori admired him for that. She only wished he had a little love left over to share with her.

In mute amazement, Tori watched the waitresses place huge bowls of food on the table, and she gaped in disbelief when her father emerged from the kitchen carrying a stack of steaks. And to her further astonishment, the swarm of men attacked and devoured their meals like pythons. Lord-a-mercy, not only were these men towering giants but they ate like a pack of starved wolves! Even Whong had tucked away his handkerchief and dove in with both hands before the food supply vanished. When this mob came to town to eat, they ate! And when they finished their meal, there was nothing but empty bowls and a platter that resembled a cattle graveyard.

While the Sullivans and Flemmings were celebrating Dru and Tori's marriage, Duke Kendrick swaggered through the back door of the Queen High Saloon to convey the information to Tyrone. "Guess what I just found out," he snorted as he negligently dropped into a chair and poured himself a glass of Tyrone's most expensive liquor.

"I'm not in the mood for guessing games," Tyrone grumbled grouchily.

"That sassy little bitch who barged in here yesterday is married to Dru Sullivan," Duke imparted.

Tyrone choked on the swallow of whiskey that had just passed his lips. Frog-eyed, he stared at Duke's whiskered face while the gunslinger nodded in confirmation. Dabbing at the dribbles of liquor that clung to his goatee,

Tyrone leaned back in his chair and grinned diabolically. "I think I know how I can get exactly what I want from both Flemming and Sullivan . . ."

While his mind teemed with sinister thoughts, Tyrone sipped his whiskey and formulated his scheme. He had waited a year to get his hands on Flemming's hotel and restaurant and the Sullivan's vast land holdings that dwarfed his own ranch on the outskirts of Virginia City. Tyrone's scare tactics hadn't worked worth a damn until Tori came upon the scene. But now that she was here, she would be the link between those two valuable pieces of property, and Tyrone intended to use her to get what he wanted. Rustling Dru's cattle and taking shots at his youngest brother hadn't sent the eldest Sullivan storming to Tyrone's ranch for a showdown. No, Dru was too clever to face Tyrone's band of deadly gunslingers when he and his brothers were greatly outnumbered.

Since Montana had become a territory in the spring of '64, the civilized politicians frowned on vigilante justice. That had worked to Tyrone's advantage. He had forced three men out of business with strong-arm tactics and he had made a killing with his various investments in mines and stores in Virginia City. But his ranch was located beside the Sullivans and allowed him no room for expansion. The Bar S Ranch and the five brothers had cornered the market on cattle. But now that Tori had arrived, Tyrone had a pawn to utilize. He would get what he wanted from Caleb and Dru, he assured himself confidently. And before long, Tyrone would become the richest man in the territory. Flemming and the Sullivan brothers would be standing in *his* shadow!

Chapter 23

When the Sullivan brothers offered to accompany their new sister-in-law on an evening stroll through town, Caleb took the opportunity to speak privately with Dru. When he had poured them both a drink, Caleb dropped into his favorite chair in his parlor. After a long moment of meditation, he downed his drink in one swallow and focused absolute attention on Dru, who was squirming in his seat.

"Why did you marry Tori?" Caleb questioned point-blank.

"Godamighty, Caleb, don't play naive," Dru burst out. He had dreaded this encounter since he blurted his announcement the previous hour. "It was what you wanted me to do in the first place, but I was too dense to figure out your wily scheme until it was too damned late."

"I implied no such thing," Caleb protested before pouring himself and Dru another drink. "I specifically remember asking you to bring Tori back home and that was *all* I said."

Dru glared flaming arrows at his ex-partner. "If you object to the marriage, I'll have it annulled tomorrow."

"I didn't say I objected," Caleb growled. "All I asked was why you did it. For Pete's sake, you don't have to be so damned sensitive!"

"Then don't pretend you didn't give the possibility careful consideration," Dru muttered crankily. "It occurred to you that while I was teaching Tori to adapt to our way of life, I might become romantically involved with her and don't you dare deny it!"

Caleb's face turned a remarkable shade of purple. "Is that what happened? You compromised my daughter's virtues so you felt obligated to marry her? Or did you decide to have your revenge on Hubert by wedding his fiancée? It seems a mite peculiar to me that neither you nor Tori mentioned your marriage until tonight. That doesn't sound like normal behavior for a happily married couple."

"You are spoiling my good disposition, Caleb," he warned in a threatening tone, and then chugged his drink to cool his temper. It didn't help.

"You aren't doing much for mine, either," Caleb muttered sourly. "I need to know what the hell's going on between you and my daughter before that woman arrives to begin her hysterical tirade."

Dru raked his fingers through his thick raven hair and then let his arm drop loosely by his side. "How do I know what's going on?" he sighed in frustration. "She changes like the wind. First she said she loved me and then she claimed she didn't."

"So naturally you married her," Caleb smirked in a sarcastic voice. "You realize you are making absolutely no sense." He was up and pacing in a flash. "You know I want Tori to remain here, that nothing would make me happier than to catch up on lost time. But if this marriage is doomed from the beginning, if it was a spiteful retaliation against Hubert and nothing more, I want to know." He paused to glower down at Dru, who had polished off his third drink and was in the process of slopping another one into his glass. "Do you love her or don't you?"

"How the hell do I know!" Dru exploded like a keg of blasting powder. "I've never been in love before. How is a

278

man supposed to know those things?"

"Well, don't ask the advice of a man whose wife sent him searching for gold and then divorced him while he was en route! I never claimed to have women figured out!" Caleb grumbled.

There was a long pause in which the silence was so thick it could have been sliced with a knife.

"If you don't take Tori home with you tonight, it's going to look pretty damned fishy to your brothers. And if you don't treat her with the respect and courtesy she deserves, you'll answer to me!" His voice rose to a roar. "The two of you better decide whether or not you're going to give this marriage a sporting chance, and you better decide quickly. When that woman gets here I won't have the slightest idea what I'm supposed to say to her."

Dru expelled a frustrated breath. He wanted Tori with him, but he wasn't sure she would be all that crazy about the idea. Confound it, he really did miss that minx, even though he had kept himself so busy the past three days that he met himself coming and going twice and didn't even have time to say hello. But Dru balked when Caleb tried to push him around and force him into premature decisions. He was accustomed to doing things his own way in his own sweet time. Maybe that's what rankled him about this whole affair. He had felt obliged to marry Tori for Caleb's sake and now that ornery scamp was pressing him for some sort of commitment. Dru felt trapped and the tighter he was tied down, the harder he struggled. If all the rest of the world would back off and let him and Tori decide what was best for them, it would be a helluva lot better. But Caleb was looking over Dru's shoulder, and his brothers had already begun to needle him about his secretive wedding.

Godamighty, what Dru wouldn't have given to be stranded on a desert island with that comely blonde until they came to terms with their feelings for each other or decided to call it quits. And what if Gwen stormed into

279

town to retrieve her daughter before . . . ?

A fleeting thought skipped across Dru's troubled mind—the same unsettling thought that had plagued him every day since he returned to Montana. Dru scowled disgustedly. Damn "that woman." He'd like to strangle her!

"Well?" Caleb demanded impatiently. "Do you want Tori or don't you?"

Dru gulped down another drink but it didn't take the edge off his nerves. He needed the whole blessed bottle. "Pack her bags," he growled in a most unpleasant tone. "And the next time you want me to do you a favor, don't bother asking. The answer will be no."

"If you foul up the next favor as badly as you have this one, I wouldn't have asked you for help in the first place," Caleb snorted caustically.

"You and your bright ideas," Dru muttered as he unfolded himself from the chair.

"Well, if you loved Tori, it would certainly help matters," Caleb shouted as if Dru were stone deaf.

"Don't badger me, Caleb. I wasn't in the best of moods to begin with and you're making it worse." His thick brows furrowed in a warning frown that Caleb flagrantly disregarded.

"As if we don't have enough trouble with Tyrone Webster and his gang of thugs, not to mention the expected arrival of my ex-wife, now you have up and married Tori on a whim." He glared at Dru. "Or should I say you married her on a—"

"No, you shouldn't say it," Dru snapped brusquely, leveling Caleb a silencing glower. "If you were going to say what I *think* you were going to say, you damned well better not say it unless you're looking to buy a set of false teeth to replace the ones you're about to lose." He brandished a beefy fist in threat.

"Well, I'm *thinking* it," Caleb sneered in defiance. "And you obviously forgot whose daughter you were trifling with on your way back to Montana. Thanks one helluva lot, friend."

The remark set Dru's teeth on edge, but he reined in the suitably nasty comment that galloped to the tip of his tongue. It would have knocked Caleb's knees out from under him. Dru was angry, but he refused to be cruel and cutting. Although Dru and Caleb had exchanged heated words, they had been through thick and thin together and Dru valued their friendship.

"Just fetch Tori's luggage," Dru ordered.

Muttering to himself, Caleb stomped off to gather Tori's belongings. One-handed, he crammed her clothes into the satchels and then flung them at Dru's feet. "Congratulations on your recent wedding to my one and only daughter." Caleb was still in an exasperated huff and his tone lacked sincerity.

Flashing Caleb a mutinous glare, Dru scooped up the luggage and stormed out the door.

"And don't forget I need ten head of beef by Thursday," Caleb called after him. "I may never speak to you again, but business is still business and I have a lot of hungry miners to feed."

Dru rolled his eyes heavenward and stalked through the corridor. For the life of him he couldn't figure out why he and Caleb had been at each other's throats. They had always gotten along superbly until Caleb had been overcome by his fatherly instincts.

Damnit all, Caleb had what he wanted—an excuse to keep Tori in Virginia City. And all of a sudden, he demanded a commitment from Dru. Hell, how could Dru satisfy Caleb when he wasn't sure how to satisfy himself? Dru wasn't sure what he expected of this marriage except the usual things a man needed from a woman. He wasn't accustomed to sharing his life with anyone except his brothers. His family had always filled his need to be needed. And if that were true, what need would Tori satisfy? She had already outgrown her fascination for him. She was too sophisticated to settle for a life-long home on the frontier, surrounded by bawling cattle and whinnying horses. He'd known that in the beginning, but he had rationalized matters because he was so cussed attracted to that violet-eyed beauty, he couldn't think straight.

So where do we go from here? Dru asked himself miserably. Home, he answered himself. And then what? Hell's bells, he would have to figure that out when they got there. One step at a time, Dru lectured himself. He would give Tori time to adjust to his way of life. If she found it revolting, he would pack her up and haul her back to her father. And when Gwen arrived, Tori could do as she pleased. Lord, Dru didn't know what he wanted and expected from that spirited minx. Maybe he should just whip out his pistol and put himself out of his misery. Jeezus, marriage wasn't wedded bliss. It was an exercise in exasperation. And Dru was sure enough exasperated. He would feel better if he had another drink—or four before he confronted Tori!

Tori was having a perfectly marvelous time until Dru showed up, carrying her satchels and wearing a smile as brittle as eggshells.

"I hope you don't mind, honey. I took the liberty of fetching your belongings from Caleb. I know you have just begun to get reacquainted with your father, but I would like to show you around our ranch," Dru declared without pausing to take a breath.

Fine, just pack me up and tote me off like a sack of dirty laundry, Tori silently fumed. But she replied sweetly. "I'll have the rest of my life to visit Papa. I'm anxious to see our home."

Of course she was. As anxious as she was to take a swim through an alligator-infested swamp, Dru thought to himself. Wasn't she just aquiver with excitement and anticipation, not subdued anger? Hardly!

"You wirr be most preased with the house, Mrs. Surrivan," Whong assured her with a humble bow.

"I'm sure I will," she replied as she curled her hand around Dru, discreetly sinking her nails into his ribs.

Dru grimaced. It was painfully evident that Tori was silently consigning him to the fires of hell for uprooting her from Caleb's home and dragging her off to only God knew where. Not that Dru blamed her really. He would have objected to being shuffled around without having a say in the matter. Tori hadn't been allowed to make her own decisions her whole life. And as independent and self-confident as she had become, he suspected her temper had been sorely put upon during the course of the evening. And guess who would become her scapegoat when she got him alone? Dru's shoulders slumped in bleak expectation. He had the inescapable feeling that Tori was going to give him hell the first chance she got.

Still smoldering, Tori allowed John-Henry to scoop her up and set her in the carriage seat beside Whong. Tori willed her accelerated pulse to slow its pace when Dru eased up beside her. His broad shoulders and muscular thighs were pressed familiarly to hers, triggering unwanted memories of more intimate moments. Defiantly, she ignored the warm tingles that had no business tormenting her when she was furious with this impossible man. She was irritated, and she didn't want her betraying body bombarding her with conflicting emotions. But when she and Dru were finally granted privacy, Tori swore she was going to let him have it with both barrels.

A suspicious frown knitted Dru's brow when Billy-Bob declared that he was in fit enough shape to ride horseback to the ranch. Those mischievous brothers of his were up to something, Dru just knew it!

When his brothers trotted off ahead of them, Dru leaned close to Tori. "Before you rake me over the coals, you'd better know this was your father's idea," he declared. He cursed himself for being so vividly aware of Tori's luscious body brushing against his, aware of the enticing scent of her cologne.

Dru stuck his foot in his mouth again without realizing it. Hearing that it was Caleb's idea for her to leave with her husband had Tori grinding her teeth in frustration. She had been hanging on the thread of hope that she and Dru had a chance at happiness. But if he was only complying to Caleb's wishes, it suggested he didn't really want her with him. Curse his callous soul!

Resolving to hold her tongue until they arrived at the ranch, Tori clenched her fists in the folds of her gown and pretended she had a stranglehold on Dru's thick neck. Damn that man, he wouldn't recognize love if it walked up and slapped him in the face!

Chapter 24

The moment they reached the sprawling stone-and-timber ranch house that was nestled against the hills, Tori climbed down to stride alongside Whong. Her gaze swept the wide veranda that encircled the front of the house. When she stepped into the foyer, her heart sank. She fell in love with the rustic decor of the two-story home at first sight. The rooms were paneled with native wood and had been polished to a shine. The furniture had been imported from the East, giving the house a touch of luxury. She had hoped to hate Dru's sprawling house in the mountain valley, but that was not the case. It was absolutely charming.

"You see? It is a mansion in the mountains," Whong proclaimed with a contented sigh. "You rike it here? Yes?"

"Yes," Tori replied as her eyes circled to the adjacent door of Dru's study, which, she saw, was lined with shelves of books. Bewildered, Tori ambled into the spacious room to survey the library collection she hadn't expected him to have.

"Billy-Bob is the scholar around here," Dru commented, setting her satchels aside. "I saw to it that he was educated enough for all of us."

"You have a most impressive collection of classics." For the moment, Tori forget she was annoyed with Dru and thumbed through the rows of books.

"You can browse to your heart's content tomorrow." Dru steered her into the hall. "Let me show you our room now."

Our? Tori's hackles immediately went back up. If he thought she would share his bed after he had pretended affection for her all evening and carted her off without asking her permission, he thought wrong!

"Good night, Whong," Dru called over his shoulder before he started up the steps. He was anxious to get the impending argument over with. After the air was cleared, perhaps they could settle their differences . . .

Biding her time, Tori allowed Dru to escort her down the hall. But the moment he eased open the door, Tori rolled out the heavy artillery and prepared to blast away at him.

"I have had just about enough of your highhanded presumptuousness," Tori spumed.

Lord, she was lovely when her cheeks blazed with fury and her violet eyes shot sparks. When he'd first met Tori she had displayed so little emotion. It was as if she had been trudging through life, feeling nothing. But she had changed dramatically in the span of two months. And now that she had been freed from her shell, Tori had become a force to be reckoned with . . .

Dru's rambling thoughts skidded to a halt when he remembered his brothers had ridden home ahead of them. He could guess why! Gnashing his teeth, he strode over to flip back the bedspread, checking for unwanted varmints that had been planted in the bed.

"What the blazes are you doing?" Tori questioned when Dru tossed the quilt back in place and dropped down on all fours to investigate the underside of the bed.

"Checking for practical jokes," he told her hurriedly. "If I know my ornery brothers, they sabotaged this room before we arrived."

"They assured you they weren't going to play any pranks," Tori reminded him, annoyed that her tantrum had to be waylaid until Dru's suspicions had been appeased.

"That's what they said, but it was only a ruse. I'd stake my fortune on it," he declared with great conviction. "And unless you want ten years scared off your life, Chicago, I suggest you help me inspect the room for booby traps."

Tori shot him a withering glance before she unlatched her satchel to shake out the expensive gowns. "I think you're being ridiculous . . . among other things," she sniffed.

While Dru rummaged through the drawers in the dresser to search for snakes, mice, and whatever else his brothers had stashed there to scare the living daylights out of Tori, she collected her garments and strode to the closet to hang them up. "I only intend to stay a few days, for appearance' sake," she announced. "And then I'm going back to—"

A shocked shriek leaped from Tori's throat when she opened the closet door and an object resembling a human body fell on top of her. The Sullivan brothers had stuffed grain sacks inside Dru's garments and had propped the heavy effigy against the door. Before Tori could react or remove herself from the path of the falling effigy, she was knocked backward and squished flat. Limp arms dangled over her shoulders and trousers filled with grain held her legs in place. She swore the effigy weighed as much as Dru himself, and she couldn't have wriggled free to save her life.

While Tori screamed bloody murder, Dru raced across the room to drag the heavy dummy off of her. "You see? What did I tell you?" Dru smirked as he stood Tori upright and dusted the wheat grains off her gown. "My brothers wouldn't overlook the chance to harass us."

Tori might have been amused now that the ordeal was over, if she hadn't been half mad to begin with. But she was, so she wasn't. "You and your ornery passel of brothers," she seethed as she stomped over to retrieve her nightgown. "You're all peas in a pod. First you force me to marry you and then I find out I've been dragged into a family of jokesters. I'm going back to town in the morning and you can make the necessary excuses to those hoodlums you call your brothers!"

Suddenly, Dru didn't give a fig about his brothers' attempt to sabotage the room or about Caleb's demands. All he wanted was what he and Tori had shared during those secluded moments along the trail. It had been an eternity since he'd held her in his arms, casting duty and obligation to the wind. He didn't want her to leave tomorrow or the day after that. He wanted her here with him. He wanted her to be the first memory of each morning and the last pleasure he enjoyed each night. He wanted to feast on her beauty and marvel at her newfound spirit.

"I demand that you . . ." Her voice trailed off when Dru closed the distance between them. His roguish smile tore the thoughts from her mind and sent her pulse leapfrogging through her bloodstream. Quickly, Tori marshaled her defenses. She was *not* going to melt at his feet like a witless fool just because he looked at her in that devastating way that unleashed forbidden memories. "Don't you dare touch me, damn you! I'm furious with you, *Andy-Joe*."

When he reached for her, Tori darted sideways and shot around the other side of the bed. "I'm not a doll you can drag from the closet to amuse yourself with when it meets your whim . . ." Tori bounded across the bed when Dru circled the bedpost to capture her.

"Blast it, listen to me when I'm talking to you," she hissed venomously.

Dru was in no mood to listen. He'd had enough lecturing from Caleb and one too many glasses of whiskey. He was in a playful, seductive mood, and chasing this feisty pixie around the room was an intriguing challenge.

With an outraged squawk, Tori darted toward the

door. But Dru whizzed around the bed to pursue her. Before she could escape, he scooped her up in his arms and carried her across the room and onto the balcony that overlooked the moonlit hillside and jagged mountain ridges.

The view was spectacular, and Tori's fury buckled beneath the sight of rugged precipices towering in the silvery light. Stars twinkled above the craggy peaks and a gentle breeze whispered over the peaceful countryside.

As if it belonged there, Dru's hand stole around her waist. With his free arm, he gestured toward the silhouette of another ranch house in the distance. "That's where John-Henry lives with his wife Elizabeth and their two boys," he said, ignoring the fact that Tori was squirming to put a respectable space between them. He held her in front of him, just the same. "And over there . . ." He indicated a log cabin which was built against the backdrop of rugged peaks. "That's Jerry-Jeff's house. And there . . ." He directed Tori's attention to the east. "Jimmy-Pete and his new wife live there. And this is your home, Chicago. I want you to stay more than just the night . . ."

He turned her in his arms. His veiled gaze drifted over Tori's enchanting face that was framed with Montana moonfire and skipping shadows. The frustrated emotions that had hounded him for more weeks than he cared to count evaporated. It felt so right, so natural to have Tori in the circle of his arms. He and Tori had grown alike in so many ways and yet they remained in direct contrast in other respects. They had become like two pieces of a living puzzle that made no sense at all until they were together. Dru couldn't put his finger on the elusive emotion that swirled around him, but he felt oddly content when Tori was beside him. This house and its spectacular view hadn't been so dramatic the previous night when he'd stood here alone, gazing up at the moonfire and starlight. But Tori made all the difference in his perspective . . .

Entranced, Dru's lips rolled over hers, drinking freely of the kiss that was more intoxicating than cherry wine. Her feminine fragrance infiltrated his senses, clogging his mind. The feel of her curvaceous body molded familiarly to his caused fires to enflame him. Passion clouded his brain like a dense fog. Lord, why did this mere wisp of a woman drive such intense feelings from inside him? She touched his emotions in ways that no other woman ever had. When he was with her he experienced a kaleidoscope of sensations that put the wind in a whirl, bombarding him from all directions at once.

"Stay with me, Chicago," he whispered against her trembling lips. "I want you here . . ."

Tori had fully intended to reject him—out of pure contrariness. But when he gathered her in those strong sinewy arms and kissed her senseless, Tori couldn't remember why she was so annoyed with him. She was every kind of fool for submitting to her wanton desires and to his softly uttered plea, she knew. There was a vast difference between wanting and loving. And Dru was so secure in his own world that he would probably never come to love her in all the ways she loved him. Yet, Tori couldn't overcome her affection for this dynamic giant long enough to deny him or herself the pleasure she had discovered in his arms.

Her resistance came tumbling down when Dru's explosive kiss shattered her composure. He aroused her by tormenting degrees. He moved her to emotions she hadn't wanted to experience again without his promise of love. But each time he touched her, he made her realize she was every ounce a woman with a woman's needs.

Tori couldn't have formulated a protest to save her life when Dru pushed the sleeve of her gown down to bare her shoulders. A warm draft of kisses drifted over her collarbone. He tilted her head back to grant himself free access to the swanlike column of her throat. Slowly he lifted his gaze to peer at the luscious nymph who had melted in his arms. A tender smile grazed his lips when luminous amethyst eyes surrounded by thick, curly lashes stared back at him. Tori bedazzled him with her blossoming spirit and unrivaled beauty. He had made Tori what she was. He had taught her everything she knew about surviving, about passion. She had become a part of him because he had become a living breathing part of her.

Dru tried to tell himself that they had been through so much together that he had simply become accustomed to her. But he was only deluding himself if he thought that was all there was to it. Oh, he had toyed with cynical thoughts, assuring himself that he was attracted to Tori simply because she was the prettiest female he'd ever laid eyes on, that any normal, healthy male would have responded exactly the same way to her that he had. But time had proved those arrogant theories wrong.

If Tori had been no more than a conquest, he would have lost interest in her long ago. But if anything, his fascination for her had increased. He resented every moment she spent with Caleb instead of him. He envied every radiant smile she bestowed on his own brothers during the course of the evening. He wanted her the way he had never wanted another woman, her soul as well as her body. And now that she was here at his ranch, he couldn't bear to think of letting her go . . .

His rambling thoughts scattered in a thousand directions when Tori lifted a slender hand to trace the curve of his lips. She spoke not a word, but in the shadow of her smile he realized he had just been forgiven for dragging her away from her father without giving her a say in the matter.

Tori had forgiven him because the love she felt for him was stronger than wounded pride and flaming temper. She could have chewed him up one side and down the other, but it wouldn't have changed how she felt in her heart. She had forgiven him because it was impossible to forget her deeply imbedded feelings for him.

What was the use of trying to hide what she felt for him? It only frustrated her. Perhaps she should simply communicate her affection for him in physical desire and pray that one day he would long to hear her confession. After all, it was the voice of stubborn pride that flung insults at him, and wounded dignity that provoked her into temper tantrums. Why endure the torment of this hopeless attraction? So what if Dru had two devoted servants—his valet and his wife? Was it a horrendous crime for a woman to love her husband, even if he couldn't return her affection? Did it make her less of a woman to harbor a love that accepted only what a man was capable of giving?

"I want you, Montana," she whispered as she traced his craggy features. "For as long as it lasts. I want to be with you, to become a part of your life. If you wish me to play the doting wife for your brothers and my father's sake, I will. And when my mother comes to . . ."

Tori wasn't allowed to finish. His sensuous lips swooped down on hers, stealing her words and her breath. He crushed her into his hard contours, molding her pliant flesh to his. He was touched and yet tormented by her words.

"I don't deserve you," he breathed against her tempting lips.

"You're probably right," she tittered softly. "But you're stuck with me until it's time for me to go away . . ."

Tori gave herself up completely to the bubbling emotions that churned inside her. She held nothing back. For the first time ever, she intended to prove the strength of her affection for him, to teach *him* things he didn't know about the power of love. It was no longer something she gave away, expecting something in return. Her love would come with no strings attached and would no longer demand a compromise. She wouldn't say the words, but she would express her emotions in the way she made love to him.

Feeling wild and reckless, Tori wriggled from his arms to fling him a seductive smile. "And now, Andy-Joe, I'm going to teach *you* a few things for a change . . ."

His black brows jackknifed when Tori took him by the hand and led him into the room with its massive four-poster bed. He felt a certain sense of pride swell inside him when Tori played the seductress. She exuded self-confidence and displayed such great depth of character that it truly amazed him. She was in command and he allowed her to do whatever met her whim . . .

A startled gasp erupted from Dru's chest when Tori clutched her fist in the front of his shirt and sent buttons flying. He stood there gaping at her as if she had sprouted another head. When she sashayed around behind him to yank off his shirt and then carelessly flung it aside, his head swiveled on his shoulders to peer incredulously at her.

"What has gotten into you?" Dru questioned, staring at the shirt that had not one button left on it. "I swear your mind has snapped."

"I'm crazy all right," she agreed with careless laughter. "But I prefer that to sanity, and I'm tired of taking myself so seriously." From behind him, her arms slid around his bare waist to loosen his breeches. "I'm going to do what comes naturally when I'm with you, and I'm going to enjoy every delicious moment of it."

"Godamighty, Chicago!" he croaked when her adventurous hand brushed over his hips, causing his knees to fold up like an accordion.

Tori tucked her thumbs in the waistband of his breeches and tugged them downward. "I'm demanding my wifely rights," she informed him saucily. "And I want to hear no complaints from you."

When he stood in the pool of trousers that encircled his feet, Tori moved to stand directly in front of him. Her gaze ran the full length of his muscular torso, blatantly admiring his powerful physique, absorbing the magnificent sight of him as if he were a feast she were devouring.

293

"Lie down, Andy-Joe," she demanded, still raking him with feminine appreciation and an impish smile that caused his thundering heart to beat against his ribs like a drum.

"Quit calling me that," he insisted, refusing to budge from his spot.

"I'll call you whatever I please whenever I please," she countered with a saucy grin. "And when I want you in my bed, you'll be there." To emphasize her point, she pressed her palms to his chest and gave him a forceful shove.

Dru flapped his arms like a windmill to maintain his balance, but his feet became entangled in his breeches and he plopped back on the bed. He had every intention of regaining his feet until Tori pulled the pins from her hair and tossed her head. A cascade of silver-blond curls tumbled free, entrancing Dru. He watched Tori transform from an elegant sophisticate into a feisty gamin.

Flinging him a provocative smile, she peeled off her gown and tossed it toward the chair, uncaring that she missed her target and the expensive garment fluttered into a crumpled heap on the floor.

Dru swallowed with a gulp when Tori slowly pushed away her chemise and petticoats in a most scintillating manner. There was a flicker in her lavender eyes when she glanced over to gauge his reaction to her bold seduction. She wanted his eyes on her, demanded his absolute attention. For once she was going to be in total command, doing exactly as she pleased with him. To all the world Dru was a tower of strength, but for this one night Tori intended to take control and prove her power over him. She was going to spread her love all over him!

But when she playfully bounded onto the bed, it sagged unexpectedly. Just as the Sullivan brothers anticipated, the romantic mood of the moment was destroyed when the bed slats that had been sawed almost in two gave way to the additional weight of two bodies lying upon it.

"Argh!" Dru roared when the mattress collapsed to

294

the floor with a resounding crash. "Damn those brothers of mine!"

It was at that moment that the four men who had been hiding in the bushes below the balcony began to serenade the startled couple. The Sullivans accompanied themselves by clanging on pots and pans, making enough racket to raise the dead.

Being serenaded by his mischievous brothers was not what Dru had in mind during his romantic tête-à-tête with Tori. Not at all! And he was going to tell those ornery brothers of his where they could stuff their pots and pans!

Chapter 25

Spewing unprintable curses, Dru rolled to his feet and grabbed his breeches, then stamped toward the balcony, spouting profanity all the way. Hastily donning her robe, Tori scuttled behind him, stifling a grin. Dru looked so furious, she swore steam was about to billow from his ears. Now that she had gotten over her anger, she found the entire escapade amusing and she couldn't imagine why Dru was in such a snit.

"Go easy on them, Montana," Tori said, clutching his taut arm.

"Go easy?" he parroted incredulously. "I spent half my life scraping enough money together to keep those brats in breeches and food, and this is the thanks I get!"

Tori rolled her eyes skyward when Dru shook himself loose from her grasp and stormed over to the terrace railing. She had never seen him so angry. After all, it was tradition to play practical jokes on newlyweds. No harm had been done.

"That's enough!" Dru bellowed over the commotion on the lawn.

Amid the uproarious snickers and "music," John-Henry waved at his bare-chested brother who was puffed up with so much irritation that he looked like an inflated bagpipe. "We only wanted to treat you to a *charivari* and help you celebrate your marriage," he declared with a chuckle.

"Thanks for nothing," Dru snarled down at them. His fuming gaze fastened on Billy-Bob. "If you don't get rid of your pesky brothers and come into the house this instant, I'll shoot you myself! For a man who was supposedly on his deathbed three days ago, you certainly recovered in a hurry."

"Aw hell, Andy-Joe. We were just having a little fun . . ." Billy-Bob's voice trailed off when Tori appeared beside Dru on the terrace, looking enchanting. Her exquisite face was framed by a waterfall of sunbeams and moonfire. "After all, you're having yours . . ."

"Watch your mouth, brat," Dru snarled, pulling Tori protectively against him, as if to shield her from his brothers' gawking gazes. "Getting back at me is one thing, but dropping a two-hundred-pound effigy on Tori was something else again."

"Oh, for heaven's sake, my life was in no danger," Tori declared with a sporting smile to the Sullivan brothers. "And thank you for the . . . unusual initiation into the family."

"There. You see? Tori is taking this a helluva lot better than you are," Jerry-Jeff chimed in. "She's all right, Andy-Joe. In fact, she's a better sport than you are."

"Do you want us to play the Wedding March on the pots and pans before we go?" Jimmy-Pete questioned with a snicker. "There's no extra charge."

"Just get the hell out of here," Dru snapped impatiently.

"We planned a party for tomorrow night," John-Henry informed the newlyweds. "The whole town will be invited. Caleb is making the arrangements, and we're roping off the streets for a dance and refreshments and . . ."

"Fine, now why don't you boys run along home and plan all the details while we get some sleep," Dru suggested.

"Sleep?" Jerry-Jeff grinned outrageously. "How dumb do we look, Andy-Joe!"

When four pair of eyes feasted on Tori's scanty attire, Dru muttered in annoyance, "Go home, damnit. Now!"

"Okay, okay," Jimmy-Pete sighed. "Jeezus, don't work yourself into a huff. We're going . . ."

When his brothers scattered into the darkness, Dru heaved a relieved sigh. He and Tori had just begun to get back on friendly terms and his ornery family had gone and spoiled the mood of the moment. Draping an arm over Tori's shoulders, Dru guided her back to the bedroom with its collapsed bed.

"I'm sorry," he apologized. "My brothers never bypass the chance to rib me. They're a rowdy bunch."

Twinkling violet eyes sparkled in the spray of lanternlight that skipped across the room. She reached up on tiptoe to kiss away Dru's annoyed frown. "Now where were we before all that racket started . . . ?"

Dru's irritation dwindled when he was treated to a light, tempting kiss. "Mmm . . . I think we were right about here . . ." His arms glided around Tori's waist, molding her scantily clad body to his muscular torso. But to his dismay, she wriggled free and led him across the room.

"I remember exactly where we were," she declared. "I was about to teach you a few things about lovemaking. And I had insisted that I would have you in bed whenever I want you there . . . collapsed though it is." One delicate finger indicated the tangled sheets. "Lie down, Montana."

Dru did as he was told. Who would argue with a woman whose provocative smile offered intimate promises?

By the time Tori eased down beside him, Dru was aroused by the sight of her satiny skin glowing in the dim light. The living fire that flickered in her amethyst eyes stirred him. It had been an eternity since he had made wild, sweet love to Tori. Quickly, he lost himself to the turmoil of sensations she stirred in him. But when Dru reached for her, Tori stilled his wandering hands and bent to press the slightest whisper of a kiss to his lips.

"Tonight I make the rules, Montana," she insisted in a seductive purr. Her fingertips skied down the slope of his shoulder to encircle each male nipple. Dru groaned in delicious pleasure. "Tonight I'm going to make love to you . . . all night if I so desire . . ."

Another moan of torment echoed in his chest when Tori's petal-soft lips skimmed over his skin and her hands wove a tapestry of ecstasy over his muscular flesh. Her touch was like a whispering wind caressing him. Her kiss was like a butterfly hovering so near and yet incredibly far away. Dru didn't have the faintest idea what had gotten into Tori, but whatever it was, she was making him crazy with desire. Her hands flowed over him like a tide rushing to shore. He felt himself melt when she worked her seductive magic on him. She murmured intimate compliments and love words that turned his mind into mush. Her body brushed over his in a long, titillating caress that caused his heart to hammer against his ribs and created monstrous cravings that drove him over the brink.

But each time he reached for her, Tori pushed his hands away to continue her ardent fondling. It didn't take long to realize that Tori was indeed teaching him things he hadn't known about lovemaking. Her worshipping caresses were the stuff men's dreams were made of. She evoked a mindless longing that Dru doubted anything could satisfy. He was receptive to her touch, to her moist kisses. He felt as if he had been strung on a torture rack and subjected to sweet, soul-shattering torment. Her hands and lips glided everywhere at once and primal needs screamed for release.

Over and over again, she stroked his body, leaving him trembling with frustrated desire. Dru gasped for breath and found no air, only the tantalizing aroma of the siren who had entranced him. He was a prisoner of wild, hungry desire. He lived for but one purpose—to become this sweet witch's possession. She could do with him what she wanted. She had devastated him with tenderness and overpowered him with gentleness. He was her pawn to command, and he didn't care that she was in complete control of his mind and body. She could have anything she wanted for the asking, if only she would end this breathless need that was as ancient as time itself.

"Chicago . . ." Her nickname tripped off his lips in a hoarse gasp.

"Do you want me?" she murmured in question.

"Madly," he rasped.

"And I want you," she responded as her leg slid between his thighs and her roaming hand enfolded him. "You fill up my world. You're the air I breathe, the sun that lights my way . . . Touching you instills intense pleasure, and I don't care if tomorrow ever comes because I'm with you tonight . . ."

Her silken body covered his, the tips of her breasts teasing his chest. Her ravishing kiss revived him the instant before he swore he had gasped his last breath. This witch set the magical cadence of their lovemaking, and Dru drowned in the myraid of fervent sensations that splashed over him. He could feel himself losing his grasp on reality, feel himself letting go with his heart, his soul, and his body.

He had become her possession, the living flame within her. His body quivered in ineffable pleasure that burned with the heat of a thousand suns. Dru had sacrificed every smidgen of strength to be one with this imaginative sprite who had entangled him in her web of black magic. Emotions that had only been pricked in passionate moments of the past were left to bleed. Dru had no control. The fierce emotions consumed him, and he clutched Tori to him as if the world were about to end.

Like a drowning swimmer clinging to a life preserver, he held on to her, afraid he would crush her delicate body but unable to let her go. And then his body shuddered in sweet, satisfying release, siphoning his energy and strength. His mind was numb, his body spent. It was a long, dazed moment before his stampeding heart slowed its galloping pace, and even longer before the fog of passion lifted from his brain.

Tangled black lashes swept up to peer at the face of the angel who hovered above him, gracing him with an adoring smile. His hand absently slid over the curve of her back to rest intimately against her hip. Sweet mercy, he felt as if he had been flung in a hundred different directions at once.

"You are a very skillful lover," Tori complimented as she traced his sensuous lips and grinned mischievously. "Would you like to try for *exceptional?*"

Dru stared at Tori as if he had never seen her before in his life. Lord, was this the same timid bluestocking he had abducted from Chicago? Hardly! "What the devil has come over you? All of a sudden you're trying to seduce me every time I turn around," he croaked.

"Feeling threatened, Montana?" she taunted. Her hand glided the full length of his steel-honed body. "Don't you think you're man enough to satisfy me?"

"Will you stop that, for crying out loud," Dru grumbled, catching her adventurous hand in his own.

"I can't," Tori insisted as she arched against his hair-roughened flesh. "Seducing you makes me crazy . . ."

Dru was quickly growing used to being the object of her rapt attention. In fact, he delighted in this new facet of her. And from all indication, it appeared she was going to have her way with him again. He couldn't fight the ravenous feelings that overwhelmed him when Tori whispered her need for him and teased him with light, sensuous caresses.

Tori had turned his well-organized world upside down. She had shed her self-reserved cocoon and spread her velvet wings. When she came to him, creating a tempest of passion, she blew the stars around, and Dru was engulfed in a storm cloud of indescribable sensations.

And it was almost dawn when Dru finally settled down to sleep with Tori nestled in his arms. And only then it was because their long, wondrous hours of lovemaking had exhausted him.

Chapter 26

Tori swore she had awakened in someone else's dream. Her eyes fluttered open to see Dru peering down at her with a look of total possession. He had pulled away the sheet that covered her to admire her shapely figure while she was unaware.

She chided him playfully for his action while he continued to devour her with those baby-blue eyes that had long ago melted her heart.

"Horrible, aren't I?" he admitted with a soft chuckle. His hand skimmed over her luscious curves and swells, quietly marveling at her exquisite loveliness. "I can never seem to get enough of you, Chicago . . ."

His voice trailed off when a strange, inexplicable fear washed over him. It didn't have a name or a cause. It was just a fleeting premonition that rose from deep inside him, whispering that nothing this good could last, that something or someone lurked in the shadows to tear Tori from his arms.

A frown knitted Tori's brow when the indecipherable emotions chased each other across Dru's chiseled features. "What's wrong, Montana?" she questioned apprehensively.

Dru shrugged off the unsettling thought and pasted on a nonchalant smile. "I guess I'm just not accustomed to feeling quite so content," he murmured, bending to plant a kiss on her inviting lips.

"And I feel like loving you again . . ." Tori whispered, unable to contain the tender emotions that welled up inside her.

"I'm not resisting," Dru purred as he clutched her tightly to him, fighting down the nagging feeling of impending doom that hounded him.

"Breakfast!" Whong called from the hall.

Before Dru could accept or decline breakfast in bed, the door creaked and Billy-Bob sailed into the room in front of Whong, who scuttled in with a tray in hand. Muttering, Dru whipped the sheet over them and glared at the two men who had the audacity to invade their privacy without being granted permission to enter.

"The reason God made doors was for people to knock on them," Dru snapped crankily.

Billy-Bob broke into a grin, and his unguarded gaze flooded over Tori's mass of tangled blond hair and barely concealed form. "I just wanted to tell my new sister-in-law good morning," he drawled, still all eyes.

"Birry-Bob thought you might rike to be served breakfast in bed," Whong said meekly. "I tord him I didn't think it was a good idea but he insisted." Grabbing the youngest Sullivan's arm, Whong herded him toward the door. "We go now." With a forceful tug, Whong uprooted Billy-Bob from the spot where he stood devouring Tori with his all-consuming gaze.

"Thank you for being so considerate," Tori murmured, fighting down her blush. "The food smells delicious."

With a humble bow, Whong slammed the door shut before Billy-Bob could barge back in.

"I think Billy-Bob has a terrible crush on you," Dru concluded, staring thoughtfully at the door.

"And I'm terribly fascinated with his oldest brother," she whispered as she leaned over him to reach the toast that was heaped with apple butter. She broke it in two to share with Dru, but the topping plopped on his chest.

304

Grinning mischievously, Tori lifted the toast so the rest of the apple butter dripped on his shoulder.

Dru felt the familiar cravings channel through him when Tori playfully licked at the globs of jelly she had purposely slopped on him. "I thought you were hungry . . ." he squeaked, his voice one octave higher than normal.

"Mmm . . . I am," Tori attested before tasting and touching him again. "But the apple butter goes better on you than on the toast."

When Dru settled down, he and Tori gave new meaning to breakfast in bed. Dru made a meal of the beguiling minx who eagerly responded to his roaming caresses and devouring kisses. Together they explored the wondrous realm of passion, feasting on the pleasures they evoked in each other.

It was several hours later before they descended the steps to find Whong and Billy-Bob anxiously awaiting their arrival.

"You riked the breakfast I prepared for you?" Whong questioned Tori.

Tori flashed Dru a saucy smile that forced him to camouflage his snicker in a cough. "Indeed I did, Whong," she assured him enthusiastically. "In fact, I can't remember another time when I enjoyed a meal quite so much."

Billy-Bob glanced from his eldest brother to the dazzling blonde, wondering what secret they were sharing. It must have been a juicy one, judging by the twinkle in Dru's sky-blue eyes. "It's a good thing the two of you came down. John-Henry was threatening to come and get you. Tori's two sisters-in law are anxious to meet her."

The instant Tori reached the bottom of the steps, Billy-Bob grabbed her arm and whisked her away from Dru to make the introductions. It was then that Dru decided it was time for him to begin building Billy a home of his own. The kid definitely had a crush on Tori, he diagnosed. Well, Billy would just have to find his own wife because Dru wasn't prepared to give *his* up.

Tori was delighted to find that Elizabeth and Sarah were charming company. It had been weeks since she had been able to converse with women her own age. They made her welcome in the family and invited her to stop by their homes whenever it met her whim. Tori eagerly accepted the invitations and sighed happily when the congregation of Sullivans filed out the door after devouring the noon meal and relating a few dozen more anecdotes about the rowdy Sullivan brothers, replete with details of their wayward youth.

After the procession of family rode away, Dru peered down into the wide violet eyes that dominated Tori's enchanting face. Lord, what had come over him? For the past few weeks he had been so frustrated and on edge that he couldn't think straight. And now he felt as if he were lounging on a puffy cloud. My, what a difference one night had made. He and Tori hadn't exactly come to any sort of understanding, but they had silently admitted that the fragile bond between them was worth protecting. And perhaps when the Cassidys, their posse, or whomever they sent to retrieve Tori finally arrived, she wouldn't want to leave him. And maybe after a few days of peaceful harmony between them, they could . . .

"I would like to see your ranch," Tori requested, dragging him from his pensive deliberations. "Will you show me around, Montana?"

There was nothing he would have liked more than to circle the perimeters of the sprawling ranch and then find a secluded place to pick up where they had left off this morning. But he had neglected his duties during his absence and there were a million things to do. There were calves to be separated and driven into the mountain meadows to graze, and fat beeves to be cut from the herd in preparation for filling Caleb's order for meat.

"It will have to wait a day or two," Dru replied, watching Tori frown in disappointment. "I have several matters to attend to this afternoon. My brothers and I will be organizing a roundup. The bulls need to be penned up so they won't cause us trouble while we're working the calves. But maybe tomorrow we can devote the afternoon to each other."

Tori nodded agreeably. She knew she was being selfish for wanting Dru's constant attention. But the previous night and this morning had been a new beginning for them. They had begun to set aside their differences and behave like newlyweds. Tori yearned to bask in the warmth of Dru's smiles, to touch him and hold him whenever it met her whim. Well, she would just have to learn to amuse herself while he was tending his chores, she supposed. She had only asked to share his life for a time, not to monopolize every hour. She desperately wanted to win Dru's love, but she knew she would have to take each day as it came if she hoped to earn his affection. Tori reminded herself not to strangle him with her love, only to shower him with it without being overly demanding.

"Another day then," she confirmed before reaching up to sketch his craggy features.

"And tonight . . ." Dru swept her into his sinewy arms to plant a passionate kiss on her dewy lips. A roguish grin dangled on the corner of his mouth as he set her back to her feet. "Bring the peach marmalade, Chicago. I'm especially partial to that flavor."

Tori flashed him an impish smile. "Shall we say about midnight? Shortly after the party?"

"I'll be there," Dru assured her before he swaggered down the steps to fetch his horse.

"I'll be waiting with the marmalade . . ."

An embarrassed gasp erupted from her lips when she wheeled around to see Whong lingering in the open door, muffling a snicker behind a sneeze.

Composing herself, Tori squared her shoulders. "Mr.

307

Sullivan wishes a snack before he retires for the night," she explained awkwardly.

"So it seems," Whong tittered, watching Tori turn all the colors of the rainbow. "Uh . . . this marmarade?" Glistening black eyes held Tori hostage. "Does Mr. Surrivan wish to eat it or wear it?"

Gathering what was left of her dignity, Tori breezed past the giggling Chinaman whose shoulders shook in amusement, causing the long queue to ripple down his back like a winding snake. "I'll help you clear the table and wash the dishes," she volunteered for lack of a better way to divert his attention.

"I rike you very much, Mrs. Surrivan," Whong declared as he scuttled into the dining room behind her. "You have put a sparkle in Mr. Surrivan's smire. For too rong he has tried to rive his brothers' rives for them without enjoying his own. I think he is very grad he married you, even if he isn't very good at saying what he feers." A smile pursed his lips before he hurriedly grabbed his handkerchief and sneezed into it. "And I rike having you around, too."

Tori stared into Whong's gentle face. Her embarrassment faded like shadows melting in sunlight. "I like being here . . . And maybe you had better make that two jars of peach marmalade," she added with a playful wink.

Whong bowed before her. "As you wish, madam." He peeked up at Tori with a conspiratorial smile. "I wirr arso see to it that Birry-Bob doesn't disturb you in the morning."

"Thank you, I would appreciate that," Tori tittered.

"So would Mr. Surrivan . . . I think," Whong murmured before following Tori into the kitchen with a stack of dirty dishes.

Chapter 27

After rounding up and sorting cattle all afternoon, Dru hurried back to the house with enough time for a quick bath, shave, and a change of clothes. Although Dru didn't begrudge the party his brothers had organized to celebrate his marriage, he'd had quite enough of effigies dropping out of closets and slats falling out of beds to last him a lifetime. And judging by the tantalizing effect Tori had on him when he spied her in the form-fitting pink satin gown she had donned for the party, Dru knew he would have his hands full just keeping the men a respectable distance from her at the dance. What he didn't need was more pranks to distract him from his vigil tonight . . .

Dru's thoughts trailed off when Tori's hand slid over his knee to give him an affectionate pat while they journeyed to town in the carriage. He marveled at the changes that had come over this mystifying pixie since the previous night. It was as if she were making a subtle attempt to resolve the problems between them, to give their marriage a sporting chance. Dru didn't have the vaguest notion what was going to happen when the Cassidys arrived. Oh, he had a few speculations, none of which appealed to him. He wasn't sure he could endure having Tori uprooted from his life now that she had embedded herself so deeply in his mind. And even if he and Tori tried to make a go of their marriage, he suspected Gwendolyn would do all within her power to take Tori back where she supposedly belonged—and away from Caleb's influence. But Tori didn't belong in Chicago anymore, Dru mused as he urged the horses into a faster clip and tossed Tori an engaging smile. She was no longer the naive little princess, and Dru couldn't begin to imagine what his days would be like without her in them.

"Save the first and last dance for me," Billy-Bob requested as he sidled closer to Tori than necessary.

"Those two are reserved for me," Dru informed his little brother. "And I would appreciate it if you would try to remember I'm Tori's husband."

"You needn't remind me," Billy grumbled, sliding away from Tori when Dru's disapproving gaze riveted on him. "How can I forget you're the one with all the luck."

"Wirr you arso save a dance for me?" Whong questioned hopefully.

Tori glanced at the Chinaman's warm grin and eagerly accepted.

Godamighty, not Whong, too? Dru thought. The poor little man had obviously taken a fancy to Tori. With all the competition for her companionship, Dru would be fortunate to enjoy more than two dances with his much sought-after wife. Besides Billy-Bob and Whong, there were thousands of love-starved miners in Virginia City. From the look of things, Dru would find himself standing at the back of a long line of men who were anxious to dance with Tori. Damn, maybe this party wasn't such a good idea after all.

That thought resounded in his brain as he reined the team of horses to a halt on the outskirts of town. The streets were congested with so many people that they resembled a milling mob. Pianos had been rolled onto the dance area that had been roped off, and the piano music, blending with fiddles, harmonicas, and tambourines, rang in the breeze. Whiskey was flowing like a river, and laughter rippled through the evening air like a tidal wave.

In disbelief, Tori stared at the crowd. The elegant balls she had attended in Chicago were dignified affairs. This party in no way resembled the stuffy gatherings to which Tori had grown accustomed. There was laughter and shouting, the likes she had never heard.

The minute Tyrone Webster spotted the guests of honor, a wicked smile pursed his lips. He had a few surprises for the bride and groom. Tyrone hadn't taken it kindly when both Tori and Dru had barged one after the other into his office to read him the riot act. Since they had interfered in *his* business, he fully intended to reciprocate by meddling in *their* affairs.

Still sporting a diabolical grin, Tyrone watched Dru assist his new bride from the carriage and lead her to the dance area. Very soon they would both regret tangling with him, Tyrone predicted. He had every intention of spoiling their evening.

"They're here," Duke Kendrick reported as he swaggered up beside Tyrone.

"So I see," he said blandly. Tyrone lifted his arm to toast the striking couple. "We will ensure that the sassy chit and her husband get exactly what they deserve."

"I'd like to be the one to give that spitfire what she deserves," Duke mumbled, his dark eyes raking Tori with lusty anticipation.

"Keep your distance," Tyrone ordered brusquely. "I have plans for that minx and her burly husband and I don't want you botching them up."

Duke had always resented Tyrone's air of arrogant authority, but he managed to clamp down on his tongue . . . for now. But Duke had his own plans for the feisty blonde despite Tyrone's sharply barked commands.

"Before this shindig is over, Tori will be crosswise of her husband. But little does she know it's only the beginning of her troubles," Tyrone mused aloud.

As far as Tori was concerned, she didn't have a care in the world. She found herself swept into Dru's powerful

311

arms to dance in rhythm to a lively folk tune. And when Dru smiled down at her, her heart swelled with pleasure. For the first time in their rocky courtship, she felt as if they were dancing on the threshold of happiness. Dru hadn't confessed his love, but his attentive attitude toward her hinted that he had become fond of her, at least a little . . .

Tori had just begun to enjoy Dru's attention when a swarm of "calico queens" converged on them to tap her on the shoulder. Before Tori could reject their requests to dance with Dru, one of the hurdy-gurdy girls wedged her way in front of Tori and latched on to Dru. Tori found herself on the outside of the tight circle formed by a dozen females who anxiously awaited their turn to dance with the groom. But Tori had no time to concentrate on the zealous females who wrapped themselves around Dru like clinging vines. Billy-Bob was Johnny on the spot, sweeping her into his arms and twirling her in a dizzying pirouette.

"Aren't you afraid you'll rip a stitch?" Tori questioned the young man who was showing off by executing every dance step he'd ever learned.

"My wound isn't as serious as all that," he said with a careless shrug. To impress Tori, he performed a high-stepping jig. "I feel ten times better when I'm holding you." He gave her a roguish wink. "You're all the medicine I need to cure what ails me, pretty lady."

A light skirl of laughter bubbled from Tori's lips. "Billy-Bob, you are an outrageous flirt," she chided, but there was too much amusement in her voice to wound her captivated admirer.

"I learned it all from my big brother," he declared before raising his brows suggestively. "Would you like for me to show you what else Andy-Joe taught me?"

"No thank you." Tori smiled wryly. "I think I already know."

Billy-Bob's shoulders dropped deflatedly. "Yeah, and he's the one who has been doing the practicing when I'm the one who needs the experience."

Before the conversation became more intimate than Tori liked, she switched topics to distract Dru's rakish younger brother. And to her relief, Jerry-Jeff ambled up to beg a dance as soon as the music ended. Although the middle Sullivan brother wasn't married and was also an impossible flirt, he wasn't as straightforward as Billy-Bob. Tori was able to let her guard down for a few minutes, at least until she was swept into another set of arms belonging to one of the endless rabble of miners who had come into town to join in the festivities.

Although Dru was surrounded with eager dance partners, he tried to keep a watchful eye on his wife while she was being passed around like a curious and coveted treasure. A certain sense of pride consumed him, knowing the male population of Virginia City was taken with Tori's radiant beauty and keen wit. Dru took solace in the fact that when the party ended, he would be the one who would be going home with her.

The tantalizing thought caused a smile to cross his lips. He had noticed the two jars of marmalade sitting on the night stand beside the bed that Whong had prepared while Dru was tending to cattle business. Dru had great expectations for the evening that would begin where this rowdy party left off . . .

Sighing tiredly, Tori elbowed her way through the crowd to reach the refreshment table that had been placed outside her father's restaurant. She had just taken a sip of spiked punch when Caleb strolled up beside her.

"Having a good time, honey?" he inquired with a hopeful smile.

Tori nodded affirmatively. "This street dance is a new experience for me," she replied, reaching out to give her father's hand a fond squeeze.

"Nothing like the fashionable affairs your mother dragged you to, I expect," Caleb sniffed. His gaze drifted

313

across the crowd to settle on Dru, who was surrounded by a mob of eager females. "I hope things are going well for you and Dru."

"As well as can be expected, considering he married me because . . ." Tori chewed indecisively on her lip and then decided to be honest with her father. "The truth is, I think Dru is only pretending to be content with this marriage for appearance' sake. I believe he feels trapped and is only trying to make the best of the situation."

A disappointed frown gathered on Caleb's brow. "I had hoped for more than that, Tori," he said with a wistful sigh. Caleb peered at the contents of his glass. "Dru is a good man, the best. But he is not accustomed to being tied down, other than to his family. Be patient with him. He'll adjust."

Tori didn't want adjustment and concession. She desperately wanted Dru's love, even if she had resolved to settle for less.

Caleb dared to pose the same direct question to Tori that he had fired at Dru. "Do you love him?"

"Yes," she responded without hesitation. "For all the good it will probably do me."

Affectionately, Caleb slid his good arm around her trim waist and gave her an encouraging hug. "Love isn't always what it's cracked up to be," he murmured remorsefully. "But I pray your marriage turns out better than mine."

When Elizabeth Sullivan swept upon the boardwalk to beg a dance with Caleb, he handed his glass to Tori. His eyelid dropped into a wink and he graced his daughter with a smile. "Make that husband of yours realize what a good deal he got when he married you," he said as Elizabeth led him away.

Tori smiled to herself. It was nice to know her father thought she was special, even if Dru didn't. Determined to keep her spirits up, Tori set the glasses aside, intent on dancing and enjoying herself. There was still the outside chance that Dru was willing to meet her halfway. And

314

when they were alone in the privacy of their room she would quietly assure Dru that . . .

Her thought stalled when Tyrone Webster—the very last person she wanted to see—swaggered toward her, wearing a smug smile and chewing on his cigar.

"When the Sullivan brothers throw a party, they certainly try to do it up right, don't they?" Tyrone remarked. His tone hinted that he could have gone one better if this had been a party of his making. "I, however, would have been more discriminating by refusing to invite the local riffraff, gamblers, and miners. They can be a raucous bunch."

"I'm sure you find the whole affair terribly inconvenient," Tori smirked, her voice laden with sarcasm. "It must make it difficult for you to bushwack men whose property you lust after while they are surrounded by so many witnesses."

The pretentious smile slid off Tyrone's lips, and it was difficult to tell if the man had a mouth. When he sneered, there was no more than a thin slit on the bottom half of his face. "You're a fool, Mrs. Sullivan. I take offense to insults and false accusations. And it has been my policy never to get mad when I find more satisfaction in getting even."

Tori looked him up and down as if to implicate he ought to know what a fool looked like—being one himself. "And you are very presumptuous to think I feel the least bit threatened by a man like you, Mr. Webster. One day soon you will get what you deserve for using unscrupulous methods to acquire enough property to control the entire town. The instant you make one false move, you will find yourself trying out the territory's new prison system."

Tyrone couldn't believe this chit's audacity! Again he was left to wonder if she could make good her threats. Duke had learned that Tori had indeed sent a telegram to her stepfather's lawyer, requesting an investigation. But Tyrone intended to have his retaliation before reinforcements arrived. There would be no investigation because Tori wouldn't be around to file charges. There were ways to deal with this spitfire and ways to get what he wanted from Caleb and Dru. In fact, she was going to help him, even though she didn't know it.

Mockingly, Tyrone tipped his hat to the sassy sprite. "Good night, Mrs. Sullivan. Don't break a leg while you're dancing . . ."

Tori countered with a smile that was every bit as taunting as Tyrone's. "Don't wander off all by yourself, Mr. Webster. It would grieve me if one of your hired gunslingers mistook you for his next victim and blasted you to smithereens."

Gnashing his teeth, Tyrone stuffed his cigar in his mouth and stalked off stiff-legged. Tori bit back a grin. She hadn't been able to control her tongue. She knew she shouldn't have antagonized that walking scarecrow, but his insufferable arrogance brought out the worst in her. And if that man thought she was going to forget she suspected him of ambushing Caleb and Billy-Bob, he had another think coming. There was no way in hell that varmint was going to use his skullduggery to assume control of her father's or Dru's investments, not if she could do something to stop him. Tyrone might have had visions of renaming this mining metropolis Webster City in his honor, but it wasn't going to happen. When the proper authorities arrived to deal with Tyrone, she would have him kept under surveillance. Her stepfather would back her, she assured herself. And if worse came to worst, Tori would sic Edgar's railroad gang on Tyrone. He thought he was so clever. Well, he had a long way to go, and he would find himself pounded into the ground if the burly giants in the rail gangs swarmed in on him. He would be no more than a spike driven into the track!

Chapter 28

Tori was just recovering from her unpleasant conversation with Tyrone when a half dozen calico queens buzzed around the refreshment table to gulp down the spiked punch. A buxom brunette sashayed over to toss Tori a wide smile and then flung her mane of curly sable hair over her shoulder.

"You're one lucky lady, honey," Sophie drawled before guzzling another swig of punch. "Andy-Joe Sullivan is one helluva man . . ."

Tori squelched the rise of irritation. She had wondered if she would ever chance to meet one of Dru's harlots. And sure enough, it looked as though she had. Tori told herself she was above petty jealousy, and she tried to respond accordingly. "Yes, he is that," she murmured politely.

Another dance-hall girl positioned herself opposite Tori and grinned wickedly. "Andy-Joe is more than that," she declared as if she knew exactly what she was talking about. "Why, the girls at the crib wait in line to get a turn at him. Nobody makes love the way Andy-Joe does . . ."

It was with tremendous effort that Tori clamped down on the reins of her temper. But this off-color conversation was playing havoc with her disposition, and it was almost impossible to hold her tongue.

"A woman can't possibly hope to restrict a man with Andy-Joe's incredible appetite," Sophie remarked between drinks. "Why, Andy-Joe made a similar comment just the other night while we were . . ."

Her hand flew to her mouth and then she carelessly shrugged off her blunder. "Ah well, I'm sure you didn't expect fidelity when you spoke your marriage vows. Andy-Joe said he decided to get married because it was time he had a wife and settled into his position like a respectable cattle baron. Wealthy landowners always think such things," she confided with an air of authority on the subject. "I guess they presume marriage gives them prestige and respectability, even if they do frequent the cribs and bordellos." Her shoulders lifted and dropped in a gesture of casual acceptance. "That's just the way men are, and we just have to accept them."

"But you're fortunate to have acquired Andy-Joe's name," Eleanor chimed in, watching Tori place a stranglehold on her glass. "No female in these parts was able to do it. You should at least be proud of your accomplishment."

"Excuse me," Tori muttered as she wedged past the passel of painted females, holding fast to her thin thread of patience. Although she calmly set her glass aside, she was entertaining thoughts of dumping the punch bowl on Eleanor and Sophie's heads! What spiteful chits they were to reveal Dru's indiscretions. And damn him! If she were toting a pistol, she would show Dru how expertly she had learned to use it by blowing him to kingdom come.

"Give Andy-Joe a good massage for me," Sophie called after her. "He likes that after the loving is over."

With her back as stiff as a flagpole, Tori marched off the boardwalk and disappeared into the crowd. What had begun as a pleasant evening had turned sour in a matter of minutes. A *massage?* Her fingers curled at the thought. She'd strangle that philanderer. According to Sophie, Dru had been tomcatting all over town while Tori was

318

visiting Caleb. That miserable rat! He was making a laughingstock of her while he was tumbling every whore in Virginia City. The nerve of that man. Tori was making an attempt to play the loving wife, to communicate her affection for Dru without smothering him with all the affection she had kept bottled up inside her. And all the while he had been cavorting all over town with every two-bit doxie he could lay his hands on!

As luck would have it, Tori found herself face-to-face with Duke Kendrick when she veered toward the hotel to take refuge in her father's parlor. The leering glance he gave her added kindling to Tori's temper. When Duke hooked his arm around her waist and pulled her against him, Tori responded by emblazoning her hand on his cheek.

Duke's leering smile became an instant snarl. "You persnickety little bitch," he hissed, his fingers clamping into her ribs to hold her in place. "You'll regret that."

"Take your disgusting hands off me," Tori spluttered, worming for release even though he was painfully prying her ribs apart. When Duke refused her demand, her hand fastened on the butt of his revolver. With the speed of a striking snake, Tori whipped the Colt from its holster and rammed it in his belly. His snarl froze on his harsh features. "Back off." Her voice held a hushed but foreboding threat.

Begrudgingly, Duke unclamped his hand and retreated a step, but the murderous glower he flung at her indicated she had made of him an even worse enemy. "You'll live to regret this," he growled.

"And if you don't keep your distance from me, you won't live much longer," Tori snapped, her temper so sorely put upon already that she had to resist the urge to fill this cocky gunslinger with his own buckshot.

Boldly, she reached over to stuff the revolver back into the holster and then flashed Duke a glittering glower. "You may push other people around with your brutish ways, but I am not afraid of you. Now why don't you go crawl back under a rock with the rest of the snakes."

When Tori spun on her heels to stamp off, Duke thrust out an arm to snare her. Tori could count all of Duke's teeth in the torchlight when he stuck his face in hers and sneered at her.

"One of these days, little Miss High and Mighty, you and I are going to find out if you're as special as you seem to think you are." A menacing smile tightened his lips. "Being a gambler, I'd wager you couldn't please a man, even with that shapely body of yours. Sullivan is probably wishing he would have married more of a woman. I'll bet you can't satisfy him even if you tried. Saucy bits of fluff like you never can."

Tori yanked her arm free and stifled the urge to rearrange his features. "You can go to hell and take Webster with you," she spewed before she pushed bodies out of her way to reach the boardwalk that led to the hotel.

Silently fuming over her confrontation with Duke and the malicious barflies from the local saloons, Tori stamped down the street. She wasn't spending another night at Dru's ranch. And she wasn't going to make a go of this ridiculous marriage, either! It was officially over. Tori had no intention of tolerating Dru's inconsistencies. He had once claimed that he would seek affection at home if he ever took a wife. But once a roving-eyed rake, always a roving-eyed rake, she realized dispiritedly. And when Gwen or whoever she had sent to retrieve Tori arrived, she was going back to Chicago and she wasn't going to spare that cruel, unfaithful, inconsiderate Dru Sullivan another thought . . . ever!

"Where are you going, Chicago?" Dru clutched Tori's arm before she reached the hotel lobby.

"Remove your hand or lose it," she snapped furiously.

Dru's brows furrowed into a perplexed frown. "What in hell's the matter with you?"

"I hate you." Tori was on the verge of tears, but she somehow fought them back before they blinded her.

Blue eyes widened in surprise. "What did I do?"

"What didn't you do and with whom is the question," she spumed, worming her arm free. "The soiled doves of Virginia City have been briefing me on your lustful expertise. And how dare you dally with them while I was staying with my father! I'll never forgive you for that!"

"I did no such thing," Dru growled in protest.

"Well it was the unanimous testimony of your harem of lovers," Tori sputtered in outrage. "It's your word against theirs, and they certainly seemed to know what they were talking about, believe you me!" It was all she could do to prevent screaming in his face.

"My brothers!" Dru snarled ferociously. "They must have put those harlots up to this. Another of their ornery stunts, no doubt."

"Isn't it just," Tori smirked, not believing him for a second. "Sure, go ahead and blame your brothers to cover up your dalliances. Coward! Why don't you simply admit one woman isn't enough to appease your voracious, lustful appetite."

Grumbling a rapid string of oaths, Dru shackled Tori's wrist and uprooted her from her spot, even when she set her feet and refused to stir a step. In swift strides, Dru dragged his angry wife through the crowd. When he spied John-Henry dancing with Elizabeth, he propelled himself and Tori toward the couple.

Grabbing John-Henry by the shoulder, Dru spun him around to meet his menacing sneer. "Tell Tori you put those barflies up to that prank," Dru demanded sharply.

"What prank?" John-Henry's craggy features puckered bemusedly.

"You know precisely what prank, damn you," Dru snarled. "The stuffed effigy and collapsing bed I could tolerate, but this time you've gone too far."

"What the sweet loving hell are you ranting about?" John-Henry wanted to know.

Tori had heard more than enough. She flung herself away from Dru and sped through the maze of dancers. Before she could sail through the door, Dru was upon her. He scooped her into his arms and stomped down the street to the carriage, unconcerned if Whong and Billy-Bob had to walk home.

"Put me down this instant!" Tori railed.

"Not until you're willing to listen to reason," Dru growled back at her.

"If you deny you've ever had anything to do with those doxies, I'll scratch your eyes out," she vowed furiously.

"In the past, yes," Dru begrudgingly admitted. "But not since I returned to Virginia City, and that's God's truth!"

"Why is it that liars are always prepared to swear on stacks of Bibles and challenge lightning bolts to strike them when they spew their false testimony?" she asked the darkness at large. Bucking, Tori tried to launch herself from Dru's arms, but he clamped them around her like a beaver trap.

"I'm not lying to you," Dru protested.

"I'll believe that when the Sahara becomes encased in a glacier," Tori sniffed caustically.

Infuriated, Dru plunked Tori onto the carriage seat and hopped up beside her before she could bound off the other side. "Damnit, Chicago, can't you get it through that thick head of yours that I don't want anyone but you? If you don't believe me, then ask Whong if I ventured into town while you were staying with Caleb."

"Whong would defend you with his last dying breath, no matter how many sins you committed," Tori muttered bitterly. "He worships the ground you stand and *lie* on."

"And I worship the ground you walk on," Dru growled in a frustrated tone that negated his words.

"Of course you do," she smirked as she clamped onto the seat, bracing herself when the carriage skidded around the corner on two wheels and sped off into the night. "That's why I feel so wanted and needed—like a festering boil on one's bare a—"

"Godamighty, Chicago!" Dru muttered before she

322

could spout off the last word. "You're being ridiculous, and if you would calm down, you would realize this was just a prank to put us at odds."

"Well, it worked, and it wasn't a prank. John-Henry proved that!" she hissed venomously.

Muttering under his breath, Dru snapped the reins, sending the horses into their fastest clip. Damn, he'd had such wondrous visions of this evening. Now his wistful dreams had gone up in smoke. Tori was so furious that she was seeing the world through a red haze and Dru was left to defend himself against the mischievous lies that had put Tori in a snit. When he discovered who had put those ornery females up to this prank, he swore he would ensure that the guilty party or parties would never dare to execute another practical joke again!

A gloating smile pursed Tyrone's lips as he watched Dru and his sassy wife barrel down the road, leaving a cloud of dust behind them. He had managed to spoil their wedding celebration and he had far more in store for the Sullivans. Before he was through with them, they would wish they hadn't crossed him.

While Tyrone was feeling quite pleased with himself, Duke stood in the shadows, glaring at Tori's departing back. Damn, how he itched to break that feisty bitch's spirit. Their confrontation had only whetted Duke's thirst for revenge. When he had his chance with that minx, he swore he would show her no mercy.

"Send for Clark Russel and Sam Rother," Tyrone demanded, dragging Duke from his spiteful musings. "Dru Sullivan and his new bride are just learning the meaning of trouble."

"Send for them yourself," Duke grumbled. "I'm not your lackey."

Tyrone bit down on his cigar and glared at the defiant gunslinger. "I pay you to do as you're ordered," he snapped.

Duke detested Tyrone's highhanded manner. Tyrone considered himself an all-powerful force, but Duke was the one who did the dirty work, the one who took all the risks while Tyrone reaped the profits. Duke was fed up with taking orders.

"You pay me to pistol-whip and ambush your victims," Duke corrected gruffly. "And if you think I'm so easy to replace, go ahead and try. You'll find the task more difficult than you think. Even Sam and Clark don't have the stomach to rob and murder the miners you believed were cheating you out of your share of their gold strikes. Without me, you're nothing except a big bag of wind. Anybody can spout orders, but I'm the one who carries them out."

Tyrone coiled like a cobra and glowered into Duke's cold black eyes. "When I took you in, you were nothing but a small-time thief who didn't have enough brains to keep out of trouble," he snorted contemptuously. "Don't forget who put you where you are."

"And don't you forget who put you where *you* are, Webster," Duke snapped back. "Without me, you'd still be just a cocky blowhard with more ideas than ability to carry them out."

Tyrone furiously backhanded Duke across the cheek and then regretted his rashness. Duke possessed a notorious temper, and he reacted violently to physical attack and verbal insult. If Tyrone had known Tori had already pushed Duke as far as he intended to go, he might have resisted the urge to strike the gunslinger.

A pained grunt erupted from Tyrone's lips when Duke retaliated by burying a fist in his belly.

"I'll fetch Sam and Clark because I want my turn at that prissy bitch," Duke snarled as Tyrone sucked in a breath and attempted to pull himself upright. "And the next time you need an errand boy, hire one."

With that, Duke stepped back into the shadows and disappeared into the alley. Massaging his tender ribs, Tyrone scowled to himself. He was also going to have to

324

do something about Duke Kendrick. The man was no longer content with his position. Mulling over that thought, Tyrone walked back to the Queen High Saloon, methodically plotting his scheme to acquire Flemming and Sullivan's property, as well as replace the quick-tempered gunslinger who had rebelled against authority.

Chapter 29

The jaunt back to the Bar S Ranch approached breakneck speeds that left Tori breathless from swerving around hairpin curves and bouncing over washboarded roads. The rough ride tested her ability to hang on by her fingernails, not to mention the strain it put on her smoldering temper. Twice she swore she was about to be catapulted from her seat and launched in front of the thundering horses. In her estimation, it was a miracle that she had survived the trip while she was riding with the devil himself.

When Dru stamped on the brake, the carriage screeched to a halt and dust rolled over Tori. In a split second Dru bounded to the ground and yanked Tori into his arms—the very last place she wanted to be. Once he had carried her up the steps and deposited her in the bedroom, he slammed the door and glared mutinously at the outraged blonde whose answering glower was meant to maim and mutilate.

"I don't know why those women said what they did, but it was a bald-faced lie!" Dru said in a booming voice. "And I haven't been with another woman or even wanted one since I met you. Godamighty, Chicago, are you still so naive that you don't know when a man is fascinated with you? And why in hell would I settle for beans when I've got steak at home? Now answer me that!"

If that was supposed to reassure her, it did not! Dru had a bad habit of saying the wrong things. He always had and he probably always would. He made their marriage sound like a cussed meal! The man didn't have a romantic or sentimental bone in his body and there was a world of difference between wanting and loving. Although she had nobly tried to accept less when she wanted so much more, she couldn't. It was tearing her heart out to know Dru had been unfaithful to her.

Tori stood there, her breasts heaving with frustrated torment. She wanted to believe Dru hadn't betrayed her, but without his confession of love, she couldn't.

Hubert had intended to keep both of his mistresses after he married Tori. Why should she expect a virile male like Dru to give up his passel of women? Tori had been prepared to overlook Hubert's infidelity because she hadn't loved him to begin with. But she couldn't excuse Dru's. Her affection for him made all the difference, and he had the power to hurt her as Hubert never could.

Swearing under her breath, Tori stormed over to the dresser to whip out the sexy negligee she had purchased in Council Bluffs. After stomping behind the dressing screen, she tugged off her gown and wriggled into the gossamer creation that dipped low on her breasts and barely covered the curve of her hips. Yanking the pins from her hair, she slinked across the room, portraying one of the many trollops with whom Dru had no doubt cavorted.

Bug-eyed, Dru gaped at the curvaceous minx whose sheer gown did more to entice than conceal. Aware that she had the lusty oaf's attention, Tori sashayed up in front of him. One hand was braced on her hip, and the other one toyed with the silver-gold tendrils that cascaded over her shoulder. After batting her eyes a few times for good measure, Tori eased down to pose seductively on the bed.

"What's your pleasure, love?" she purred mockingly. "Would you like your massage before or after we take a tumble on the sheets?"

A muted growl rolled from Dru's taut lips. "Knock it off, Chicago. A prostitute you'll never be."

His remark only challenged her to play the role that he obviously expected of his wife. "If you've got the money, I'll do whatever you wish," she murmured with another flurry of fluttering eyelashes. "Come on, honey. Don't be bashful. It *ain't* as if this were your first time. Lord knows, you've probably spent more time on your back than on your feet." One delicate brow lifted when a thunderous growl exploded from his lips. "What's the matter, sweetie? Did you want one of the other girls instead of me tonight?"

Dru had endured all he could. Tori's attempt to ridicule the special moments they had shared the previous night and to rub in the dance-hall girls' vicious lies, stretched his temper until it snapped. In a single bound, he pounced on her, pinning her to the bed.

"You want to be treated like a doxie, do you? You want plain and simple tumble?" he growled in hateful question.

Violet eyes drilled into him. "That's all we've ever had anyway," she lashed out to hurt him the same way she was hurting. "I've never been more than your private whore and that's all you expect of me in this marriage. Private?" Bitter laughter gurgled forth when she realized she wasn't the only woman who had slept in his powerful arms and thrilled to his masterful touch. "I hadn't expected to be the first woman you'd ever known, but I had wanted to be the last and the only." Shiny tears swam in her eyes, but Tori angrily brushed them away, determined to speak her piece. "You betrayed my trust in you, and I won't forgive you for that. If I am to be no more than one of the many harlots whose room you frequent, than I fully intend to behave like one!"

Dru was furious. He could have talked until he was blue in the face and it wouldn't have changed Tori's stubborn mind. In her opinion, he was guilty until he could prove himself innocent, and even if he could, she would probably accuse him of bribing his witnesses.

And as much as he wanted this gorgeous sprite, as much as he had anticipated tonight, she had spoiled it with her childish tirade and her attempt to portray a shameless doxie.

Pushing away from the bed, Dru shoved his hand into his pocket and tossed a fistful of coins and gold nuggets at her. "Take the money," he said brutally. "Buy yourself a tutor to teach you how to seduce a man, sweetheart. You could damn sure use the practice. And if you think I've been cavorting all over town, maybe I should, just to prove you right!"

It was a cruel, cutting thing to say, but anger and frustration had a hold of Dru's tongue, putting hateful words in his mouth. The fact that Duke Kendrick had voiced a similar remark a few hours earlier made it doubly difficult for Tori to restrain her tears. Dru might as well have said she couldn't measure up to the women he had known, that her lack of experience bored him.

Now the truth was out and Tori couldn't endure another moment in the same room with this big, brawny beast. She was prepared to crash through the nearest wall to avoid him if need be. The knot in the pit of her belly twisted even tighter, and she swore she had thorns in her throat. Dru couldn't have wounded her more if he had physically attacked her.

With a muffled curse, Tori snatched up her pillow and sheet and dashed toward the door. When Dru caught her arm, she wheeled to kick him in the shins, using another of the techniques he had taught her. But when he didn't let go, Tori bit down on the hand that was clenched around her wrist. With a yelp, Dru released her before she bit a chunk out of his fingers.

Like a bullet, Tori shot down the hall and sailed out the back door, determined to become one of the swaying shadows before Dru could track her. She didn't care where she spent the night, as long as it wasn't with that horrible, infuriating man!

"Damnit, Chicago, come back here!" Dru bellowed at her departing back.

Anger and humiliation had put wings on Tori's feet. She was long gone before Dru reached the back door. Keen blue eyes scanned the shadows, searching for the five-foot-two-inch headache he was having. Muttering under his breath, Dru stamped around the corner of the house, wondering which of the dozen trees Tori was hiding behind.

With the silence of a cat, Tori circled the house, darting in and out of the row of shrubs until she reached the barn. Following the path of moonlight that sprayed across the center section of the open-ended stable, Tori moved quietly past the row of stalls that lined the breezeway. The livestock that had been pinned inside the stalls shifted uneasily. But to Tori's relief, none of them betrayed her by whinnying, braying, or bawling.

The huge-stone-and-timber barn with its spacious loft would become her bedchamber, she decided. She preferred to sleep in the straw rather than with that haystack-headed husband of hers. Talk about insensitive! He had referred to her as a steak, for crying out loud. Tori spitefully wished he was one. She would have delighted in slicing him into bite-sized pieces!

With the pillow and sheet tucked under one arm, Tori made her ascent into the loft that was open in the middle so hay could easily be dropped into the stalls and mangers below. The dark loft made it difficult to navigate and Tori, unfamiliar with her surroundings, reached up to clutch the rope and pulley that stretched from one end of the loft to the other. Employing it as her guide line, she inched across the straw. In the darkness she could barely make out the heaping stack of hay in the corner, but that was her destination—a fluffy straw pallet.

An unidentified noise caused her to glance over her shoulder. Two round eyes that glowed in the faint light peered back at her. It was apparent the barn owl that had perched on the rafter didn't appreciate sharing his accommodations, not that Tori cared one whit. The loft was certainly big enough for the both of them . . .

Her foot landed on the discarded pitchfork that lay

directly in her path, catapulting the handle upward to club her in the shoulder. A startled squawk burst from her lips, putting the owl to flight. The disturbed bird swooped down from his perch to flutter over Tori's head and whizzed through the opening where hay was hoisted into the loft from outside the barn. Instinctively, Tori let go of the rope and ducked away when the hooting owl soared past her.

Another frightened shriek erupted from her lips when her foot slid over the rim of the rectangular opening that gave access to the stalls below. Frantic, Tori dropped the pillow and sheet and flapped her arms like a windmill. But it did no good whatsoever. She couldn't maintain her footing. Knowing she was about to fall, Tori launched herself forward just as both feet dropped off the ledge. Tori scratched and clawed to drag herself back to safety, soundly cursing whoever had designed the loft with a hole in the middle of it. It might have been handy for those who were feeding the livestock but it was disastrous for Tori!

The excess straw that lined the edge of the loft made it impossible for Tori to pull herself up. With a blood-curdling squeal, she dropped down, still clutching the loose hay in both fists. Tori landed with a thud and a groan in the stall below. As luck would have it, Dru had two of his prize bulls penned in the barn until all the cows and calves had been separated. Tori literally dropped in on one of them. The bull, who was nowhere near sociable to begin with, did not take kindly to sharing his stall. With an indignant snort, the two-thousand-pound creature lowered his head and charged while Tori screamed bloody murder.

Now there are some folks whose fear paralyzes them when they run headlong into adversity. And there are other folks who turn tail and run. Tori belonged in the latter category. When the bull pawed the ground and lunged at her, Tori bounded to her feet and leaped into the wide manger, just in the nick of time. The bull's horned head collided with the wood railing, jarring Tori sideways. Her heart very nearly popped from her chest when she felt the huge animal's hot breath on her neck.

With another snort, the bull backed up to butt her again, and Tori flattened herself in the straw and prayed. And oh how she prayed the lumber Dru had used to construct the sides of the manger was strong enough to withstand another collision. If the timber cracked, Tori was in serious trouble.

"Montana!" Tori hadn't meant to scream for assistance, but Dru's nickname involuntarily flew from her bone-dry lips.

Dru was on the far side of the house when he heard Tori's first shrill shriek. He shot down the hill to locate his missing wife who was obviously in trouble or she wouldn't have screamed at the top of her lungs. Dru had just reached the entrance of the barn when Tori yelped for his assistance.

The sounds erupting from the barn reminded Dru of a novice orchestra tuning up for a performance. Hens were clucking on their roosts, horses and mules were neighing and braying while they nervously slammed against the rails of their stalls. Milk cows were bawling, and both bulls were snorting and pawing.

The shaft of moonlight spotlighted Tori, who was desperately trying to throw one leg over the manger and climb over the stall before the bull smashed the railing and tore her to pieces. Frantically, Dru groped for the whip that hung on the left side of the entrance.

With whip in hand, he dashed forward to pop the bull on the nose before he gored Tori through the railing with his deadly horns. The white-faced bull didn't appreciate having the hide snapped off his snout any more than he wanted to share the same space with a human. He backed up four paces and chugged forward like a locomotive.

Quick as a wink, Dru reached over the rail to hook his arm around Tori's waist. Swinging her out of the way, and none too gently in his haste to discourage the charging bull, Dru lashed out at the crazed creature before he smashed the manger to smithereens. With the unwanted intruder out of his private quarters, the bull ceased his assault and stamped around his stall.

Inhaling a gasping breath, Tori wobbled onto weak legs after Dru had roughly tossed her aside. She had been positively furious with Dru and then she'd had the living daylights scared out of her. She was not in the best of moods!

"Are you all right?" Dru questioned, scooping Tori into his arms and striding outside the barn.

"Considering I hate you and I fell from the loft into a stall with a mad bull who had it in mind to make mashed potatoes out of me, I'm in splendid shape," Tori sputtered. "Now put me down!"

Dru ignored her. He had seen the way this dazed sprite had been staggering around on rubbery knees. He wasn't setting her to her feet until he returned to their room, and that was that.

"That was a stupid thing to do," Dru growled at her. "You nearly got yourself killed."

"And you would have made a far better widower than a husband," she parried insultingly. "I can well imagine you would have sought solace in the arms of one of your many paramours the moment after you stuck me in the ground."

"For Chrissake, I told you there haven't been any other women. What will it take to convince you?" Dru exploded, still unnerved by Tori's near brush with calamity and this frustrating topic of conversation that had put them at odds in the first place.

"A sworn confession signed in blood, plus a human sacrifice—both yours—might convince me," she sniped.

Tori squirmed to free herself, but to no avail. Dru was as strong as an ox and he refused to set her to her feet until he had her exactly where he wanted her!

Chapter 30

When Dru reached the bedroom, he tossed Tori on the bed. They were right back where they had started exactly one hour earlier. She was spitting fire and he was blowing smoke.

While Dru stood there struggling to put his tangled thoughts in order, Tori vaulted off the edge of the bed to pluck out the straw that clung to her hair and gown. This done, she snatched up the quilt that lay at the foot of the bed, rolled it lengthwise, and flung Dru a fuming glare. Placing the improvised division line squarely in the middle, Tori plopped down on her half of the bed and presented her back.

"I have heard it said that husbands and wives should never go to bed fighting with each other," Dru muttered to the back of her head.

"We aren't fighting. I'm simply not speaking to you ever again for the rest of my life," Tori qualified as she reached over to swipe his pillow. Hers was somewhere in the barn and she wasn't about to retrieve it, not after the harrowing incident with Dru's lunatic bull!

When Dru stamped around to her side of the bed to glower at her, Tori defiantly flounced onto her right side and looked the other way. Dru refused to tolerate the silent treatment. With a muted growl, he peeled off his shirt and boots and straddled his brooding wife.

"This is my half of the bed," Tori protested, trying to buck him off and spitefully wishing the sap would topple off and land on his wooden head. But two hundred thirty pounds of solid muscle wasn't easily moved, and Dru remained where he was.

When Dru leaned down to take her lips under his, Tori turned the other cheek. She refused to feel anything but anger, now or ever again. Dru wasn't going to woo her with his masterful kisses and skillful caresses. No sirree. She would lie there like a corpse, feeling nothing, wanting nothing to do with him, now and forevermore.

"So that's the way it is, is it?" Dru muttered in frustration.

"That's the way it is," Tori grumbled in confirmation. "If you're so fond of your harlots, you can have them and not me. I don't want you ever again!"

A taunting smile bracketed his mouth as he traced her pouting lips. No matter what his contrary minx said, they were going to bed loving, not fighting. Determined to melt the wall of ice that had formed around Tori's heart, Dru bent to spread a path of butterfly kisses along the trim column of her neck and down her bare shoulder. His hands glided up her thigh and down again, subtly soothing away the tension that plagued her. His hair-matted chest brushed against her breasts as he eased down beside her, holding her exactly where he wanted her.

Tori promised herself that she wasn't going to be stirred by his sensuous assault. Famous last words! Her traitorous body rebelled against the commands sent out by her brain. Forbidden sensations spilled over her as Dru's practiced caresses freed the emotions Tori had desperately tried to hold in check. Involuntarily, her body arched toward his seeking hands, wanting his touch, craving the pleasure he could provide.

"I do hate you," Tori chirped, wondering if she were trying to convince him or herself.

"So you told me," he whispered against the swells of

336

her breasts.

"And I'm really never going to speak to you again," she declared, her voice on the shaky side.

"I understand perfectly," he murmured before his tongue flicked at the dusky peak, dragging a soft moan from Tori's lips.

Like a consuming shadow, passion fell over her, clouding her thoughts, leaving her susceptible to Dru's gentle touch. When his lips made their slow, tormenting ascent back to her lips, Tori helplessly surrendered to the maelstrom of sensations that swamped and buffeted her. Her body became putty formed to fit his hands. Her senses were full of the scent, the taste, the feel of his sinewy contours molded familiarly to hers. The world shrank to fill the space the exact size this exasperating man occupied.

When he touched her so tenderly, as if she were special to him, Tori let herself believe he truly cared for her, that he hadn't betrayed her with other women. It was impossible to think past the moment, to feel anything except the wondrous sensations that piled atop each other like the towering clouds of a thunderstorm. Her heart rumbled in her chest and pleasure sizzled through her like lightning. She was instantly and totally aware of the man who kissed and caressed her. This wizard had cast his spell of passion on her and Tori became a prisoner of her own needs as well as his.

Over and over again, his hands scaled the peaks of her breasts, teasing, tantalizing, leaving her wanting him in the most incredible ways. His lips feathered over her quaking flesh, tasting her as if she were a delicious treat. He whispered love words against her skin, confessing his desire for her. He assured her that she pleased him, and he begged forgiveness for the cruel words that indicated otherwise when he had spoken in anger.

Tori was hopelessly lost. She had the feeling she would get over hating him for betraying her, but she knew she would never get over loving him. It would take an act of

337

God to destroy the fierce hold he had on her body and heart.

Wild tingles flew up Dru's backbone when he felt Tori involuntarily surrender to his amorous assault. Dru ached up to his eyebrows with wanting, yearned to forget the harsh words that had flung them apart. He wanted to surrender—body, mind, and soul—to the fiery desire that channeled through him.

Instinctively, his arms folded around Tori, bringing her silken body into intimate contact with his. He could feel the taut peaks of her breasts against his heaving chest, feel the soft texture of her thighs beneath his. He wanted to absorb her luscious body, to soar through time and space to passion's paradise.

Her arms, as if they possessed a mind of their own, glided over the rock-hard muscles of his shoulder. A ragged sigh tripped from her lips when Dru's scorching kisses seared across her cheek to seek out her lips. Emotions that had been suppressed by wounded pride and anger bubbled forth to spread through every part of her being. Tori felt her body surge eagerly against his as he came to her. Her fingertips tunneled through his raven hair, holding his head to hers while she kissed him with all the fervent feelings that churned inside her.

"Love me, Chicago . . ." Dru commanded hoarsely. "I need you. I've always needed you and no other . . ."

Tori died a thousand deaths when she drowned in the sea of passion that flooded over her. He was whispering words to appease her. But fool that she had always been when it came to this man, Tori succumbed to his quietly uttered plea. She knew he only wanted to satisfy his male desires. She knew he was loving her with his body, not his heart. But Tori couldn't deny him when it meant sacrificing her own wanton needs. He could make her soul sing and she knew the ecstasy that awaited her when they were flesh to flesh, sharing a splendor that defied description.

Her thoughts evaporated when his body drove into

338

hers, causing hot sparks to leap through every muscle and nerve ending. Tori was burning with a fever that only this one man could cure. She matched him, thrust for thrust, kiss for kiss. She experienced the paradox of passion when Dru clutched her tightly to him, making it impossible to breathe. Although she was engulfed in his sinewy arms, she felt as wild and free as an eagle soaring above the craggy mountain precipices. The emotions that avalanched upon her were fierce and intense and she could almost feel the restrictive garments of the soul fall away as she glided past the horizon.

Tori dug in her nails when a maelstrom of sensations pelleted her like driving rain. Shards of pure white light bombarded her just before the universe exploded in a spectrum of brilliant colors. It was as if she were standing apart from the multitude of emotions that assaulted her body, as if she had transcended the realm of reality. She was drifting in paradise, reveling in each magical sensation that had converged upon her . . .

A gasp tumbled from Tori's lips when the star world into which she had skyrocketed collapsed upon her. She was catapulted back through time and space like a meteor blazing back to the earth to be consumed in a holocaust of fire. Her body shuddered convulsively as Dru clutched her to him and held on for dear life.

Dru felt as if he were being sped along a swift-flowing current that sent him tumbling over a frothy waterfall. He dropped into a tranquil pool to bob on rippling waves. He felt drained, as if he had given his all to share the ineffable passion that had wracked his body and numbed his brain. When he made wild passionate love to this feisty vixen, no emotion was left untouched. She shattered his self-control and left him feeling like a mountain that had been blown to bits by a blast of gunpowder.

Affectionately, Dru nuzzled his nose against Tori's and smiled down into her passion-drugged features. "Why should I search elsewhere when you satisfy every need, little minx?" he rasped.

"Why, indeed," Tori choked out, hating him for using the passion between them as an argument for his defense.

Knowing what a lusty lover Dru was, she imagined he would feel the same satisfaction within any woman's arms, even when she would have preferred to believe otherwise. But it just wasn't so. Eleanor and Sophie had convinced her that they had enjoyed the same pleasures Tori had experienced.

A wary frown plowed Dru's brow. He had the unshakable feeling that his attempt to convince Tori that she made lovemaking rare and unique and that he hadn't betrayed her had worked in reverse. The look she gave him suggested he had just cut his own throat instead of proclaimed his innocence.

"Confound it, Chicago, there has been no one else," he muttered in exasperation.

"Of course there hasn't," she muttered sarcastically, biting her trembling lips. "Now if you will kindly crawl onto your side of the bed and leave me to mine, I would like to get some sleep. I will be busy packing in the morning for my return trip to town."

Dru flounced on his side of the bed, but not without flinging her a fuming glower. "You're *not* leaving," he snapped in a tone that invited no argument. "You can visit Caleb anytime you wish, but come dusk, you had damned well better be in our bed—divided though it is!"

"I hate you!" Tori burst out in frustration.

"Really?" Dru smirked as he reached over to retrieve his pillow that lay under Tori's head. "You've told me that so enough that I believe it."

"As well you should," she grumbled, starting a tug-of-war with the one and only pillow. When she gained possession of it, she promptly hit Dru over the head, wishing it were an anvil instead of a feather pillow. Then she turned her back on him. "I'm going home the minute my mother or stepfather come to rescue me."

"Good riddance," he growled spitefully. "It will

probably be the best for both of us."

"Amen to that!" Tori sniffed furiously.

"I'm through trying to cater to you, Chicago. I have enough obligation without a shrewish wife underfoot."

That really hurt! Tori wanted to wail like an abandoned child. But she didn't. She was too angry to cry. "And I'm sick to death of pretending to care for you when I don't. I've been playing a charade for your family's benefit. I want to go home and forget I ever met you!" she said to hurt him the way she was hurting.

"Good!" Dru muttered between clenched teeth.

"Fine! I'll have the marriage annulled the instant I set foot in Chicago."

Tori knotted her fists so tightly that her nails dug into her palms. Flinging cutting remarks at Dru hadn't helped one whit. She was still positively miserable, and she swore the ache in the pit of her belly would never go away. Her marriage was crumbling like a dam disintegrating beneath fierce floodwaters. Where there was no trust there could be no love, Tori mused despairingly. The fragile bond that had once held them together was gone. She would endure Dru's presence until she could return to Chicago. And when she was back where she belonged she would erase this frustrating chapter of her life as if it had never existed!

Love was indeed a cruel, tormenting curse and she knew exactly how her father had felt when Gwen broke his heart. It was pure and simple hell on earth!

Chapter 31

After the fiasco the previous night, Tori felt the need to put a safe distance between herself and her infuriating husband. Dru had stomped out of the house without announcing his destination, and Tori vowed not to be around when he came back. Garbed in her buckskins, she breezed out the door to retrieve a mount. Knowing the Sullivan brothers were scheduled to drive part of their cattle herd northwest into the mountain meadows, Tori aimed herself south to admire the beauty of the rugged precipices and to be alone with her thoughts. She wanted to erase every memory of Dru from her tormented mind. But Montana itself reminded her of Dru. The Montana sky was the color of his eyes. The mountains resembled his striking physique—bold, awesome, and handsome in their ruggedly unique way.

A remorseful smile brimmed Tori's lips when she reflected on their night together. She had behaved like a child throwing a temper tantrum and Dru's good disposition had turned sour as a lemon. She had said terrible things to him and he to her, and she knew they could never smooth out the latest wrinkles in their relationship. Tori had finally resigned herself to the fact that their marriage was a lost cause. And after Dru's humiliating betrayal Tori would never be able to forgive him. Now they couldn't go back to what they'd had just a few short days ago. Dru had spoiled any chance of that . . .

The crunch of rocks above her caused Tori to jerk up her head and glance warily at her surroundings. To her horror, she spied Duke Kendrick and his two scraggly sidekicks poised on the ledge. Gouging her steed, Tori wheeled around to make a dash for the safety of the ranch house. But Duke leaped down at her like a bloodthirsty panther. Tori's shriek of alarm transformed into a pained groan when she was hurtled from the saddle and crushed to Duke's lean frame. His arms fastened around her like a steel trap.

Tori tried to pry one of his revolvers loose. But after their confrontation at the party, Duke had begrudgingly come to respect Tori's resourcefulness, and he made certain she couldn't get her hands on his pistol or knife. As a last resort, Tori scratched and clawed to gain her freedom, but she couldn't escape. The wounds she inflicted on her captor only infuriated him and he pelleted her with a barrage of salty curses.

"You feisty little bitch," Duke snarled as he straddled Tori and braced her arms above her head. "I oughta take you here and now."

Clark Russel grasped the reins of Tori's steed before it bolted and galloped back to the barn. "You better leave her be," he warned Duke. "Webster said to bring her back in one piece so her pa and husband would know she was still alive, at least until he gets them to sign over the property."

Duke was already annoyed with Webster after their heated exchange the previous night, and he was far more interested in settling his score with this blond-haired hellion than in what Tyrone wanted with Tori. But Clark Russel and Sam Rother had been hired to shoot straight and not to think for themselves. They always did exactly what Tyrone told them. When Duke defied Clark by ramming his knees between Tori's thighs and reaching down with one hand to loose his breeches, Sam Rother

344

swore vehemently.

"Get off her, you sonofabitch. We got our orders. You'll get yer turn with her, but not here and not now. If somebody was to see us, Webster's plans would fall through and we wouldn't get paid."

When Duke defied the order, Sam clenched his hand in the nape of Duke's shirt and yanked him backward. "You think you're so goddamn smart, but sometimes you don't seem to have a lick of sense, Duke. Leave her alone until we get her to the shack."

With a sour growl, Duke bounded to his feet and roughly jerked Tori up beside him. "You lay another hand on me, bitch, and I'll make you wish you hadn't," he vowed viciously.

Tori didn't lay a hand on him. But she did spit in his puckered face and received a backhand across the cheek for her daring defiance. When she stumbled back, Duke lunged to maintain his bone-crushing grasp on her arm. Tori screamed bloody murder and the distraught sound bounced off the looming peaks to echo in all directions. Muttering, Sam clamped his hand over her mouth to shut her up. Furious and frantic, Tori bit into his fingers, causing Sam to erupt in a volley of curses that would have burned the ears off a priest.

All three men descended on Tori like a swarm of angry hornets. Before she could scream at the top of her lungs again, a handkerchief was stuffed in her mouth and her hands were bound behind her. In a flurry, the three henchmen scurried around to tie Tori to her mount. In helpless frustration, Tori stared down the narrow path that led to the ranch, wishing her wanderings had taken her another direction, wishing with all her heart that Dru would have been within shouting distance. But only God knew where that man had gone. If he had known Tori had been abducted he probably wouldn't have cared. The path Tori had chosen to ensure she wasn't around when Dru came back had certainly served its purpose, but not in the way she had intended. She had put herself on a collision course with disaster!

Dru might come looking for her when she didn't return by dark, but it appeared he would arrive too late to rescue her. In grim silence, Tori sat atop her steed as they wound through the rocky terrain that led up the western slope of the mountain. To her dismay, the three henchmen veered north, taking them farther away from town and the ranch.

An hour later Tori was yanked from the saddle and propelled into a small, dilapidated shack that was nestled in a clump of pines. A muddled frown creased her brow when she spied the homespun garments that lay on the table. What the blazes was going on?

Sam untied her hands and thrust the tattered clothes at her. "Go in the back room and put these on," he demanded curtly. "And don't try anything, honey. Clark is standing guard at the back window and I'll be posted at the front door. If you cause us any trouble, I just might let Duke at you."

Flashing Duke and Sam murderous glowers, Tori stamped into the bedroom to change her clothes. Her mind raced, wondering how she could escape these hooligans without sacrificing her life in the process. When she returned with her buckskin clothes in hand, Duke yanked them from her fingertips and swaggered out the door.

"Sit down," Sam commanded gruffly.

Tori did as she was told, resenting every minute of her captivity. Her nose wrinkled distastefully when Clark lumbered inside with saddlebags in hand. To her chagrin, he fished into the leather pouch to retrieve the meal they were about to share.

Beans. Tori stared at the can and her whisker-faced captors. She thought she had seen the last of those disgusting meals, but she was about to consume another one while keeping the worst company!

*   *   *

346

Dru never broke stride as he shoved his bootheel against the door of the cottage where Sophie and Eleanor entertained their male patrons. He had thundered into town with the sole purpose of learning who had put these harlots up to feeding Tori that crock of lies the previous night. Because of the malicious tale, he and Tori were at odds again.

Four pair of wide eyes gaped at the brawny giant who stood in the hall, staring into one bedroom and then the other. In each hand was a Colt that was aimed at the occupants of each bed. Dru didn't waste time with greetings, and the mutinous frown on his lips indicated that he was sitting on a short fuse.

"Who put you up to telling my wife that I had been intimate with the two of you when you know damned good and well I wasn't?" he growled in question.

Neither Sophie nor Eleanor volunteered the information. Their tongues were frozen. Muttering, Dru fired a shot at the wall above Sophie and her lover. With a shriek, they both dived beneath the quilts. Likewise, Dru treated Eleanor and her beau to the same drastic measure of interrogation. The second set of shots gained answers.

"Tyrone Webster paid us to say those things," Sophie chirped, peeking up at the ominous giant who glowered flaming arrows at her. "He said it was just a prank and that he'd own up to it before the night was out."

"He paid us fifty dollars apiece," Eleanor squeaked, eyeing Dru's stony expression apprehensively.

Muttering under his breath, Dru rammed the Colts into their holsters and spun on his heels. He had just about enough of Tyrone's underhanded tactics and cruel pranks. And Dru was in the perfect frame of mind to take on Tyrone and tear him to pieces with his bare hands. Determined of purpose, Dru stormed down the street to the Queen High Saloon, leaving doors sagging on their hinges as he went. But to his irritation, Tyrone had yet to make the drive into town from his ranch and Dru was unable to take out his frustration on its true source.

Swinging into the saddle, Dru pointed himself toward the ranch. He had several duties to attend to and his vengeance against Tyrone would have to wait until he got the scoundrel alone. Dru had no intention of storming Tyrone's headquarters, which was surrounded by his mercenary army of bodyguards—not without reinforcements anyway. But at least now he knew who had thrown stumbling blocks in his and Tori's path the previous night. She would probably never forgive him for the cutting remarks he had made and the shameful way he had treated her. But for what it was worth, she would know that he hadn't been unfaithful to her . . .

The sound of pistols barking in the distance provoked Dru to grumble under his breath. He had barely reached the outskirts of the ranch and he had hoped to confront Tori before tending his chores. Now Tori would have to wait. From the sound of things, rustlers had launched another attack against the cattle herd Jimmy-Pete and Jerry-Jeff and the other ranch hands were trailing into the mountain meadows for fall grazing.

Gouging his steed, Dru thundered off in the direction the shots had come. In the distance, he saw Billy-Bob aiming himself toward trouble, leaving the steers Caleb had ordered for his restaurant unattended.

When he intercepted Billy-Bob, Dru hitched his thumb over his shoulder. "You get those cattle back to the corrals and pen them up," Dru ordered hurriedly.

"But I . . ." Billy tried to protest.

"No," Dru snapped in a tone that anticipated no argument. "You're still on the mend and I have no intention of chasing down Caleb's steers again."

Pressing his knees against his steed, Dru thundered off to assist his other two brothers. Muttering, Billy-Bob reined his horse around to drive the cattle to the stock pens.

John-Henry, who had also heard the commotion, came charging across the valley at breakneck speed. Following at Dru's heels, he veered around the steep bluff. A wordless scowl erupted from Dru's lips when he spied Jimmy-Pete, Jerry-Jeff, and the ranch hands pinned down behind the boulders by volleys of gunfire. Startled cattle were scattered hither and yon. Ten masked men were blasting away at them from their vantage point on the ridge above the narrow chasm.

Kicking his steed into a gallop, Dru made a daredevil charge straight up the hill. His brothers followed suit, firing from both hips as they vaulted onto horses and lunged up the slopes. While Dru and his brothers provided cover with their rapid fire, the ranch hands circled the rustlers. Sensing disaster, the band of thieves hightailed it along the winding path to disappear into the canopy of trees that rimmed the jagged slopes.

"I'm getting damned tired of this," Jerry-Jeff grumbled grouchily. "Every time we try to move cattle, Webster's buscaderos bushwack us and scatter the herd from here to hell."

"And how are you going to go about bringing Webster to justice when we have no proof that he's behind the attack?" Dru growled in frustration. "This new territorial government of ours frowns on vigilante justice. But they haven't provided any solution to guard against men like Webster."

"I say we drag Tyrone out of that fancy saloon of his and string him up," John-Henry suggested. "He'll confess with a noose around his neck."

Dru expelled an exasperated sigh. The U.S. marshal who was supposed to have been sent to keep a lid on Virginia City and the surrounding area had never arrived and he suspected Webster was responsible for the man's absence. Tyrone wanted control of the Bar S Ranch and the money-making businesses in town and he had employed every tactic imaginable to force Dru and Caleb out.

According to his brothers, person or persons unknown had blocked the spring that fed the creek which watered Sullivan cattle the previous month. When they went to

349

investigate they found a rock dam. If not for John-Henry's astuteness, the water would have been turned loose and the thirsty cattle in the valley below would have died of poisoning, for the water had been contaminated with strychnine.

It was time to do something about Webster. The territorial government was inefficient. The legislature was trying to civilize Montana, but thus far, the politicians had done little. The problem was, Tyrone Webster was shrewd and deceptive and he worked every situation to his advantage. He was careful to have an alibi and always made sure that he wasn't around when calamity befell his victims.

Dru was fed up with justice and laws that protected the guilty and victimized the innocent. Caleb and Billy-Bob had already suffered because of Tyrone's cunning tactics. Dru and Tori were at odds again because of Tyrone's treachery. Dru was tired of waiting for a marshal to show up. He could lose one of his brothers trying to observe laws of justice that had proven ineffective, especially in Tyrone's case.

"After we get these cattle gathered, I'm going to talk to Webster," he announced as he nudged his steed down the rocky slope.

"The best way to solve the problem is to eliminate its source," John-Henry snorted. "It would make more sense to lynch Webster and scare off his road agents than to talk to him."

John-Henry had always been one to go off half-cocked while Dru contemplated his alternatives. Tyrone was an easy target because the Sullivans had been crosswise of the man for almost a year. But the fact was, Dru had no concrete proof that Tyrone was the ringleader of the road agents and rustlers that terrorized the countryside. And as much as he would have preferred to lynch Webster, he expected that he and his brothers would be severely reprimanded for calling the Montana vigilantes into action once again.

While John-Henry grumbled about Dru's refusal to permit them to drop what they were doing and storm into town to string Tyrone up, Whong came thundering through the valley like a house afire. After several sneezes caused by the dust he had raised, Whong erupted in rapid-fire Chinese and waved his arms in expansive gestures.

"Confound it, speak English," Dru demanded.

Whong dabbed the perspiration from his forehead, blew his nose, and rattled in broken English. "Mr. Fremming says come quick. He's got prenty of troubre in town and he needs your herp."

"I've got plenty of trouble here," Dru grumbled, staring after the cattle that had scattered to kingdom come. "Tell Caleb's messenger that I'll be there as quick as I can."

Nodding in compliance, Whong wheeled his steed around and galloped off with his queue flapping behind him and his blousy shirt billowing in the breeze.

For two hours, Dru and his brother trekked through the timbered foothills, rounding up the frightened herd. When the cattle were finally squeezed into an orderly procession, Jimmy-Pete, Jerry-Jeff, and the other cowboys aimed them toward the meadows in the high country. Dru had just pointed himself toward home when Whong reappeared, babbling in Chinese the way he always did when he was overly excited.

"Godamighty, Whong, what is it now?" Dru muttered grumpily.

The taut expression on Whong's face testified to the extent of his concern. "It's Mrs. Surrivan," he burst out.

Sickening dread swamped Dru. "What about her?"

"She never came back from her ride," Whong reported grimly.

"Damn," Dru scowled as he nudged his steed toward headquarters.

Her and her newfound independence! he grumbled under his breath. He had given that woman a few basic lessons in riding and survival and she thought she was an expert! No doubt their conflicts had sent her on a reckless excursion—anything to ensure that she wasn't around when her unwanted husband returned. Blast it, he should have cautioned Tori about riding off alone. She could have been anywhere in a hundred square miles and it would take days to locate her if she had been thrown from her horse and injured.

Riding at breakneck speed, Dru raced back to the ranch house to determine if Tori had returned during Whong's absence. But Dru found hide nor hair of his missing wife, only the note from Caleb. His eyes blazed over the message that had gone into greater detail than Whong had suggested, at least not in plain English!

"Confound it, why didn't you tell me what Caleb's emergency was?" he growled sharply.

With head downcast, Whong stood first on one foot and then on the other. "Because you said Mr. Fremming's emergency courd wait and you had troubre of your own," he quietly defended himself.

Dru rolled his eyes in exasperation. Whong was as good as gold, but there were times when the language barrier between them caused difficulties. This was one of those times. Whong could speak English far better than he could read it.

Of course, in all fairness to Whong, the Chinaman didn't know that Gwen and Edgar Cassidy and Hubert Frazier's arrival indicated disaster. The names meant nothing to him since he hadn't accompanied Dru all the way to Chicago when he whisked Tori away from her intended wedding. And what a terrible time for the group to arrive in Virginia City! Tori was most likely making preparations for the return trip. Dru speculated that Tori's disappearance was somehow connected with Caleb's message. Most likely, the messenger had happened onto Tori and she had trotted off to town to greet her mother, stepfather, and ex-fiancé. What other logical explanation was there? Besides, it would give Tori the perfect excuse to abandon her husband again, just as she had done when they had first returned from their trek west.

Hastily shrugging on fresh clothes, Dru pointed himself toward town, just as the sun made its final descent behind the jagged peaks. He had the uneasy feeling a battle was being waged at Flemming's hotel. It wasn't going to be a happy reunion with an ex-husband, a wife, and her second husband meeting face-to-face. And the situation would be even more ticklish since Hubert Carrington Frazier II had accompanied the Cassidys. That uppity aristocrat was going to be madder than blue blazes when he discovered his fiancée had married the man who had knocked him silly the previous year.

Dru was anxious to settle the dispute and escort Tori home where she belonged. Once he explained that Tyrone was responsible for the lies that had driven wedges between them at the dance, perhaps he and Tori could make a fresh start. God, he certainly hoped so. The thought of watching her ride off with the Cassidys and her ex-fiancé tied his stomach in knots!

Had Dru known Tori wasn't anywhere near Virginia City and hadn't been for the past several hours, he would have been tearing the countryside apart to locate her. But he didn't know. And more was the pity that Tori had wandered off alone to scout out the majestic mountains. There was enough trouble brewing without her stumbling into catastrophe.

Chapter 32

Looking rumpled, Gwendolyn marched through the corridor and pounded on the door that the hotel clerk indicated to be Caleb's residence. When the portal swung open, Gwen braced herself for her confrontation with her ex-husband.

"Where is she?" Gwendolyn demanded to know without bothering with a civilized greeting.

"Why, Gwen, what a pleasure it is to see you again after all these years," Caleb smirked, his tone suggesting it was nothing of the kind.

With wicked glee he surveyed his ex-wife's bedraggled appearance. Judging by her dusty clothes and puckered expression, her long, tedious journey had been nothing short of hell for her. She reminded him of a goose that had roasted overly long over a campfire. Her fair skin was dried and burned. Her pouting lips were cracked, and her tangled blond hair looked as if it had been styled during a sandstorm. Now wasn't that a shame, Caleb thought spitefully.

Drawing herself up, Gwen tilted a haughty chin to stare down her nose at Caleb. "Don't pretend you don't know why we are here," she bit off as she shouldered her way through the door and flounced into Caleb's favorite chair. "We have come to fetch Victoria home where she belongs. And if you don't hand her over to us immediately, we will press criminal charges against you and you can rot away in jail for all I care."

The threat rolled off Caleb like water down a duck's back. There was no one within shouting distance to whom Gwen could demand Caleb's immediate arrest. In these parts it was still every man for himself. Although the jail had been erected, there was no one to stand guard over it. Gwen would have to take him into custody by herself, and he'd like to see her try it!

"I don't have the faintest notion what you're babbling about," Caleb insisted as he ambled over to stare down into Gwen's sunburned features. "Tori isn't here." And it was no lie he gave.

Hubert pushed past Edgar, who had decided to let Gwen have her way and approach Caleb alone. Edgar had graciously allowed his wife to do all the talking since that was her wont. That was, after all, what Gwen did best. But Hubert was plagued with several of Gwen's failing graces and also delighted in throwing his weight around to make himself feel important.

"We know who abducted Victoria," Hubert snapped testily. He strutted across the parlor like a peacock displaying his fine feathers. "You sent that brawny gorilla named Sullivan to fetch her for you! I demand that you hand my fiancé over to me at once!"

Caleb looked Hubert over once or twice and decided Dru's description of the spindly-legged dandy was accurate. Hubert had definitely grown up to be a big, spoiled pipsqueak. "Did I?" Caleb countered, looking properly astonished. "Now why in the world would I do something like that?"

"Because you wanted to get back at me," Gwen sniffed in irritation. "You can drop the pretense, Caleb. We all know you had a hand in Victoria's disappearance. You saw your chance to get even with me and you pounced on it."

Caleb carefully assessed his ex-wife. For years he had harbored the remnants of a frustrated love that refused to die. But the lingering affection he had once felt for her died a quick and painless death when he was forced to tolerate Gwen's arrogant demeanor. Edgar's vast wealth had gone to her head and Gwen flaunted her haughty airs, her expensive gowns, and her sparkling jewels most effectively. She definitely looked the part of a stuffy, arrogant aristocrat.

All these years Caleb had cursed Edgar for stealing Gwen away, luring her back to him with the fortune he had made in his railroad business. But the fact was, Caleb almost pitied Edgar Cassidy. The man who lounged against the doorjamb without jumping down Caleb's throat looked terribly beleaguered and had aged considerably since his marriage to Gwendolyn. Caleb wouldn't have exchanged places with Edgar for all the gold in the federal treasury! Edgar was welcome to this haughty witch.

"We have endured a horrendous journey," Hubert growled, sticking his face in Caleb's unconcerned one. "We are in no mood for your vengeful games. Now, hand Victoria over to us at once!"

"If you are weary from your travels, I suggest you rent rooms at my hotel," Caleb smirked. "I have the best accommodations in town, and may I add that I do a thriving business with my restaurant as well."

"Confound it, Caleb!" Gwen vaulted from her chair to stamp her foot. "You have had your revenge on me. Now return Victoria to us! As you can see, Hubert is beside himself with concern over his fiancée."

It didn't look that way to Caleb. *Indignant* was nearer the mark. Damn, if only Dru would hotfoot it to town, thought Caleb. The instant he had seen the elegant coach pull into the street, he had sent a courier racing to the Bar S Ranch. But Dru had been detained, and Caleb was left to greet his hostile guests alone.

"While you get settled into your rooms, I'll find out what I can about . . ." A mock-innocent frown plowed his brows. "What did you say this man's name was who supposedly kidnapped Victoria? Simpson? Sturdivant?"

Hubert's hazel eyes narrowed in agitation. "Sullivan, as if you didn't know!"

"Ah yes, Sullivan," Caleb replied with a nod. "Let us hope he has seen Victoria. If she is in town I would like to see her myself." His eyes drilled into Gwen, who wisely chose to look the other way. "After all, I haven't been allowed to see my one and only daughter in ten years."

Silently seething, Gwen followed Caleb out the door and then verbally exhibited her ill temper when her ex-husband had the audacity to charge them twice the normal fee for renting rooms. After stamping down the street to inspect the other establishments, Gwen discovered that Caleb's hotel did indeed resemble a palace in comparison to the other crude accommodations. Under no circumstances would she have stayed at those shabby inns that were undoubtedly crawling with bed bugs and only God knew what other disgusting creatures!

"This is highway robbery," Gwen muttered as she watched Edgar fork over the full amount without complaining.

"So is stealing one's daughter away for ten years without allowing her father to see her," Caleb parried, casting Gwen the evil eye.

Gwen gnashed her teeth and sent Hubert a discreet glance, hoping he had paid little attention to Caleb's biting remark.

When the threesome struggled upstairs with enough luggage to keep them in fresh clothes for six months, Caleb broke into a devilish grin. He had Gwen right where he wanted her. He couldn't wait for Dru to show up and announce that he had married Tori. Gwen would be fit to be roped and tied, and Hubert would be hopping up and down in outraged fury.

Now, if only Dru and Tori had come to terms. Caleb crossed his fingers and hoped the hasty marriage wouldn't fall apart before Gwen convinced Tori to return to Chicago. His daughter and his best friend could certainly uncomplicate matters if they fell in love and decided to make a success of their marriage. Caleb prayed fast and furiously that they had. Nothing would make him happier than to see Dru and Tori on the best of terms and to send Gwen, Edgar, and Hubert packing. He and Dru could have the last laugh on that pack of aristocrats!

While Caleb's visitors from Chicago settled into their rooms at the hotel and Dru was thundering toward town, Tori was attempting to worm her hands from the ropes that held her arms behind her. Sam and Clark had ambled outside to stand as posted lookouts, giving Tori an opportunity to wrestle with the rope. The only sharp-edged instrument at her disposal was the jagged lid on the empty can of beans she had choked down. It had taken some doing to scoot the can to the edge of the table with her chin and shove it into her lap, but she had accomplished the feat while keeping one eye on the door. Tori had also managed to maneuver the can beside her on the chair and then wedge it behind her with her hip. She was still a long way from freedom, but Tori had become a determined soul these days. The formerly helpless, defenseless little girl had found herself in enough scrapes to employ her cunning and imagination when necessity dictated.

At the risk of slashing her wrists, Tori sawed at the rope with the rough-edged can lid. At irregular intervals, she stole nervous glances at the door, praying the two thugs who had been hired to hold her prisoner would remain outside for a few minutes longer. Feverishly, Tori frayed the rope that burned her wrists. If only she were granted enough time, she could cut herself loose and make her escape! Ten more minutes were all she asked. That wasn't an unreasonable prayer, was it?

Her heart leaped into triple time when she heard footsteps and voices on the stoop. Sam poked his head inside to double check on Tori, and she paused from her frantic labor to sit as still as a marble statue. Satisfied that their hostage was exactly where they'd left her, Sam eased the door shut and stared off into the distance.

Once she was left alone, Tori continued to rake the ropes across the lid of the can. Her arms felt like boiled noodles, but she gritted her teeth and tended her task until she had no strength left. It was hopeless. She was doomed to spend the last few hours of her life confined to this crude shack.

No, it was *not* hopeless, Tori told herself fiercely. Willfully, she mustered her sagging spirits. Lifting her weary arms, she sawed on the ropes until her muscles screamed, once again, in agony . . .

A relieved sigh gushed from her lips when the rope finally gave way. Thank God for beans! Tori thought as she peered at the jagged lid of the can. She would never ever utter a discouraging word about them again. They had inadvertently saved her life.

Scooping up the can, Tori rose from her chair and tiptoed into the back room to ease open the window. Once outside, she inched toward the corner of the shack to locate the horses. A thoughtful frown knitted her brow while she calculated the time required to dash to the steeds and make her escape without being gunned down in the process.

Backing as far away from the cabin as she dared, Tori took aim at the open window. The moment the empty can of beans sailed into the back room and clattered against the wall, she shot toward the horses like a discharging cannon. While Sam and Clark charged through the front door with a pistol clenched in each fist to determine what had caused the racket, Tori leaped onto one horse in a single bound and snatched up the reins to the others.

A volley of eardrum-shattering curses reverberated around the shack as the two men searched for their missing captive. With her heart beating wildly, Tori galloped down the steep slopes, clinging to her steed. Hearing the thundering hooves, Sam and Clark stampeded out the door to blast away at the escaped hostage. Tori flattened herself against the saddle, dodging the bullets that whizzed past her in rapid succession.

When Tori disappeared in the distance, Sam shoved his revolvers into his holsters and erupted in another string of colorful profanity. "Now what are we gonna do?"

Clark's bulky shoulders lifted in a shrug and he spat a wad of tobacco before replying. "Damned if I know. But I don't want to be the one to tell Tyrone that we lost that wench. He's already made plans to use her to get to Flemming and Sullivan. He was going to stuff her clothes full of rags and set it on a horse and pretend to shove her off a cliff to put the fear of God in them two stubborn men. But that won't do no good if that chit's running around loose."

Sam heaved a disgusted sigh. "Well, we ain't got no choice except to go after her and bring her back."

"Afoot?" Clark croaked in disbelief.

"It's only four miles, and most of it is downhill to the Bar S Ranch," Sam reminded him as he stepped off the stoop to begin his walk.

Muttering, Clark followed in Sam's wake. And next time he promised himself not to take Tori Sullivan for granted. She looked like a dainty, incompetent female, but she was anything but! It got his goat to be hornswoggled by a woman. But, with his goat gotten, Clark paced off the steps in hopes of recapturing the inventive sprite who had cut herself loose with an empty can of beans.

"Will you just look at this place!" Gwen groused, turning up her nose at the modest furnishings that surrounded her. "I wouldn't put it past Caleb to give us the worst room in his shabby hotel. It was humiliating enough to find a skull and crossbones carved into our door, but the place is probably lousy with insects as well."

Hesitantly, she peeled away the well-worn bedspread to check for roaches and whatever other critters might have taken up residence in the room. A horrified gasp burst from her lips when she spied the bloodstains that all the washing in the world hadn't removed from the sheets that Webster's hoodlums had planted on them.

"Somebody was probably murdered right here where they slept," she croaked, her face white as flour.

Edgar shucked his expensive but dusty jacket and heaved a long-suffering sigh. "Don't let your imagination run wild, Gwen. I'm sure no murders have occurred in our room. Caleb isn't that vindictive. I suspect all he wanted all along was to get even with us and to be reunited with Tori."

"Victoria," Gwen hastily corrected. "Why you persist in calling her by that unsophisticated nickname is beyond me. It doesn't become a dignified young lady." She picked up a pillow and beat it against the headboard to encourage any varmint that might be inside to crawl out. "And if you don't think Caleb is out for revenge, you're an utter fool, Edgar. And why you are taking all this so calmly is beyond me! After all, I'm not the only one Caleb despises around here. And if it ever occurs to him that you—"

"And there have been times I've wondered if you didn't plan it all," Edgar grumbled, abruptly cutting her off in midsentence. "Caleb will never know unless you get overly excited and blurt it out—which is exactly what you might do if you don't get a firm grip on yourself. You would fly into a fit of hysterics if Hubert learned what really happened. Your reputation in Chicago would be soiled and I know full well how the thought of losing face terrifies you."

Gwen was indeed in a frazzled state. Having Hubert constantly underfoot made her as nervous as a caged cat.

If they weren't careful, Hubert would discover that Gwen had lied on a number of occasions about her first husband. Lord, the scandal Hubert could cause! Gwen was walking on pins and needles and had been for a month. Seeing Caleb again rattled her. The threat of having Hubert discover more about her first marriage than he needed to know unnerved her. And the fact that Caleb had hidden Victoria for safekeeping infuriated her beyond words. Damn that spiteful man. She thought she was well rid of him years ago. He was her one mistake in life, and he plagued her like a swarm of locusts.

"How long do you suppose Caleb is going to play these cat-and-mouse games of his before he allows us to see Victoria?" Gwen questioned as she covered the unsightly stains on the sheets.

"I haven't the slightest idea," Edgar replied before he poured water into the basin to shave the stubble from his face. "But he has ten years' worth of revenge built up inside him. And whatever he has in mind for us, we probably deserve it."

Gwen gaped incredulously at her husband's back. "What kind of remark is that?"

"An honest one." Edgar lathered his face. "At the time I didn't care what Caleb thought or about the hell we put him through. But he's suffered enough because of us. I, for one, think we should be frying in our grease for a while."

"Edgar, what in God's name has come over you?" Gwen snapped. "I swear, the dust has filtered into your brain after that dreadful journey and it has clogged the cogs of your mind. We have endured the most distasteful trip imaginable, lived like heathens in the backwoods, and were forced to survive on rations that a starved dog would turn up his nose at. And if that wasn't hell enough, we have to endure Caleb's ridicule and reside at his hotel! If Caleb has sabotaged Victoria's thinking and has convinced her to stay in this godforsaken . . . "

Gwen shuddered at the unsettling thought. "We may

never get Victoria back without a full-fledged fight. Hubert and his family will be outraged if this wedding doesn't take place, and we will be the laughingstocks of Chicago! Your reputation is also at stake here, Edgar. I should think you would be as upset as I am."

Edgar rolled his eyes, requesting divine patience. He had listened to his wife rant and rave for well over a month. Having spent so much time with her lately, it left him wondering why he had fallen in love with her in the first place. At the time, Edgar thought Gwen was all he needed to make his life complete. But it had dawned on him too late that it was only his wealth that appealed to Gwendolyn—and had always been the case. She had used him as a stepping-stone into the ranks of high society and he had been too concerned with winning her back from Caleb to notice. But Gwen's true selfish nature had come pouring out the past few weeks. A man never really got to know his wife until he was forced to spend countless hours with her in an enclosed carriage. And even more depressing to Edgar was the fact that Gwen seemed more concerned about scandal than Tori's welfare . . .

"I'm starved to death for a decent meal, Edgar," Gwen fussed as she paced back and forth in front of the door.

"I doubt Caleb serves gourmet meals in his restaurant," Edgar mumbled, contorting his face to shave the hard-to-reach place under his nose.

Gwen punished him with a blistering glare. "Well, I am not settling for rancid bacon floating in its own foul-smelling grease, I can tell you that! I saw enough of that revolting pork at the stage stations where we stopped to eat!"

"Just don't set your heart on escargots and caviar," Edgar replied with a smirk. "Virginia City isn't known for five-course meals and exotic cuisine. From what I've seen of this town, it is a haven for miners, gamblers, and ruffians who not only can't pronounce escargots but never even heard of them. I rather like the wild, half-civilized atmosphere."

"I don't find you the least bit amusing, Edgar," Gwen admonished peevishly.

And your disposition isn't anything to brag about, either, thought Edgar. But being a gentleman, he kept the snide remark to himself.

The rap at the door heralded Hubert's arrival. Pasting on a pleasant smile, Gwen greeted her future son-in-law. With Edgar ambling a few steps behind, the threesome adjourned to the restaurant. As expected, Gwen complained about the proper arrangement of the silverware, the water spots on the glasses, and everything else that didn't meet the high standards of formal dining to which she had grown accustomed.

Edgar was beginning to wish he had never agreed to allow Gwen and Hubert to accompany him on the journey. He was finding out things about Gwen and Hubert that he would have been much happier not knowing. Gwen was a constant complainer, and Hubert was so arrogant and spoiled that he provided boorish company during the long hours of traveling. In fact, Edgar had the feeling that Tori, the victim of this kidnapping and the subsequent cross-country chase, was actually the lucky one. Edgar would have given his fortune to exchange places with Tori—wherever she was! It couldn't have been worse than tolerating the company of two of the world's most spoiled aristocrats!

Tyrone glanced up when Duke moseyed through the back entrance of his office at the saloon. "Did you take care of that little matter for me?" he questioned as he puffed on his cigar.

Duke tossed Tori's buckskin clothes on the desk. "She's tied up. Sam and Clark are keeping a watchful eye on her," he reported.

An annoyed frown furrowed Tyrone's winged brows when he noticed the claw marks on Duke's cheeks. "That woman had better still be in one piece until I have no more need for her," he growled in venomous threat.

Duke touched his fingertips to the wounds and swore under his breath. That feisty bitch hadn't seen the last of him. No matter what Tyrone had planned, Duke was going to exact a few pounds of Tori's flesh to compensate for the scrapes on his face.

"She's still in one piece," Duke grumbled.

"Well, she had damned well better be." Tyrone bounded to his feet. "If you botch this scheme, you can find yourself a new job, Kendrick."

Duke was fed up with that repetitious threat and with taking orders from a man who never dirtied his hands with killings and ambushes. "Just keep in mind that if I seek other employment, I'll tell everything I know about your activities," he snorted in warning.

A mutinous frown puckered Tyrone's homely features. He didn't like the sound of that challenge and he was definitely going to have to do something about Duke when he finished his dealings with Tori.

Clamping down his temper, Tyrone hitched his thumb toward the back door. "Go fetch me a horse and some feed sacks to stuff in Tori's clothes," he demanded. "We'll scare the living daylights out of Flemming and Sullivan by letting them think Tori plunged to her death. When they come searching for her, we'll be there to bargain with them. After they discover it was only a dummy in her clothes that tumbled off the cliff, they will be willing to give me anything I want to ensure she doesn't truly suffer that fatal fall."

For a long moment, Duke stared at Webster, wondering whether or not to tell that bossy varmint where he could stuff his orders. But Duke chose to do what Tyrone requested because he still wanted to even the score with Tori. The sassy firebrand had become Duke's obsession. For the past few hours he had visualized taking her again and again, making her beg for mercy to make up for the humiliation she had caused him at the dance and in Tyrone's office earlier in the week.

For that reason and no other, Duke dropped Tori's buckskin clothes on the desk and reversed direction to do as Tyrone demanded.

"Cocky bastard," Tyrone growled when the door slammed shut behind Duke. He was going to have to dispose of that bloodthirsty gunslinger, and quickly. Duke was getting a mite too big for his breeches and his arrogant attitude clashed with Tyrone's. When Duke had accomplished his mission, Tyrone made a mental note to get rid of the gunslinger . . . permanently.

A muddled frown knitted Tori's brow when she reached the ranch and found it deserted. Glancing down at the tattered homespun clothes she had been wearing, Tori decided to take time to bathe and change. There was no telling who had worn the oversized breeches and shirt before she had been forced to shrug them on. And she was not wearing these foul-smelling garments one minute longer than necessary!

After heating water, Tori trudged up the steps to fill the tub. It was with great relief that she sank into the warm bath to scrub away the dust, perspiration, and the revolting scent of Duke Kendrick. And while she sat there, recovering from her near brush with catastrophe, she cursed the vision that rose above her.

Damn that Tyrone Webster. He had intended to use her to get at Caleb and Dru and to dispose of her for daring to threaten him. Well, he wasn't getting away with that, not if Tori had any say in the matter, which she most certainly did! She had heard Sam Rother remind Duke that Tyrone had given them orders to capture her. Tori had more than enough evidence to incriminate Tyrone. Maybe she couldn't have him tossed in the deserted jail for bushwhacking Caleb and Billy-Bob, but she could damned well accuse him of having her kidnapped by his three henchmen.

Chomping on that vindictive thought, Tori hurriedly

dried herself and stepped into her gown. Since Dru and Whong were nowhere to be found, Tori decided to assume the crusade single-handed. But this time she armed herself with a pistol and knife—one weapon in her purse and the other tucked in her garter that encircled her thigh. Never again would Tori go sauntering off without being armed to the teeth, not until Webster and his dim-witted hoodlums were mildewing in jail!

Determined of purpose, Tori sailed out the door and pulled herself into the saddle to ride astride. Darkness had enveloped the countryside long before she reached the ranch, and she had ridden like a disembodied spirit floating in the night. On a mission of vengeance, Tori raced off to town with her lavender gown billowing around her.

While Tori was galloping down the moonlit path that led to Virginia City, Sam and Clark erupted in another string of oaths. They had just veered around the jagged rocks to make their last quarter-of-a-mile jaunt to the Bar S Ranch when Tori thundered off in the opposite direction. Quickening their steps, Sam and Clark scuttled toward the barn to retrieve the two saddled horses Tori had left behind. Kicking their mounts into canters, they trailed after their escaping hostage.

"What do you suppose she's plannin' to do now?" Clark muttered.

"Hell if I know, but if we don't catch her before she alerts everybody in town, Tyrone will have our heads," Sam grumbled sourly. "That woman is a peck of trouble. She never stays put long enough to get the jump on her."

Forcing their steeds into their swiftest paces, Sam and Clark charged off in pursuit of Tori who was setting a reckless pace to reach Tyrone Webster's office and repay him for the torment his henchmen had put her through.

Chapter 33

Exhausted and in the worst of all possible moods, Dru strode through the hotel lobby and into Caleb's parlor. His gaze swept the empty room and riveted on Caleb, who had just ambled out of his bedroom.

"Well, it's about time you got here," Caleb grumbled. "You missed all the fireworks."

Dru didn't bother with pleasantries. He was worried about Tori, who didn't appear to be here with her father. Godamighty, where was that woman? Had Gwen taken her and hustled her out of town before Dru had a chance to speak with her?

"Where is she?" he demanded.

"In the restaurant by now, I suspect," Caleb replied, tugging at the shirt-sleeves beneath his velvet jacket. "But I doubt the menu will suit her, particular as she is."

A muddled frown knitted Dru's brow. After a moment it dawned on him that the *she* to whom he had referred was not the same *she* to whom Caleb had referred. "No, I mean Tori," he clarified.

Caleb paused in midstep and glanced in bewilderment at Dru. "How the devil should I know? I thought she was at the ranch with you." Concern etched his weather-beaten features. "Where the blazes do you suppose she could be?"

Caleb peered apprehensively at Dru, who peered

apprehensively back at him. The speculation that Tyrone could have somehow gotten hold of Tori to utilize as leverage struck both of them at the same moment. Caleb and Dru made a beeline for the door and attempted to push their way through the exit that wasn't wide enough to accommodate both of the oversized men.

"Get out of my way," Caleb growled, lowering his shoulder to give Dru a nudge.

"*You* get out of *my* way," Dru snapped as he rammed Caleb against the doorjamb.

When Dru squeezed his way through the door first, Caleb glared daggers at his ex-partner's departing back. "You don't have to pretend you're worried about her," he muttered disdainfully. "You made your feelings clear enough the other night. And Tori admitted that you were only being nice to her at the party for appearance' sake."

"I didn't say one way or the other either time," Dru bit off as he took the corridor to the hotel lobby in swift, impatient steps.

"My point exactly," Caleb parried, quickening his step to keep up with Dru's long, graceful strides.

"I care," Dru admitted, although his tone negated his confession.

"Sure you do," he sniffed caustically. "That's why you don't even know where my daughter is when she is supposed to be with you. It's a wonder to me that you didn't lose her during the trek west!"

Dru halted so abruptly that Caleb rammed into him, forcing his breath out in a whoosh. Pivoting, Dru glared into Caleb's agitated frown. "For your information, your daughter has developed a fierce sense of independence, just as you hoped she would. You requested that I teach her to fend for herself in the wilds, and she gained great confidence in her abilities to take care of herself. And as she so loudly reminded me last night, she is perfectly capable of going where she pleases whenever she pleases. And if she has managed to embroil herself in trouble, she also managed it *all by herself* because she is not giving me the time of day at present!" Dru all but yelled into Caleb's face.

"Well, you're a helluva lot bigger than she is," he pointed out. "I should think you would be able to exert some control over her, no matter what she says to the contrary."

Dru wheeled about to continue on his way. "Yeah, well, I'll have to catch her first before I exert my superior strength over her . . . that is, if Tyrone hasn't beat me to it."

Muttering at that dreadful possibility, Dru marched onto the street. Knowing Tyrone had deliberately caused trouble between him and Tori left Dru wondering what else that treacherous scoundrel had up his sleeve— probably the queen of spades that had been up his sleeve when he cheated the former owner of the saloon out of his business in that fateful poker hand ten months earlier.

As luck would have it, Hubert and the Cassidys had just strolled outside the restaurant the moment before Dru and Caleb whizzed out of the hotel, determined to interrogate Tyrone. Upon seeing his rival, Hubert growled furiously. Like a charging bull, he lowered his head and attacked Dru's blind side. A pained grunt erupted from Dru's lips when he was butted to the ground and pelted about the shoulders and ears with doubled fists.

Unfortunately for Hubert, whose skills in hand-to-hand combat were sorely outclassed, Dru came up fighting. With a vicious snarl, Dru cocked his arm and lambasted Hubert with an uppercut that sent the dandy skidding backward through the dirt. Spitting blood and vengeful curses, Hubert bounded to his feet like a mountain goat. Poising himself like the professional boxers whose matches he had observed on occasion, Hubert prepared to go several rounds with the sinewy giant. Hubert danced around Dru, displaying his fancy footwork and issuing challenges and threats. Dru surveyed the dancing dandy the way a hunter glances at a rabbit on his way to fell a lion. While Hubert hopped around, just out of reach, Dru reared back a meaty fist, pounced, and socked Hubert squarely in the nose.

Gwendolyn stood on the boardwalk, emitting a spasm of hisses and furious squawks, encouraging Hubert to beat Dru to a pulp. But when Hubert kerplopped in the street, coldcocked by a powerful blow, Gwen flew into hysterics and began spewing sobs in great gulps.

Edgar simply stood there, assessing the man who had knocked Hubert silly. He supposed he should have pitied Hubert, whose nose was lying limply on the left side of his face. But frankly, there had been several times the past few weeks when Edgar would have enjoyed doing exactly what Dru had done. Hubert had gotten on Edgar's nerves with his constant complaints and haughty attitude. Yet, being a gentleman, Edgar had refrained from punching Hubert in the mouth and doing likewise to his cranky wife.

The beaming smile that radiated from Caleb's face could have led a lost traveler through a blizzard. Nothing made him happier than seeing Dru knock the living daylights out of Tori's arrogant ex-fiancé. The man was a stuffed shirt if ever Caleb saw one. Another grin pursed Caleb's lips when he glanced back to view Gwen's horrified reaction. Seeing her blubbering in tears and hopping up and down in indignation did Caleb's heart good. When Gwen was most miserable, Caleb was delighted. For years it had been the other way around.

With a gloating glance at Gwen, Caleb stepped over Hubert's unconscious form and followed in Dru's wake. As much as he would have reveled in watching Gwen's fit of hysterics, Caleb was anxious to know if Tyrone had gotten his hands on Tori.

"Don't just stand there, Edgar," Gwen wailed. "Do something!"

Edgar did. He stepped over Hubert to trail after Dru and Caleb. "I would like to see Tori," he called after Dru.

"So would I," Dru mumbled with a backward glance.

A perplexed frown flattened Edgar's brow as he hurried to catch up with Caleb. "Doesn't he know where she is?"

Caleb stared at the man he had despised for a decade. Of the three, Edgar was the only one who seemed sincerely worried about Tori after her harrowing journey through rough and unfamiliar terrain. Gwen and Hubert were more concerned about salvaging their pride and exacting revenge than Tori's welfare—which was definitely in question at the moment. Caleb wasn't prepared to like Edgar, but he begrudgingly admired the man who had obviously taken an interest in his step-daughter.

"I'm afraid Tori might have gotten herself into serious trouble," Caleb reported bleakly.

Edgar's face whitewashed. With grim resignation he followed Dru and Caleb, silently praying that Tori hadn't met with some unanticipated form of catastrophe.

Frantic, Tori stepped back into the alley from whence she had come and quietly eased Tyrone's back door shut behind her. Her heart was pounding like hailstones and her hands refused to stop shaking. Her mind raced and then faltered, unsure what she should do next. She had kept telling herself the world was better off without Tyrone in it, but she never should have confronted Tyrone by herself. It had been foolhardy disaster and now she . . .

Tori's wild thoughts came to a skidding halt when an unidentified assassin leaped at her from the looming shadows. Before she could scream at the top of her lungs, a calloused hand clamped over her mouth and she was yanked back so quickly that it knocked the breath out of her. Damn, what a rotten day she was having . . .

That was the last thought to flit across Tori's mind. When the butt of a pistol clanked against her skull, she

373

folded up at the knees and wilted like a flower buckling beneath the scorching summer sun.

Sam Rother stared down at the limp form that was draped over Duke's shoulder. A smug smile hovered on his lips. It was immensely satisfying to see the wild-haired misfit oblivious to the world after all the trouble she had caused. He and Clark had ridden like bats out of hell to run this feisty tart down after she had eluded them twice. Luckily, he and Clark had happened onto Duke and together they had recaptured the elusive spitfire.

"You take this note to Flemming's house," Duke instructed Sam. He fished the other note from his pocket. "Clark, make sure this is delivered to the Bar S Ranch."

Nodding mutely, both men darted through the alley, leaving Duke to bind and gag Tori. Silently, Duke strode back to the horses and deposited Tori's unconscious body over the saddle. A satanical smile hovered on his lips as he pointed himself toward the shack from which Tori had first escaped. Before he disposed of this troublesome minx, he would have his revenge for the claw marks she'd left on his face. Sam and Clark had stopped him from having his way with this blond-haired she-cat earlier in the day. But no one would stand in his way now. He would have her all to himself.

A wicked chuckle burst from his lips as he entertained throughts of ridiculing this defiant beauty and reducing her to pleading tears. He'd make her beg for him to kill her before he was through with her. The money Tyrone had intended to extort from Flemming and Sullivan for Tori's return would be all his. And before the Sullivan brothers chased him down, he would be long gone with the ransom money that Sam and Clark had been sent to collect.

Another sinister burst of laughter erupted from Duke's lips. Tyrone Webster thought he was such a clever mastermind. But Duke had taken his last order from that cocky varmint who wanted Virginia City in the palm of his hand. This time Duke was going to swagger off with enough gold to keep him in the manner that Tyrone had taught him to enjoy while he did that scoundrel's dirty work for him. This time it was Tyrone who had been double-crossed. Tyrone would never get his hands on the money or the deeds to Caleb and Dru's property. Duke would be laughing as he rode away with his saddlebags heaping with gold!

Chapter 34

When Dru barged into the saloon and aimed himself toward Tyrone's office, Caleb and Edgar scuttled behind him.

"You'll have to stand in line to get to Tyrone," Caleb growled, rushing toward the door through which Dru had disappeared. "He's all mine!"

Caleb came to a screeching halt beside Dru, who was staring curiously at the floor. "It looks as if we're all too late," Dru muttered, peering at the corpse that was sprawled facedown on the floor.

"Oh, my God!" Caleb chirped like a sick cricket.

"What's wrong . . . ?" Edgar wedged his way past Caleb and Dru to see Webster's lifeless body lying on the floor like a misplaced doormat.

"Somebody already killed Webster," Dru declared without the least bit of sympathy.

"But who?" Caleb mused aloud.

"It's hard to say. Everbody who knew him hated him," Dru said frankly. "The whole town is suspect."

Dru found himself wondering if one of his brothers had taken it upon himself to dispose of the source of trouble in Virginia City. All four of his brothers indicated that vigilante justice was the best method of dealing with Tyrone, expecially John-Henry who was plain-spoken and a bit too radical at times for his own good. And considering how unpopular Tyrone was, there probably wouldn't be an investigation in his murder. Whoever killed the scoundrel without anyone witnessing the murder would probably get off scott free, as well they should . . .

Gloomy apprehension flooded over Dru when he recognized the buckskin clothes that were clutched in Tyrone's hand. Glumly, he hunkered down on his haunches to loose the garments from Tyrone's fist. "Tori's," he mumbled before he rolled Tyrone over to survey the knife wound in his belly.

Edgar didn't have an inkling what was going on, but the taut expressions on Dru and Caleb's faces alerted him to disaster—but of what sort, he wasn't certain.

The swish of petticoats and the sound of half-muttered curses broke the strained silence. Dru pivoted to see Gwen barreling toward the office, her face skewed up in a murderous sneer.

"I'm going to have you arrested for attacking Hubert, as well as for abducting Victoria," she spumed furiously at Dru. "You think just because you live in this godawful country that you can beat the tar out of everyone and kidnap the daughter of the most respectable citizens in—"

"Be quiet, Gwen," Caleb snapped at his ex-wife. "We have enough trouble without listening to another of your babbling tirades."

"How dare you speak like that to me!" Gwen howled, her breasts heaving with indignation. "As soon as I locate the law official in charge of this rowdy town, I'm going to have you and your vicious accomplice arrested . . ."

"You heard him, Gwen," Edgar barked in a tone he rarely used on his wife. "Keep your mouth shut up for once!"

Gwen blinked like a disturbed owl. Never in ten years had Edgar raised his voice or called her down. Her jaw sagged on its hinges. Nonplussed, she gaped at her husband.

When the grim procession filed out of the office, Gwen's gaze dropped to the body that lay in a limp heap. "My God, you killed him," she railed at Dru, instantly suspecting him of the crime. "Murderer! Butcher!"

"Somebody shut that woman up," Dru growled as he pushed his way through the crowd that had suddenly gathered in the saloon.

Edgar thrust out a hand to grab Gwen's wrist, yanking her beside him. When she opened her mouth to repeat the cry of alarm, Edgar clamped his hand over her lips. "You saw what Sullivan did to Hubert and his second victim," he said for dramatic effect. "If you don't stop harassing Dru Sullivan, you're liable to be his third victim."

The threat shut Gwen up like a clam. Wild violet eyes flew to Dru's broad back and then dropped to the holsters that were draped on his lean hips. There was deadly menace in the way Dru shoved bodies aside as he stalked through the saloon. Gwen decided not to tangle with Dru until she was equipped with an army of law officials as reinforcement. Whatever Dru Sullivan intended to do next, it looked as if all the cowardly citizens in Virginia City were going to let him get away with it! Not one soul stepped forward to stop the sinewy giant who had propelled himself through the saloon door and into the street.

By the time Dru shouldered his way through the crowd of onlookers that had gathered in the street, Hubert had roused to consciousness. Wiping the blood from his nose and lips, he staggered to his feet, glancing in all directions at once. A furious growl spurted from his puffy lips when the congregation who clogged the entrance to the Queen High Saloon parted like the Red Sea to reveal the ominous giant who had kidnapped Victoria and pounded Hubert into the ground.

"Where's my fiancée?" Hubert snarled out of the side of his mouth that wasn't quite as swollen as the other.

378

Dru shot Caleb a hasty glance. "Did you tell him?"

"No, I thought it was your place to tell him," Caleb retorted, still stunned by the sight of Tyrone lying on the floor in a pool of his own blood and by the implication of Tori's involvement.

Dru exhaled a frustrated breath. Godamighty, this evening had evolved into a nightmare. Gwen and Hubert were making this intolerable situation more intolerable. And from all indication, Tori had taken it upon herself to confront Tyrone. But what in heaven's name was Tyrone doing with Tori's tattered buckskins? Dru couldn't imagine. Had she clashed with Tyrone and then taken it upon herself to relieve Dru and Caleb of their biggest headache—Tyrone Webster?

The office certainly bore evidence of a struggle. Chairs had been overturned and the paraphernalia that usually lay atop Tyrone's desk was scattered helter-skelter. Dru had no doubt that Tori had stabbed Tyrone in self-defense. But he couldn't imagine why she would have gone there in the first place, unless he had taken her captive. But she had obviously eluded him and left him in a lifeless heap.

But that still didn't explain why Tyrone was clutching Tori's clothes in his fist. Where the devil was Tori now? And could all his conjectures be completely wrong? Maybe one of his brothers had clashed with Tyrone against Dru's orders. Damnit, where in hell was Tori? And why the blazes did Hubert have to be blocking his path when he was anxious to catch up with that female hurricane who had apparently whizzed through town leaving a path of destruction in her wake?

Before Dru could conjure up logical answers to the myriad of questions that raced through his mind, Hubert started issuing another round of threats and demanding explanations. The babbling dandy intensified Dru's black mood.

"I'm going to have you lynched in the street!" Hubert sneered as he rearranged his twisted clothes and stomped forward. "First you kidnapped my fiancée and then you

379

assaulted me."

"And he murdered that poor man in the saloon!" Gwen burst out.

A murmur rippled through the crowd like a tidal wave upon the ocean. Dru expelled a disdainful snort. "I did no such thing. Webster was already dead before I could tear him to pieces."

"Then who killed him?" Gwen sniffed, her tone indicating she didn't believe his testimony for a minute, which of course she didn't since Edgar had declared Dru was responsible, if only to get her to pipe down.

"Your daughter was most likely responsible," Dru growled, intending to set Gwen back on her heels. But just as Edgar had discovered, the tactic had the reverse effect.

"Liar! Victoria would never harm a living soul. She is a proper lady!" Gwen loudly protested and then broke into a mumbled though shrill-voiced tirade.

"You haven't seen your daughter lately," Dru scoffed when Gwen finally paused to inhale a breath. "She can hold her own against any man."

That should throw that pesky termagant for a loop, he reckoned. And it did. Gwen's face turned the color of raw liver.

"You beast! You turned my daughter into a heathen, just like you are! Now she's a fugitive of justice." Gwen wailed like a banshee. "My God, Edgar! I was afraid something like this would happen. Caleb and his cohort have turned poor Victoria into a monster!"

It was clearly evident that Gwen was having another fit of hysterics. Dru wasted not one ounce of sympathy on her. In his estimation, it was a wonder Tori had turned out as well as she had with Gwen as her example. The woman was ranting on and on about how the Cassidys' reputation would be ruined and the family disgraced in Chicago's high society. Gwen babbled about how she would face a barrage of embarrassing questions and how she would be unable to hold up her head when the whole world discovered her daughter had become a murdering outlaw.

"I'll have your head for this," Hubert seethed. "I'll ruin you, Sullivan. You'll never sell another herd of cattle at any railhead that delivers to my stockyard and slaughterhouse, or any of the others in Chicago. I'll see that you're run out of this town and hunted down like the worthless scoundrel you are!"

There Hubert went again, issuing threats that he wasn't man enough to back up. Dru wasn't the least bit intimidated. His only concern was locating Tori before she got herself into more trouble. If she had gone into hiding after her tussle with Tyrone, there was no telling where she was or when she would come back!

"*You're* the one who is leaving town," Dru muttered as he stalked toward Hubert. "Tori is my wife and my responsibility. And I wouldn't want to sell one steer at your slaughterhouse. The only thief around here is you, Frazier. You tried to rob me blind and I have half a mind to stomp you into the ground. Every cattleman in the county would applaud me because you cheated them, one and all."

Hubert's mouth dropped open like a pelican's. Victoria had married this . . . this despicable cretin? She must have gone mad! Why else would she have committed a dastardly crime? Insanity was the only logical explanation, Hubert decided.

While Gwen erupted in another ear-shattering howl, Dru stamped toward Caleb's parlor. Lord, he needed to sit down and hack his way through the jungle of thoughts that hounded him. He couldn't think straight or decide what to do when that woman was throwing a hysterical tantrum and Hubert was spouting like a geyser.

When Dru stomped off with Caleb one step behind him, Edgar tried in vain to calm Gwen down. But she wouldn't cease her bubbling tirade long enough to listen. Throwing up his hands in resignation, Edgar left Gwen standing in the middle of the street, making a spectacle of

381

herself, and marched off behind Caleb.

No sooner had Dru breezed into Caleb's parlor than he spied the note laying on the sofa. He unfolded it, anticipating a message from Tori. A murderous growl exploded from his lips when he read the unsigned ransom note. What the sweet loving hell was going on? Had Tyrone's thugs latched onto Tori after her confrontation at the Queen High Saloon? Dru didn't know what to think, only that Tori's chances of survival were slim . . .

Caleb snatched away the note, read it, and erupted in fluent profanity. While he was swearing, Edgar yanked the message from Caleb and all three men cursed the air blue.

Like a shot, Caleb blazed down the hall to gather the gold demanded in the ransom note. Within minutes, he returned with two heaping pouches of nuggets.

The hopelessness of the situation struck Dru like a physical blow. He thought of the horror Tori was probably enduring at the hands of her abductors and he shuddered in revulsion. There was no guarantee that Tori would be returned alive, especially since Tyrone had turned up dead. And what were the odds of finding her after dark in this rugged country of jagged mountains and gulches? He might be able to set a trap and ambush whoever came to retrieve the ransom money, but that wouldn't do Tori a helluva lot of good.

A pain, the likes of which Dru had never known, stabbed at his soul. Tori's hauntingly lovely image rose above him like a specter in the night. He remembered with vivid clarity every moment he had spent with her. He had learned her moods and had become sensitive to her needs. He had reveled in the splendor of her passion, chided her for her tears, and delighted in her laughter. He had watched her transform from a shy debutante into a strong, independent tigress who was brimming with confidence and resourcefulness. She had done more living in the course of three months than she had done in a decade. She had begun to reach her potential and Dru

382

had been there to watch her pass each and every milestone . . .

The door slammed against the wall, causing a dribble of dirt to trickle from the woodwork. Dru glanced up to see Whong burst in, waving a note and rattling in rapid Chinese. Behind Whong stood all four of the other Sullivan brothers. The look on their faces were four grim copies of the expression that was chiseled in Dru's stony features. Too upset to translate into English, Whong flailed his arms in frantic gestures and chattered like a disturbed magpie until he was overcome by a barrage of consecutive sneezes.

"This note came flying through the window, attached to a rock," John-Henry reported when Whong, in his extreme state of duress, was unable to make the transition from Chinese to English.

Dru snatched away the message Whong was flapping in front of his face. "Caleb received one just like it," he said gloomily.

Edgar Cassidy dug into his vest pocket to retrieve his wallet and offered the money to Dru. For a long moment, Dru peered at Edgar's anxious expression. "You're making it very difficult for me to condemn you for what you did to Caleb," he murmured with the faintest hint of a smile.

Edgar shifted uneasily beneath Dru's piercing blue eyes. "I'd give ten times this amount of money to get Tori back and to turn back the hands of time." He grabbed Dru's hand and laid the money in his palm. "But all I care about is getting her back safe and sound. Living with my mistakes is punishment enough, believe me," he murmured quietly.

Dru's penetrating gaze shifted to his brothers. "Tyrone Webster is dead, stabbed with a knife," he reported bleakly. "I don't suppose any of you know anything about that, do you?"

Four shocked faces peered back at him. Dru assessed his brothers and then heaved a frustrated sigh. "I was afraid you didn't." If his brothers weren't responsible, that left only one prime suspect—Tori. And only God knew who had a hold of her now!

While Whong sniffed and sneezed between outbursts of his native tongue, Caleb paced as he was prone to do when he was upset. Five pairs of sky-blue eyes watched him circle the room, waiting until the designated hour of midnight to deliver the money.

During the next hour, Dru did some serious praying. He could only hope Tori would utilize some of the techniques he had taught her along the way. Dru felt positively helpless. The one time Tori needed him, he didn't have a clue where to begin to search for her and she had no way of leaving a trail for him to follow unless she . . .

Dru bolted to his feet and dashed toward the door. The group of men automatically fell into step behind him.

"Where are we going?" Caleb questioned. "It's two hours before we were told to leave the ransom south of the stage station."

"We're going looking for clues," Dru murmured absently. "I pray to God Tori has the presence of mind to lead us to her."

"In the dark?" Jerry-Jeff snorted incredulously.

Dru didn't respond. He kept right on walking.

After retrieving improvised torches that Caleb had gathered from the dance the previous night, Dru strode down the alley behind the Queen High Saloon. When he spied Tori's discarded purse in the dirt, he held up the torch to survey the tracks that led off in three different directions. Dru gloomily observed that Tori's tracks led to Tyrone's office and then disappeared altogether. His astute gaze shifted to the most deeply embedded bootprints, wondering if Tori had been carried away, either unconscious or . . .

Refusing to believe the worst, Dru followed the trail to the spot where the hoofprints indicated the horses had been tethered earlier. Ordering Jimmy-Pete to gather their mounts, Dru trekked beside the prints of two horses that had veered from the alley into the street. From there, the tracks mingled with dozens of others, and Dru could only guess the general direction Tori's abductor had taken. But even if Dru was leading this procession on a wild-goose chase, it was far better than parking himself in a chair in Caleb's parlor, waiting the moment of impending doom.

There was only a shred of hope that Tori could lead him to her, and he wondered if she would remember what he had told her an eternity ago. He didn't dare hope she would remember, but he prayed desperation would be her salvation in this critical moment when her life hung in the balance. The thought of never seeing Tori again tore him to pieces, bit by agonizing bit . . .

Chapter 35

Although an excruciating headache plowed through Tori's skull, she pried open her eyes to stare upside down at the dark world. The tension that had sustained her thoughout the day gave way and depression crowded in on her like a dense fog. It seemed no matter how valiantly she struggled, she couldn't escape her fate. She had exhausted every technique of self-preservation Dru had taught her just to survive these past ten hours.

Tori wasn't a fool. She knew Duke Kendrick didn't have a merciful bone in his body. Whatever he was planning, he didn't intend to have her around to point an accusing finger at him. He was going to kill her sooner or later, and Tori had no chance to save herself, not while she was draped over the horse with her wrists and ankles bound with rope. She couldn't reach the dagger in her garter to cut herself free.

Fighting her way through the tangled cobwebs caused by her throbbing headache, Tori wracked her brain. Surely there was some vital tidbit of information that Dru had given her along the way that she had overlooked. If there wasn't, Tori was as good as dead!

Tori reflected on every moment she had spent with Dru, mulling over every incident, everything he had told her. But sentiment kept getting in her way when she faced the stark realization that she would never see Dru again, not on this side of eternity leastways. All the wondrous sensations they had shared would never again collide with reality. She could never express the love she had harbored for him, the deep affection that had never been allowed to blossom. She would go to her grave loving him with her heart, body, and soul and he would never know it.

Tori wondered idly if Dru would miss her, if he had come to care for her during the trials they had faced together, during the moments of splendor when she had attempted to convey her love without words. Would she simply be just another of the many women he'd had, the one he had felt obligated to marry to salvage his friendship with Caleb, the responsibility he had begrudgingly undertaken? More than likely, especially after all the hateful things she had said to him the previous night, Tori mused dispiritedly. There had been times when Tori thought perhaps Dru had begun to care for her, that he also harbored some special feeling. But he had never made a declaration to her and he had betrayed her. The one time she had confessed her affection, he had reduced it to logical equations . . .

Think, Chicago! Tori scolded herself fiercely. It would do no good whatsoever to muddle through the sweet, forbidden memories of Dru during this crisis. She could muck about, praying for a miracle and pining for a lost love while she was standing at the pearly gates, waiting for Saint Peter to fit her with her wings and a halo . . . And Lord, the way her luck had been running of late, she would probably wind up roasting over a blazing fire in hell beside Tyrone instead of drifting on her own private cloud in heaven.

Blast it, there had to be some way of saving herself from impending doom. Tori conjured up and discarded a score of imaginative ideas, finding nothing to suit this situation. God, what she wouldn't give for a can of beans to sprinkle behind her, leaving a trail for Dru to—

The whimsical thought jostled a flash from the past.

Suddenly Tori remembered Dru standing before her, poking fun at her for refusing to remove the strand of pearls her father had given her so long ago. They had been a symbol of that time in her life before Caleb went away. Because of their sentimental value, Tori had never parted with them. Dru had laughed at her comical costume of buckskins and pearls and flippantly remarked that if she needed him, she could always leave a path of pearls for him to follow.

A wry smile pursed Tori's lips as she uplifted her bound hands to tug at the necklace. It was a long shot, she knew. But if Hansel and Gretel could leave a trail of bread crumbs to find their way out of the forest, then she could string a path of pearls to lead Dru to her, if he even bothered to hunt for her. Of course, he probably wouldn't remember the comment he had made in jest and it would probably be impossible to see the pearls among the pebbles, especially in the dark. Desperation was said to be the mother of invention, Tori misquoted to herself, and so she called upon her ingenuity.

Tori could hear the clop of Duke's steed moving methodically up the slopes in front of her. Pretending to still be unconscious, Tori made as little movement as possible to draw suspicion. At regular intervals, Tori dropped a pearl from her fist, watching the moonlight glisten against the jewels that fell among the stones that paved the road leading away from Virginia City. She knew she didn't have so much as a prayer of surviving the night, but the path of pearls gave her one glimmer of hope, whimsical though it was. It was far better than drowning in self-pity and wishing she could have gone to her grave cherishing the memories of Dru's devoted love.

When a woman had nothing to lose, it seemed she clung desperately to fleeting clouds of hope. Pensively, Tori dropped another pearl when Duke veered up another steep path that led higher into the mountain range. She was probably wasting her time, but what else did she have to do while she waited for Duke to dispose of her in his vile, tormenting way? Tori dropped another pearl and sighed defeatedly. This hadn't been her day. She could kick herself for not staying in bed. This was definitely one of those times when it hadn't paid to get up!

Dru released an exasperated breath as he meandered from one side of the road to the other. "Damnit, Chicago, if you're conscious, use your head," he muttered half aloud.

"Would you mind telling me what we're looking for?" John-Henry questioned. "All I see is our tracks and that of a dozen other riders going one way and the other."

"For God's sake, Andy-Joe, if we don't deliver the money pretty quick, Tori's captors are going to—" Jerry-Jeff was cut off by Dru's harsh scowl.

"Don't say it," Dru snapped, flinging his brother a silencing glare. "Don't even think it."

Holding the torch high above his head, Dru trotted down the road while the rest of the congregation of men stared dismally after him. Oh, what was the use? Dru thought despairingly. There was no sign of Tori. He was chasing rainbows, and Tori wasn't going to be sitting at the end of one . . .

The glimmer of a pearl caught his attention just before he turned back toward his brothers. Dru felt his heart leap with hope as he bounded from the saddle to pluck up the pearl among the stones.

"She remembered!" Dru burst out in relieved laughter.

Caleb glanced in bewilderment at Edgar and the Sullivan brothers, who shrugged in response to the silent question. No one knew what Dru was babbling about. When Dru summoned them, the group clattered down the road, certain the eldest Sullivan's mind had snapped. Beaming with satisfaction, Dru unfolded his hand to reveal the delicate jewel.

"Tori's necklace," he announced to the bemused crowd of men who stared at Dru as if he were addle-witted. "She's leaving us a trail of pearls to follow."

Clinging to their one thread of hope, the men rode abreast, their torches held high, searching for another pearl to lead their way.

"Over here!" Billy-Bob called as he swung down to retrieve the fallen jewel.

Crowding in front of his youngest brother, Dru led the way up the winding path that wove into the mountains. Pride swelled inside Dru while he trekked along the narrow trail, picking up pearls as he went. He hadn't realized how much Tori had meant to him until he came to grips with the bleak thought of losing her. This ordeal was far from over and the outcome was still uncertain, but Tori had kept her wits about her and that gave Dru hope. She had learned to think like him, to react like him. When he met her they had been as different as dawn and midnight, but they had grown so similar these past few months, it was as if they were one . . .

"Hang on, Chicago," Dru whispered to the haunting vision of violet eyes and silver-gold hair.

Sam and Clark rose from the bushes and stared at the spot where the money was supposed to be delivered. There was nothing but skipping moonshadows and the muffled sounds of crickets chirping somewhere in the distance.

"What are we gonna do if Sullivan don't pay to get his wife back?" Clark murmured, scanning the surroundings.

"How in hell should I know," Sam grumbled irritably. "Tyrone don't pay us to do the thinking."

"Maybe one of us should ride back to town and ask him what we're supposed to do if we don't get the money," Clark suggested.

Sam gave the idea a moment's consideration and then gestured toward the tethered horses. "You go ask him.

I'll stay here and wait for Sullivan and Flemming."

Nodding in compliance, Clark scurried through the brush and stuffed his foot in the stirrup. As he trotted off, Sam sank down in the brush to wait. In less than thirty minutes, Clark returned, his face frozen in an expression of stunned disbelief.

"Well, what did Webster say?" Sam queried impatiently.

"He didn't say nothin'," Clark replied.

"Didn't you talk to him?" A befuddled frown plowed Sam's brow.

"I couldn't," Clark reported. "Dead men don't talk."

"What?" Sam bolted to his feet.

"Somebody stabbed Webster. He's layin' in his office and it's been torn upside down."

Swearing under his breath, Sam stalked toward his horse. "We better tell Duke what's going on. He'll be at the shack wondering where the hell we are. And if the Sullivans killed Webster, they'll be coming after us next. Those vigilantes are on the warpath again. Damn . . ."

Like streak lightning, the gunslingers galloped down the deserted road, speculating on what the Sullivans had in mind for them after they had disposed of Tyrone. This scheme had suddenly taken a turn for the worse. First Tori had escaped them and had to be recaptured. And now the ransom money hadn't been delivered and Tyrone had wound up dead!

Anxious to give Duke the unsettling news, Sam and Clark thundered up the trail that Flemming and the Sullivans were following. Had they known what lay ahead of them, they would have turned tail and ridden off into parts unknown. Dru Sullivan was short on patience at the moment, as Sam and Clark were about to find out!

At the first sound of thundering hooves, Dru ordered the lanterns doused. "What now?" he muttered to himself.

392

Leading their horses behind the boulders that lined the trail, Dru scanned the moonlit path, waiting to pounce on whomever approached. The instant Sam and Clark veered around the bend in the road, the Sullivans leaped down on them like a swarm of angry bees. Surprised squawks erupted from the lips of Sam and Clark when they were shoved to the ground and hammered by punishing blows.

"Who's holding Tori for ransom?" Dru snarled as he jerked Sam to his feet to give him such a fierce shaking that the man's teeth rattled.

"Tori who?" Sam smarted off.

It was not a wise thing to say, considering Dru's frustrated frame of mind. Dru didn't repeat the question, not in verbal form anyway. He merely cocked his arm and drove Sam's navel against his backbone. Sam grunted in pain and his knees buckled. When John-Henry yanked the scoundrel upright, Dru reared back to deliver another staggering blow.

"Duke Kendrick." Sam sang like a bird before Dru could deliver the third blow. "Webster told us to take her captive, but she got away and we had to go after her. We caught up with her when she shot out of Tyrone's office and—"

"Shut up, Sam," Clark barked.

Jerry-Jeff uncoiled like a rattlesnake. When Clark went down, Sam's loose tongue wagged even faster.

"Are you gonna lynch us? We didn't do nothing to your wife. We was just following orders. All we did was—"

"Where did Duke take Tori?" Dru interrupted impatiently.

"Are you gonna hang us?" Sam demanded to know.

"If you don't answer my questions, you'll be swinging from a rope in ten minutes," Dru growled in vicious threat.

"Duke took Tori back to the shack while we went to collect the ransom," Sam reported.

393

"And who took that shot at Caleb?" Dru interrogated him.

When Sam didn't answer immediately, Jimmy-Pete pushed his way forward. "Let me have a turn at him, big brother."

"I did," Sam admitted before he became the recipient of another bruising blow.

"And what about Billy-Bob?" John-Henry quizzed him.

"That was Clark's doing," Sam confessed since Clark didn't have enough breath left in him to speak for himself.

Spinning about, Dru tossed ropes to Caleb and Edgar who thus far had been only spectators. "Tie them up," he commanded as he strode toward his horse. "If they give you any trouble, just shoot 'em. It will save us the trouble of lynching them."

"With pleasure," Caleb enthused. A devilish smile pursed his lips. One-handed, he dallied the rope around Sam's neck and strung it down his back to manacle his wrists.

"You promised you wouldn't hang us!" Sam sputtered.

A menacing smile pursed Dru's lips as he trotted his steed past the wide-eyed hooligan. "I lied . . ."

While Caleb and Edgar tied the gunslingers in Gordian knots, the Sullivan brothers bounded into the saddle. As they trotted northwest, Dru cursed vehemently, imagining the horror Tori must have endured. He hadn't known she had been abducted once and escaped before being recaptured. It was a wonder she was still in command of her senses after her ordeals and he couldn't blame her one bit for seeking vengeance and burying her dagger in Tyrone's midsection. Webster had put her through hell and she had sent him on a one-way trip to that eternal inferno. That was exactly where the miserable vermin belonged. And Duke Kendrick was next in line for a flight to Hades. Dru only hoped Tori would live to see her abductor punished for the torment he was putting her through.

Webster and Kendrick had used Tori as a pawn to extort money from Caleb and Dru, hoping to bankrupt them and take control of the hotel and Bar S Ranch. If Dru had known that, he would have stabbed Tyrone before Tori got to him! Damn Webster's black soul and double damn Kendrick!

If Tori survived, Dru swore never to let her out of his sight again. She had the most incredible knack for attracting trouble. Maybe there was good reason for Edgar and Gwen to keep Tori secluded in the ranks of the socially elite. Tori had never met with disaster until Dru dragged her to Montana. Now she had more trouble than one woman could be expected to handle. Godamighty, he should have left that lavender-eyed nymph in Chicago.

Chapter 36

Still pretending to be unconscious, Tori remained as
limp as a rag doll while Duke heaved her over his
shoulder and carried her into the shack. To her dismay,
Duke deposited her on the bed and strapped her arms to
the bedposts. And to further frustrate her, Duke didn't
seem to care if she were unconscious or awake when he
abused her. Although he did untie her ankles, she didn't
have to be a genius to guess why he had!

The instant Duke shoved his knee between her thighs
and attempted to hike up her gown, Tori came to life like
an enraged wildcat. She jerked up her knees and rammed
her feet into his groin with the force of a kicking mule.
Duke's breath came out in a guttural growl, but in the
batting of an eyelash, his ferocious temper erupted. Duke
was as violent and bloodthirsty as they came when he was
physically attacked. To his distorted way of thinking, it
was perfectly all right for him to inflict pain on everyone
else, but he took offense when he was on the receiving
end of a punishing blow.

"You little bitch," he hissed, grazing Tori's cheek with
a doubled fist. "Nobody lays a hand on me without
suffering the consequences. Webster tried to dispose of
me and he wound up dead. The same thing is going to
happen to you after I've taken you and you beg for
mercy."

397

Tori barely had time to digest his words before Duke hurled himself at her like a snarling tiger. He clawed at Tori's elegant gown, ripping the seams and sending buttons flying in all directions. But Tori was going out in a blaze of glory, fighting this crazed murderer with her last dying breath. She writhed and twisted and struck out with her knees and heels, despite another blow to her cheek. Had she been able to grab hold of the dagger that Duke had yet to notice in his attempt to stifle her struggles, she would have buried it in his ruthless heart without one smidgen of regret.

Althought Tori battled with every ounce of energy she could muster, she was no match for Duke's brute strength and vicious temper. His body uncurled upon hers and Tori felt her skin crawl with revulsion. She refused to be subjected to his vile abuse, preferred to provoke him into killing her before she was subjected to his despicable violation. Tori blocked out the fierce pain in her jaw, willfully ignoring the groping hands and fighting tooth and nail to unseat the lusty beast . . .

A growl that sounded almost inhuman orbited around the room. Dru barreled through the door, leaving it sagging on its hinges. Icy blue eyes riveted on Duke, who had twisted to clutch at his Colt. But before Duke could snatch up his pistol and blow Dru to smithereens, Dru pounced on him. The pistol rolled over Duke's knuckles and plunked down beside Tori, doing her absolutely no good since her hands were still bound to the bedpost.

Luminous violet eyes blinked owlishly when Dru hurled Duke against the wall as if the varmint were as light as a feather. Never had she seen such a murderous snarl plastered on Dru's craggy features. There was a deadly glint in his eyes, a venomous curl on his lips. He looked one hundred percent savage beast when he hurled himself at Duke, who was having difficulty getting his bearings after his head crashed into the wall. Before Duke could react, Dru was upon him, beating him to a pulp with fists of steel. Groans and grunts erupted from

Duke while he attempted to ward off the vicious blows that sank deep in his belly and hammered his face.

It was no contest. Even desperate fury couldn't save Duke as he was pitted against this giant of a man whose temper was at a rolling boil. Dru had come through the ranks of life the hard way, scratching and clawing, taking his knocks and battling for survival. All the bottled-up fear and frustration that had hounded him during his frantic search for Tori erupted like a volcano. Flesh cracked against flesh, jarring bone and teeth. A spasm of furious hisses and curses erupted from Dru's lips and hung over the room like a cloud as he made mincemeat of Duke Kendrick.

When Duke slumped against the wall, bleeding all over himself and unable to counter even one devastating blow, Dru finally gained control of his temper. Heaving a shuddering breath, he unfolded himself to pivot toward the bed. The sight of Tori's torn gown and the huge splatters of tears that shimmered in her amethyst eyes tugged at his heartstrings. He couldn't find the words to express his sympathy and regret for the terror she had endured. Even though he had been forceful and violent with Duke, he was incredibly gentle when he eased down to remove the gag and loose Tori's hands. Emotions welled up inside him, struggling to translate themselves into words. But his feelings were much too jumbled to express and he was visibly shaken by the sight of her ripped clothes and bruised cheek.

Tori promised herself she wasn't going to cry, knowing how Dru disliked tears and the weakness it displayed. In disbelief, she peered through the mist that clouded her own eyes to see the moist fog that hovered on the pools of azure blue. Never did she expect to see the day that Dru expressed enough emotion to form a single tear!

Since the tragic death of his parents, Dru had kept all his feelings under lock and key. He had never let anyone but his family get close to him, never allowed himself to care deeply for a female. He had never wanted to suffer the agony of needing someone so much that he could be thoroughly devastated by the loss. He had been strong and dependable because his brothers had needed him, tough when he had to be, vicious if the situation demanded. He had been a tower of strength. But Tori's horrendous ordeal got to him when nothing else had for years.

Battling for hard-won self-control, Dru reached down to brush his quivering hand over the welt on her cheek. "You've had one helluva day, Chicago," he murmured shakily.

"Ain't it the truth," she agreed, muffling a sniff and forcing the semblance of a smile.

"*Isn't* it," he corrected. His features finally relaxed enough to curve into a grin, feeble though it was. Tenderly, Dru traced her puffy lips. "I know I haven't made life easy for you the past couple of months, but I want you to know I . . ."

Shock registered on his face when Tori abruptly snatched up the pistol that lay beside her and cocked the trigger. Reflexively, Dru darted sideways when the barrel swung toward his chest. Tori had very nearly blown his head off with a shotgun once, and that thought provoked him to dive for cover before she repeated the action. Dru didn't have the faintest notion what had gotten into her, but he decided to duck now and pose questions later.

The pistol exploded so close to his head that it nearly burst his eardrums. A second shot ricocheted off the metal bedframe and embedded itself in the wall beside Tori's head.

Wheeling about, Dru stared over his shoulder to watch Duke's left hand and his pistol drop lifelessly to his side. From all indication, Duke had regained consciousness and had grasped the other revolver in hopes of burying a bullet in Dru's back. If not for Tori's quick reflexes, he would have been pushing up daisies.

"*You* almost had one helluva night, Montana," Tori chirped, dropping the pistol as if she were handling live coals. She turned a sickened shade of green. The thought of watching Duke gun Dru down left Tori shaking like a leaf in a windstorm.

The two shots caused a stampede of footsteps to thunder across the porch. Within seconds, Dru's four brothers appeared at the door, aiming their Colts in every direction at once. Dru had instructed his brothers not to charge until he signaled, but the barking pistols sent them to their oldest brother's rescue, despite his specific orders for them to stay put.

Although Dru was bombarded with questions, he never took his eyes off Tori as he shucked his shirt to cover her ripped gown. "Let's go home, Chicago," he whispered, scooping her up in his brawny arms.

Home. If only Tori knew exactly where that was! She knew she no longer belonged in Chicago, living the life of the idle rich, married to a blustering fool like Hubert. But she wasn't so sure she would fit in Montana, either. There were some individuals who, because of unforseen circumstances and drastic changes in their lives, didn't have a place to call home. Tori had become one of those individuals. She was a misfit who didn't really belong anywhere . . . except in the protective circle of Dru's powerful arms, and she wasn't sure he wanted her there, not really. She was just another responsibility he had assumed and he pitied her because of the perilous trials she had encountered.

Although Tori was thankful to be alive, she knew she shouldn't dare ask for anything more. But what she wanted more than anything was to make a place for herself in Dru's life, to earn his love. Yet, deep down in her heart, she knew she would never be more than an obligation, the wife he took because circumstances demanded it.

When Dru swung into the saddle behind her and cradled her close, Tori died a little inside. She knew the only reason he was being so protective and attentive was because he sympathized with her plight. Dru wasn't offering love, only compassion.

Though her spirits plummeted, Tori mustered a smile when Caleb and Edgar rushed toward her to ensure she was alive and well after her long ordeal. They insisted on accompanying her to the ranch while the two youngest Sullivan brothers marched their captives to jail to await their hanging.

Tori was completely exhausted by the time they wound down the mountain to reach the ranch house. And she was certainly in no mood for the reception that awaited them in the parlor of Dru's home. Although Whong jumped for joy when he spied her and then repeatedly bowed and jabbered in rapid Chinese, the other two guests dampened her homecoming. Gwen and Hubert lashed out at Dru the instant he set foot in the door, and two men whom Tori couldn't recall seeing in all her life bolted forward to take charge.

A lean, lanky man who appeared to be pushing forty, strode across the parlor with pistol in hand. Behind him was a stocky, trail-weary man who was also toting two revolvers. To Tori's astonishment, the strangers trained their Colts on Dru.

"Dru Sullivan, you are under arrest for kidnapping, physical assault, and for the murder of Tyrone Webster," Tom Bates announced.

Tori's head jerked up to see Gwen and Hubert beaming in smug satisfaction.

"That's ridiculous," Caleb scowled. "He was—"

"And you are also under arrest, Mr. Flemming," William Fogg chimed in. "You have been charged with withholding information and in aiding in the young lady's kidnapping."

"Who the hell are these men?" Dru growled in question.

"Pinkerton agents," Hubert gloated. "They just arrived on the Wells Fargo stage after following you cross-country for the past seven weeks. I hired them to track you down. It took them long enough, but at least

402

there are two representatives of law and order to see that you pay for your crimes."

Dru looked as if he would like to stomp over and punch Hubert squarely between the eyes!

"Do your duty, gentlemen," Gwendolyn insisted, tilting a haughty chin. "We have a long ride back to town with our prisoners in tow."

"Dru didn't kill Webster," Tori interjected.

It was bad enough that Dru was about to be indicted for abduction and assault, and it was clearly evident who had been on the receiving end of Dru's beefy fists—Hubert Carrington Frazier II. But she refused to let Dru take the blame for a crime he didn't commit.

"Clam up, Chicago," Dru muttered.

When Tori stared bemusedly at him, Dru glanced over at the Pinkerton detectives. "I stabbed Webster and shot Kendrick."

"You most certainly did not!" Tori pivoted, wondering why the devil Dru was confessing to those crimes.

"Yes I did," he bellowed at her.

"Godamighty, Montana, stop trying to take the blame," Tori snapped. "I killed Kendrick before he shot you in the back and you darned well know it."

"And Webster?" Caleb prodded, hoping the detectives would be lenient with Tori, who looked as though she had been through hell, which she most certainly had!

Tori stared curiously at Dru, who was scowling under his breath. It dawned on her just then that Dru assumed she had stabbed Webster and that he was trying to protect her. Always the fearless protector, she mused, staring at Dru. Well, she didn't need his protection or his sympathy. If not for her own ingenuity and an open can of beans, she would have been dead hours ago!

"I didn't kill Webster. He was already dead before I burst into his office," Tori declared. "Duke Kendrick admitted he had killed Tyrone when Tyrone tried to dispose of him."

Hubert muttered in annoyance. "Sullivan is still

wanted for kidnapping and assault, and I want him behind bars before the night is out!"

"And the same goes for Caleb Flemming," Gwen trumpeted, glaring daggers at her ex-husband.

When the Pinkerton detectives homed in on Dru and Caleb, Edgar elbowed his way past Tori to speak his piece. "There was no kidnapping," he announced, only to hear Gwen burst into an outraged squawk. "I telegraphed Caleb to inform him of Tori's upcoming wedding. He only sent Mr. Sullivan to accompany her across difficult terrain for a visit. I knew exactly where Victoria was the entire time, and I knew she would be in capable hands."

"You?" Caleb, Gwen, and Hubert hooted in unison.

Tori sat down before she fell down. It was beyond her understanding why her stepfather had contacted her father and why he was now coming to the defense of Caleb and Dru. Apparently, Gwen was every bit as stunned by the news. She fainted in a dead heap and no one bothered to catch her as she hit the floor with a decisive thud.

The Pinkerton agents looked at each other and frowned in confusion.

"And as far as the assault on Hubert is concerned, there wasn't one," Edgar went on to say. "Hubert instigated the attack and Dru countered in self-defense. Dru is innocent of any wrongdoing and I refuse to press charges against him. All that he has done is save Tori's life . . . in more ways than one," he added, casting Hubert a meaningful glance. "Dru is to be commended, not punished."

"If you keep this up, Edgar, I'm going to wind up liking you," Caleb chortled. Respect twinkled in his brown eyes.

Hubert was so frustrated that he couldn't stand still. He was outraged by Edgar's betrayal and by the fact that Dru was about to escape unscathed. When the detectives holstered their Colts, Hubert spewed curses.

"If you think I'm going to pay the two of you for your

time, you are sorely mistaken! I found Sullivan long before you did and I intend to give a report of your poor abilities to Pinkerton! You might as well start looking for another line of work because I'll see to it that you two bungling baboons are out of a job!"

Calmly, Edgar fished into his pocket to pay the agents their wages. "You have no need to fear for your jobs," he assured Tom and William. "Hubert can spout until he is blue in the face, but I will be presenting a conflicting report that commends your work. As I'm sure you have discovered by now, Hubert is just a big bag of wind."

After grinning at Edgar, Tom Bates and William Fogg pocketed their money and went on their way. But Hubert was still fit to be tied. Nothing had turned out as he had anticipated and he wasn't enjoying one iota of satisfaction.

"You're every kind of fool if you remain married to this brutish maniac, Victoria," Hubert growled at the rumpled beauty. "Sullivan only married you to get back at me. When he was in Chicago last year, he lost his temper and struck me like the barbarian he is. And he married you just to have his revenge on me. You were just his pawn to have the last laugh."

Tori's bewildered gaze lifted to see Dru muttering under his breath. He had never indicated that he knew Hubert or that he'd had any previous dealings with the man. Obligation and revenge against his archrival? That was what this marriage was based on? God, it was even worse than she thought!

Seeing the torment in Tori's eyes, Hubert went for the throat. "Go ahead, deny it, Sullivan," he challenged, grinning triumphantly when Tori looked as if she had suffered a blow to the heart. "You didn't bother to tell her, did you? No, of course you didn't. It would have spoiled your scheme, wouldn't it? But you did use her to get back at me." Hubert raked Dru with scornful mockery. "I shudder to think of all the other lies and lurid ways you used Victoria during your trek to Montana."

405

Tori took the second verbal blow courageously, but she was thoroughly crushed by Hubert's scathing accusations and the ridiculing glare directed at her.

"Get out of my house before I throw you out," Dru roared, his voice vibrating off the walls to come at Hubert from all directions.

Hubert glanced down at Tori, whose downcast eyes were focused on the clenched fists that were knotted in the folds of her crumpled gown. "I hope you are proud of yourself, Victoria. You were his gambit, his whore . . ."

When Dru launched himself at Hubert, the smaller man shrieked in terror. Before Hubert could scamper away, Dru grabbed him by the nape of his jacket and the seat of his pants and carried him out the door. Hubert kicked and squawked like a disturbed rooster. With a mutinous growl, Dru heaved Hubert out the front door. A pained grunt gushed from Hubert's lips when he hit the ground, jarring every bone in his miserable body.

Growling in disgust, Dru stamped back inside to find Tori bookended by Caleb and Edgar.

"Please take me back to the hotel," she requested, tilting a proud chin, refusing to glance in Dru's direction. "It has been a long, harrowing day and I'm exhausted."

Helplessly, Caleb stared at Dru who was swearing under his breath.

"Don't go, Chicago," Dru demanded.

His sharp voice caused her back to stiffen like a ramrod. Defiantly, Tori stared at the air over Dru's head. "I will send someone to retrieve my belongings in the morning," she announced in a curt tone.

When Gwen roused, moaning and groaning, Edgar pivoted to hoist his wife to her feet and scuttle her out the door before she threw another tantrum.

As the foursome disappeared into the darkness, Dru slumped against the doorjamb to expel a harsh breath. Mumbling to himself, Whong scurried around the parlor, uprighting the end table Gwen had inadvertently knocked over when she wilted on the floor.

"You wirr be very sorry if you ret her go, Mr. Surrivan," Whong had the gall to say.

Dru glowered at the Chinaman from his towering height. It was unlike Whong to spout his opinions. Whong was meek and devoted to a fault and he usually kept his thoughts to himself. He never interfered. He merely went about his business like a dutiful servant.

"And just how do you propose I get her back?" Dru scoffed, disgruntled. "You saw the look she flung at me. If looks could kill, I'd have been a dead duck!"

"Most women rike to be showered with gifts," Whong declared, his dark eyes focused on Dru's agitated scowl.

"What can I possibly give Tori that she doesn't already have?" he questioned in exasperation. "Edgar has blessed her with every luxury known to womankind, and Caleb has bestowed a new wardrobe on her that's befitting a queen. She thinks I used her to . . ."

"Didn't you?" Whong had the audacity to ask.

That really did it! Dru had been abandoned by his wife and now his devoted servant was glaring accusingly at him. And that was a first! The mild-mannered Whong had never raised his voice or ridiculed Dru in any manner. Or at least he hadn't until now.

"If you're so damned fond of her, then why don't *you* marry her," Dru suggested flippantly. "It's for sure she wants out of the marriage in which she presently finds herself!"

Whong sadly shook his head and his queue rippled down his back. "Because I cannot give the rady the gift she wants and needs," he said ruefully.

Dru fished into his pocket to stuff several gold nuggets in Whong's hand. "There, go buy her what you think she wants, though I cannot imagine what it could be. She has two fathers catering to her. Some of us don't even have one! And if you think gifts will win her affection, you're in for one helluva surprise, Whong."

His gaze lifted to stare Dru squarely in the eye. Calmly, he handed the nuggets back to Dru. "For such an interrigent man, Mr. Surrivan, sometimes you can be very stupid."

Dru puffed up with so much indignation he would have popped the buttons off his shirt. But Tori was wearing it at the moment. "Thank you for insulting me, friend," he sniffed sarcastically.

"You're very wercome," Whong snapped before he stormed out of the room.

Tossing up his arms in a gesture of futility, Dru stomped up the steps to his room. But therein lay another round of torment. The aroma of Tori's perfume clung to the chamber, and her gowns were crowded in his closet. Everywhere he looked there were visual reminders of Tori's intrusion in his life.

And Godamighty, he couldn't even collapse in bed without being haunted by the sweet memories they had made there. Even when Dru stared up into the darkness, he was hounded by the image that materialized above him like a specter in the night. Luminous violet eyes surrounded by long silky lashes and streams of silver-blond hair shimmered in the Montana moonlight . . . Moonfire . . . That flowing mass of tendrils that surrounded Tori's enchanting face reminded him of moonfire—the beguiling combination of glowing silver and shimmering gold.

Dru expelled a deep sigh. There weren't nights anywhere on the continent that compared to the ones beneath the wide Montana sky. Nothing rivaled the Indian moon when it hung on the horizon like a circular gold nugget amid the silvery starlight. The nights were as spectacular as Tori. Well, almost, Dru reluctantly amended. The truth was, even Montana moonfire couldn't hold a candle to Tori. And she, like his full-grown brothers, didn't need him all that much anymore. Dru had lived up to his family obligation. Now his brothers were managing quite well on their own and Tori didn't need a protector . . .

Dru pummeled his pillow until the feathers flew. Give

408

her gifts to soothe her irritation with him? That wouldn't work worth a damn, and Dru knew it. Whong wasn't so smart if he thought a gift would ease her anger long enough for him to apologize. Hubert's words had planted seeds of doubt and hounded Tori with humiliation. If Dru had admitted he had dealt with that weasel once before, Tori might not have taken such offense now. Dru couldn't really blame her for what she was thinking. He had, after all, considered that his marriage to Tori would really get Hubert's goat. And it had. But if only he was allowed to explain . . .

And just what the devil would I say to her? Dru asked himself. *Would I declare revenge never crossed my mind? That I didn't feel obligated after our romantic interlude in Des Moines?* he quizzed himself. Tori wouldn't believe him for a minute!

Dru exhaled another exasperated breath and flounced on his bed, begging for sleep. Well, what did he have to lose by going to Tori, bearing gifts as peace offerings? If he could get a foot in the door, maybe he could explain that he hadn't exactly used her for his own selfish purposes. After all, they had been through thick and thin and he was accustomed to having her around, *liked* having her around. It would kill him if Tori left Montana hating him. There were too many precious memories at stake, and Dru felt the need to make an attempt to explain his feelings before she left him for good.

Maybe he *would* shower her with presents, he decided, giving the idea second consideration. What did he have to lose? Only everything that had come to mean anything to him, he realized dismally. Damnit, if Hubert had kept his big mouth shut, Tori would have been beside him tonight. Instead, Dru was left alone, reflecting on every moment he had spent with that stunning nymph, visualizing what his life would be like when Tori was no longer in it. It wasn't a pretty picture. Not a pretty picture at all!

Part V

Her look, her love, her form, her touch!
  The least seemed most by blissful turn
Blissful but that it pleased too much,
  And taught the wayward soul to yearn.
It was as if a harp with wires
  Was traversed by the breath I drew;
And; oh sweet meeting of desires!
  She, answering, owned that she loved too.
                              —Coventry Patmore

Chapter 37

All decked out in the most fashionable suit he owned and carrying a bouquet of flowers that he ordered Whong to pluck from the garden, Dru rapped on Caleb's door. When the portal swung open, Dru displayed his most beguiling smile. But it was not well received. Tori glared poison arrows at him.

"For you," he murmured in a seductive voice as he offered her the bouquet.

Tori accepted the flowers. With defiance glittering in her violet eyes, she snapped the fragile blossoms from their stems, threw the flowers in his face, and handed the stems back to him. Flinging her nose high in the air, she promptly shut the door.

Dru's shoulders slumped dejectedly. Grumbling, he brushed the blossoms from his black jacket.

Whong let loose with a whistle and sadly shook his head. "Mrs. Surrivan is rearry mad at you," he observed. A muddled frown puckered his brow when Dru pivoted on his heels, bowed his neck, and marched down the corridor. "Where are you going, Mr. Surrivan?"

"If she doesn't want flowers, maybe bonbons will tempt her to spare me five minutes of her precious time," Dru mumbled, whizzing through the hotel lobby.

While Dru was making his purchase, Tori was trying to regain control of her temper. With her mouth

413

compressed in a thin line, she sank back in her chair across from Hubert and Gwen, who had come to talk some sense into her.

"I'm willing to put the past behind us," Hubert declared nobly. "And I regret the degrading remarks I made to you last night. I was angry and upset and distraught to learn you had married that oversized ape. But I'm sure, being the bully he is, Sullivan left you with little choice in the matter. If you have this outrageous marriage of yours annulled, we will return to Chicago and pretend nothing has happened. No one has to know about this unfortunate incident."

"Hubert and I will ensure there is no gossip," Gwen insisted. She reached over to pat Tori's hand, as if gossip was Tori's foremost concern instead of Gwen's. "You can't stay here with Caleb. Montana is no place for a civilized, properly bred lady. And Hubert is being very understanding and forgiving."

Tori's gaze lanced off her mother, who had expressed more concern over the family reputation than the ordeal of her kidnapping and the subsequent murders. Her attention shifted to Hubert, who was sporting a black eye that was the identical size of Dru's fist. In Tori's opinion, Hubert's only reason for wanting to marry her was to save face in Chicago and to have his revenge on Dru. And Gwen, who had also been too socially sensitive to suit Tori, was more concerned about scandalous tales than Tori's happiness.

In fact, Tori could safely say, now that she had come to think of it, Edgar was the only one of the three who had treated her with consideration and respect. Edgar could have had Dru strung up by his heels. And Dru probably should have been, the miserable rat!

When Tori considered all the love she had wasted on that insensitive brute, it annoyed her. He truly had used her. She had been no more than the time he was killing while he toted her to Caleb. Spurred by revenge against Hubert and an obligation to a long-time friend, Dru had married her. But he had wed Tori because of what she was to Caleb and to his adversary—Hubert Carrington Frazier II. That really hurt! It also made Tori furious. She was sick to death of being manipulated and maneuvered. Even Caleb's purpose in sending Dru after her had been selfish. He wanted his revenge on Gwen, and now she wanted hers because Caleb had his and she considered turn about fair play.

The only one whose motives Tori couldn't quite figure was Edgar. Why had he gone behind Gwen's back to inform Caleb of the marriage in Chicago? And why had he saved Dru's neck and spared Caleb from Hubert and Gwen's wrath? Considering all that had happened, Tori was spitefully contemplating returning to Chicago with Edgar and leaving her mother and her ex-fiancé to muddle back home by themselves. Tori was beginning to think they deserved each other. As for herself, Tori just wanted to be left alone to sort out her tangled emotions . . .

Another firm rap at the door jostled her from her musings and her annoying conversation with Hubert and Gwen. Since Caleb and Edgar had left together to inspect the businesses Tyrone Webster had once owned, Tori was left to answer the door and portray the hostess. She was miffed by the blooming friendship between Edgar and Caleb and irritated by the interruption in an already frustrating conversation with her mother and ex-fiancé.

The moment Tori swung open the door, her thoughts became even more troubled. There stood Dru, still dressed in his Sunday best, bearing bonbons from the bakery.

"Sweets for the sweet," he announced, sorting through his repertoire of disarming smiles to grace Tori with one of superb quality.

Gnashing her teeth, Tori opened the box, scooped up a bonbon, and smeared it all over Dru's charming face. Surely he would get the message this time, Tori mused as she slammed the door in his gooey face.

"Now as I was saying . . ." Hubert cleared his throat and formulated his thoughts while Tori sank back in her chair. "The only possible way for all of us to salvage our dignity and . . ."

While Hubert rattled on, Dru stood in the corridor, wiping the globs of bonbon from his face. "You and your bright ideas," he scowled at Whong.

"I have heard that the third time is supposed to be a charm," Whong commented, stifling a grin. "Perhaps if you were to offer Mrs. Surrivan the gift of . . ."

If the third time was the charm, Dru was game. Since he stood to lose everything he wanted if Tori returned to Chicago, he decided to give it one last try. Wheeling about, he left Whong in midsentence to purchase another gift for Tori. It would be something no one else had given her. If nothing else, it would at least get her attention.

Rolling his eyes, Whong propped himself against the wall to await Dru's return. "Foorish man," he muttered. Dru was going about this gift-giving all wrong. Whong didn't claim to be an authority on women, but he knew what made Tori happy and what didn't. Tori needed only one gift, but Dru was too blind to realize what that was.

A crow of disbelief gurgled from Whong's throat when Dru returned fifteen minutes later with his unusual gift. The mere fact that Dru had the audacity to bring it through the hotel lobby was laughable. But Dru was desperate. If nothing else, this particular gift would hold Tori's attention long enough for Dru to rattle off what he intended to say. This had to work. Dru had already received the rapt attention of the crowd that milled around the hotel! Surely it would also leave Tori thunderstruck and allow Dru to speak his piece.

"The stage leaves in an hour," Gwen informed her daughter. "I want you to come home where you belong, Victoria. You don't fit into this raucous mining town any

416

better than I do."

Tori heaved a sigh. She could think of no reason to stay in Virginia City and no reason to go, either. But she supposed it would be to her best interest to put great distances between herself and Dru. The only reason he had come bearing gifts was because he felt obligated to make amends to his wife—one he hadn't wanted in the first place. As always, Dru's overactive sense of responsibility spurred him to action. He had come because he thought he should, not necessarily because he wanted to.

Her only salvation was Edgar, Tori mused pensively. He had shown himself to be compassionate, fair, and just throughout the entire ordeal. Tori scolded herself for not being more receptive to Edgar the past few years. She had erected an invisible wall between them because he was her stepfather and she would have preferred to spend those years with her own father. But the best friend she'd had the past decade had been right under her nose and Tori had purposely overlooked him because he had tried to take Caleb's place in her heart. She had faulted him for that, but it certainly wasn't a crime. In fact, it was damned noble of Edgar to think of her as his daughter and to attempt to treat her as such.

Finally, Tori made her decision. She intended to return to Chicago. But from now on she would give Edgar the respect he deserved. And she wasn't going to marry Hubert, no matter how hard Gwen pushed and prodded. Those days of meekly accepting her fate were over. Edgar would stand up for Tori, just as he had interceded when Gwen and Hubert tried to file charges against Caleb and Dru. Edgar was a good man. He had tried to express fatherly love, and now Tori was going to accept his affection.

Squaring her shoulders, Tori peered first at Hubert and then at her mother. "I have decided to return to Chicago, but—"

The sharp, insistent rap at the door brought quick

417

death to her announcement.

"Who the blazes keeps interrupting us?" Hubert muttered sourly.

Tori didn't reply. There was enough tension between Hubert and Dru without creating another awkward confrontation. Gracefully, Tori swept through the parlor and into the hall. When she flung open the door to tell Dru where he could stuff his peace-treaty gifts, her eyes bulged from their sockets.

While Whong stood there sneezing into his handkerchief and muttering in his native tongue, Dru mustered another blinding smile. "For you, Chicago. I wanted to get you something you didn't already have."

Tori's jaw fell off its hinges as she surveyed the sleek, muscular palomino mare that stared back at her. The whisper of voices and amused snickers wafted through the corridor where two dozen men and women gauged Tori's reaction to her unique gift and the fact that Dru had the gall to lead the steed through the hotel lobby.

"I bought her because she reminds me of you," he murmured, his eyes drifting possessively over Tori's curvaceous figure that was accentuated by the trim-fitting blue satin gown.

"Oh really?" she smirked when she finally regained her tongue. "Which end of her?" Tori stomped around to the horse's rump and then glanced disdainfully at Dru. "Funny thing that you should mention it. From this end, she reminds me of *you!*"

Dru gritted his teeth and clamped an iron will on his temper. "While you are taking Moonfire on a ride around town, I'd like to speak privately with you," Dru requested as politely as possible after Tori lambasted him with a stinging jibe.

Tori flashed him a withering glance. The man was impossible. She had insulted him, and it hadn't seemed to faze him.

"What in the hell is going on here?" Caleb's shocked voice clanged down the corridor like a pealing bell.

418

As calmly as you please, Dru glanced over his shoulder to see Caleb and Edgar elbowing their way through the crowd of snickering onlookers who clogged the entryway. "I brought Tori a gift."

"Well, you could have taken her outside to see it instead of the other way around," Caleb spluttered. "Get that animal out of here before the hotel starts smelling like a stable!"

"The horse and I aren't leaving until Tori agrees to speak with me in private," Dru said in a no-nonsense tone.

"For God's sake, Tori go talk to him—outside," Caleb pleaded.

"No," she protested. "We have nothing left to say except good-bye. I'm leaving on the stage in an hour."

Dru could pretend to be a polished-mannered gentleman for just so long before he told propriety to take a hike. Tori wasn't going anywhere until he had the chance to speak his piece. Without preamble, his hand snaked out to grab Tori's wrist. Swiftly he deposited her atop the palomino mare. In the batting of an eyelash, Dru swung up behind her.

"What is going on out there?" Hubert grumbled as he unfolded his bruised body from the sofa to have a look.

Gwen gasped in astonishment when she peered around Hubert's shoulders to see Tori and Dru sitting atop the horse in the corridor that connected Caleb's home to the hotel lobby. "Victoria, get down from there this instant! We have a stage to catch!" Gwen squawked. "Edgar, for God's sake, do something!"

Edgar did. He pressed himself against the wall when Dru backed the mare out of the narrow corridor. When Hubert dashed forward to retrieve Tori from Dru's clutches, a booted foot caught him in the chest and knocked him into the wall.

"She's my wife," Dru growled down at Hubert.

"She is *my* fiancée," Hubert crowed like an indignant rooster. "She is going to have your marriage annulled so she can marry me in Chicago!"

The news, whether it was true or not, caused Dru's temper to snap. "I refuse to have my marriage annulled!" he all but shouted at anyone who cared to listen.

"What you want is of no importance," Hubert spewed contemptuously. "There are ways around stubborn, uncultured barbarians like you. I have the wealth and the power to get things done. You should have learned that after our dealings last fall."

Tori squirmed to slide from the saddle, but Dru held her tightly. "I am going to Chicago," she insisted.

"Maybe so, but I have something to say to you and you're damned well going to listen!" Dru breathed fire down her neck.

Again Tori attempted to fling herself off the mare, but sinewy arms clamped around her, mashing her against Dru's rock-hard chest. As he backed from the hall, the crowd parted to let him pass. Reining Moonfire around, Dru clomped through the lobby and pushed Tori forward before she smacked her head on the top of the doorway.

Before Tori could protest, Dru was out the door, gouging Moonfire into her swiftest pace. And he didn't rein the steed to a halt until they were on the outskirts of town.

Chapter 38

Tori was furious. She had been abducted so many
times the past few months that it had finally and totally
loosed her temper. The minute Moonfire skidded to a halt
and Dru dragged her from the saddle, Tori lit into him.
She pounded him with her fists and called him every
disrespectful name that came to mind, even if she wasn't
much good at getting her curse words in the proper order.

Dru had a full-fledged fight on his hands, trying to
restrain Tori from clawing him to shreds. She was all
teeth and fists and flying fur, and Dru had to dance
around in circles to dodge her swinging arms and striking
feet. Godamighty! All he had wanted was to talk to her!

When Tori threw herself off balance with a blow that
connected only with air, Dru lunged like a tiger. His full
lips swooped down on hers, stealing the breath from her
lungs. He bent her into his masculine contours, making
her far more aware of him than she wanted to be, leaving
her cursing her volatile reaction to him.

"Don't leave me, Chicago," he rasped when he came
up for air. His hands wandered down her spine to brush
familiarly over her derrière. "I've grown accustomed to
having you around."

"That is hardly reason for me to stay," Tori choked
out, fighting down those infuriating tingles that Dru so
easily aroused in her. "You had your revenge on Hubert,

421

and my father had his on my mother. And I'm Godamighty tired of being used as a device for everyone around here to get even with somebody else!"

Once Tori got started, all her pent-up frustrations came pouring out like floodwaters. "All my life I seem to have been caught in the middle of one feud or another. I've been ordered about, commanded to do what proper ladies are expected to do precisely when they are supposed to do it. For once in my life I'm going to do what's best for me, and your misdirected sense of responsibility and your devious ploys be damned! You don't want me and you never did. I was only a duty you accepted. I was the naive, inexperienced innocent you trained to survive in the wilds. I was the wife you married because you felt honorbound to salvage my reputation and pacify my father."

Tori inhaled a quick breath and raged on. "I was the love you didn't want or need because you had your brothers to care for and look after. I don't mean anything to you and the only reason you want me to stay is because you think it is the responsibile, sensible thing to do!" Violet eyes blazed up at him. "Admit it, Montana, and then take me back to the hotel," she yelled at him as if he were deaf.

"All right, damnit, I'll admit I derived some wicked amusement from marrying Hubert's fiancée," Dru grumbled. "Seeing the look on his face when I told him satisfied my vengeance. Hubert cost me a fortune last year when I drove my cattle herd to the stock yards. After our fracas he used his influence to prevent me from selling to other buyers and I was forced to accept his rock-bottom price. Of course I wanted to have my revenge on that weasel! Who wouldn't?"

Dru held Tori at arm's length and stared her squarely in the eye. "And it's true that I felt obligated to do the right thing by you after we became intimate. But confound it, Chicago, even if you think you have me all figured out, there are three things you don't know that you should know before you spirit off on that stage.

"The first thing is that I didn't betray you, as you were led to believe by that passel of calico queens. I paid Eleanor and Sophie a visit while they were entertaining two of their regular clients. After a little forceful persuasion, they admitted that Tyrone had bribed them to feed you that crock of lies."

"Curse that man's black heart for deceiving me," Tori muttered under her breath.

"My sentiments exactly," Dru concurred. "Tyrone was notorious for causing dissension and trouble every chance he got. He probably decided to attempt to dispose of Duke Kendrick because the hired gunslinger had an ego the exact size as Tyrone's. Webster never did care for competition."

"I suppose his cruel prank was his way of getting back at me for threatening him when I barged in on him and his three henchmen," Tori mused aloud.

"You did *what!*" Dru croaked, his eyes popping from their sockets. "Jeezus, Chicago! What were you thinking? It's a wonder Webster didn't have Duke shoot you on the spot!"

"I wanted it known that I would not tolerate another attempt on my father's life," Tori defended. "The man kept getting away with murder, and my sense of justice refused to overlook Tyrone's tyranny, so I confronted him."

While Dru was grumbling about Tori's foolhardy bravura, she frowned curiously at the towering giant. "And what were the other two things you declared I needed to know, Montana?" she questioned impatiently. "I have a stage to catch and time is short. Say what you intended to say and be quick about it."

His bronzed finger lifted to trace her cupid's-bow lips. "The second and most important point I want to make is that I love you, and I don't want you to go away and leave me alone. Last night without you was pure and simple hell. I couldn't sleep a wink. I lay there like a floundering

423

fish, trying to figure out some way to get you back, to make things between us like they were, only better."

His expression softened when Tori stared up at him in mute disbelief. "I hadn't planned to fall in love with you, you know. I told myself my reaction to you was a perfectly natural one for a man who was left alone with a beautiful woman, a man whose job it was to teach you to adapt to a world that was as foreign to you as China. And I told myself I married you to infuriate Hubert and because I thought that's what Caleb wanted me to do. I did feel obligated to you after our night together in Des Moines. But those were all flimsy excuses to conceal the truth from you and from myself. I have never been very good at talking about my emotions. And I'm not as demonstrative as I should be. But from here on out I'm going to be."

Dru expelled a sigh as he combed his fingers through the glorious mass of silver-blond hair that was the exact color of Moonfire's mane and tail. "I didn't want to need you, but I do. You satisfy a craving that I never knew existed before you came into my life. You fill up my world and you've tormented my thoughts for so long that I haven't been able to think straight since I don't know when . . ."

Her index finger pressed against his lips to silence him. "You are not obligated to confess what you don't really feel," Tori insisted with a rueful smile. "You have mistaken responsibility for love. I told you once that I loved you and I have loved you from the very beginning without expecting anything in return, even if your love was what I wanted most. But you can't give me what I need because you don't really love me and I doubt you ever will. And because you cannot, I think it would be best for me to return to Chicago before we make each other more miserable than we already have."

Tori had thoroughly convinced herself that Dru could never honestly love her and she refused to believe him now. He was a man with a strong sense of obligation to his family and friends. He was saying only what he thought she wanted to hear.

"Just accept my love for you and let this marriage be over before you wind up loathing me for tying you down," Tori pleaded with him.

"Noble to the very end, aren't you, Chicago?" he teased with a rakish grin.

Lord, what a relief it was to hear she loved him. She had told him she hated him so many times the past few days that he believed it.

"From the beginning you were prepared to give your love away, certain that I had no love to give." Dru sank down on the carpet of grass beside the road and pulled Tori on top of him. "But you failed to give yourself credit. You cast a potent spell on a man, sweet witch." His hand glided up to brush across the blue satin that concealed her breasts. "Perhaps it's time I showed you what my brand of love is all about. You seem to think you have the corner on the market, Little Miss Sophisticated. Well, you don't. I said I love you and I do, so don't try to talk me out of feeling what I feel. I've never felt this way about a woman in all my life." His hand cupped her chin, uplifting her face to his. "Look into these eyes and tell me what you see. It is love staring back at you. Don't you recognize it?"

His dark head tilted and his face moved deliberately toward hers. Ever so tenderly, his lips courted hers with intimate promises, watching her watch him while he kissed her with all the suppressed emotion that churned inside him.

The kiss made Tori's legs go boneless and sent her heart leapfrogging around her chest. There was more than passion in his embrace, more than wanting. He was loving her, not only with his body but with his heart. She could see the tender emotions chasing each other through his sky-blue eyes . . .

Tori blinked in astonishment. "You do love me, don't you, Montana?" she realized and said so. A pleased smile

425

captured her enchanting features when he nodded affirmatively and then crossed his heart.

"Well, you don't have to look so damned smug," Dru teased in a playful tone.

Tori looped her arms around his broad shoulders and beamed in satisfaction. "I can if I wish," she declared saucily. "I consider your love a priceless gift. The only one I have ever wanted, in fact."

It suddenly dawned on Dru what Whong had been trying to tell him. The gift to which Whong had referred was the gift of love. That little Chinaman had far more insight than Dru had given him credit for. And thanks to Whong's insistence, Dru had Tori back in his arms where he had wanted her all along. He had been too blind and stubborn to admit how much this lavender-eyed elf meant to him.

"You're quite something, Chicago," Dru murmured, raking her with masculine appreciation.

"Ain't I though?" she replied with a carefree giggle.

"*Aren't,*" he corrected. Dru's smile was as wide as Montana Territory.

"I certainly *are,*" she teased before dropping a kiss to his sensuous lips.

"Your English is going to hell," Dru declared, unable to suppress another blinding smile. He peered into Tori's dazzling features, and he broke into a chuckle without knowing why. He supposed the irrepressible pleasure that swelled inside him had simply bubbled to the surface like an eternal spring.

"My grammar may be deteriorating, but my love life is definitely showing signs of improvement," she parried in a provocative tone. "Suppose you prove this love of yours, Montana. I never did care much for a man who was all talk and no action."

"Right here? Right now?" Dru croaked, glancing in all directions at once. "Somebody might see us!"

"Are you ashamed to let the world know you love me?" she questioned, her delicate brow elevating to a

426

challenging angle. "Perhaps you love me, but maybe you don't love me enough."

"I'll be happy to tell anybody who cares to listen," Dru proclaimed with great conviction. "But I draw the line at letting anyone watch me communicate my affection for my gorgeous wife. There are some things left better to privacy . . ."

His voice trailed off when, lo and behold, his four brothers came galloping from the direction of the ranch and the Cassidys and company came rumbling from town in a rented carriage.

Lord, just what he needed so soon after he and Tori had finally come to grips with their feelings for each other. Godamighty, couldn't a man be alone with his wife for a few minutes without all his relatives arriving upon the scene?

Chapter 39

John-Henry and his younger brothers brought their steeds to skidding halts to assess the brawny giant who lay on his back with the stunning bundle of femininity sprawled on top of him. It wasn't every day that travelers came across a couple lounging in the grass by the side of the road. The unusual sight had the four Sullivans snickering.

"What's the matter, Andy-Joe? Did you take a fall?" John-Henry inquired with a teasing grin.

A rakish smile encompassed Dru's craggy features when Tori's violet eyes silently challenged him. "I took a fall all right," Dru chuckled as he lifted his raven head to press a kiss to Tori's lips. "I fell hopelessly in love with my wife. Now all I have to do is to convince her to stay in Montana with me." The smile faded as he peered into Tori's luminous eyes. "Will you, Chicago?"

Before Tori could respond, the carriage rolled to a halt.

"She most certainly will not be staying in this godforsaken country!" Gwen sputtered as she clambered from the coach. "This heathen is not the man for you, Victoria. Hubert is your rightful fiancé, and this ridiculous marriage is going to be annulled posthaste! You are not remaining married to this beast and that is that." Gwen swiveled her blond head to focus on her husband. "Edgar, tell Victoria she is coming home with us."

All eyes fastened on Edgar who leisurely unfolded himself and climbed down from the carriage. Somberly, Edgar approached husband and wife, who were still lying in each other's arms by the side of the road. Clasping his hands behind him, Edgar stared down into Tori's enchanting features.

"Tori, what exactly do you want to do?" Edgar wanted to know.

Gwen gasped in outrage. "Don't *ask* her, Edgar. *Tell* her!" she spewed at her husband.

Dru stared up at Edgar, noting that same expression he had observed on his features on several other occasions. With bated breath Dru waited, glancing first at Tori and then at Edgar.

"Tori, you have had demands placed on you since the day you and your mother came to live with me," Edgar commented. "Your mother has never allowed you to speak your mind or follow your own heart. Tell me what you want and I will see to it that you have your whim. Gwen and Hubert's threats count for nothing. I will deal with the two of them."

"Edgar Cassidy!" Gwen puffed up like an offended toad. "Have you gone mad?"

"No, Gwendolyn," he replied without taking his eyes off Tori. "I've given in to you for the very last time. Both Tori and I are announcing our independence."

"Edgar, if you don't come to your senses, I'm going to . . ." Gwen spluttered, stamping her foot.

Edgar pivoted to arch a thick brow. "You're going to do *what?* Leave me as you threatened to leave Caleb when he didn't jump when you snapped your fingers?"

His sober gaze swung to Caleb, who had climbed down to stare bemusedly at him. "Losing Gwen was your reward, Caleb. Loving her to distraction was my punishment. I won't beg for your forgiveness, but I want it known that I deeply regret the torment I put you through. I like to think I'm a better man than I was

430

twenty years ago. I suppose I wanted Gwen because I couldn't have her all those years. And once we were married, I realized I was much better off without her. Having Tori underfoot was my only enjoyment. In the ten years you were with Gwen, I'm sure she threatened to leave you to come to me. And this past decade she has reversed that threat when I didn't give her her way— which I'm afraid I have done too often."

"I don't have to stand here and listen to this verbal abuse!" Gwen snapped furiously. "You are making a spectacle of all of us, Edgar, and I will not permit it!"

"You'll permit it because you've had it coming for twenty years," Edgar growled. His mild-mannered demeanor cracked as he glared at his persnickety wife. "I have purchased several businesses in Virginia City and I intend to reside here during the summer months. And when my railroad lines build farther west next year, I'll set up headquarters somewhere other than Chicago. The house is yours, Gwen. I hope you enjoy puttering around in it all by yourself."

Tori supposed she should have mustered some sympathy for her mother, but there was none forthcoming. For years she had manipulated both Edgar and Tori to have her own way. Gwen had never showered Tori with love, only with endless lists of rules on how to behave and what to think. In fact, Gwen would have made a far better prison warden than a mother. She was too vain, selfish, and too conscious of social position for motherhood.

When Dru rolled to his feet and then hoisted Tori up beside him, her attention shifted to the blue-eyed giant who peered expectantly at her.

"Tell us what you want, Chicago," Dru requested softly. "You have more than earned the right to make your own decisions."

It was as if the world had faded into oblivion. Tori looked up into that ruggedly handsome face that was framed with midnight hair and blessed with eyes to match

431

the wide Montana sky and she knew where she would always want to be.

"I want you to love me the same way I love you," she murmured, tracing the smile lines that bracketed his sensuous mouth. "Like the evergreen—forever fresh, forever new. I want to feel this magic every day for the rest of my life . . ."

Her words and the soft whisper in which she conveyed them caused Dru to tremble uncontrollably. He looked back through the window of time, recalling Tori's cryptic references to evergreen. She truly had loved him all along and he had been too blind to notice. And how aptly had she summed up what he felt for her, even in the beginning. With Tori, each time they made wild, sweet love was like the very first time. The world had changed from day to day, but his feelings for this beguiling blond nymph had been ever-constant, even when he denied the emotions that tugged at his heartstrings.

Dru bent to grace Tori with a kiss that expressed his tender feelings and his everlasting tie to her. "I love you, Chicago, and I always will—even more tomorrow than today . . ."

"Then it's settled," Edgar declared, pivoting to hustle everyone back into the carriage. "Victoria stays in Montana with her husband."

"Not everything is settled," Dru called after Edgar. "Are you going to tell her or am I?"

Edgar spun about. Astonishment was written on his distinguished-looking face. Edgar watched Dru glance at him and then at Tori. "How did you know?"

A wry smile pursed Dru's lips as he hugged Tori close. "As Whong reminded me not so long ago, I can sometimes be very blind. But in other instances I see a little too clearly."

No one seemed to know what Dru and Edgar were trying not to say to each other, which was just as well since Edgar and Dru had no intention of imparting information in front of the whole crowd.

432

"Perhaps later," Edgar mumbled before stepping into the carriage. "At present the stage awaits, and Gwen and Hubert are going to be on it."

While the Cassidys and company piled into the coach, the Sullivans filed past Tori and Dru, grinning in roguish delight. At long last their big brother had tied himself to something other than his family. He had finally found what had been missing from his life, that for which he had compensated by spouting orders to his four full-grown brothers. Not that the Sullivans didn't admire and appreciate all Andy-Joe's sacrifices and all he had done to ensure their prosperity, mind you. But the foursome wanted to lead separate lives without being bossed around. Now Andy-Joe had a wife who was more than a handful. Keeping this bewitching blonde out of trouble would be a full-time job that would occupy the eldest Sullivan.

When the Sullivans trotted off behind the carriage, Tori stared curiously at Dru. "Would you mind explaining that peculiar conversation between you and Edgar?"

"Perhaps it is Edgar's place to tell you," Dru murmured, staring thoughtfully after the coach.

"Tell me what?" Tori prodded. "What is going on?"

"Nothing is going on." Dru dismissed her with a shrug. "I think it best if we send your mother and Hubert off with a civil farewell. Despite how poorly she has treated you, she is still your mother."

Tori supposed Dru was right. His sense of obligation was cropping up again. But it was difficult for Tori to feel much sentimental attachment when Gwen had never displayed an ounce of affection for her. Gwen and Tori were related to each other but that was about the extent of it.

And sure enough, Gwen proved herself again the spoiled termagant when Tori bid her farewell. Gwen's parting words were another lecture on Tori's foolish decision to remain in Montana with her barbarian husband when she could have been lounging in the lap of luxury in Chicago. Gwen also scolded Tori for leaving her mother to battle the scandalous gossip she would inevitably encounter upon her return to civilization. That seemed to be Gwen's foremost concern and always had been. It certainly wasn't Tori's happiness that had any bearing on Gwen's thoughts.

When the stage rolled down the street of Virginia City, Dru's shoulders slumped in relief. He had always regretted losing his parents, but having one like Gwendolyn wasn't one whit better, he reckoned. It was a shame Gwen had to be such a shrew.

"Lord, I'm glad that's over with," Caleb said with a thankful sigh.

"That makes two of us," Edgar murmured, peering pensively at the stagecoach.

"This moment calls for a celebration," Caleb announced. "The Sullivans and I would like to properly welcome you to Virginia City and toast your new business endeavors, Edgar."

Edgar thanked him kindly. "I'll join you momentarily. But I would like to have a few moments alone with Tori and Dru first."

When Caleb and the Sullivans ambled into the hotel, Tori stared curiously at her stepfather. Awkwardly, Edgar shifted from one foot to the other.

"Dru seems to think you and I should have a heart-to-heart talk, though I'm not sure it is the wise thing to do."

Edgar exhaled nervously, glanced at Dru, and then drew himself up in front of Tori. "Tori, I want you to know I love you very much and I always have. I have tried to be a good father to you the last ten years. I do regret that I have allowed Gwen to take such a dominant hand in your raising. But I couldn't stand aside and allow you to marry until you had seen a bit of the world and

434

were reunited with Caleb. I knew how much he meant to you."

Uneasily, Edgar removed his hat and twirled it in his hand. "I never approved of Gwen's methods of deceiving you about Caleb and his supposed lack of interest in you. But as devious as Gwen has been to protect herself and her precious reputation from scandalous gossip, I cannot say that I have behaved much better. I suppose I was a coward when Gwen demanded that I stick to the railroad business while she took command of raising you to be a dignified young lady who appreciated the luxuries of life. The fact is . . ." Edgar stared into Tori's inquisitive eyes and lost his nerve. "The fact . . . is . . ." he himhawed. After plunking his hat on his head, Edgar shoved his hands into his pockets and stared at the dirt beneath his feet.

Dru rolled his eyes and waited for Edgar to spit out the truth. But the man kept his secret so long that he couldn't bring himself to put the confession to tongue. "What Edgar is having difficulty telling you, probably because he is apprehensive of your reaction, is that he is your natural father, not Caleb."

There. It was out in the open. Now he and Edgar had naught else to do but wait for Tori to digest the truth and to cope with it. Apprehensively, Dru and Edgar watched the color ebb from Tori's cheeks and her mouth drop wide open.

"You'll probably wind up hating me, and you have every right to," Edgar said before Tori could locate her tongue and lambast him with insults. "But I was young and in love and very foolish. I was captivated by Gwen's beauty and she was the first woman I ever loved. These past years I've watched you grow up, marveling at the striking resemblance between you and Gwen—or at least the Gwen I used to know before power and wealth came to have such a disastrous influence on her. I would look at you and remember how much I cared for Gwen so many years ago."

435

Edgar's pale-blue eyes lifted to meet Tori's frozen expression of disbelief. "When Gwen turned from me to Caleb because he was such a lively adventurer who swept her off her feet, I was absolutely devastated. I even tried to stop the marriage and made a bigger fool of myself. Caleb and Gwen hadn't been married a month before she came to me in tears, vowing she had made the wrong choice and that Caleb couldn't support her in the manner she craved. Fool that I was, I didn't realize it was only my money she wanted and not me. I have always wondered if she had deviously planned that moment so that if she had a child it would be mine instead of Caleb's. What Gwen always needed was wealth and prestige to make her happy. She yearned for the life of high society far more than she desired to love and be loved."

His gaze dropped. "Gwen stayed the night with me and I begged her to leave Caleb. He was away from home in search of work that would offer the money Gwen thought she needed to be content. He never knew she had strayed, but Gwen told her father in hopes he would agree to let her leave Caleb permanently. Her father was outraged and he demanded that Gwen honor her wedding vows. When Gwen knew for certain she was carrying my child, she again tried to leave Caleb, but her father swore he would ruin her reputation and disown her. He refused to allow a divorce in his family and it was not until he passed on that Gwen dared to leave Caleb without the threat of scandalous gossip."

"Is Caleb aware of the truth?" Tori murmured, her eyes swimming with shiny tears.

It suddenly dawned on her that this was the third thing Dru thought she should know before she left Virginia City. But they had been interrupted earlier and Dru hadn't gotten around to making the third point. Tori had been so elated to learn she had earned his love that she forgot all else.

Edgar gave his head a negative shake. "Caleb was hurt enough by my foolish obsession and Gwen's craving for

436

influence and prosperity. It was her idea for Caleb to strike out in search of gold. And the moment he was gone, she came running to me to dissolve their marriage. But Gwen refused to let anyone know you were my child. Her reputation has always meant the world to her. It was to her advantage to let everyone think Caleb was a thoughtless vagabond who abandoned his wife and child. Gwen preyed on pity and utilized it during her ascent to the pinnacle of high society that meant so much to her. Too late I realized Gwen had never loved me, that she wanted what my money could buy. When I suggested telling you the truth, she threatened to take you and leave me. She would have denied me my own flesh and blood, just to save her reputation. You then became the device she held over my head. I tolerated her arrogance just to be with you, to watch you grow into a lovely young woman, and I couldn't let you go . . ."

His voice cracked, and it was a long moment before Edgar could compose himself and continue. "Now perhaps you understand why I insisted that you were to inherit from me, even if I was supposedly your stepfather. My cross to bear these past twenty years was that you might never know the truth and to come to think of me as your father. I have kept the secret so long I probably wouldn't have told you if not for Dru's insistence." A muddled frown knitted his brow. "And just how the blazes did you find out?" he questioned Dru.

Dru glanced at Tori, then smiled at Edgar. "It was right there, staring me in the face the first time I met both of you. Your expressions, the shape of your eyes, and the resemblances in your smiles made me curious the day I saw you and Tori on the steps of the church. But I shrugged off the resemblances and attributed them to spending ten years living under the same roof with each other. But when you arrived in Virginia City, I noticed it again and again. The fact that you had waited ten years to wed a woman who had once been your childhood sweetheart left me wondering," he added pensively. "I

437

figured there had to be more to the story than I had heard from Caleb. The fact that you came to Tori's defense several times strengthened my speculations."

Edgar focused on Tori's tormented features. A melancholy smile hovered on his lips. "Love can sometimes be disastrous, Tori. I feel I have paid for my obsession ten times over. I wish more for you than the agony I've endured. I was forced to live a lie while I loved in vain. But I think perhaps you and Dru have discovered something rare and special, something that doesn't come around even once in a lifetime for many of us."

His hand folded around Tori's, giving it a fond squeeze. "Love can be a tragedy or a treasure. I want for you what I couldn't have. You have been blessed with a husband who cares so much for you that he didn't even care if he made a spectacle of himself by dragging a horse through the hotel lobby just to get your attention. And you have two fathers who love you dearly. Caleb is just beginning to like me, and I would very much prefer to keep it that way. We have a great deal in common." A faint smile brushed his lips. "We both fell in love with the wrong woman and we both cherish our daughter."

For a contemplative moment, Tori sorted through the past ten years of her life, scolding herself for being remote and distant when Edgar had been nothing but kind and considerate. It was difficult to accept what he had told her, and yet she couldn't find it in her heart to hold Edgar in contempt. He was generous enough in soul to allow Caleb to go on believing Gwen had been faithful to him, even if their marriage had been a disaster. Gwen had never known how to love, never learned to sacrifice. For that Tori pitied her. Gwen had made two men's lives miserable. Tori couldn't bear to hurt Caleb or Edgar more than they had already been hurt. Until the past few months Gwen, for her own selfish purposes, had kept both of Tori's fathers from her.

"Then it shall remain our secret, if that is what you wish," Tori whispered as she hugged Edgar closer than

438

she had in their ten years together. "I only regret that I didn't reach out to you when you were always there."

"And I'm sorry I couldn't give Caleb more notice about your ill-fated marriage to Hubert," Edgar replied, cuddling Tori to him and cherishing every moment of it. It was the first honest affection that he remembered her showing toward him. "But you dragged your feet about the wedding date until Gwen interceded and set it for you. I'm thankful your new husband arrived when he did. I had almost given up hope that Caleb would come to your rescue in time."

Dru exchanged smiles with Edgar. "I wondered why there weren't bloodhounds on our heels the moment we lit out cross-country," he chuckled.

"If Gwen and Hubert would have had their way, there would have been a pack of dogs and detectives trailing you," Edgar admitted. "I postponed sending out Pinkerton's agents as long as I possibly could by speculating that you might send a ransom note. But Hubert recognized you, and Gwen suspected Caleb. I gave you all the time I could without drawing their suspicion."

Tori curled her arms around Dru and Edgar's elbows and propelled them toward the hotel. "We had better rejoin Caleb before he comes looking for us."

With her heart bursting with happiness, Tori ambled into the hotel lobby. She felt as if she were walking on air. She had finally earned Dru's love and had come to know both of her fathers. Life had suddenly taken a marvelous turn and Tori vowed to relish every moment!

Chapter 40

Impatiently, Tori paced around the bedroom, wondering what had detained Dru. With a seductive smile and a wink, he had sent her upstairs. He promised to join her after he attended some mysterious mission that he refused to reveal no matter how hard she pressed him . . .

The creak of the door brought Tori's head up to survey the brawny giant who filled the entrance to overflowing. Lord, he was a magnificent figure of a man with eyes as clear and bright as the Montana sky, hair as black as a raven's wing, and a rugged, massive body that reminded her of the awe-inspiring mountains. Even now, Dru's mere presence could put her heart on a drumroll. Dru was the most vital man Tori had ever met and she loved him so deeply that sometimes it frightened her. Having earned his love, Tori couldn't bear the thought of ever losing him . . .

That sentimental thought sent Tori sailing into Dru's arms to squeeze the stuffing out of him. When she felt Dru's chuckle vibrate through his broad chest, she tilted her head back to peer into his chiseled, smiling features.

"What did I do to deserve that, Chicago?" he questioned before pressing a light kiss to the tip of her upturned nose.

"You fell in love with me when I thought you'd never

get around to it," she replied, reaching up on tiptoe to grace him with a steamy kiss. "It certainly took you long enough, Montana. All this time love has been staring *you* in the face and *you* didn't recognize it."

The smile slid off Dru's lips. Adoringly, he lifted a big hand to sketch Tori's delicate features. "To tell the truth, I thought you were too good for me." His rich baritone voice was soft and husky. "And you were such an innocent the first time you confessed your love for me. I was sure you were only suffering a naive infatuation that wouldn't last the duration of the journey."

"There was nothing temporary about it," Tori assured him. She looped her arms over his shoulders and flung him a saucy grin. "I knew what I wanted all along, but you were too stingy to let me have it."

His hands slid down her ribs to rest familiarly on her hips. "Do you know, I think I fell in love with you the instant you floated up the steps of the church, looking like a sad little princess out of a fairy tale." He lowered his head to nibble at her lips. "I envied Hubert for getting such a prize when he didn't deserve it. And the more time I spent with you, the more possessive I became. I wanted you to transform from a naive debutante into a competent woman so you would fit into my world. And when you did, I couldn't let go of you or the memories . . ."

His tender confession touched her soul and she blessed him with a smile that sparkled like Montana moonfire. "I love you so much . . . too much I think . . ."

Dru gave his dark head a contradictory shake. "Too much isn't anywhere near enough, Chicago," he murmured. "Smother me with your love . . ." He reached into his pocket to retrieve the pearls and fastened the necklace around her swanlike throat. "I saved the jewels you left on the trail to lead me to you. I had them restrung and they're good as new." His forefinger glided over the strand that encircled her neck. "I want these pearls to mean twice as much as they did

442

before, just like in the poem you recited to Caleb. I want each one of them to be a reminder of the memories we've made and all the ones to come."

Tori intended to begin making new memories this very moment. But when she lifted parted lips, Dru suddenly jerked away, leaving her frowning in bemusement.

"Godamighty, you're so distracting that I almost forgot!" Latching on to her hand, Dru towed her across the room and onto the balcony.

"What in heaven's name . . . ?" Tori came to a screeching halt when she spied the two objects silhouetted against the moonlight that hadn't been in the landscape the last time she admired the view. There, standing fifty yards from the back of the house, were two three-foot tall ponderosa pines. Her thick lashes swept up to see Dru grinning down at her.

"We planted two more evergreens on either side of the front door, so no matter which way you look, you'll see the symbol of my affection for you. Everlasting . . . evergreen . . ." Dru draped a muscled arm over Tori's shoulder, giving her a heart-felt squeeze. "Whong has strict orders to see that the trees never lack water, that they grow strong and tall and remain constant fixtures on our ranch, as constant and enduring as my love for you . . ."

When a stream of sentimental tears trickled down her cheeks, Dru brushed them away with the back of his hand. "No tears, Chicago," he whispered. "All I want is to hear your laughter and to bask in the warmth of your love." Sporting a roguish smile, Dru glanced over his shoulder toward the bedroom. "What flavor of marmalade are we having tonight?"

The reference to that marvelous morning she had enjoyed an eternity ago put an impish grin on Tori's lips. "Peach."

Effortlessly, Dru lifted her into his arms and carried her to bed. "My favorite flavor," he murmured, his blue eyes twinkling with rakish anticipation.

443

When Dru fell back on the bed, clutching Tori to him, her soft laughter filled up his senses. Her violet eyes shimmered in the lanternlight that illuminated their room. Her silver-gold hair glistened like sun and moonfire, and Dru felt more alive than he had in all his thirty years. He wanted to spend the rest of his days in Tori's silky arms, reveling in a love he'd never expected to find. He had always thought his married brothers had become gushy and sentimental when they wed the women of their dreams. But Dru was feeling a little gushy and sentimental himself. This dazzling sprite had tapped the deep well of emotion inside him, leaving the bubbling sensations spewing forth like a geyser.

"Lord, Chicago, what I feel for you is so overwhelming I can't quite put it into words," he breathed in frustration.

Tori tunneled her hands beneath his shirt to make tantalizing contact with the muscular flesh of his chest and slid her knee suggestively between his legs. "If the words are difficult, Montana, why don't you show me how much you love me. Indeed, I would prefer it . . ."

In less than a heartbeat, Dru reversed positions and watched the wild spray of blond hair tumble across the pillow. With deliberate slowness he ran a tanned finger along her shoulder, inching her gown away to expose her creamy flesh to his all-consuming gaze. "My pleasure, Chicago." His voice was thick with caressing huskiness. "I hope you don't have anything else planned for the rest of the evening. I intend to be very thorough in demonstrating my love for you."

His seductive smile and the glint of passion in his eyes assured Tori that their lovemaking would last the whole night through. There was nothing she would have liked better than to make up for the nights of splendor she had missed out on because of all the misunderstandings and obstacles that had stood between them the past few days.

"Do you think maybe just once you could call me by my name," she murmured as her hands mapped the steel-honed contours of his masculine body.

"Victoria was the name of that sophisticated child-woman I met three months ago," Dru whispered as he peeled away the blue satin gown that deprived him of seeing every luscious inch of her exquisite body. "And Chicago is the nickname I gave you to taunt you and to remind myself that we were worlds apart." A wry smile dangled on the corners of his sensuous lips as he nibbled at her lips. "But there is one name by which I'll call you from this day forward—*my one and only love . . .*"

Dru came to her, expressing his devotion in ways she had never dreamed possible. And while the two lovers were setting out on the most intimate of journeys, Montana moonfire glittered down on the evergreens Dru and his brothers had planted to symbolize his affection for the spirited pixie who had taught him the meaning of love. Over and over again, Dru proved his everlasting need for her.

Tori, not to be outdone, devised inventive ways to dazzle this mountain of a man who had become her sun, moon, and world. She silently thanked her lucky stars that Dru had kidnapped her from her wedding to reveal a new way of life to her that was flooded with a kaleidoscope of wondrous emotions. Now that she had Dru's love she wanted nothing else. He had taught her to live up to her potential and to love with her heart, body, and soul . . .

"I adore you," Dru murmured, his voice rattling with overwhelming emotion.

"I know, Andy-Joe," she whispered as she lifted sparkling violet eyes to shimmering blue.

Dru cocked a thick brow. "Don't you have anything to say back to me?" he prodded, yearning to hear her confession of love until it echoed softly through his mind.

An impish smile pursed her lips. "Indeed I do . . ." A dainty forefinger indicated the nightstand. "Fetch the peach marmalade . . ."

A deep skirl of laughter erupted from Dru's throat when Tori took the jar from his hand and etched the words *I love you* on his chest with the marmalade. Her playful antics amused him . . . until she created a unique way to erase the message she had printed on his skin.

By that time their playfulness had transformed into a fiery passion that fed upon itself. Dru surrendered to the blazing sensations that boiled inside him, and to the all-consuming love he felt for this blond-haired nymph. His love for Tori burned bright against the night, assuring him that the wondrous pleasures that had escaped him all his life had only just begun to sparkle like mystical beams of Montana moonfire . . .

A Note to My Readers

I hope you enjoyed this lighthearted romp from Chicago to Montana with Tori and Dru. The next book will take you to the imposing mountains of New Mexico and Arizona for an action-packed adventure.

Moriah Laverty has been soured on civilization in general and men in particular after her stepfather attempts to dispose of her to gain control of her inheritance. Determined to become a hermit, now and forevermore, Moriah seeks refuge in the mountains. But Devlin Granger, who is known as White Shadow to his blood-brother Apaches, doesn't want some incompetent female crowding his space while he is involved in his private feud with the commander of the cavalry.

Only time can resolve Devlin's deadly conflicts between the Army and the Apaches. But he soon realizes nothing will diminish his craving for the stubborn firebrand who has invaded his domain.

It is my sincere wish that Moriah and Devlin's tale of adventure, romance, and danger will bring you an occasional smile and several hours of reading pleasure.